CAPE BRETON ROAD

Joe

For all the memories
of the "Cape Breton Road".

ALSO BY D. R. MacDONALD

Eyestone

CAPE BRETON ROAD

D. R. MacDonald

Doubleday Canada

Doubleday Canada and colophon are trademarks.

Canadian Cataloguing in Publication Data
MacDonald, D. R.
Cape Breton Road : a novel

ISBN 0-385-25901-8

I. Title.

PS8575.D6295C36 2001   C813'.54   C00-932138-1
PR9199.3.M23C36 2001

Text set in Stempel Garamond
Designed by Lori McThomas Buley
Printed and bound in the USA

Published in Canada by
Doubleday Canada, a division of
Random House of Canada Limited

Visit Random House of Canada Limited's website: www.randomhouse.ca

RRD   10   9   8   7   6   5   4   3   2   1

For Emma, with love and hope

An cuir tobar a mach as an aon shùil
uisge milis is searbh?

Will a spring send forth from the same opening
water both bitter and sweet?

—GAELIC SAYING

*The author wishes to thank the following
for their help, direct or indirect:*

Richard J. Schrader
Mike Mullery
Jack MacDonald
Jessie MacDonald
Russell Leblanc
Dr. Mahmoud and Rae Naqvi
the late Rev. Randolph MacLean
June Bonner Arnold
Gerrit Schuurkamp
And, in ways beyond measure, Sheila

CAPE BRETON ROAD

1

The power line cut like a firebreak through the wooded ridge and Innis could follow it easily now, his private road, could take it a long way beyond his uncle's boundary and cross, unseen here in the upland, other people's woods, veering down into them when something caught his eye. The afternoon was growing colder under a lazy snowfall and he captured on his tongue the cool taste of a downy flake. He carried a bucksaw loosely in one hand, in the other his walking stick that beat snow out of boughs, showed him snow depth, ice thinness, heard but unseen water, and if he found himself without the stick, he would retrace his steps in a crouch until he saw where he had set it down, distracted by something he wanted to inspect— tracks, a bush, a hole in the snow that said an animal lives here. Back in his uncle's woods he'd been thinning young spruce, improving a clearing well above the power line, the spot he had staked out in the fall for his own seedlings. Starr never went up in the trees anymore, would never know what went on there, one way or the other. For what Innis had in mind, summer light in that clearing would do. And it would, by fall, light his way out of here, though at the moment collas swaying in the sun were not easy to conjure.

His tracks were filling so quickly he could barely see how he'd meandered along the break. He liked his tracks to dip into the lower trees, then out again, a snaking trail someone might follow, looking for whatever creature was at the end of it. Overhead, the power line, two widely spaced cables, sagged gracefully toward a wooden pylon visible on the next rise, then disappeared into the snowgreyed air. If he were to follow it in that direction, east for maybe an hour, he could hit the TransCanada highway and thumb down a car or a semi the way he had last October. People still hitched in this part of the world, even women. But he was not ready for it. He was not a prisoner after all, except to himself, but he knew now the ride out would have to be a long one, all westward. He hadn't the nerve yet to go it alone in this country, though he would never admit that to Starr, not for a second. He had once wished for nothing but to be back in the streets of Watertown, of Boston better yet, but that city, that whole country down there, was closed to him now, forbidden—a hurt he woke to some days like a bruise in his chest. With some real bucks in his pocket, he kept telling himself, he would find his way maybe to Montreal or Toronto, even all the way to Vancouver, cities big enough to start over in. But last night when he'd looked at a map in Starr's old atlas, Canada's vastness disheartened him, diffusing him into its indefinite spaces, unmoored and anonymous, a nobody.

Now the snow whirled down, gently blinding him in the grey light, and he was weary of this relentless season. A hatred for North St. Aubin seized him so strongly he nearly fell to his knees. That ragged skyline of thick spruce wherever he looked, one little store with a gas pump. March in Watertown could be nasty, sure, but winter wasn't nailed down like this. Pot plants growing in these woods? A pipedream. In the deep wall of trees below him he saw a few different evergreens, a small grove, stately, fuller, and when he took a branch in his hand and shook it free of snow and felt the long needles like coarse hair, he knew it was a pine, a Scotch pine. A soft swirl of wind soughed through it, a timbre he never heard in the other needled trees. In all his trampings he had come across but a single pine, a white pine hidden in spruce, so old its crown was out of sight. Christmas presents had this smell on them when he was a kid, his mother urging him to tear them open when he tried to save the pretty paper, to hell with it, never mind, she'd say, but he'd liked the figures on the wrapping, the designs. They'd had no Christmas, he and his uncle, Starr said it was mushy, the whole sentimental business, and he spent Christmas day and night in Sydney with some woman, clear of any duties toward or expectations from his nephew boarder. Innis's mother had always wanted Scotch pine for Christmas. So how about this fifteen-footer, Mom? I'll ship it to you, you can save it for next year, I won't be there to haul it up the stairs but your boyfriend can do the honors. He ducked under its branches, snow trembling down his neck as the saw ripped into bark, the blade pungent with resin, sawdust dribbling into the wooly snow like cornmeal, and when the tree fell away from him with a hiss, he drew back and inhaled the turpentine smell. Resin. Jesus, it jacked him up, like that other resin he loved to smoke. He stood panting, snow in his eyelashes, his hair. His back muscles burned, water trickled cool then warm along his spine, over the chill of sweat. The pine lay humbled against the snow. But his angry exhilaration faded with every smoky breath, the satisfaction seared through him so fast he didn't know what made him do it, just take it down like that. When he heard the faint squeak of footsteps behind him, he thought first, it's getting colder, the snow is noisy, and then his mind was already racing toward a lie.

"God, if my dad wasn't near ninety, he'd kill you." The man stood planted like a stout child dressed up and sent out into the snow, his big mittened hands at his sides. His face was flushed beneath the brim of a green stocking cap. "He'll have the Mounties on you, boy, and that's the least of it."

Innis picked up the bucksaw he'd flung down: Starr's name was carved into the handle, and Starr would be wild anyway if Mounties showed up at the door. Well I knew you'd bring them sooner or later, you have this thing with the police, eh?

"These trees yours?" Innis hated the boyish supplication in his voice, the register it always rose to when he'd been caught. "I didn't see any signs or anything. I figured they were just anybody's."

The man swung his weight slowly about as if he wore snowshoes, not heavy galoshes. "Trees are always some-body's," he said. "You can't come into our woods with a saw in your hand. You haven't the right, you see."

Don't get in trouble like you did in Boston, Starr told him when he first set foot in the house. There's not the chance, b'y, for one. And for another, they'll put you away so quick you'll think you'd never been here.

"I only cut the one," Innis said.

"For what?" The man lifted the pine by its tip like a dead animal.

"Listen, I'll pay you, whatever you think it's worth."

The man didn't seem to hear. "Only stand of trees like this on the whole goddamn island," he said. He touched the oozing tree stump, then sniffed his glove. "Where you from? Not from here, are you. I can tell by your talk."

Innis wanted to tell him I *am* from here, I left here a baby and my folks are from here clean back to my great-grandfathers. But he didn't feel the truth of that, it was just what he had been told, and when you were seized in the act, it was not the time to open up a genealogical cupboard the man could rummage in. Like it or not, you're a Corbett, Starr told him. You don't have to care about that, I can't make you. But I care. Your great-grandpa built this house. Don't shame it.

"Sydney," he said. He'd been into Sydney twice with Starr, the big town, malls and all.

"Who do you belong to? I know all kinds of people in Sydney."

"You wouldn't know mine."

"But your name, what's your name?"

"MacAskill." Innis knew there were no MacAskills in North St. Aubin.

"You Englishtown MacAskills? North River?"

"No. We haven't lived here very long."

"Queer place to be cutting down a tree, if you live forty miles away. What did you mean by it?"

"How the hell did you know I was up here?"

"My dad," the man said. "'Finlay,' he said to me, 'somebody is at the trees.' He always knows when somebody's in the woods what don't belong."

"You mean he saw me?" Innis looked into the dark trees around them, blacker now in the late afternoon light. There was no house near, he knew that. "That's crazy."

"He saw you, in a way. My dad sees things the rest of us don't. What MacAskill are you? Not Jimmy Angus's family? No." Snow had whitened the man's cap, gathered on his thick mackinaw like a shawl. Innis was tensed to run, the slow whirl of flakes closing around him, his heart beating harder now. The guy couldn't give chase, could he, chubby as he was, and if he sicced the Mounties on him they wouldn't get here for an hour, spread as thin as they were, and they'd be looking for a car anyway, a car he didn't have, not a young guy on foot and where would they look in the woods? Would they even give a damn, for a pine tree? But he didn't run.

"I want you to come with me," the man said calmly, as if it were the natural step now.

"I'm not going to hang around waiting for the Mounties, if that's what you're thinking. I'm not as young as I look."

"You come meet my dad. You come meet Dan Rory. He's a man you should know and you just cut down a tree he likes very much."

Innis backed away a couple steps.

"I can disappear pretty damn quick. I know these woods."

"Odd, that, for a Sydney boy. You hunt up here? Oh, you won't disappear, it's not that easy, is it? Run if you like. Walk away." He turned slowly and started back. "We know who you are, me and my dad," he said over his shoulder.

Innis picked up his walking stick and watched him. "What do you mean?" he yelled. "I've never seen you before, or your old man either!" The man kept on, not hurrying, retracing his tracks down the hill until he slipped out of sight in the dark trees.

Hunched into his parka, shivering, his toes numb, Innis let the snow gather in his hair. He did not want to get in trouble here, and so far he hadn't. Trouble you saved up like coupons and he didn't want to cash them in on this. A bottle of aftershave under his coat at a drugstore in The Mines, okay, and a sawbuck one afternoon from Starr's battered till, but nothing that would bring the Mounties down on him, no hotwired cars, no joyrides. Not that it would take a hell of a lot for a deportee, the Mounties probably had a file on him. A pine, a nice full, sweet tree? Maybe, but shit, he wasn't going to follow that guy, he wasn't a kid anymore, and he turned angrily toward the break. He'd have a long hike back, he'd been walking longer than usual. The kitchen would be warm, if Starr was home from The Mines they'd fry up some meat and potatoes like a couple of country bachelors, and that was okay too. His uncle preferred that

Innis have things going in the kitchen if he could, nothing worse in winter than coming into a cold empty house, he said, no fire or food in sight, my old dad used to call that feeling it gave you *fuar-larach*. They got on pretty well most of the time, except for the women issue, the ones Starr had and the one Innis didn't. Listen, Starr said once, kidding but not quite, I was your age too, you're a walking hard-on, but you've been in enough trouble for now, you're broke anyway and nothing bores a woman faster than a broke man.

Deer tracks, feathering over, crossed Innis's path, heading up toward a spring, a dark wound in a white hill. Deer were in velvet now, new antlers growing. In snowy silence, there was nothing like catching an animal in the corner of your eye, a bit of intense life in that stillness of cold air. He wanted a joint but he'd have to fumble it out and get it lit and maybe what he didn't need was a downer flash, like that first day at Starr's kitchen table when he felt like he'd just put down in the Yukon, sleepless, wrung out, the windows lashed with cold rain while his uncle squinted at him over a cup of coffee, What in God's name made you steal cars and get yourself booted out of the country? Even if he hadn't been so numb, he would have had no answer to give. Innis followed the tracks to the point where the deer had blown into flight, the kicked-up snow barely settled. Something had spooked them from their drink, off into the upper woods. The spring had formed a small cave in the snowbank. Deep in its shadow, water plinked steadily. Innis knelt down and put his hand into the colder air of the opening. Then he saw the prints beside him: an animal had drunk here maybe minutes ago. Not hooves but paws, broad in the soft snow where it had rested and lapped. Innis could imagine the crisp sound of its tongue snatching water and he felt again a kind of current in the still trees and he stiffened as it passed through him. He knew there was nobody there, nothing as tangible as a man. Had this been a family's spring, had there been a house up here once? The woods rose like a dark cliff. He had come upon such sites before, no paths to them, buried in trees, stones and fallen beams thick with moss. He had sketched such a place in his book, but his stiff fingers wouldn't hold a pencil now. In the city, even a derelict house was seen, was passed by, there were photos of it, drawings somewhere, records. Thirsty, he knelt into the cold chamber of the spring and lapped water until his mouth pained. The coming dark was above the snow and the woods at night asked things of you he didn't have. The knees of his jeans had soaked through. No, he did not want trouble. Not for a tree, not with his own seeds waiting for their artificial spring.

The path the man had taken was an old one, narrow, without the faint marks of his feet Innis would have lost it quickly. A rabbit shot out of a thicket, a blur of fur and snow, and he cursed it, where the hell was this house anyway. An old barn appeared finally when the trees thinned out, much older than Starr's, a saltbox, swaybacked, grey as driftwood, and beyond it the house stood out, its shingles the blue of a washed-out sky. He smelled the chimney smoke merging thinly into the falling snow. The rear windows had light in them. What could he say? He had no bread, just a few bucks from odd jobs. But if things went right with his seeds and his plants, he'd have money come fall, not that he could say wait till September, fellas, my dope will be ready to sell and I'll be flush, can I owe you awhile? It seemed outrageous, this plan of his, crazy, but other times it lifted him up.

Who do you belong to? the man had said.

The back step was crudely shovelled. He could hear a fiddle starting and quitting and the sound covered his knock and he knocked again. The man looked different in the open door, bulky in a red sweater, his grey hair mussed from the cap he'd pulled off. "Yes yes, come inside. Daddy, it's the lumberjack!" he called into the house, and the fiddle music quit. Innis kicked snow from his boots. Maybe this was a mistake, but he'd made enough of them in the last year, so he'd see it through. Something simmered on the huge stove, ornate as an old car, flourishes of engraved nickel and black iron. The kitchen was stuffy with smells, the cooking, drying wool, linoleum, wood, brine. The man led him into the next room where his father sat by the window in a high-backed rocker, his huge hands cupped on the armrests, the dark varnish worn clean where he'd worked it. He was handy to his needs—pipe and tobacco pouch on a small table, magazines, binoculars. Powerful glasses, if he could see clear through the woods to the power line break. His dark eyes, stern but not unkind, sized up Innis keenly. A thick white moustache hid the expression of his mouth.

"You look like a Corbett, not a MacAskill at all. No relation to The Giant, by the looks of you, though you're taller than a lot of us."

"My mother's people were tall, so she told me. This man here says you know who I am anyway."

"Starr Corbett's family. Not his young fella, because we know Starr takes women but not wives. Alec at the store, he says there's a young man living with Starr since fall."

"He's just my uncle."

"Yiss. You'd be Munro's boy, I see him in your face. But your mother, her it was had the red hair, eh?"

"Pretty grey now."

"Did you put the grey in it?"

"Some. But that's between me and my mother."

"Sally Ann. Sally Ann Lamont, from down Middle River. A tall girl herself, but so was her dad, wasn't he, Finlay?"

"He was so, Daddy. At least."

"You know everybody around here?" Innis said.

"All that's is and been," Finlay said behind him.

"Your dad and your mother came to this house, more than once, before they went off to Boston. You'd be Boston too then."

"Watertown, west of it. But Boston, yeah."

"Your grandpa and me were great friends. A better farmer he was, God, yiss, I never cared for the farming a damn bit but I had to do it. And here we are, me and Finlay, the last of the nine of us. All we grow is potatoes and trees. The spruce are put in by the devil, but the pines we put in ourselves. That pine, now, the one you brought down. What made you?"

"I don't know, hard to explain. It just happened. Before I knew it, it was down. I'll pay you for it."

"Don't think of it like money. There's too much of that. But yiss, hard to explain. Well. You'll be staying in North St. Aubin, working and such?"

"Not long. I'll be going out west, by fall anyway." It was good to declare that to them: a sure thing. Nothing to prevent it, even if in September he was still a broke man. What else did the old guy know about him? Starr had said, I won't tell anybody that immigration men escorted you to your airplane seat, we'll keep that to ourselves, that's what you want and that's what I want. "Not much work around here anyway."

"Hard to come by. But you got to find work where there is work. Cape Bretoners been going off since my own dad's days. He did it, carpentering all the way to Montana. Myself, I did threshing trains to Alberta after the war. But he came back and so did I. So I guess you're coming back. Work that pays money always been short in this place. Work to be done though. Och, lots of that. Now, that pine, that was a special tree. A son of mine was killed and I planted it, up there."

"I didn't know. I mean, it's not like there was a plaque on it."

"It's plaques he needs, Finlay. Better get up there and nail some on for this fella."

"Tomorrow, Daddy, first thing."

"How the hell did you know I was up there?" Innis said. He still couldn't believe he'd been caught like that, surprised in that territory he thought of as his.

The old man reached for his pipe and slowly tamped tobacco into the bowl. "You were at the spring too. My dad's brother, John Allan, built him a little stone house up there. Lived up there alone, 1860 something. He went down to The States and we lost track. North Carolina, someplace there where they had the Gaelic." He struck a wooden match under the chair and sucked flame into his pipe.

Finlay said, "He has the *taibhsearachd,* you know, the Second Sight. He's seen you before. But you don't need to know about that now."

"Why shouldn't I?" Innis felt hot, lightheaded. A sweet tobacco smell, like cooked apples, seemed to come out of the dark wainscoting. He unzipped his jacket. He was suddenly uneasy about his planned set-up in the attic corner, it had seemed so clever a little while ago. "My uncle'll be getting home soon, for supper. He expects me there."

"Och, you'll have some supper with us," the old man said firmly. "We didn't expect you either. We'll talk a little. Set a plate for the young man, Finlay." He reached for a stout cane and raised himself out of the rocker, collecting his strength. Despite a stoop he was taller than Innis. "Dan Rory is who I am. Come along, Innis. I want to show you something. Not the fiddle there, I used to play it but my hands went slow on me, they won't follow my head. Only thing worse than a bad fiddler is a poor piper."

He led him into a small cluttered room off the parlor,

most of its space taken up with a cot whose sag suggested the long body of the old man himself. A blind hung halfway down the window where light snow fluttered past. Maybe his mother had fled a house like this, this light in winter, where she'd felt as Innis did, trapped and drowsy, inert, living like these men, back up here alone with white fields and woods and a drab sun in the curtains. From the crammed closet Dan Rory pulled out a khaki uniform, laying it out carefully on the cot as if it were alive. The dull brass badges on the shoulders said "Canada" and on the sleeves were sergeant's stripes.

"The Great War," the old man said. "I learned about death. You know about death?"

"Not that way. Not war."

"What way then?"

"My dad was killed by a car. I've been to a funeral or two. The way most people know it."

"A good fella, your dad. Sad, he was young." The old man smiled. "I can see him in the kitchen there, naked as the day he was born, hands clapped over his *clachan*, doing a little dance in front of the stove, and the women, well, drying him off, terrible for teasing him. He fell through the ice in our old pond, must've been six or seven."

"What was he doing on the pond?" Innis said, anxious to capture this memory of his father.

"He was looking for fish."

"Fish?"

Dan Rory poked open the tunic with the tip of his cane and exposed the dark tartan of the kilt, lifted its hem. Light shone in a tiny mothhole. "Blood and mud washed out of her now. When they formed up the Highland Brigade, the 185th, I said right, I'm ready, that's for me. Wear the kilt, I'll look so grand in it. I was older, see. Should have known better."

They both stared at the uniform. "You were wounded?" Innis said.

"Twice. Gas is the worst. Awful. Mustard gas goes where you sweat. We had to give up the kilt in battle." He shifted his cane-tip to the belt buckle, s-shaped bits of brass.

"That's a snake buckle. We liked those. *Mheall an nathair Eubh*. You know the Gaelic?"

"Not a word."

"Starr should give you some then. You can call a man down to the lowest of the low in Gaelic, or praise him to the highest. The Language of The Garden."

"What garden?"

Dan Rory raised his eyebrows. "Eden, of course. Eden. Your uncle should've told you that."

"He throws out bits of it but not so I'd learn. It's for things he doesn't want me to know. What would I do with it anyway?"

"There's things said in Gaelic you can't say any other way, or hear any other way. But no, that wouldn't matter to you, not in Boston. I see you've got no belt on your trousers." The old man pulled the leather belt from the tunic. "Here, run it through your loops."

"I couldn't take this."

"Och, I was skinny as you then. Buckle it up. How old are you?"

"I'll be twenty. This is part of your old uniform."

"They're not going to bury me in it. You want to keep your trousers up. Starr has trouble with that, always did."

Finlay called them into the kitchen and they sat solemnly at the wooden table while Dan Rory said grace. "Lord, we thank thee for this bountiful food, and for bringing this young man Innis to our table, may he benefit like we have from the blessing and nourishment of God, The Father, Amen." They quietly passed around the bowls of chowder and the plate of bread and Innis felt the ritual more than the meal, a ceremony, but he ate hungrily, buttering the bread thickly and savoring the white fish.

"Now, the pine," Dan Rory said after a few sips of tea that had simmered on the stove until it was black. "We'll take work, not money. There's work here needs doing."

"Trees that need cutting," Finlay said, setting down his spoon. "There's budwormed spruce in the lower woods dead to their roots. And a mess of windfalls. We'd like a path cleaned through that thrash to the road and I'm old for that."

"The old path to the brook," Dan Rory said. "I want to walk to that water without breaking my neck."

"Not a chainsaw," Finlay said. "We don't like the racket. We got a double-bit axe sharp as a razor, and a good cross-cut can make short work of a tree, eh? It's not easy work, but we'll call it square when you're done."

Innis sipped the last of his tea, cooled by a stream of canned milk Finlay had added without asking, and set the cup carefully on its saucer. "Look, I don't want my uncle to know. All right? And the other thing is, what money I make is from odd jobs around, so I can't spend all my time at it. I owe Starr for board as it is."

"Work it around your other duties. It's not a great rush," Finlay said. "The woods isn't going anywhere."

"What about that priest with the old cottage?" Dan Rory said. "Alec says he's looking for somebody to paint it up or something."

"Father Lesperance, down by the ferry wharf. There's a job for you, Innis, his summer place there. He's not rich but it'd bring you a few dollars."

"We're not Roman Catholic," Dan Rory said, "and neither are you, not that I've seen your uncle in church since I can't remember."

"He doesn't go, no." Starr had said, I told my dad when I got home from the navy I wasn't going to church, not any day, anymore. He nearly froze me out when he saw I meant it. He could turn to stone for long spells, my dad. Quiet as a shut door for days on end. He hated that he couldn't talk, that he didn't have the kind of heart to do that, sit down and say, listen, this is what's on my mind. Oh, Jesus, no. Clam up. God, we were all that way, when I think about it, the whole damn bunch of us.

"The priest is a decent fella. Am I right, Finlay?"

"He is so. Had that cottage a few years now, and he's not the sort to convert you, I don't think."

"Nothing to convert," Innis said. "If he's got work, okay with me."

There was an air of business having been settled and they relaxed into an apple pie Finlay had baked, tough crust and all. Why in the hell had he cut down that pine? Two or three minutes of fury just to see it fall, and here he was bound up with these guys. He felt found out, more known than he wanted: people didn't just look at you here, they looked into you, they inquired, and if you had a family connection, some of them expected, even at first meeting, if not your family tree, then at least a hefty branch of it. The maroon teapot was trimmed in gold leaf, similar to one his mother had, one of her "old things" she'd brought with her to Watertown. She'd known what it was like to be sheltered by family, to have strangers care about you because they knew who your grandfather was, your mother, uncle, aunt. But family could suffocate you too, want to know too much about you, and that's what his mother had never missed in Boston: after her husband died she could disappear for an evening with another man and no one knew or cared whose daughter she was, or sister or neice, who she belonged to or how far back they went.

"Starr shown you cousins?" Dan Rory said. "No Corbetts left here in St. Aubin, but you'd have MacKinnons and Campbells in other places."

"We haven't got around much." That was close to true, though Starr had taken him to see two aging sisters who shared a house in Sydney, Campbells, Netta was one and Innis couldn't recall the other one's name, skinny as a crane. They had talked around and over Innis as if he were a decent topic of conversation but didn't need to be there, and they soon moved on to people they really wanted to discuss, those who'd had interesting surgery, real excavations, or awful deaths or a trajectory of decline even Starr could appreciate. And Alec who ran the store in North St. Aubin was a cousin too, friendly but distant, taciturn, not a prober or a gossip, and Innis liked him for that since he seemed to expect nothing more private from you than he was willing to give himself and that was very little. And Starr had mentioned cousins over on Southside St. Aubin and up the east coast of Cape Breton Island but didn't seem keen to expose them to his nephew, fine with Innis since the less he saw of kin, the better chance to be taken on his own terms, the less enmeshed his fabrications, the less strain between him and his uncle who didn't like the lies to begin with. We should be telling the truth about yourself, Starr said, that's the way to start over, not like this. But I'm not starting over *here*, Innis said, am I? Can't you understand that? I'm going west when I'm ready, but I'm not ready yet. No, Starr said, ready you're not.

Dan Rory lit his pipe and Finlay a cigarette, blowing smoke thoughtfully. "Saw your uncle Starr with a new ladyfriend yesterday," Finlay said. "In Sydney." But for the creases around his eyes he had the face of an old child, innocent but canny.

"She's not real new," Innis said. "I haven't seen her myself."

"Very pretty she was, yes. Arm in arm on Charlotte Street. He looked mighty pleased."

"He was always a good dancer, Starr Corbett," Dan Rory said.

"Liked a good fight sometimes too, at the dances." Finlay took a deep drag. "Well, didn't we all. Not so much of it now, even the youngsters."

Starr had never mentioned dancing, or fighting either, but sometimes if he felt good or nicely toasted he might break into a brief stepdance on the kitchen floor while Innis watched, amused.

"I'll drive you up home," Finlay said. "A long walk from here."

Innis fetched his jacket from the parlor. He noticed on the wall a framed photograph of Dan Rory in the army kilt, young, all bony knees, a feather in the badge of his cap. The snake belt was clasped around his tunic.

"What color was that feather?" Innis said, pointing at the photograph.

"Green," Dan Rory said. "It was a green feather. The feather is the first to go."

2

Innis stepped into the attic room at the end of the hallway, into the shock of its March air and the dusty scent of dry wood. He shut the door carefully: there might be times when he would be inside here with his uncle somewhere in the house and he had to know every board that creaked, where he could crouch without announcing it, how gently he need latch the door. In the sooty darkness the door boards emitted cracks of light. He played his flashlight over the hewn rafters, the pegged beams, the trunks and boxes and pieces of furniture. The big wooden loom sat as his grandmother had left it years ago, a piece of rough grey cloth in the heddles. Her husband had built it for her, put it together right here in the attic, "over the kitchen," and there she wove in the wintertime until arthritis crippled her. Innis had tried to imagine how she looked as she worked the loom, her feet and her hands moving, but he couldn't, he didn't know enough about that, not yet. He squatted beside the equipment he had collected within the loom's frame, the old fluorescent shop fixtures he'd bought two new plant bulbs for, a simple timer, a warming tray. Start them off at maybe eighteen hours or so and see how they went. He had the pots, the soil, a small watering can, an old crock to store water in, tinfoil to drape over the length of the lamp to direct it down toward the seedlings. The loom was perfect to hang the fixture from: he could make a tent out of it with two blankets that would conceal the light and hold warmth. Even if Starr stuck his head in the door, he wouldn't necessarily see much. If he poked around, well, the game was up, but such was the risk of secrets, and better found out now than later. Innis had pried up a floorboard and tapped a multiple socket into the wires in the kitchen ceiling. He was proud of his set-up, practically above Starr's dinner plate. None of it had cost much, from a secondhand store in The Mines mostly, and he was keen to get this under way. Even in June there might be killing frosts, Starr said, and Innis's seedlings needed this jump start if they were to grow well and amount to money: a dozen plants even half the size of the ones in the marijuana book, healthy *sinsemilla* with good flowers, could bring him a grand apiece, and no middleman. Find that trucker and fire up a sample for him, there'd be no problem unloading it. And then Innis could leave North St. Aubin, he would strike out on his own.

The fluorescents flickered and balked and then hummed into a steady pinkish light. He touched the warming platter:

not too hot, just warm enough to make them happy. He'd germinate the seeds in a wet cloth, start tonight. Last night he had spread them out on a sheet of paper and, like a jeweller, poised a finger above them, selecting slowly, deliberately, each promising seed he would devote his risks to. Maybe here and there sat that one just waiting to sprout in a place like Cape Breton, one that had in it the desire for a new locale, far north, a need to rise out of cool boreal clay and grow like crazy, for the sheer hell of it. He draped the blankets over the loom: it looked like some old sheepherder's hut out on a dark moor, he liked that. He killed the flashlight and stood there shivering, daring something to lay hold of him, in the dark sometimes he could feel it, if he'd had a few tokes. The first time he shut himself in here, things seemed to rush out of the wood, but they did not make him uneasy, not anymore. He could not say what they were, spirits maybe, but hell, he was probably related to them, it wasn't as if they were strange. Pieces of the house's history had been pushed into the attic. In this dark he felt most strongly what kind of house it had been. Mothholes of light appeared in the blankets, his grandmother had woven them, they were old. He had only known her when she visited them back in Boston, him a small boy at the time, but he was certain she wouldn't want her loom sheltering a garden like his.

Innis went about the house as if nothing had changed, despite the shrouded light in the attic, his little plot set up and sown. Downstairs, back upstairs, he was tense, a bit wired. Starr would be out late, that new woman was making demands on his attention. In the hall Innis dustpanned a spill of potting soil, searched for other traces of his hidden activities. Finding none, he flipped open a sketchpad under his bedroom lamp, unable to settle into the details of anything, scribbling a rough sketch of a woman's face, boldly pretty, her hair swirls of dark pencil. Tomorrow he'd go back to the upper woods, far up where he'd staked out that spot, a clearing nicely concealed for summer planting. Still some work to be done there. His plants would need good light without being easily noticed by browsing deer or nosy humans. Apart from Finlay scaring the shit out of him that afternoon way down the break, he'd never run into a soul in all his wanderings up there, just three hunters he'd hidden from back in the fall when the woods were as new and foreign as everything else. You're a Boston kid, Starr had told him, you get lost up there and we'll have to send the Mounties in after you. But he knew the woods now, the woods were his.

When he'd first driven into The Mines with Starr to give him a hand at the TV repair shop and seen it in all its dreary clutter, he'd nearly left that very day. But he had nothing to take him anywhere, no money, no friends or destinations, he was starting from scratch in a new country, it didn't matter that he had been born here, and The Mines itself, with its rundown storefronts and air of commercial despair, offered nothing. Starr was bound that Innis should learn to repair televisions, be his cheap apprentice for awhile. It was a skill you could stay afloat with, Starr said, get you on your own no matter where because every goddamn person everywhere has a TV. Go to the backwardest spot on earth and they'll have a TV before a toilet, even in Outer Mongolia or someplace, and sooner or later their favorite yak program will suddenly turn to snow and there'll be no man between them and heaven they would rather see standing at the door of their hut than you with your tools because no kind of prayer can bring a TV picture back, nobody's god deals with that. But Starr's shop, with its blank dusty screens stunned every which way, its spill of haphazard parts and testing devices and wire, reminded Innis of a correctional school, and Starr its dead-end instructor hunched under a lamp, a man, it seemed to Innis, who'd settled for the least ambition he could get away with. A few episodes of sparks and smoke and cursing and Innis got what he preferred—staying back in North St. Aubin, picking up odd jobs with people Starr knew, cleaning yards, painting, cutting wood, doing handyman carpentry from junior high woodshop. Sometimes he was less than handy, a jackknife carpenter for sure, but he learned fast from his mistakes and faster yet how to cover them up. I don't care, Starr had said, if that's what you want to do, you don't have the knack for circuits, you handle a TV like a trash barrel. Bring in something toward your board, that's all I ask for now, and there's no temptations out there in North St. Aubin, at least I'm not finding many. You can settle down and keep straight. Don't give your mother any more grief. Jesus Christ, Starr, who's got the grief? If she'd made me a citizen, I wouldn't be here. Starr said no, you got the sleigh before the horse, was it her that stole the cars?

He was kneeling beside the tub testing the water for a bath when he heard the Lada skid down the driveway to a halt. His uncle's laughter, a door slamming, then Starr pounding up the stairs. What the hell was he doing home so soon? Innis turned the taps on full for the noise, sweeping his hand through the water now nicely hot. Little chance that his uncle would blunder into the attic, but Innis stumbled into his jeans and by the time he had buttoned his shirt Starr was rapping on the bathroom door.

"Hey, save me some hot water! I might need it later."

When his pulse had calmed, Innis stood at the door to Starr's bedroom. His legs felt too light under him as he looked in at his uncle groping into a lower drawer of the dresser, yanking out shirts.

"Back early," Innis said.

"I'm not back, I'm just refueling. What you up to?"

"Come on, Starr, what could I be up to? A hot bath. Wild, huh?"

"Your age, I had a bath on Saturday night in a tin tub in the middle of the kitchen."

"Okay, I'm really grateful for the hot running water."

"If you had to heat it on a coal stove, you'd damn well be grateful."

Starr pushed some bills into his wallet and kicked the drawer shut, stooping toward the dresser mirror. He patted his face with both hands, a tough face, darker than Innis's, its angles squared and solid, like the men in the old photographs downstairs. A deep cleft in his chin—like a stroke Innis might make with a soft pencil—gave to his face the possibility of humor even when he set his jaw. And that's what had saved them when they got in each other's face, when the strain of Innis's living there was too much for either of them, the release of a few laughs. Starr stroked a brush carefully through the tight waves of his steel-grey hair, pursed his lips at himself. "I have to piss and get out of here. There's a woman waiting, she's not the sort to wait for long."

From the hall window Innis looked down at the Lada sputtering and trembling in the dark. In its headlights snow danced like moths. Kitchen light faintly reached the open car door, the leg of a woman in jeans, her black fur-trimmed boot resting on the running board. Radio music was going and her foot tapped to it. A hand appeared gracefully, palm up, received a few flakes of snow, and then withdrew. Innis could make out the edge of a wide-brimmed hat but not the face beneath it. Jesus, his uncle never brought a woman into the house, not since Innis had been here. You won't be driving, he'd told Innis the first day, I don't have to tell you you won't get near the wheel of a car while you're in this house. I'm not turning my life around to make room for you, but we'll be okay for the time it takes you to get straightened away.

Starr came out of the bathroom zipping up. "Now you

know where my money is," he said. On his uncle, alcohol always seemed like cologne, definite but not dangerous. He gazed into Innis's face with mock gravity but he meant it. "And I know it will always be there. Eh?"

"You mean I can't skim any?"

"I'll skim it off your hide."

"Another Friday and I'm trapped here, Starr. No wheels, nowhere to get to, nothing."

"Look, you had wheels back in Boston, but they didn't belong to you, did they? They shipped you back here and you're not exactly our idea of an A1 immigrant. Felony deportees don't deserve much, not for awhile, now do they? It's a probation, like."

"In your eyes maybe. I left all that at the border, I paid my dues in the States. It's a clean slate here."

"And clean we'll keep it."

"I been here seven months clean as a whistle. I bet I've walked more woods than you have in a lifetime."

"You'd like to think so. Just because you don't see me doesn't mean I'm never up there."

A polite toot came from the driveway.

"She's antsy, I'm off. Don't use so much damn water. Oil isn't cheap, you know."

"Why didn't you ask her to come in?"

Starr cocked his head, looked him up and down slowly. "With a dangerous man like you in here?"

He laughed and started down the stairs singing without words, then stopped and looked back at Innis. "Let's keep it simple. That's best for me and you too. Right?"

"Whatever you say, Uncle Starr."

"And don't call me Uncle. It makes me sound like a geezer."

When he was gone, Innis looked again into the attic dark. Satisfied, he closed the door and locked it. Where did Starr get his ideas of what was best? What was Innis, a freak?

So, no women, a cold Friday night, but at least the house was his. Drafty as a barn anyway. To hell with the bath. Leave it for Starr, he could cool his nuts in it when he got home. Innis jacked up the basement oil furnace and pokered the coal in the big iron stove his uncle used for heat in the kitchen and sometimes for cooking when he felt nostalgic, shifting pots about on its flat surface as he recounted how skilled Granny had been, boiling water here, and simmering fish over there, baking the best bannock in the oven at the same time. The sink tap pattered on the black skillet and its crescent of chilled grease. After warming his hands over the stove, he fished out upstairs a small wooden stash box, hidden in a boot in his bedroom closet. He unwrapped with great care a ball of tinfoil: his beautiful seeds, the ones he hadn't used. In his palm he worked them around with his finger like diamonds. The party at Mohney's brother's apartment back in Boston where the hippie guy pressed the seeds into his hand like they were magic: Put them in the earth, man, they'll bring you joy. Right on. Promising plumpness and color, so said the book Innis kept under his mattress. Miraculous things, seeds. He squeezed them in his fist. Summer. Heat. Green leaves spreading like hands, flower tops dense as bullrushes. But God, when would this winter let go?

He rolled a thin joint, then held his baggie of pot up to the light: had to go easy on this. Some floating around in town probably, in The Mines, in Sydney for sure, but he couldn't afford to get busted, he had to pick his risks carefully. Ned Mohney, the crazy bastard, had brazenly mailed this weed to him from Boston, two cleaned and tightly-compressed ounces from the last kilo they had scored to deal over in Cambridge, and it got here through customs, despite the wrong box number packed in a big bag of M&Ms, a note inside: Something for the munchies, pal. Keep your energy up. Keeping anything else up? Sure, Ned,

I've never seen so many women. He hadn't heard from Ned since. Why would he? Innis was banished, gone from the conversation of the few friends they'd had back there in Watertown. He'd been a topic for a while, did you hear what they're doing to Innis, they're deporting the guy to Canada, can you believe that? For what, dope? No, that Porsche he stole. His mother had called at Christmas, just smalltalk, she seemed nervous and the line was bad. How could you have a private conversation anyway on that old wooden crank phone on the kitchen wall with another dozen people up and down the road bending their ears to it? Alexander Graham Bell lived a few miles from here, Starr said, up at Red Head, and we're still using the phone he invented, we're getting dial next year, but that's no excuse for not calling your mother. We've said all we have to say, Innis told him.

Starr might come home tonight, and he might not. Unsure still if his uncle knew the smell of grass, he lit up and stepped outside the back door, huddling against the jamb. He drew deeply, held it until his eyes welled and the smoke blended with his breath. Even so, Starr didn't miss much, and he kept a lot of things to himself. On the radio one night they heard about a pot bust on the mainland, and Starr said, Marijuana, hell, they used to grow it for rope, and now they hang you with it. Folk doctors concocted it for nerve medicine and perking up appetites, not just for food but sex, eh? If you think country people didn't know much, there you are. Your Granny, she knew the wild plants and herbs, she was a healer, a midwife, many a night she was called out in terrible weather.

The telephone rang and Innis counted reflexively, three longs, three shorts, not ours, a shaky hand at the crank, it sounded like. People had styles of cranking out rings— some bold, urgent, loud, others hesitant, tripping along. Innis was getting so he hardly listened at all, the phone simply trilled out a few times and went silent. No one was phoning for him anyway, he'd fielded enough calls for Starr, from women even, one in particular who seemed put out that he was never available lately, though when he had been he'd sweettalked her in low tones, as charming as he could be in code, on a party line. But this new woman with the hat and snow on her hand, she had Starr jumping, avoiding the shop some days, often gone in the evenings. Innis himself felt older now, beyond teenage girls, what he saw of them on his few visits to The Mines seemed just that to him, girls who would not understand what had happened to him or why. Why should they. And what could he offer the older ones, floating in space the way he was? Starr had told him, Look, you don't have a license anymore and I'm damn sure not going to take you somewhere looking for a date, better you stay out here for a while, you've had enough problems out on the town, you don't need women, have a drink instead. He'd pushed the rum bottle across the table, *Dìreach boinneag,* but Innis said no, that stuff's poison to me, I don't touch it anymore.

In Watertown he and Ned had loved beer, not just in bars but at home because pot made them thirsty and they could glide nicely on a sixpack or two. But later on when Innis was facing his final INS hearing, they thought hard liquor was maybe the way to go, more miles per gallon, Ned said, and in a loud bar they went for bourbon, flat-out, and Innis reached a point where it slid down like pop. He began to flip unshelled peanuts at people passing their table, laughing at first, but then grimly flinging them, taunting anyone his bleary gaze could fix on. To save him from a sure beating, Ned coaxed him into the street and drove him home, Sleep it off, man, go to bed. But when Innis, stumbling and cursing, saw his mother glowering at the top of the stairs, something flipped, he was on the verge of striking her before he pulled back, somehow it was her fault that his simple life had turned hopelessly complicated. After throwing up in the bathroom, he smashed the mirror, the toilet. It was the toilet that freaked her out, seeing him lift the lid off the back and break up the tank, yelling and slipping, collapsing finally on the wet tiles, water gushing everywhere, so mad drunk no one would come near him, and if he hadn't been in deep trouble already, she would have had the cops in, such was her disgust. No alcohol since, not even a beer. He did not miss it: it lit flames in his nerves, made his mind thick and stupid. But grass was clear, thoughtful, mellow, most of the time. Every so often, though not enough to put him off, bitterness rose up in him when he smoked, his grievances vivid, he tasted them, felt their sting. But he kept them in his head, talked them out with himself, found the words that would have worked if he'd had the wits when he'd needed them. Sometimes, stoned and alone, he would realize that he was talking out loud, fists clenched, pumping his anger as if the person were right there in the room with him. But he calmed down when he came down. Maybe it was good after all, that he could work it out this way alone. And if grass stoked his fantasies, better that than nothing. By fall, he would have plenty weed, not just for himself, but for the right people with money to spare.

His only call had been from his mother a few weeks ago, and though there were times back home when she'd been tough with him, formidable, and he'd feared her temper, he was struck by how distant she sounded, her voice thin, almost pleading. When he'd lived with her, she knew a good bit about his life, if not as much as she wanted to know, but now she had no real idea what he was up to and that seemed to shake her up. Don't worry, Ma, Innis told her before he hung up, conscious of the bad line and the eavesdroppers, I hitched my wagon to a Starr. She didn't laugh.

He squinted at the dark shape of the barn set back in the old pasture. Hard to imagine there'd ever been life in it, horses and cows coming and going, rumbling in their own hot stink, but warm nevertheless even on a night like this. Starr had hated farming, he let the place go after Grandpa died, the equipment wasn't touched again, even the old pick-up behind the toolshed was sunk to its hubs, the tires rotting, a load of snow in the truckbed. I shovelled so much shit I ran off to the navy, he said, and I wouldn't grow anything here now that God didn't give me for nothing, not even a blade of grass. Okay, Starr, I'll put in a crop for you. Grass it is.

The trucker who'd picked Innis up that day last fall outside New Glasgow said, Listen, stuff this good you could move easy, no problem at all around here, and don't give me another hit or I'll have us in the ditch. Jesus, it's a damn shame we don't grow it here, look at all this land, gesturing at the hills they were passing, black with spruce, and the old neglected fields. But you can, you know, Innis told him, explaining that he'd read how you could develop a strain for your own climate, they grew it all over the States, down South it was replacing moonshine, was what he'd heard. Well I never heard tell of that in Cape Breton, the trucker said, but if a man could and he did, he'd make a real go of it, good weed like you got in your hand there. Real money in that. What would we call it, eh? Cape Breton Gold? Canso Red? He laughed. He was a heavy guy with a blond neatly groomed beard and a darker ponytail, hauling drums of herbicide to some Swedish pulp company over in Port Hawkesbury, and Innis envied him, on the move, heading out every day. If guys like him wanted weed, Innis could, maybe by September, with some luck and good weather, provide it. And no middleman.

But without money, without a car, you were helpless, no more than a kid anyway. When the INS officer told him, Son, you are barred for life and that means what it says, it knocked him back, he felt like a bum. He couldn't live in the country he'd grown up in, couldn't even do time there anymore, they did not want him in the United States, period. He had told his mother, for Christ's sake, hard criminals don't even get thrown out of here, Ma, people a hundred times worse than me walk the streets free every day, killers, rapists, the worst kind of scum. They do time, they get to go back home when it's over. But his mother said, You *are* a criminal, Innis, that's what they call you when you keep stealing automobiles, and they are sending you home, that's where you were born, down east. You can live with Uncle Starr until you get on your feet. His feet? What about the rest of him?

He had thought, Cape Breton, it's just a name I'm going to, he heard it in his first memories, fluttering through his mother and dad's conversation, always with a peculiar and specific warmth whether their tone was anger or nostalgia, he'd heard it on the telephone as they talked with friends, it was a place where the people in his parents' kitchen came from because they had so many stories about it, Cape Bretoners they laughed over or admired or recalled with affection, the room full of cigarette smoke, bottles of beer or rum or Canadian whisky on the table, names tossed back and forth, you remember Johnny MacPhail, Johnny Nookie we called him? Lord, yes, he put out the bushline on the ice until he was too old to stand. And old Archie Bain, he told my dad, Listen, if you want to farm good you got to get the sheepses. But the names just drifted past, Innis never dreamed he'd be going there, "down home" belonged to his parents, to their time and their past, not to his, and Starr was just another name he had heard. A road to Cape Breton, that's how he'd thought of it as a kid, there was a road that went there and back to Boston, and all these people who gathered in the kitchen and called on the phone had travelled it one time or another, some just yesterday, last

night, fresh with news and stories, and others a long time
ago, but they had stories too and memories and people they
loved to talk about, and they all seemed to want to go back
over that road, sometime, even the ones who never would.
Innis had thought it an awful long road to where they all
had come from and where they all were going, and even the
ones who said they were glad they'd left sounded like they
couldn't forget this road either, and if Innis could get on it,
if somebody would put him in a car and take him there,
he would understand what they were all talking about and
he wouldn't be outside their passions and joys. But as he got
older, it was not a road Innis wanted to take, he wasn't listening in the kitchen anymore, it wasn't his road, it was
theirs.

Innis took another hit and pinched the roach into his
pocket. That day he had run from this place, a couple weeks
after he arrived, he'd turned back just beyond New Glasgow when he realized how broke and how dumb he was, no
idea where he was headed except away from North St.
Aubin, and it had taken him most of the day to get off Cape
Breton Island, Canada already feeling like just one great
westward space, blank, cold. By dark he was back on the Island, not far beyond the Canso Causeway. Two short rides
and his thumb was out again, hitching to the Ferry Road, to
Starr Corbett's house. He had to laugh. Grubby, stoned,
swaying like a loose road sign while cars blew by him, toss-
ing his long hair. A new Pontiac with two young women in
the front seat slowed down long enough to get a good look
at him, then took off. What scared them? Doper? Axe mur-
derer? Deportee? For the first time he'd felt ugly, conscious
that he could be seen entirely different from how he saw
himself. Across the road some kind of small trees ran up
a hillside clearing like rows of young corn. Pulp saplings,
he'd thought, spruce. Bands of Mi'kmaq Indians had torn
up acres of them, Starr said, so a big pulpwood company

couldn't spray from the air to kill off hardwood, it's useless for pulp. Spraying poisoned their springs, the Indians said. Brooks, game, the forest is not your farm, not a plantation, it has life you can see and life you can't see. But the spray had come anyway, misting over the new woods from helicopters, carried beyond its targets by shifts of wind not officially predicted but which any local would have warned them about. All right, he'd seen Indians along the highway and had never met one, but here was something for the Mi'kmaqs. He charged up the hill, yanking out the young trees, flinging them about like carcasses until he noticed the soft needles in his hand: damn, these were pines, hundreds of them, meant for bubble lights and tin angels. He found a plastic garbage bag in the road ditch and began to work the roots out gently instead of ripping them up, setting each seedling into the bag. He did not intend them for anyone's Christmas: he would plant them in the higher woods, a cover for his own crop of weed, an excuse to his uncle for going up there, if Starr should ever ask. Did his uncle even care what Innis did up there? The moonlight had made everything hard and still, the shadows of the tiny pines diminishing up the hill behind him. Another truck had finally given him a lift and the driver, tired in the dashboard light, kidded Innis about the sack that filled the cab with a smell of balsam and damp dirt. They got to talking about the Indians and the property owners who were fighting the herbicides, and the driver said, Listen to treehuggers and we'll all be out of work. We're out of it anyway, Innis said, trying to sound like a local, fellas like me. And what kind of fella are you? the man said. There's always work for them that wants it. Innis just smiled. He had a plan now, something of his own. He'd leaned his head back on the seat and watched the dark stream of trees rushing by, the road parting like a dark sea these woods he would slowly get to know.

Snow twirled powdery off the toolshed roof. The distance between houses widened in the winter months, the year-round residents fewer now, some houses empty until summer. He hugged himself. Beside the back field ran the dark gulley, its trees bare and black as iron. He was still afraid of the woods at night, of going deep into them, he couldn't shake that: when they turned dark, something powerful came into them, and he had never known it in a city. It was not menace, the way he felt in parts of Boston just driving through, places where he wouldn't even walk because what might happen there was easily imaginable— mugging, beating, being chased down, hassled. But in the woods he felt things he didn't understand: nothing to fear in the usual way, but something messed with his sense of what was real. Right now he wanted spring, a warm wind, color. The brook down there was hard as stone. Last fall seemed years away, that play of light and shadow where the hardwood canopies closed over him and he was glad to be lost. If you've lived a winter here, you know something about this place, Starr said, anybody can live a summer. Well, Innis knew the woods in winter, the mysterious tracks, the dry creak of wood in the wind—all had been welcome to his loneliness then, sheltering, the black trees at dusk like a drape across a window, losing him in a numbness, no one demanding to know who he was, where from, why he was here. He had felt like the convict in that movie set in Siberia, a man staggering through a stark waste of conifers and snowfields that went on and on like a dream further than anyone could see, escaped from a prison into the endless trees (It's crazy, ordering you out of the goddamn country, Mohney had said, you're American like me, you're from here, and Innis said no, I was born up there and I have to go back to it, for good). Whatever had watched him in those trees, it wasn't a person. Deer, sure, from a safe distance, poised for flight, but they had no opinions about him. Birds he couldn't name then, a script of tracks looping delicately through fresh snow, and their wings crisp as scissors when they flew. A rabbit would bolt from its cowering place, whips of fur and feet, its little pink brain unwinding through the brush like a top. But he liked to be near the road when dark came down, maybe where a streetlamp shone through the trees, not deep in the woods.

He stepped back into the mudroom, into the smell of the big salt cod a friend of Starr's had brought, holding it up by the tail like an animal pelt. It hung from a nail in the entryway giving off a rich odor, like salty cheese, and was there weeks later untouched until Innis wondered if maybe it was a trophy and not to be eaten at all. Starr would give its hard skin a stroke whenever he passed, Jesus, you don't find that size much anymore, and one time you'd haul them in and need two arms to carry them. Finally he began to break off pieces and soak them overnight and they ate boiled cod and potatoes and Innis got a taste for it. He tore off a shred and chewed it to sate the munchies, then stuffed himself with crackers and cheese in the warm kitchen. A rush of optimism made him smile at the ceiling light, right up there it was in the attic, in operation, things were moving at last. Outside, each flake spun lazily past the window, he could feel snow now even when his back was turned, even before he opened his eyes in the morning, it gave a tone to the air.

In the hallway, he studied the old photographs framed haphazardly on the wall, Granny hung them there, Starr said, I just left them the way they were. Innis liked to get right inside them, smell them, feel them. On some the glass was smoky, their corners held pinches of dust. These are people you came from, Starr told him, some of them. They seemed to Innis distant, removed, trapped in sepia shades and the blurry edges of box camera snapshots. Nothing candid in their poses, no fooling around. When Granny Corbett had stayed with them that time in Watertown when he was little, she was grey and heavy and ancient, wincing from room to room on bad feet, talking quietly to his dad in a language neither Innis nor his mother knew, saying things she didn't want them to hear and his mother got angry and slammed doors. Granny mailed him knitted socks at Christmas that itched and brown wool mittens he never wore when he was out of sight because he wanted gloves. But she never came back, and here she was in a chair on a porch, her hair darker, her folded hands big and capable in her lap, a woman he did not know, in some summer of her life where roses curled from a trellis, and there was Starr's brother, Munro, Innis's dad, on a haywagon at the reins of a big dark horse, the horse turning its head as the shutter clicked, smudging its face, his dad squinting in a bright sun, solemn, uncertain. How old was he there? Younger than Innis? A Cape Breton farm boy who would, like so many others, head for Boston or beyond, and who would be struck by a car near Scollay Square years later. Worst drivers in the world, his dad was always saying, they're right crazy, I wouldn't own a car in Boston if I had the money to buy one. Me too, Innis had said, only nine, and he never did own one. Leaving a bar he liked on a Friday, heading for the hot flat where they lived, his dad stepped too quickly off the curb and the car threw him amazingly high and far, or so Innis had imagined it, overhearing his mother on the phone, talking long distance to Cape Breton. Later she would tell friends how bystanders heard a great thump, like a deer getting struck someone said, and then saw him flying, stiff as a store dummy. Innis seized that picture of him, took it to his bed and dreamed it, enlarged it, drew it slowly and carefully with crayons, his father frozen there above a street, a puzzling mannequin in the air, dressed nicely in a suit they buried him in, light grey, his eyes dark circles of surprise. He had worked in a tool factory where Innis would never want to work, nights that left a man a hump in a daytime bed, grumpy at supper, his wife forgetting what she'd loved him for and drifting out in the evenings with women friends, just an hour or two, at first. She was pregnant when they married, Starr said, miscarried on that one, right here in this house, and maybe another in Watertown, if I'm not mistaken, before you came along. She wanted out of here. She never came back that I can remember, not here. I could say things about your mother, he told Innis, but I won't, she has her weaknesses and I got mine. Munro loved her, he did, and he wasn't an easy man himself. I know it was some hard there in Boston for a long time, for her and for your dad too, so no, I won't say a word. But what could he have said that Innis didn't know already? He had grown up with her, slept next to her bedroom.

In his room Innis danced on the linoleum cold enough to skate on as he searched his drawer for wool socks. A bitter draft from the window blew about his feet. When he was a kid he'd raise the window a crack before he jumped into bed and inhale the new snow on the sill, the wind soughing outside, then warm up under the big patched quilt his Granny had sewn and sent.

He poured water from the chipped pitcher into the washbowl glazed with yellow roses and splashed his face. He was tired enough, whacked out from getting his plants set up and tucked away, tight and edgy every moment he was doing it lest his uncle show up. But the thought of sleep depressed him, of giving himself up to it on another Friday night, marooned in the old house, Starr out with the mysterious woman. Newly wed, Innis's mother and dad had come to this bedroom, used it until they had their own place. The very day Innis was to leave Boston she had taken his hand and whispered to him, Innis, honey, when you get there see if that commode is still in the bedroom, would you? Starr has a bathroom now but we washed with that pitcher and bowl winter and summer, cold water every morning, and I didn't care at all at the time. Jesus, telling him that and him not two hours away from a plane flight out of the country for good. Did she have a clue how he felt that day? All the cockiness knocked out of him like they'd punched him in the heart? What do you want? she had yelled at him after he smashed the toilet, are you just crazy or what? The guy she was going with, a man she really liked, grabbed his coat and left that night, said no thanks, that kid is nuts. Innis lay in bed the next morning listening to two plumbers murmuring in the bathroom, his mind grey as mud, feeling like shit. What did he want? Only one thing: to stay where he lived, and had lived. If they had pondered day and night the worst way to punish him, the one penalty that would bring him up short, they had found it.

In this bedroom now he had collected objects his mother and probably his father too would never have wanted. The limestone rock, water-carved, sculptured by the brook he'd pulled it out of, a piece of art. His walking stick, a thin spruce he'd whittled and peeled, oiled from his hands now, a crutch his first days in the woods when he'd fallen often, fooled by level runs of bracken fern, hidden holes, windfalls, brooks. The antlered skull of a deer he'd found wedged in the crook of a tree and soaked in bleach until it was white: it had chilled him a little when he first hung it on the wall, in night shadows or waking to it (It's customary to keep the hide on them, you know, Starr said, when you mount them like that, with nice glass eyes, not ugly sockets, don't ever bring a woman in here, you'll scare her stone cold), but Innis wanted that charge of fright when he opened his eyes in the dark, it seemed necessary to get some of the city out of him. A cluster of feathers—raven, eagle, gull, grouse. Three paperback books, one on plants and flowers, another on birds, grubby and thumbed before he ever bought them at that secondhand shop in The Mines, and the book about growing marijuana he'd hidden in his suitcase at the last minute, disguised in a dust jacket snatched from one of his mother's crappy novels, *The Romance of Red Rock Castle*, a kind of pretty guy in a kilt closing in on a startled woman in a strapless gown. A shed snakeskin from under the toolshed, its dry transparence had fascinated him, the faint pattern of its markings. When Starr saw it he said, hang on to it, it'll keep the house from burning, that's what your Granny would say. Innis had been leery of snakes, he'd leapt away from the first one that quicksilvered across his path, but Starr said not to worry, no poisonous snakes on this island or Cape Breton Island either, no poison ivy, no poison oak. He'd pinned a few of his drawings to the wallpaper, scenes of the woods, the old barn. Others he concealed under his mattress, the ones that came out of his own head. He'd done one of Starr sitting at the kitchen table, Starr grumbled about it but cooperated long enough for a pencil sketch. Innis handed it to him when he was done and Starr stared at it frowning, nodding, well you've got something of me there but I'm not sure what, and he handed it back.

Innis got under a quilt, a sketchpad on his knees. It wasn't so much that he was good with a pencil or a pen, he was, his teachers had always told him so, it was just something he'd always had to do since he was tiny. Whatever impressed him, good or bad, he liked to draw it later when he was alone. Older, and stoned, what he got on the page was stranger, more interesting, some way of looking at it he wouldn't otherwise find.

He started with her hat, wide and floppy, but left her face in shadow. He picked out the fur trim of her boots and gave her a fur collar, high about the neck, graceful, like her legs,

one drawn up and clasped in elegant hands, the other outstretched. For company, for familiar noise, he flipped on the
transistor radio by his bed, looking for that CBC station
that played rock. Sometimes he'd hear a band that had been
popular back home, that he might have shared with a girl
as they rode in one of his borrowed cars, the girls never
knew they were stolen. Background music, life needed it
sometimes. But he stopped the dial when it crossed over a
woman's voice. French. Sexy, its own kind of music. He
didn't know French any more than he did his grandmother's
Gaelic, but this woman seemed to be telling a story, he
could hear its rhythm. What it might be about didn't matter, because he was imagining the woman herself: he quickly
sketched her face under the hat, in lines he considered
French, slender and sultry, mature, her mouth forming a
word like a kiss, in her hands pages of her story. On another
of his pages he could strip her if he wanted, do her nude, in
beautiful detail, he had that skill. Schoolmates used to press
around him, urging him to draw a woman naked. At first,
when he was young, the simplest figure would satisfy them,
a cartoon of curving, swelling flesh, the pubis a dark daub,
and they sucked that up, it was so illicit, oh Jesus, Innis,
what if the teacher sees it, they howled, groaned, went mute
with awe. And as his skills improved, they wanted details,
hairs, clefts, openings, a zoom shot between the thighs, they
wanted anatomy, couplings, horseplay, dumb fantasies. So
he added men, acrobats of erectile tissue, probing, joining
from the few angles his newfound friends could think of,
their imaginations were not ready for the Kama Sutra. His
intricate drawings began to bore them, they drifted away,
they no longer whispered, Come on, Innis, draw us a good
one, they were looking for skin. Innis drew only for himself after that. His mother had saved his drawings until they
got weird. I didn't want to show those to my friends, now

did I? she told him, women undressed from every angle you could imagine? You shouldn't have been nosing around, Ma. That's not nosing around, not as long as you're under this roof, it isn't.

Women here, if he could meet any he wanted to get next to, would only ask questions as soon as he opened his mouth, where you from? and he'd have to lie and he was tired of making himself up just so no one would dig any deeper. In Watertown, the last girl he dated, an Italian, his mother told him not to bring home because she was Catholic. So he stole a car to take her to a big dance, a Cadillac convertible, deep purple with a white top, beautiful and absurd, and they left the dance early to drive around, playing tapes. He told her an uncle loaned it to him and they parked down by the Charles River awhile, then drove into the wooded area outside Boston and had sex on the deep leather seats, great to get naked on, cushioned in music. After he dropped her home, the car full of perfume and pot smoke, Innis drove around the rest of the night because the car felt so fine he couldn't give it up, and just after sunrise, as he was about to ditch it in a back street, the police caught him cruising with the top down. Wearing his pale blue sportcoat, the sun on his face, he had thought that white steering wheel belonged in his hands, but apparently he didn't look it, they were on him so fast. After his mother bailed him out, he called the girl but she wouldn't come to the phone. You're a bum, her mother screamed at him and hung up. That was the last fun car before his mother saw him in the Lincoln. He was on probation then already. She was wild, she pulled up beside him at a traffic light honking her horn and he had to floor it to shake her, cutting down side streets. When he got home after midnight she was still up. I've got the license number of that car you stole, she said, they're probably still out there looking for it.

You don't pick cheap ones, do you? What was that, a Lincoln Continental? I was taking it somewhere, Ma, for a friend. Stop lying to me, damn you, Innis. If they nail you again, you'll be out of here, they'll ship you home. Home? he said, I *am* home. She said, don't kid yourself, they'll show you where home is. Bullshit, Ma. I've lived here since I was what, two? I'm as American as anybody. She said, sometimes I don't think you're wrapped too tight. If they find out you're not a citizen, they'll deport you, they'll let the Canadians have you. Listen, I want you to get yourself to Cape Breton and stay with your Uncle Starr a couple months, now, tomorrow. You haven't been there since you were a tot, but that's okay. You do this, you disappear up there or so help me I will turn you in myself. They don't know half the cars you took. They'll be around soon enough, if they're not at the door in the morning, I'll be damn surprised, they got plenty on you. He said, I'm not going back there and you can't make me go back. They got nothing on me. I'm not driving the car now, am I? Is it parked outside or something? I wore gloves. No prints, nothing. His mother put her face close to his, God, you're a stupid boy, oh Jesus, you are.

That had happened before the Porsche, before he stole for someone else. They made him pay for that one: he was over eighteen.

Thirsty from the grass, Innis ran the sink tap in the kitchen, the water instantly cold. He took a glass from the cupboard: on its rim was the perfect impress of a woman's lips, translucent, pink. When did Starr have a ladyfriend in here, the bastard? Could've washed the glass at least. Innis filled it. He tasted the lipstick, its faint scent, and then the water, sweet and cold. Far up in the woods, under its rickety wooden shelter, the old spring trickled out of rock.

3

The snow had turned wet under a bright sun and Innis left off splitting stove wood to pack a snowball. He shaped it hard and baseballed it into the side of the woodshed with a satisfying thump. He peppered a few more, then quit. In Watertown at night he and Ned Mohney used to whump cars as they passed, fleeing when brakelights lit up. Kid stuff. Harmless excitements. He didn't hear from Mohney, just the note in the M&Ms. The prick, where was he now? Down at Danny's place? Cruising around? Innis tossed another snowball far into the back field, sending two ravens lumbering into the air, their deep scolding croaks fading into the lower woods. The sun felt great but that chill east wind was still blowing across the drift ice. With the sea so close the weather could turn quickly. He could see white floes in the channel water beyond the woods, and above that the long mountain ridge showed nothing but winter, grey swatches of hardwood and the darker evergreens touched with snow. Sometimes it didn't feel that he was on an island, from the house the strait looked more like a wide river, in many shades and moods, taking on the skies, the shadows from the mountain. Now over the trees it was afternoon blue, bits of pan ice ebbing brightly in the tide. He should call that Father Lesperance but he wasn't in the mood today. Maybe he'd get away to the shore for a while, he hadn't spent much time in the lower woods, they ended at the beach and you'd have to be pretty dim to get lost in them since all you had to do was go downhill or uphill and you were in the clear.

Innis glanced up at the snow-streaked roof. His seeds hadn't popped yet and that worried him, but what could he do? He split a few more logs, then embedded the maul in the chopping block and headed down the back field, past

the carrion ravens had been picking at, gobs of rabbit fur
and blood, and as he reached the border of the trees he
heard the Lada's rattling diesel and looked back to see it
rolling slowly down the long driveway through the front
field. He ducked behind a spruce. Starr wouldn't like a cold
kitchen but tough luck, what was he doing home so early?
The man seemed to have no hours lately, going to the shop
when he felt like it, closing up at odd hours in the afternoon. Innis had seen him printing out a cardboard sign on
the kitchen table, *If the vertical's no good, try the horizontal. Closed till tomorrow.* Someone with him now, another
face behind the windshield. At the back door his uncle got
out, left the engine running while he dashed inside, returning immediately shaking his head, at his nephew, no doubt,
and opened the passenger door. A woman emerging? The
hat with the big brim, holding it in her hand while she did
a slow turn, taking things in. Too far to see her clearly, black
hair, dark coat with a colorful belt. Starr kissed her on the
mouth and they stood there in an embrace, talking. Innis
watched, resenting Starr in a way he could not have predicted, he didn't know who the hell this woman was but
just that closeness to her he could feel right now, her breath
warm in this cold wind, the perfume of her. He was in no
mood to go up there now, let them start their own fire, upstairs too if they wanted. Try the horizontal, it's all vertical
for me.

On the old shore path Innis patted his pockets for that
roach he'd saved for later but needed now. He sheltered in
alders long enough to toke up, annoyed that he had to ra-
tion his weed. Hiding there alone, he was soon flirting with
self-pity, with blame, but no, he wouldn't let that eat him
up, lashing out at his mother. No, he'd done this to himself.
Those fall days drifted back to him, roaming the woods up
above, further and further beyond the power line break to
where the land flattened out, not giving a damn if he got

lost or not. Until it happened. He had whispered the word over and over, *lost, lost,* like a dare. Then in those woods he thought by then he knew like a city block, he lost his way, on that overcast November afternoon, as confused as any city boy could be. You're too fucking cocky, Starr had told him only the day before, tramping way back up in the trees like that, you don't know the lay of things, you'll disappear, there's no taxis up there, b'y, no street signs, it's not Watertown, and it sure isn't Boston. And Innis flared at him, it doesn't take a genius, I've been up there and back a hundred times. True, he'd known nothing about forest when he came to Cape Breton, not even what trees were called, or how you made your way safely through a few miles of them. But they were a place to hide himself, and they absorbed him in their indifference. Slowly he'd begun to see that the qualities of leaves meant something, that bark was not just a commonplace word but a mark, a signal, here smooth and grey, there ridged and deeply brown, and that trunk and branch grew in different contours, and that when stricken by worms and blight and lightning, when light-starved and scarred and ripped by windfalls, they kept unmistakable features, and you could use those features to braid an invisible tether and that would lead you back where you wanted to return. He'd extended himself deeper and deeper, testing what he learned, what he observed. He'd felt that something lay back there deep, if he kept going. At first he'd just sketched it in his small notepad whenever a shape struck him. He'd come to hate asking Starr anything about the woods, he wanted to learn them on his own, but he had asked him the name of a tree here and there, and after he bought the paperback book on trees, he saw that his uncle was sometimes wrong (You called this one silver maple but it's not maple at all, look at this leaf, poplar, silver poplar, and Starr said, That's what we always called them here so that's what I'll call them, does the fella who wrote that book live here?), and when Innis knew the trees he walked through, had detailed them in pencil, he felt he'd mapped the woods in his own way, that they were not blinding and trackless anymore but navigable, subject to his wits, not like streets back in Boston but like an almost private sanctuary where he was the only man. Yet, there he was, lost. The sun he'd kept on his left shoulder had gone, absorbed into a sky cold as milk, and the wind that he'd remembered as east, east on his face, had dodged somehow around, leaping at him in different directions, confusing him in showers of dry leaves. Small clearings of light in deep spruce and fir and stripped hardwoods mocked him as he plunged first toward one, then another. The deadfalls he had taken bearings on, noting the angles they had fallen at, the peculiar ways they'd crashed and split or snagged strangely on the way down, seemed to have vanished in the vague sunless shadows. The spiny green monotony of the spruce would bring night down thoroughly and fast, and that frightened him— everything he had learned would dissolve in darkness. He tried to will the woods around him into a pattern he could recognize, an arrangement of foliage and branch and light that had to be there. But in the wind the dead and half-dead trees, swooning in the branches of the living ones, rubbed and sawed, a conversation of sounds he would not want to hear at night. Where was that head-high stump he could not fail to see, it would fairly shout at you, its ragged neckhole, its oxblood core torn open in the high winds of two weeks ago? Where was the ant-brown bole of that old white birch? Without sun to give a slant of light, any deer trail looked convincing, luring him a few paces until another one appeared to draw him innocently away, and then, with a quick breath of panic, he sensed how deeply wrong his steps were, and the woods deepened and turned in on him, became the dark abstraction he once had of them. City boy without a city. He walked harder as if the sheer gravity of his step would guide him out, bringing his feet down harshly in the leafy duff. He swore, he gnawed his lips, he did not want to feel like a kid who had to be found, he was nineteen, but that feeling was taking hold in him. Jesus, Starr would be home from work by now, he might be knocking some supper together, muttering where in the hell is Innis. I'm here, damn you, in somebody's woods spread all over creation, acres of it, left to itself. He rested on a trunk so long on the ground brilliant blades of fungus grew from its bare, mossed flanks. How long would it be before an alarm was sent out? Surely not until it was well dark, before Starr would make a phone call or two and then drive the Ferry Road, squinting through the windshield. Or would he think his nephew had taken off again, maybe even in someone's automobile like the car thief he'd been, I never expected Innis to stay in Cape Breton anyway, it's not Boston, it's not enough that he was born here, this is not his place. Innis was afraid he'd end up like the woman up the road, a city person like himself, just visiting her brother, and she went into the woods above his house to hunt mushrooms and got lost so sure and solid she might have been in South America. Innis knew now how it happened, how she must have seen a mushroom she wanted off the trail, an appealing yellow cluster more satisfying than flowers, and she'd stepped a ways here, then there, and then she stood up suddenly and felt something like what Innis was feeling now—tricked, and small. The Mounties came and wouldn't let anyone local go up here looking for her because a tracking dog had been called in and they didn't want the scent disturbed by searchers, and before the dog showed up a helicopter came all the way up from Shubenacadie around dusk and swept over the trees ineffectually for a while and then landed in a yard, useless. The tracking dog did it, a German shepherd, meticulously circling along the woman's frightened and spiraling trail, tracing almost minute by minute the time it took the hook of her fright to set deeply, that pathetic, aimless tramping through tangled brush and wild, relentless trees, praying for luck. The dog found her near a bog about midnight standing in the middle of berries she was too scared to eat, swollen with fly and mosquito bites, scratched, but pale and okay in the harsh beams of flashlights. But Innis did not want the attention of Mounties, or to be taken out of here by a dog and kindly rescuers, he did not want to see his uncle's sarcastic smile, he did not want to be written up in the paper or be on the news, they would all know what had brought him back here. He had closed his eyes. This was a big step backward, territory lost. So he'd just listened. In the rush and noise of the trees a sound was there for a second and it made him shiver—footfalls so soft in the leaves, so new his ears seized it from other noises, even the surge of his heartbeat. He stood up quickly, sensed rather than saw a flick of fur behind a heap of greying spruce. But that was all. Movement, unhurried flight. Not a deer but something quiet and lower to the ground. Soundless, just eyes. The chill of it held him for a few moments, then he calmed down. Jesus, how many times had he flushed an animal, a bird up here, a rabbit? Why fear it now? He set off again deliberately, ignoring direction, ignoring the wind. There was a brook, and the brook should slope down toward the road somewhere, that he knew. He followed it until its meagre water went dry underground and it became just a slick mat of leaves. He stopped: the sky took on an odd brightness for a moment and the trees seemed to turn suddenly, like those trick cards whose images change when light hits them a certain way, and he spotted a high straight pine, this one as familiar as a house, and when he circled it, there was the blaze mark he'd made in its dark trunk a month ago, dirty with the bleed of sap, it was like seeing his name carved there.

Innis heard the Lada horn, that irritating hoot, what a lame automobile, any woman worth your time wouldn't be seen in it. Starr must have noticed his tracks leading away from the woodpile. He hurried the rest of the way through the lower woods, stumbling once nearly to his knees, whoops, that roach had a wallop. He leaped from the shore-bank to the beach and tramped through its mix of snow and ice, feeling the bite of the wind. The mountain seemed higher across the strait, the wooded hills of St. Aubin at his back. In January it had been all still ice, clear across to the other side. But now the dark cold water was moving, waves eating tangled floes from shore rocks and ragged driftwood. The storms had driven in a huge tree trunk, its amputated roots already sea-worn, tipped with claws of ice. He hauled on yellow rope snaked under the snow and drew out a lobster buoy, a gay red and white, and he twirled it around and around his head and away into the water. The waves would wash it in again, or would the eddy get it and bob it out with the tide, down there beyond the big bridge, out to sea? A thick hemp towline was woven among the beach debris like a weathered python. Starr had played here as a kid, swum here. Hard to imagine it ever warm enough. A tree stump, so often soaked and dried out it had opened out like a book, long laminations of wooden pages.

For an island, Starr had told him when Innis first came, St. Aubin's as much land as sea, land being close on three sides of us, we're a long loaf of an island tucked into Cape Breton Island, and the water to the west and south is the heart of us, the big lake, saltwater, the tides run in the strait you see toward the mountain there, but we got the ocean on the northeast end, can't see it from here unless you're way high, the sea isn't far, she's out there bright and wide. So you could be worse places, it's not like you're on St. Kilda. Innis had thought he'd prefer an island clean and isolated, where you couldn't see anything but ocean, but that was the early days after his arrival when he didn't care much what happened to him. It didn't help when Starr told him, I've lived by myself a long time and if I had a choice it'd be a woman bedding down in here, not a nephew who's made a hash of his life. Sure, Uncle. Who could blame you for that? Though the tide was twisting through its dark surface, the strait had been frozen across to the mountain shore for over a month, and he had walked out on it once with Starr who warned him that you had to know how to read the ice or it can take you into a quick black hole, the current trapping you under and sweeping you away. In the days before paved roads people travelled the ice all over, when solid it was a good highway, you could hit another shore just about any-where that mattered. Only patches of ice were travelling today, gliding seaward.

He poked along the beach, kicking ice, his eyes tearing in the wind. Objects had more than common interest when he was high, even a rum bottle, its colorful Jamaican label half peeled away. Jamaica sun, wow. And *ganja.* His hands were cold already but he brushed snow off the big log and sat. He took out his pad, sketching not the shore—it was too new to him and he wasn't sure how he felt about it, the water un-nerved him a little this close, level with it—but the spring up in the woods where the animal had drunk and he had drunk just after it, it had to be a cat, that shy stealth, so quiet, crouched at the lip of the spring, nothing else moving but the lap and flicker of its tongue and the last, light snow, and the fringe of its fur in the wind. Innis used a black ball-point to get the feeling of the woods, the feathery, spiraling snow, the stark silence in simple lines, black against white, and the dark mouth of the spring, that little pattering cave, the faint pawprints. The cat, whatever it was, would have to wait until it revealed itself, or he might invent it, he wanted to imagine a snow leopard. Who would stop him? He could draw what he liked. The penpoint began to skip, he put the sketchpad in his pocket and wandered further, into the cove where he investigated a long hump set back beyond the highwater line, covered with a blue tarpaulin, its edges held down with stones. He knocked on it. Wood. Anyone home? Kneeling, he lifted the tarp like a skirt: a boat, dull white paint. The blade of an oar was visible. There were the remnants of a nest in the rocky sand. He stood up and looked out at the water leaping with waves and sun, tips whitened with wind. Jesus, who would dare row in that? It stirred and excited him, as much because he was safe on the shore as the prospect itself. Maybe you wouldn't even have to row, maybe the currents would take you all the way to the bridge and beyond, cold spray in your face. One warm spring morning in Boston he was on the bank of the Charles River, lying on the grass, mellowed out, glad to be alone, traffic a distant noise, when he heard the synchronized grunts of a rowing crew, college boys, Harvard in their crimson shirts, and he sat up to watch their shell cut sleekly past, the oars as efficient as wings, the rowers blind to anything but their task, and he longed to have his heart pounding like theirs, to share their exhaustion, their camaraderie, their kind of learning he would never know. Starr said, your grandmother lived over there on the other side and my father rowed across to see her, in some mean weather too, he wanted to see her that bad.

Innis shaded his eyes but the mountain trees ran ridge to shore, holding within them the life that was left there. He could glimpse but a house or two embedded in the trees like white chips of wood but he could not tell if they were old enough to have held a grandmother. Colder now, grass always made him cold, a clear memory flew into his mind, he was four years old and his mother took him with her into the ladies section of a department store, and he let go her hand to push through the racks of dresses, eager for the smell, the feel of women's cloth against his face, and, taken with a slender mannequin, he'd gotten on his knees to peer underneath her skirt, and above him the women laughed, his mother too, he could hear her laughter now. There was no telling what weed would call up, what taste of memory.

4

"Claire, that's Innis. The Backwoodsman from Boston."

"That's me," Innis said, flashing the peace sign. "Hello." The kitchen killed the last of his high but enough of it lingered to ride with his uncle's mood. He was sweating and a bit lightheaded from the long walk up and there was surely a better time to meet this woman sitting at the table, her high cheekbones rouged with winter air, her eyes dark, bright with cold. She looked at him with a calm frankness, taking him in, then she smiled.

"Hello, Innis."

"Sorry the kitchen was cool. I got sidetracked."

"Innis spends a lot of time on sidetracks," Starr said, spearing a stove lid with a lifter. Innis had to smile, slightly: that was true, he did, but he didn't like his uncle saying it. Starr clanged the poker around in the stove hole and fire flared up. He slammed the lid back in place. "Listen, Claire's staying here for a while."

"A short while," Claire put in. She seemed to suspect that Innis would not be thrilled. She was right: another person crashing here, someone else who might open that attic door on a whim.

"Sure," Innis said. "Fine. I'm just a boarder myself."

"She's had some trouble," Starr said, "with an ex-boyfriend, ex-partner. Whatever he is, the bastard hit her.

Look at this." He gently lifted her chin, so the ceiling light caught a dark welt along the edge of her eye.

"Nothing serious," she said, taking his hand away with equal gentleness. "He's sorry already. He'd never laid a hand on me before."

"He won't get another chance, and that's a fact," Starr said, grabbing a green wool scarf off the wall hook. He wound it round his neck, tucking the ends behind the lapels of a black wool sportcoat that had seen some wear, but never in the daytime that Innis could remember, and the scarf was a new touch, a little rakish for Starr, who favored blinding-white shirts, soaked in bleach you could smell in the kitchen sink on Saturdays, he ironed them himself with great seriousness, cursing and kissing his fingers as he slowly steamed out the wrinkles. He'd been to the barber too, his wavy grey hair smoothly groomed, shiny with barber's oil. Maybe she enhanced him somehow, this Claire, but he looked handsome in a rough-edged way and Innis, still warmed by the weed, almost told him so, but he'd learned to rein back his tongue at those very moments when effusiveness or embarrassing affection seized him: he usually regretted it when he came down. Even so, there was an air of elopement about Starr and this Claire, as if he'd brought a bride home for Innis's approval, his blessing, here on the other side of the threshold, because he came with the house now. But no: that was stoned-think, so don't say anything unnecessary.

Starr leaned close to her, talking low. "Okay, now, I'm going back there to get your things. Better give me your keys. You say your suitcases were already packed?"

"Two, in the hallway. He kicked one open, kicked the stuff around. Don't bother about it. But Starr, if Russ is there? Just forget it, all right?"

"Does he own a gun?"

"I don't think so. He never said so. But please..."

"Please? Yes, that's what I'll tell him if he's there, You like to hit women? Try me instead. Please, I'd like that, I would."

"Starr Corbett to the rescue," Innis said.

"You should know, Tiny Tim."

Innis felt heat rise to his face. "Come on, Starr," he said, touching his hair. "It's shorter than when I came."

What had Starr told her about him? Any of the truth? If he had, there was no chance for harmony here. "He thinks I'm a hippie, Claire. He's never met one, of course."

"Like hell." Starr pulled on leather gloves and smacked a fist into one palm and then the other. "We had a house full of them down the road, MacLeans' old place. They squatted there, they set up shop. Vietnam War scared them up here like a flock of chickens, but we didn't give much of a damn for a while. Then one afternoon Alec Grant's coming along in his car and one walks right in front of him crossing the road, all dreamy looking, naked as a peeled egg. Now, a woman, Alec wouldn't have cared so much. But a longhaired hippie with a big beard, his ass hanging out, no thank you. A few of us went up there and helped them leave."

"Hippies don't fight," Innis said. "That wouldn't be hard."

"You're right, it wasn't. But they weren't all peaceful, I can tell you that. You have any work to do or you just goofing off? I haven't seen the color of your money lately."

"I'm owed some, and there's a priest with a cottage needs fixing up, down by the old wharf."

"A priest? That should bring a bundle. Claire, there's rum in the cupboard, dear. Innis, show her. You need a drink, girl. I'm off." He opened the back door but stopped as if something had just occurred to him. He looked back at Innis. "None for you, though. You don't drink."

"Right on, Uncle. I wouldn't touch it. Those your Lada racing gloves?"

"You're too damn saucy. And don't call me Uncle." He gave Claire a wave and closed the door. Innis sighed but didn't move while the Lada revved and revved and clattered off up the driveway. Then he sat at the table, pulling his parka open. "Hot," he said. He smiled at Claire who was lighting a cigarette. She blew smoke at the ceiling, revealing a pretty throat, elegant and muscular.

"The hair thing's a big deal with him, is it?" she said. "Lord, when I was your age I'd have given a lot for long straight hair."

"Why?" Innis said. "Your hair is beautiful." It reminded him of crows' black, the way light caught their wings.

She smiled. "Listen, I'm not moving in. Just lying low for a week or two."

"I'll be out of here by maybe September myself. At the latest."

"You don't like it here?"

She had seen most of her thirties, and places beyond Starr, beyond Cape Breton, Innis guessed. She didn't look like any woman he had seen here, not up close, not on the street, in The Mines or Sydney either. She knew she was attractive, he could tell, but it wasn't an issue with her.

"What I like about here I can't explain," Innis said. "Anyway, it isn't enough."

"A young man like you, he wants to get away, sure. I came out from Ontario with my boyfriend, the one Starr is not going to meet up with, I hope. He bought a hundred acres to raise trotters on."

"Where?"

"Here on St. Aubin, down at Black Rock."

"Never been there."

"Cliffs at the back of his place, the ocean's right there. I almost said our place. It was his project, but it took a lot of my money."

"Money in horses."

"Not for him, not for Russ. It was a dream of his."

"Is that bad?"

"Not if your feet are on the ground. His money is gone too, along with some other things."

"Bummer."

"He didn't take it too well. I wouldn't mind a little of that rum?"

"Hey. Sorry." He had the rum out fast and a glass, sighting it at the light to see if he'd washed it. "Anything with it?"

"Water and ice. Is it decent rum?"

"Captain Morgan."

"Jesus."

"Starr's not fussy. If it gets him toasted..."

"I'm raising his tastes. He'll take a good bottle of wine now, if you can find one."

"I suppose it must be the boonies here, compared to Ontario. Toronto?"

"Close. I was an air hostess. But no, Cape Breton is beautiful. You'd be surprised what you can find here, if good wine isn't one of them. Sydney's not Boston, of course, is it."

"Not what I've seen of it, and that isn't much. I don't tool around a lot."

"Why?"

"No wheels."

"That must be a real handicap, living out here. Starr won't lend you his?"

"That rattletrap? I'd rather hitch. Hot in here, isn't it?" Innis flung off his parka and checked the stove damper. "Starr tell you anything about me?" he said, his back to her.

"A little. You're his nephew, after all. But I don't know why you came up here from Boston. You can tell me about yourself. I'll listen."

"I've led a boring life. The good stuff's all ahead of me, is the way I look at it. Come on, I'll show you around."

She was taller than he thought, tall as Starr anyway, her long black sweater cinched at the waist in a wide lavender belt. Innis directed her into the hall, flipping on the light so he could point out the old photographs, making up names if he couldn't recall what Starr had told him, "But that's my mother's father with one of his pals, out on the town, I guess, see the bowler hat in his hand? My mother's dad, he was a bricklayer, in the steel mill in Sydney mostly, bricking the furnaces." "He's handsome," Claire said, and Innis wanted to tell her, People think I look like him. "This is the parlor," he said, "the furniture's old as hell, most of it. I guess my great-uncle made the tables, the beds and dressers upstairs, a good carpenter, like my grandfather. The rockers are his, the pine cupboard. People here flung a lot of stuff in the fire, Starr says, they thought it was dreary, they wanted new things, especially after the war, you know? But the folks hung on to it in this house. It's dreary all right, that old dark varnish." "Not really," she said, "they're antiques now. They have the atmosphere of another time, that's all. Sometimes atmosphere is everything." She ran her finger across the mantle of the fireplace and held it up to him, smiling. "Okay, okay," he said, "we're behind in our dusting. The fireplace is always cold, Starr doesn't use it. That TV is something, isn't it? I think my grandfather built it."

Innis let her go ahead of him up the stairs, watching her hips move under her wool skirt, her expensive leather boots allowing him just a glimpse of her leg. Too much to hope that his uncle would get held up and he'd have this woman to entertain into the evening. Maybe this Russ guy would be more than Starr bargained for, a real tussle, the Mounties would be called in.... He moved ahead of her, turning on lights. He showed her the bathroom first. "This was a little bedroom once, until the plumbing came in. Starr has lots of outhouse tales. You know, how rugged it was, the slop bucket and all that, chamberpots, cold water." She shivered. "It is cold up here. Big quilts, I hope." "Trunkfuls. Here's the spare bedroom. I'll do the bed up for you, I know where the sheets are. Unless, I mean..." He had passed Starr's bedroom without a word even though the door was wide open, the bed neatly made. He didn't even want to consider that she and Starr might share it, yet he felt like a hostelkeeper or somebody's dad, steering her to the safe bedroom, next to his own. But she touched his arm to put him at ease. "This room will do fine. A big tree out the window. And wallpaper!" "I hate it," he said, "but it's not as bad as mine." He pointed her to the next room. "Look."

"Oh," she said. "You draw."

Innis stayed in the doorway while Claire went from sketch to sketch, peering close, then leaning back. "Nice, you're very good. That old man's face, terrific. Who is he?"

"Old guy up the road. He's about a hundred years old. I put the army cap on him, with the feather. He didn't pose that way, I just did him from memory. Dan Rory MacRitchie." He watched her long slender fingers drift absently over the glass shade of his lamp, his radio, the feathers in a cracked vase. A woman in his room. Too much. "Sometime I'll draw you, since you're going to be around."

"I'd like that. But flatter me if you can."

"Piece of cake."

"Good God, are you a hunter?" She reached up to touch the deer skull. "That's gruesome."

"He's like a pal now, I can't go to sleep without him. I don't hunt, I found him in the woods."

At the head of the stairs she paused by a closed door. "Another bedroom?"

"God, no. The attic, full of junk. I mean, to the rafters. Just step in the door and you're filthy."

She stared at it until Innis felt his heart pick up. For a few moments he had the urge to tell her everything, to open it and show her there was something in there that was only his. Instead he reached out and rattled the knob. "See? Locked. Hey, you haven't seen the little corner cellar where they used to store their food."

"Maybe I'll skip that, Innis, for now."

"If you hear cracking and groaning, by the way, it's not me, it's the foundation. Unmortared stones."

"I should call my old number. I don't know what's going on over there."

"Don't reveal any secrets. There's always about six dozen locals tuning in."

She laughed. "The same in Black Rock. I'm used to it."

There was no answer at her old address but Starr was back just after dark, banging two suitcases through the back door, flushed, out of breath, highly pleased with himself and ready for talk. If anyone phones, he told Innis, we are not at home. He brought in sacks of groceries and sat at the table smoking cigarettes and drinking rum while Claire cooked them thick steaks and potatoes and peas on the big old stove instead of the smaller propane one, amused, Starr coaching her, You got to be a bit of a fireman, dear, to run that thing. Russ the ex-whatever had not been home after all, his car was gone, and Starr had gathered up the suitcases, one of them lying open in the yard, her underthings a scatter of color. Innis stayed out of the conversation, content with his meal, listening, cadging looks at Claire. He'd thought her eyes were dark brown but they were really an intense, inky blue.

"My dad was a crackerjack farmer, Claire, you know," Starr said. "Maybe we could get this place going again, you and me."

"What about Innis?" she said.

"Innis is just passing through. He's got other fish to fry, if he can hook them."

"Yep, I'm always on the move." Innis tried to sound flippant but he was hurt. His uncle's plans were fantasies anyway, so all the more reason to include him. "I need a city. A big city."

"Yeah," Starr said. "One without cars in it."

Innis shot him a look but Starr, his hands working the air, had already forgotten, his scenario was expanding with each glass of rum as he gabbed away to Claire as if they were newlyweds. He would sell the old farm and move to British Columbia, good work and wages there, or he'd re-enlist in the navy, they had such good pensions now he could put in ten more years and be sitting pretty. He could get his license on the Great Lakes, the lakeboats needed men with his background, engineer types. Good money, but maybe he shouldn't be away from home that long. No, he wanted to be here, he was sure they could make something of this land again. Hell, at the very least he would turn his woodlands over to silviculture, the government would kick in the money for that and he'd have an income steady as trees. Full circle, he was back on the farm, even ready to pull Innis into it.

"My father ran this place almost alone. Him and his brother, Uncle Malcolm, they could make damn well anything they needed, iron or wood, b'y, they had their own forge. We could get into the swing of it, sure, we'll bring the old orchard back, we'll plow a few acres, get us a few cows, pigs, some laying hens, we have great water here. Sheep I don't care for, though I know people who do. We could farm this, me and you. Eh, Innis? Couple strong lads like us? Claire behind us?" Their eyes met and for an instant Innis wanted to believe him, believe in some wild idea of work, of family, brown furrows trailing behind them, the clash of machinery, grain running through their fingers, their hungry talk in a hot kitchen at noon, hollyhocks under the window like he'd seen in a photo in the hall, someone calling them home, a woman like Claire in the house. "What would we grow?" Innis said, and Starr's grin brought them back to earth. "You'd want to raise opium poppies or something along that line, eh?" and Innis, his mouth suddenly dry, smiled stupidly. Were his precious seeds waking, right over their heads?

"Not me," he said, turning away. "How about potatoes?"

Innis rinsed dishes slowly in the sink. He did not want to leave Claire to his uncle, she looked wiped out, chin in her hand, smiling now and then by way of reply while Starr pulled his horizons back to the borders of his own land. "B.C.? It's full of hippies. There's not a speck of farmer in me or Innis either. Leave here? God, I joined the navy to get away from it. Then home I come and my dad dies sudden, before I figured anything out." He laughed, there was a scrape of a match as he lit another Export. "Jesus, Claire, can you see me out there haying? You bringing me out a jar of spring water sweetened with oatmeal?"

"Perhaps," she said. "I wouldn't know unless I tried it."

Surely she knew by now, after weeks of seeing him, how wound up Starr could get when the rum was in him, and of course her very presence fueled his main weakness: even on the work days of his life there was always just under the surface an urge to celebrate if there was a promise of a woman's company. Innis had seen it before: a phone call, a coded conversation to thwart the eavesdroppers and Innis as well, and soon he was dressed and gone. But now she was here, at home, in his own place.

"What about that silviculture you mentioned, Starr?" she said calmly. "All those acres of trees, and Innis to help you."

"I'm not growing wood for the goddamn government, them and their chemicals. Leave the trees like they are. They don't need poisons. Right, Innis? He's a wood rat. He knows. Been up above lately? Check the *fuaran* when you're up there, the water's a little slow."

Innis could have told him, No wonder the spring is low, all the baths you're taking lately, but he didn't because he wanted Claire to feel she could bathe whenever she liked.

"I'll have a look tomorrow, Starr. There's a bed for Claire made up. Two quilts and another folded if she needs it."

"You're right on top of things," Starr said. "We'll ring if we need you."

"Thank you, Innis," Claire said. "I'm going to need that bed pretty soon."

He left them talking and wandered outside. The wind had turned damp, he tasted fog in the air. Through the steam-streaked window he could see his uncle leaning across the table, taking Claire's hand. She said something to him, smiled, stood up. Then she stretched, arching her back slowly, and Innis ached watching her bend toward Starr and kiss him.

In the toolshed, the lightbulb above him smudged from his dirty hands, Innis pushed tools around, lifted them, dropped them noisily. He honed the big axe with a whetstone, brightening the blade-edge. There was a smell of old grease and metal and rust. He'd started on those goddamn woods of Dan Rory and Finlay's, busting his ass for nothing, not a penny. He slipped off his belt and buffed the brass snake with a bit of steel wool, rubbed an oily cloth over the leather. Wind gusted in the door and he looked out at the house: a light in Starr's room, and the bathroom. They were going to bed. He'd wait for awhile after the lights were out.

The cold air of the attic surprised him and he feared for his seeds. Surely they were getting heat from the kitchen ceiling, this had been Granny's weaving room, it couldn't have been too cold for her. He had not looked under the loom for three days or so and the seeds were overdue to pop up. He lifted the tinfoil curtain a few slow inches, prepared to scuttle his vision of five-lobed leaves swaying in a hot breeze. But God, there they were, all of them, sprouts curling out of the soil in odd little postures, lifting their seed heads out of sleep, their jackets open and still clinging, duller than when he'd peered at them in his palm. He held them one by one, puffed motes of dry soil from their heads and stalks. Underneath the small peat pots tiny white roots were already probing and soon he'd have to put them in bigger pots. He dipped each one in the water crock to soak the peat and set them back on their bed of gravel, the fine stone warm to the touch. Good. Cold water was fine to taste but not for growing. He could not stop smiling, he wanted to squat there and watch them ease their heads toward the light, be there when the first leaves appeared. But he was already shivering, as much from nerves as from the early April air. He had followed the book like a catechism. The author, a portly young man in a bushy black beard and a T-shirt that said FLOWER POWER, wrote in a chummy tone Innis had liked immediately: they were both engaged in a conspiracy against authoritarian forces devoted to coming between them and good weed. This enterprise involved high risk and a measure of love. The book was more like talk than a text, like maybe the way Innis's grandfather had instructed Starr about farming, in a commonsense but feeling way, even if the crops were different, to be sure, and Starr had come to enjoy reminiscing about that hard work, not performing it, whereas for Innis the pleasures and rewards had just begun. Soil? the author said. Just dirt, pardner, and if it ain't good dirt, you don't get good weed. Innis had studied the illustrations of cartoon pot plants: overfertilized, their mouths rounded in alarm; water-starved, they hung withered and mournful. Chemical stuff is poison, pardner, if you don't use it right, so go easy. But water is life. Innis knew that the ten-foot marijuana stalk the man stood next to on the last page of the book had not grown anywhere near Nova Scotia, not in Cape Breton for sure. The guy didn't know the conditions on this island, the short summers and killing frosts in June. So Innis was writing a chapter of his own. Make them happy any way you can, the author said, they have to be happy to thrive. That made sense. Innis could not say he was happy himself, but he was harder and wiser than he had been, and that was good enough for now. He lowered the moth-shot blankets over the loom, preserving his corner of early summer.

5

Innis's axe sounded sharply through the trees as he notched a tall spruce, dead from top to root and ready to fall with the next storm, its crown lost in mist. A fine dry rain of needles flickered into his hair. He had worked up a good sweat and sore hands, coming up here early in the morning out of a restless sleep, certain he had heard Claire's dreamy murmurs through the wall of the next bedroom. But maybe he'd been dreaming, though when he woke he remembered only feelings, a tender, unfocussed desire that had everything to do with her. Sure, he had a boner but he had that every morning: sex or death, that flag would fly. He drove the axe bit in so deep he had to rest before he levered it out. Jesus, he'd listened at his bedroom wall a good many times until his mother realized that he was growing up on the other side. He'd been just her little boy in the next room who was supposed to have other things on his mind than putting his ear to the plaster. She couldn't guess how he was deciphering what he heard, that his imagination made up in power what it lacked in accuracy. But Claire, well. Claire.

He rubbed the calluses on his hands, hard but raw, then took up the crosscut and put his back into it, biting quickly through the bole of the tree, drawing the damp morning air deep into his lungs. Did Dan Rory know he was down here slaving away? Ought to, with that X-ray vision or whatever it was. Around noon he would meet the priest. Innis and a padre. Celibate life. Good, clean. That's what he needed. Smother his unclean thoughts. He stepped away as the trunk gave out a tentative crack, shifted slightly above his blade, and then plunged with gathering force, striking the debris around it like an enormous switch. He stood panting amid vibrations of dry branches, the dust of dead needles and bark. Around him lay trees already tumbled, busted deadfalls, splintered trunks, spikes of broken branches you could barely climb through. Out of this mess he was supposed to clear a path, to the brook and beyond? Green spears of spruce were struggling up through it. Good luck.

As the sounds died away he heard it, again and always, in autumn and winter too, at some distance in the trees, the snap of a dry branch, then silence, then the slow compression of leafy matter, of duff, of crusted snow, the satiny sweep of a needled branch springing back, held, released. Deer, he'd thought at first. Or, later, the big cat who'd left his marks up by the spring, who would never let you see him. Starr said, Sure, you're hearing a buck up there keeping clear of you, checking you out, and one afternoon a doe had busted out of the trees, scaring him so good he froze until its white-tailed rump disappeared in its crashing flight. But this sound he heard now and then seemed different, heavier, oddly careful, even cunning. He knew a good deal now about what noise the woods could make. And after he smoked a joint, his ears were so tuned he could hear bugs breathe, the fine trembling of a spider's web strummed by sunlight, a hawk's feathers swimming through air. Nothing could get by his ears when he had smoke in his blood, and this sound seemed to him like footfall, neither nearing nor receding, but simply there. He strained to pick it up again but couldn't. There was only the fog now into which the trees were sinking back, slowly advancing as if it were rising from fissures in the ground. Innis hacked away branches, sawed the tree into sections he could kick away. Bushy brittle foliage was sticking up every which way and he wanted some level sight here, an indication of progress. He piled the thrash for burning, broke for a few swigs of water, and then made his way out to meet Father Lesperance.

AS THE WHARF ROAD curved down toward the derelict pier, the priest's cottage came in sight, small and square, once a store when the ferry was running. The dirty white shingles could use some paint all right. A slush-streaked Chevrolet sat at the curb. The only other dwelling on this short stretch of road was the house of a retired Great Lakes captain across from the cottage, old too but newly shingled in red cedar, with a new dormer gazing toward the strait and the mountain, the broken concrete piers of the wharf. The captain lived in Florida most of the year—a snowbird, Starr called him, he flies back when it's warm. The attached garage looked a bit rickety despite the fresh shingles. What kind of car would a captain drive?

Innis expected a man in black, the collar and all, but a big man appeared from the direction of the wharf, hunched into a long grey mule coat, a red earflapped cap on his head, moving up the sloped street in labored strides. He had his hand out long before he reached Innis.

"Well, well, I think I know who you are." He was breathing hard, his blue eyes tearing. "Innis, is it?" He gripped Innis's hand and gestured toward the cottage. "Come inside, young man. I was down there at the water. She's calm and dark today, not a bit of wind. But oh that's a mean current there sometimes. Eh? I'm Henri. I've misplaced the front door key, Innis, we'll do the back."

"Father Lesperance, right?"

"Right you are. Henri's fine."

The priest ignored the lock and shouldered open the back door, exclaiming at the state of the kitchen. Dirty dishes and a skillet were piled in the sink, a cold smell of frying in the air.

"They've been here again. The little rats." He didn't sound angry. He opened the fridge. "Well they didn't eat everything, Innis," he said heartily, "left us baloney and bread. Sandwich?"

"Sure. Thanks."

He put together their lunch as he explained that the lock had been forced several times already by the kids— "troubled boys"—he brought out here from the industrial towns in the summer. "A dose of country life," he said. But a few had returned on their own at night and ripped off the few valuables he'd had—his TV, old golf clubs, an electric kettle, the binoculars he liked to watch passing boats with. He admitted that it hurt, but he shrugged it off. "There wasn't much here in the first place, and there's even less for them now, so maybe they will have to do good and shape up. You didn't come here to watch TV anyway, did you?" he said, handing him a hefty sandwich.

"There isn't much on to watch. I'm here to work."

"But look, make yourself at home when you're working, Innis, whatever's in the fridge, whatever."

Innis could tell that the priest was a little tight, his eyes puffy like he hadn't slept, a high color to his face and it wasn't just from walking in cold air. But he was in a good mood, showing Innis the other two rooms, one for living, he said, one for sleeping. He pointed to an odd piece of furniture. " A prie-dieu, Innis. A woman gave that to me, when I had a parish, and anytime you wish to kneel on it and pray, go right ahead. It's about the only thing they didn't steal. Hard to fence, I suppose. Not much call for them in Sydney."

"What kind of trouble do these kids get into, Father, if you don't mind me asking?"

"Breaking and entering mostly. The Cape Breton vice. Fighting, boozing, the two go hand in hand. Drugs now too. Marijuana, even young ones get into that."

"That's something they sure don't need." Jesus, he sounded like a kiss-ass, a choirboy. He had needed it, needed it now. Innis swallowed the last of his baloney and white bread, enough mustard on it to make his eyes tear. Ned Mohney had given him that first hit of pot. Not primo, what they got ahold of, but they worked the tobacco out of two cigarettes and tamped the grass in with a pencil. They'd seen Ned's brother smoke it, so they took their puffs and held them down until they coughed and were soon giggling and rolling around and half-sick. It was the day Innis knew he was not a kid anymore: something crazy but sharp had colored his mind, and it wouldn't let him be young the way he had been, no matter how he might seem to others, to his mother, his few friends. No one could fool him again, he was sure of it, not while he was high, not in any way that mattered, though there were times when he had managed to fool himself. A couple years later he and Mohney would take the MBTA over to Cambridge and deal some weed in Harvard Square, small-time, mostly college kids, enough to keep things moving.

The priest flung the curtains open and turned on the lone table lamp in the front room. The kerosene heater gave off whiffs of smoke, but when that cleared away the room began to warm, like the tubes in the old brown radio, its red glow dead center in a big round dial the priest turned until the sounds of a French station emerged. "My sound system," he said. "They lifted my cassette player. Do you know any French, Innis?"

"I don't, Father."

"*Tant pis,* but that wouldn't single you out, my friend, not in much of Cape Breton. But there are parts of it where French is king, oh yes."

The priest cocked his ear toward the radio, even in French it had the cranked-up urgency of news, but even the CBC news in English had little to say about the U.S.: it didn't matter that much anymore, not in detail, The States weren't the center of the universe here, and Innis himself wanted to hear less about a place he could never go back to. Starr always passed over French stations in a flash, as if angry that the language was there at all.

"Well, Innis, what color should we put on these drab walls? Something bright?"

"How about yellow? Not loud, I mean, pale."

The priest ran his hand over his bald pate slowly as he looked at ceiling and wall. "You pick it." He pulled out a paint store chart from under his coat and laid it on the chair. "Pick the color you think best. I'll be back in a few days with paint. The walls need washing anyway, wouldn't you say? A little scraping on the woodwork?"

"I'll clean it all up first, Father."

"Well." The priest clapped his hands together. "We'll make this place like summer. It's for summer, after all. I bought it for a song, Innis, as they say, not that there was much music here. No land came with it to speak of but I've got the wharf and the beach down there, and the water and the mountain to enjoy. I hope you enjoy them as well, my friend. Just don't leave anything valuable here."

"I don't have anything valuable."

"I don't think that's true."

The priest showed him where he stored cleaning implements, and where to turn the water on and off under the house: there would be more freezing weather and you had to protect the pipes. In the little bathroom he kept a bowl of 15-amp fuses for the fuse box. The old well-pump blew the circuit if you had too many lights on.

"Innis, it's all yours," he said. He pulled on his cap, shook Innis's hand, and drove away, trailing exhaust and a rattling bumper.

Innis was pleased to be alone, relieved that the priest hadn't pumped him for information about himself but just took him as he was. There was a stack of *National Geographic* and outdated *Maclean's* to thumb through, and he could nap on the nubby blue couch after the room got toasty. His back and shoulders hurt. Chopping and sawing. What a future. Grunt work. Innis touched his breast pocket, then worked out a roach like a piece of lint. A lipscorcher but it would do. He squeezed a couple good hits out of it and stared out the kitchen window at the stretch of shore, water the color of lead, the tide slack beneath the gently drifting fog. A cold, frozen beach. He could not envision warm sand and swimsuited girls lying around in it, but oh man, thinking about them hurt more than his muscles.

He wandered into the priest's bedroom, spare as a jail. The juvenile housebreakers had snatched a good lamp from the little table, the priest said, and the grey wool blanket he'd used as a spread. But they'd spared the crucifix on the wall. Good Catholic boys. Like Ned Mohney, who always, on the way to or from a bit of sin, crossed himself when he passed his church in Watertown, St. Patrick's, or any church of his kind, even St. Theresa's of the Child Jesus, a name that made Innis want to look inside that church but he never had. The crazy bastard, mailing him this dope, but the package had got through and nobody showed up to arrest him. Without Innis, was he still dealing pot on his own, selling it to the college kids, his baggies on the light side of an ounce? Mohney wasn't the sort for a letter, and what could they share now? For letters, you had to have a future.

Innis was gone, a dead-end. Send him some smoke and forget about him. But Innis had envied Ned the religious rituals that seemed always available to him, and that Ned never questioned regardless of what trouble he got into. Whenever he crossed himself, his hard, humorous face was fleetingly meek and peaceful. Innis sometimes had longed for that feeling, whatever it was. He wanted to call upon those names, murmur those phrases, pull rosary beads from his pocket and work them through his fingers. Ned had given him a St. Christopher medal, said he could wear it for a while since Innis wasn't really anything, didn't go to church at all so maybe he could turn Catholic sooner or later. But Innis's mother yanked it off his neck like it was a voodoo charm and threw it out the kitchen window. Sometimes when Innis got stoned he could still feel the thin chain, the metal resting on his breastbone.

When he was young, the Easter after his father was killed his mother took him to a Presbyterian church, dressed him in a new wool jacket the weave of which was on his fingertips right now. The church was filled upstairs and down. Pale yellow paint on the walls, and cream and white. Flowers and people, flowers on the altar, everywhere, all those once-a-year souls pressed in stiffly side by side, dressed to the teeth. Straw hats and white hats and bright corsaged dresses, and the little girls in white shoes, small boys like himself stiffwalking in suits and sportcoats, flowers in their buttonholes. The only time his mother ever took him, ever went herself, so far as he knew. I had enough church at home to last a lifetime, she'd told him once, my dad was Gospel Hall and I ran screaming from it first chance I got. Tough? Lord! No dancing for those people, no make-up, no movies, no music in the house but hymns, not a drink stronger than tea. The mackerelsnappers were allowed to have fun, God, she'd say that for them.

Innis lay back on the bed. The mattress gave off its damp coolness along the backs of his legs. Upside down, the crucifix looked a little worse for wear. Maybe the damp salt air dulled the finish. Father Lesperance probably had a better one at home. The sermon from that Easter morning was about an orchid, about two girls who felt sorry for their hardworking mother and saved their meagre coins until they could buy her this orchid on her birthday. But instead of being cheered by it, the mother scolded the girls because they were poor and the flower was merely beautiful, a waste when they needed things to eat and to wear. But the orchid, in the minister's way of looking at it, was really love, he said, and he approved of it, he took the girls' side. Sometimes we need an orchid, the minister said. By that time the church was filled with rustling sounds, as if the flowers were stirring on their own, but it was all that Sunday clothing, all that new cloth. He remembered how sweet the air smelled, how he sniffed it until he felt dizzy.

Marijuana. If he whispered it slowly, he could make it sound like the words Ned had mumbled. Better not, with a crucifix over his head.

Be something else to bring a woman here, lie with her on the padre's bed. An extra dimension, but dangerous. This bed was wired to that crucifix, had to be. Zap.

Claire dressed to kill this morning, heading out with Starr, she looked a knockout. Her clothing, her smile, the whole house seemed lighter. She and Starr were still just having fun for a few days, getting away alone, getting off the island, anywhere to leave St. Aubin behind. Innis dug out a sketchpad from his backpack and drew her quickly in the light through the window curtain, rapid strokes, not so much her as an impression of her, whirling, caught in a dance. This morning, lying awake as he often did, he'd heard her, first up, bare feet on the floor, into the bathroom. First the tub running, hard, her hands swishing hot and cold water, back and forth. Then the taps turned off, the cold tap, the little screech of the hot one. Water dripped, *plink, plink,* loud in the steamy air. He heard the fall of her robe. He closed his eyes. She said *ouch* and the cold tap came on for a blast. Then she eased into the tub, her skin rumping against the porcelain as she settled, water cascading through her hands. Innis's bare feet swung out from the bed and touched the floor like feathers. He knew each board between his door and the bathroom, which noisy, which quiet, and he glided over them and knelt in one motion, his eye barely touching the keyhole. He'd spied on his mother's friends, long after he was old enough to let it go. Watching a woman unaware she was watched, hey. Such excitement, those fractions of flesh: all he'd needed was a blur of panties sliding down, skin suddenly pale beneath a line of tan, a few seconds of moist cleavage, hair. He could not stop imagining his own body against Claire's on a cold night like last night, with its icy moon, the taste of her skin on his tongue, and there was a sweet center he could only agonize about. But he stood up and just listened to her swirl the water, scoop it over her body. Her skin would be hot when she rose up. He had thought she heard him standing there, she could have heard his heartbeats sure enough: she went quiet in the water for what seemed like minutes and Innis, hearing Starr get out of bed, had backed away carefully into his room.

He fell into a nap, woke, heart pounding, the room darkened, depressing even after he realized where he was. He lay there sore, inert, a weight he hadn't the will to lift. What was he doing here? He felt a bit crazy, like a part of his youth had been amputated, snatched away. He could never get on a plane to Boston or hitchhike there or even walk across the border. He might have left Watertown anyway, but that wasn't the same thing as not being allowed back, ever, not the same at all. The walls suddenly oppressive, he pushed off the bed and looked at himself in the mirror of the tiny bathroom. His face was thinner, the bones showed more, his long chin stubbled red. That dark skin under his eyes hadn't been there before but it made his green eyes look older. He cut a piece of lacing off his boot, gathered his long hair in both hands and drew it into a ponytail, tying it off. He grinned wearily at himself: a man to be reckoned with.

In the fog-dimmed afternoon he swerved across the road to the Captain's house and put his eye to a crack in the garage door. Was that a streak of chrome? A car in there? Probably an old heap. He gave the door a kick and trudged off to the road where he'd have to stick his thumb out or face a long walk home.

6

Innis expected a spring with warm rains, Boston in April, but instead it had come in with snow, and a strong northeast storm pushed drift ice back up the strait and into the lake beyond, and in the morning's calm water, green as old metal from the shadow of the mountain, pan ice ebbed in white patches slowly toward the sea, steaming faintly in the sun. Spring, Starr said, it's just an appendage of winter here, so don't get your hopes up. For a spell the snow did give way to rain but cold rain, though the temperature rose enough to notice as Innis worked in Dan Rory's woods in the mornings where he was beginning to see a path take shape through the broken trees and the tough brush underneath, windfalls crisscrossed like tossed sticks, snared in each other by branch stubs hard as steel. Finlay appeared one day, told him things were looking better and laid two sawbucks on him, Here, he said, a man your age needs something in his pocket. That's not all I need, Innis said, and Finlay said, That's as true for me as it is for you, if you can believe it, and then he was gone again into the trees. It embarrassed Innis now to recall his crazy fury in the winter pines: must've been the resin, a bad high. He stood back from the slash fires, his face hot in their raging crackle and snap, glad for the rest, the bright noise, wind swelling their red cores, turning them to ash that scattered and danced in the heated air. He was getting stronger, he could feel it in this wild heat, he was using his whole body now, could drive that crosscut saw through a hefty trunk without a break, lost, almost dazed in the rhythm, nothing in his head but motion. When he finished, his long arms were no longer limp and trembling, he wasn't spitting on busted blisters, and he could swing the axe again and again deep into wood, widening the notch, the blade spitting chips hard and fast. He liked to watch the heap of slash slowly sink, the logs collapse, slip down until, icy grey and blackened, they smoldered in feathery ash.

This morning he moved closer to the embers, drying the sweat from his clothes. That first week his muscles had been so tender, even his legs, he groaned when he sat down to eat, and one afternoon Claire put her fork down and came around behind him and began kneading his shoulders, the back of his neck, working her fingers deep into the muscle, deeper, it seemed, it felt so good Innis flushed and shut his eyes and when he opened them Starr was squinting at him over a cup of coffee. That's enough of that, Starr said, this isn't a massage parlor, but Claire continued long enough to let him know she didn't care for his remark, then she sat down and finished her supper. Claire had gone back to work, in Sydney, taking reservations for the airline. Starr had told her, Don't worry about money, you've got a place to stay and I'll take care of the rest, but she'd said no, she always paid her way, she preferred it, even with Russ her old boyfriend she'd put up her half and watched her savings evaporate in horse feed and stables and vet bills. Starr went with her to retrieve her car from Black Rock, Russ having calmed down enough to talk at the front door. But when he saw Starr behind her, things got tense until Claire talked Starr into backing off, both men flinging harsh words at each other, things, she said later, that men don't forget.

That incident seemed to make Starr more possessive of her, and glad she was rarely alone in the house with Innis. His uncle could barely hide his annoyance when he came upon them talking in the parlor or the kitchen, as if she and Innis should not have anything to say to each other when he was not a part of it. But Innis thought it was a trip that he could spark jealousy in his uncle, that the man might view him as a threat just because he was alone in the same room with Claire. They only chatted and joked anyway. Okay, she was a fox, what could Innis do about that? When Starr was upstairs, Innis purposely kept his voice low, just as Starr did when he didn't want Innis to overhear. But he had overheard one night when he was squatting down in the attic checking his plants, afraid to breathe after they both came into the kitchen below him. You shouldn't be alone here with him, Starr said, it's not a good idea, and she said, Starr, explain what you mean by that, would you please? But Starr didn't even try, he just mumbled into another subject and they were soon out the door. They were not home often in the evenings, she and his uncle. Once in a while they didn't show up at all, crashing overnight somewhere in Sydney, Innis supposed, she had a girlfriend or two down there, more private than this house could be, free of his eyes and his ears which, he had to admit, were tuned, with Claire moving through the house, to an immeasurable tolerance. Starr had a cot in the back of his shop but Claire would never go for that, Innis was certain. Of course you never knew what women would go for, they were full of surprises, he'd spent enough time around them to know that.

When the fire was no more than lazy wisps of smoke, Innis walked to the priest's. He warmed up the cottage, going room to room with a mug of coffee in his hands until the dampness was gone. Today he would draw some light in. After he ate, he cut in the trim in Father Lesperance's bedroom, pleased with the ragged yellow glow along the borders. He lifted the crucifix off the wall, set it on the storm-washed lobster crate the priest had dragged up from the beach (proud of it—Innis, he'd said, look at this, a made-to-order table!), the grit of sand still in its slats. Innis rolled a stripe of paint from ceiling to floor over the faded shape of the cross, then he covered the whole rectangle of the wall, moved on to the next until he was done. He soaked the roller in a pail and sat on the edge of the narrow bed, crinkling the plastic dropcloth he'd laid over it. It was early for a joint, he had to portion it out, but he lit the smaller of two roaches from his breast pocket. He watched smoke leak between his pressed lips, followed it up the window, then saw Father Lesperance pulling up out front. Innis grabbed his coat and whirled the air toward the kitchen, toward an open window, then ran to the curb to intercept the priest as he was pulling a flat package from the back seat.

"Ah, Innis, my man!"

"Father."

"I'm just swinging by, Innis, on my way to Baddeck. I found this at a yard sale. We'll make use of it, in the front room, shall we?" He ripped the brown paper away and held up a painting, several men in black cassocks gazing up at a heavenly sky, smaller figures below them in a woodsy scene, Indians, a campfire, a lake.

"Good colors in it," Innis said. "Those angels in the clouds?"

"They are, Innis, if a little cute." He looked toward the mountain ridge where sooty black clouds were riding, tattered by a northeast wind. "Nothing angelic up there. I'd say we've got a storm on the way, maybe rain this time."

"I'm tired of snow, Father. I better get off home myself."

"Been painting?" He pointed to the spatters on Innis's denim shirt.

"I did the bedroom. It needs another coat."

"Wonderful, let's look."

Before Innis could slow him down the priest charged into the cottage, pausing in the front room to sniff the air. "Odd smell, that paint." But he didn't even glance at Innis. "So much better, that room, isn't it? Oh, that's a nice yellow, that's summer, Innis."

"Seems a long way off, Father."

"Don't you worry. When it comes, it's glorious. I'll give you a lift home? Yes."

They shut all the windows and went back to the car. The priest flipped his felt hat into the back seat. A light rain had begun and he hunched toward the windshield. "Not a Catholic family on this part of the island, that I know of."

"You know Dan Rory and Finlay, I guess. MacRitchies?"

"I do. Good men."

"You can drop me off anywhere, Father," Innis said, wanting to clear his head before he got home.

"No, no. Just tell me where."

Father Lesperance was no slouch at the wheel, he drove faster than he talked, the car rocking around curves on its bad shocks. They idled at Starr's mailbox while the priest worked his wallet loose under the big coat. The rain was light but beginning to gust, smearing the windshield.

"No hurry to pay me," Innis said. "When I'm done is fine."

"Here's an installment anyway. Is that your uncle down there?"

They both looked down the long sloping driveway where Starr had the hood of the Lada up. He had just crawled from underneath the engine and directed a wild kick at the front fender. Claire's car was parked ahead of it at the back door.

"That commie car bums him out sometimes," Innis said.

"Yes, I see. A man of passions. A lady's man, I hear."

"Who would you hear that from?"

"He doesn't keep it a secret, does he?" The priest smiled and stuffed bills in Innis's shirt pocket. "Here's fifty."

"Too much, Father." Innis plucked it out but the priest just shook his big bald head.

"I don't see how. A lot of work remains, my friend."

As Innis walked down the driveway, scuffing crusted snow, he could hear Starr cursing steadily.

"I wouldn't give you a nickel for that car," Innis said, hating the sight of it anyway, its chalky blue paint, the dreary dents.

Starr extracted himself from under the hood, a smear of grease across his brow. "You got a nickel for any car? That job at the padre's is short on money and long on time, b'y. What's he got down there, a cottage or a cathedral?"

Innis yanked the bills from his pocket. "Here. Take it."

"Not a lot, is it?"

"I'm not finished. Claire home?"

"She doesn't feel good, came home early and called me. Got a fever. But I have to go to North Sydney, pick up a goddamn shipment of parts. If I can get this piece of shit to start." He booted the bumper. "I could've been there and back by now. Communists put this thing together, did you know that? Cold country car, eh? Canada eats this car for breakfast. Help me rock the son of a bitch, I think the starter's locked up."

Innis rocked the car while Starr tried the ignition, but nothing came to life. He banged his head against the steering wheel.

"Sure it's the starter?" Innis said, wishing he knew enough about engines to tell his uncle precisely what was wrong.

"Look, Innis, you steal cars, you don't fix them. Remember? Just let me rest here a minute, let me think. Is that the damn phone again? They're like kids—no TV, they don't know what the fuck to do with themselves."

"I don't think it's our ring. Sounded like four-ring-five."

"Four-ring-arsehole, it'll wake Claire up." Starr stared at the back door. "I hope she's all right. She was damned glad to come here and stay. Walked into my shop that day lugging her busted stereo. Can you fix this? Damn right, I said, I'd fix anything for you, if it takes glue or nails I'll do it. God, she looked awful good. Women like her don't come through the door of my broken-down shop very often, I can tell you. Then I saw her at the North Sydney Mall, she just stood out, and I think, what the hell, I said hello. We talked, good talk, fun. So I said, I'd like to take you out to dinner. If you like to dance, we'll do that too. She laughed, she looked at me real hard. I'm in a relationship, she said. I said, I don't think you're in so deep you can't have dinner with me. And I was right, I knew it, I knew there was something wrong there with her and that boyfriend. That's the kind of thing you wouldn't notice, Innis, you wouldn't have scoped that out. Now she knows what I'm like, I know what she's like."

"What is she like?"

Starr squinted at him. "Never you mind."

"You going to marry her or what?"

"Christ, you're nosy as a cat. You can stow that subject."

"We're sure eating better," Innis said.

"Food! That's all a kid would understand."

"Come on, I'm not a kid," Innis said solemnly. "About time you realized that."

"I realize more than you think, believe me. Now shut up and push."

Innis heaved his shoulder into the Lada, he'd push this thing all the way to The Mines just to get his uncle out of here. Starr leapt out of the car, ah, the battery terminal was loose! He tightened it viciously and flung the wrench aside. The engine groaned, kicked in, and he sat there racing it, his hands clasped above his head in triumph. He leaned out, surveyed the darkening sky, his face damp with rain.

"Jesus, I'm going to get caught in the middle of this. You'll have to make supper, Claire's not up to it. I might be late." He rolled the window up, then partway down. "But not very late."

Innis watched him buck his way to the road, fearing the car would stall, come drifting back. Well, he still had the twenty bucks from Finlay.

He rubbed his hands over the kitchen stove. Bread rolls she'd baked yesterday sat on the counter and he tore one open and layered it with butter, chewing it slowly. He wanted to ask Claire, hey, where did you learn how to cook, I thought stewardesses just handed out bad ready-made food. But he could not find her downstairs, and upstairs her door was closed. Hell. He wouldn't knock on it, his mother always told him when a woman's bedroom door is shut, let her be.

Innis crept into the attic room, cold as the barn, and pulled back the blankets, the foil, exposing the green seedlings, healthy, a few inches high, their leaves that unmistakable shape that could still get him arrested in many parts of the world, including here. That did not worry him much, only that it would be such a long time before they were really worth anything, before they began to metabolize that resin that would get you ripped. In the meantime he had to defend them and protect them, and they were not even safely up in the woods yet where their roots could worm deep. He raised the lights a bit higher, then took each plant and brushed its leaves with his fingertips: the book said to do that. The man believed they responded to touch, just as we do, that they enjoyed a gentle hand on them, a caress. It made sense. He'd like to show Claire what he had going here, a horticultural operation right under his uncle's nose. Too risky, she was still tight with Starr and something might slip. She seemed mellow enough, but you could never be sure what a person thought about weed until you had some clues. He recalled the nickname Starr had tossed at him once when he was drunk: Cock Roddy. Cock Roddy, he sang, caught his nuts in the niddy-noddy. What the hell is that? Innis said, and Starr said you'll find one in the attic, by the old loom. Wind yarn on it. Let's go up to that attic, lots of stuff in there maybe you should know about. But Innis told him no, he didn't care about it, and he went out to the toolshed, his knees so weak he had to sit on the stool, afraid Starr would stagger up there on his own. But he didn't. His uncle had already asked him about the electric bill. You leaving lights on, Innis? Shouldn't be this high, and Innis said, There's three of us now, Claire has a hair dryer and stuff, and Starr said, Oh.

Innis rearranged the seedlings on their trays, rotating their places under the lights. He dangled a hundred-watt bulb nearby to give more heat. The thermometer under the loom said 58 degrees: could be worse, at least they were growing, though God knew where they thought they were. A dense, whipping rain resounded over the roof. But, yes, Starr was right, not warm, not spring. There were no buds anywhere in the woods, no sign of leaf. Except here, under the faintly lavender fluorescence of his artificial sun.

The hall, the whole house, felt gloomy after the focussed cheeriness of his little garden. He lay on his bed listening, but through the rain could hear nothing of Claire beyond the wall. Had she heard him moving about? Be great to stretch out beside her, just lie there with her while she slept.

The weight of his exile suddenly bore down on him, physical, oppressive. Despite the odd objects he'd brought to it, this room seemed to hold him in some vague past where only the old lived. The pitcher and bowl his mother and father and how many before them had washed in, the antique flowers on the wall, tiny sprigs of grey roses once pink, the oil lamps, their yellowing kerosene, the spool bedstead his grandfather had made on a treadle lathe. His mother had poured water into that bowl as a young bride, and his dad scooped water over his face, and they'd struck a match to that brass lamp, blown it out at bedtime. But Innis was born in a hospital in North Sydney and they left eventually for Boston, for Watertown. His mother wanted no more fields or woods or barns. I didn't like people knowing everything I did, she'd told Innis, they all know you and they know about you. Where did her need for men begin, when not just one would do? Here? There?

He heard Claire walk past his door, her footsteps on the stair. The tap ran in the kitchen. He didn't feel like talking. The reception on his small transistor was bad, crackling with static now, but he kept it on low, picking up a rock song murmuring with a memory of Watertown, of lying on the floor in Mohney's basement den smoking pot and bull-shitting about joining the Marines, then breaking up with laughter, they could never get out of bed that early. Maybe they'd go saltwater instead, a tramp steamer. But then there was the spiral of arrests, convictions, a reckless pattern Innis himself could not explain and could not stop, and then they'd stopped it for him. Jesus Christ, Mohney had said, sending you clean out of the country and you can't ever come back? Rain drove hard against the dark window. Why not snow? It was cold enough, the temperature had dropped. Around him were not streets or homes or buildings but woods and fields and hills, and the water in the strait would be a nightmare now, he wouldn't go near it, wind and tide clashing, whitecaps leaping up. His humiliation seemed to fade like a long moan into the countryside, into dark wooded spaces. He got up and poured water from the pitcher to the bowl. He dangled his fingers in it: waking and washing.

From the hall landing he could see a light in the parlor. "Claire?"

She was half-lying on the sofa, her long legs stretched out. Her eyes had a dazed shine to them.

"Innis, dear, I feel rotten, I really do. I almost passed out here. Fever. Feel."

He pressed her forehead the way his mother used to, as if she were telling his fortune. "Jesus, you're burning. You better get back in bed. I'll bring you whatever you need."

"It's the damn flu, I know it is. I had it last year. It takes the legs out from under me."

His arm around her, holding her against him, he helped her upstairs. "I don't want any fuss," she said. She had come down for a bite to eat but was not hungry, just thirsty. "But you, you must be starved, Innis. I'm sorry nothing's made."

"How do you think we got by before you came? I'm a mean cook."

Innis turned on the dresser lamp as she tumbled back onto the bed, her arm over her eyes. "Too hot," she whispered, pulling at her clothes.

"Hey, get under the covers. You don't want to get chilled too. I know that much."

When he returned with a glass of water, she asked him to help her undress. "What? Me?" He laughed, a little too loud, and threw up his hands in mock horror. "Starr would love that."

"Innis, I'm weak as a kitten, I don't care." Her cheeks had fiery patches. "I can hardly lift my eyelids."

Her eyes were already closing as he drew her sweater up and over her hair, a breath of damp heat released from the wool. Her breasts were bare, her nipples small and dark. God. How could she stand that wool next to her skin? He tugged her jeans down carefully, trying to be quick without seeming to strip her. If Starr showed up, that would be something. No, not this soon, not in this weather, and so what, she was sick and he was seeing to her. And how could he not look at her, her pale blue panties, her smooth legs? Did that make him a bug? He pulled the blankets over her and tucked them in.

Innis felt dizzy himself, hot. Was he getting sick too? Outside, the big maple drooped deeply, its branches glittering in the dim light from the streetlamp up at the road. Claire was sleeping already, her mouth open in a soft snore. Innis examined her belongings that lay strewn on the dresser. Some makeup. She didn't wear much, didn't need much. A touch of mascara, lipstick just bright enough to bring out her olive skin. A headband of summery yellow he had never seen her wear. A long-handled hairbrush, its bristles entangled with her hair. He ran it through his own and set it back, hoping he'd left a few strands, red woven into black. He quietly opened a drawer. The colors of her underwear startled him, scarlets and yellows and lavender, a shade she liked. He moved his hand through the silkiness, plucked out a pair and stuffed them in his back pocket fast, like a shoplifter. Claire had flung her covers aside, shivering now, drawn up like a child, and Innis covered her quickly and laid on a quilt from the old blanket chest at the foot of the bed. Her eyelids were darker than the skin around them. Were they always? He should call up Starr, ask him if he should get a doctor or come take her to one.

But on his way downstairs the house went black, so deep he grabbed the bannister and froze, disoriented until he heard rain sweeping across the house. He felt his way back to his room, to the old oil lamp he'd never lit. He struck several matches to the mantle, his hands shaking, he didn't know why, he wasn't afraid, he just had to have a light quickly. The wick flared high and smoky, reeking of old carbon, but he finally got an even burn and slipped the dirty chimney into place. The room seemed to constrict within the glow of the lamp: this was the old light they'd lived by, died by, and he carried it to Claire's bed, her face, composed in a gentle frown, glistening with sweat as he held it above her. Worried, he fetched the washbowl from his room and a facecloth, wringing it to a chill dampness and daubing her face, her neck, her arms. He dipped it again into the bowl and twisted out the cold water. He'd take care of her alone even if it scared him. His mother's hands, when he was sick in bed, had hovered over him in a kind of talk sometimes, and she would touch his face like a blind person when she kissed him good night. He drew the bedclothes further down and lightly wiped her throat, her chest, between her breasts. Her nipples hardened under the cool cloth and he jerked back as if he'd burned her. She looked calmer, breathing in a deep whisper. What feverish dreams was she lost in? He took in the sight of her, then bent down and put his lips to the soft muscular flesh of her belly, its salty heat. He sat back and her eyes fluttered open and fixed on him a confused gaze before she slipped away again. Did she feel that kiss? She didn't see it, not in this shadowy light, but his heart drummed as he snugged the covers under her chin. He folded the damp cloth and pressed it across her brow. That's what they always did in the old movies when someone had a fever. He would stay awake all night if he had to. Give her apirin when she woke. Home remedies, that's all they had here in this house once, that and prayer. Your grandmother was a healer, a midwife, Starr said. Maybe this was in Innis's blood, this instinct.

His legs trembled when he stood. He'd leave the lamp with Claire, she wouldn't like waking in pitch dark. He couldn't hear the rain anymore and wandered downstairs, the dark no bother now, and found a dim flashlight in a kitchen drawer. His seedlings, their cycle would be thrown off, there in the chilly dark, they could be stunted, traumatized. The phone had not given out its crazy rings for a long while: the receiver was dead against his ear. Lines down. He stoked up the stove in the kitchen until the embers snapped and hissed. He was thirsty, and Claire would need water too. But as he stood filling a pitcher at the sink a loud muffled crack came up from the lower field, too loud for a gun. He grabbed his jacket and stepped outside the back door into a stillness that stopped his breath. Ice, everywhere, every object he could make out was thickened, confected with ice. And the silence, like something had just come to rest a million miles deep. The junked pickup truck glassed like a huge ornament, the woodshed an iced box. Everything had been stilled so quickly time dangled or hung: there was not a tick or a drip anywhere. The rain had been caught, captured by all solid things, wind-whipped and frozen onto their shapes. It had blown like hair from the raingutter above him, rigid now, icicles angled as the wind had left them. Innis inhaled the cold, utterly quiet air. A silver thaw they called this, Innis had heard about it, but now, under a piercing moon the clouds had set free, the solitary trees were like teetering, translucent sculptures, laden with a lovely weight some could not hold, their crowns bent to the ground, their trunks bowed, gracefully tensed. Innis walked out into it, dead grass crunching under his shoes, every rut and depression giving way like delicate windows, every bare bush and cane turned to crystal. He wondered what the pines would look like way up behind Finlay and Dan Rory's, how the rain had iced in their branches, leaning and bright. A breeze swept over the fields, a soft and brittle music, and the moon was closed away in cloud. Claire, she should see this, this alone would break her fever. The priest was wrong: not summer but this was glorious. He would draw it for her, in pen, all this nodding, hanging, suspended glass. As he turned shivering toward the house, somewhere in the dark a tree broke like the shot of a rifle.

7

Wrapped in a wool blanket, Innis sat watching Claire in a deep sleep. She wasn't thrashing around anymore, coiling the bedclothes, tearing them loose. Good. She'd be better now. But he fell into a doze in the chair until an early sun woke him. Claire was awake too, in a bathrobe, straightening the quilts he'd laid over her. Then she sat on the bed and pressed her hands to her face, said if she looked like she felt, she must be a vision indeed, she felt so weak, she just wanted to sleep.

"Claire," Innis said at the window, "take a look at the sun in that ice. Look."

She stood beside him, puffy-eyed and pale, and he held her up with his arm. "It's lovely," she whispered. "Like blown glass, everywhere."

Neither of them had heard the Lada arrive, and just as his footsteps distracted them, Starr was at the bedroom door.

"What's this?" Unshaven, he looked haggard and older. "The house so cold you got to warm each other up?"

"I've got flu, Starr." Claire said, sitting on the bed, pulling the robe over her knees. He touched her face. "I can see that. But what's his excuse?" He yanked open Innis's blanket and Innis yanked it back. "Hanging around in his underwear."

"I looked in on her, that's all, I fell asleep in the chair."

"He was a help, Starr, he was. I had a fever, I was out of my head. Let him alone."

"He's got a fever too, I think. You going to help him with that?"

"Oh, Starr, please shut up."

Innis turned away but his uncle caught him in the hall and wheeled him around to face him. Innis gripped the blanket tightly in his fists, he would hit Starr if he touched him again.

"Stay out of her room. Anytime, day or night."

"She was burning up, Starr. She looked real sick, you weren't here, the phones were out. Don't come tearing in here like I did something awful."

"Go get some goddamn clothes on."

"You want me to move out?"

Starr grunted, looked him up and down. "I told your mother I'd see you through the year."

"You don't need to see me through anything, nothing."

They were a few hot words away from blows, Innis saw that suddenly and clearly and he backed away because the look in his uncle's eyes was poisonous. They were both tired, frayed. And he did not want to move out, not now. "Fuck it," Innis said. "Go see to Claire. You're the doctor."

As he dressed he listened to Starr in the next room, fussing over her, telling her he'd been trapped in The Mines, the damned silver thaw had made the roads murder, so he'd done a little work in the shop, napped until the salt truck was out, did she want some breakfast.

Innis drank a cup of coffee quickly and left the kitchen's warmth for the upper woods, shaky, disgusted. The sun was painful, glaring in the thawing ice. An apple tree was beginning to drip, its wild branches flickering with sunlight. Meltwater everywhere, shedding the bowed trees slowly of their burdens. Brush and dead grass were turning wet, the butt end of winter once again. If this kept up there'd be mud, sure as hell. His plants would have to wait. He'd see how tough they were when he got a chance, but right now he wanted to put some distance between himself and that house.

The footing was bad and he went sprawling on his back, knocking the wind out of him, he lay in the driveway gasping. His hip was sore by the time he limped to the road, past the Lada Starr had left on the shoulder, no wonder they hadn't heard him coming. Up the right-of-way road to the power line it was already slick, the bare clay still hard but taking his boot print faintly where the filmy ice was gone. He passed a birch that had lost branches, then others, maples too, leaning, limbs torn. The crystal show was over. The more flexible fir and spruce had fared better, ice still glistened deep in the shade of their needles. He combed ice bits out of a bushy branch and watched them melt in his hand. He could have touched her any way he wanted. He could have done the worst of what Starr might be thinking, but he didn't. Yes, he could feel his blood in his face right now, how could he not think of her, lying there hardly aware of him, but his desire was mixed up with something else, something he and Ned Mohney would never have discussed, never have known about.

How long would it take a car to get clean off the island, not just St. Aubin but the whole of Cape Breton Island around them, a good car, not a truck grinding up the grades?

Innis crossed the break to check the spring, Starr found the water cloudy last week and he wasn't keen to make his way up here anymore, too long a climb, he said. Innis was winded himself when he leaned into the damp air of the little shed that sheltered the water. There seemed to be an almost invisible layer of ice on the surface and he tapped his fingers through: the water struck like an electric current it was so cold. He stirred it quickly. No, nothing there, no silt or anything that he could see. Starr was always holding a tumbler of it up to the light like a chemist. Best water in the world, he'd say. But it was open to things that might wander into it up here, this very water that ran from their taps. Later in the morning, if she felt better, Claire might bathe in it, it might rush into a glass she held. Innis touched his tongue to it, drew it back numb. He latched the door. There was a pawprint frozen in the clay mud of the entrance, the same one he'd seen in the snow by that other spring way up the power line. The big cat? But it hadn't drunk here, not since a while ago when someone left the door unlatched.

He was ragged out. He'd slip and slide back to the road and try to hitch to the old wharf, walk if he had to. Father Lesperance's place seemed highly appealing, peaceful, almost his own. Starr had crossed a line, he'd never been this uptight before about anything. But there was sun in the sky, warm on Innis's face when the wind let up. All around him the sheaths of ice were thinning, brightly transparent, trickling away.

HE RAISED THE front room window of the cottage and leaned out, inhaling the air. He had napped on the couch for a little and now he studied the Captain's house across the road. Captain John MacQueen. Grew up in North St. Aubin. Lived in Florida until summer was well-arrived, then came back for three months, to that house. Snowbird. Snow goose. Who looked after it while he was gone? Nobody within sight, even on a clear day rising out of an ice storm.

No, it wouldn't be a break-in. He wouldn't break a thing.

Innis squinted into the crawl space: room enough. Cold pipes. The grey tufts of old spider nests. Stored lumber toward one corner said there must be a hatch nearby, and there it was not far from the water pump. He pushed up through a throw rug in the bedroom and did not move: fear and thrill of a strange house, of surprise, of alarm. Someone home, or not? The furniture was draped with plastic and old sheets, but he barely took a breath as he crept tensely through all five rooms, everything at rest and unused. He picked the receiver off the wooden wall phone, startled to hear a voice: the phone was still connected. Feeling as if his own breath might give him away, he started to hang up but caught a few words the woman was saying in her gentle, un-hurried brogue: "...no, she's just living there with him and the young fella, hhyes, well, you know what he's like," and the woman at the other end said, laughing, "Don't I ever!" He wanted to hear more but was afraid to stand there with a receiver in his hand.

It had never occurred to him they were local topics, Starr and Claire and himself. Things got around fast here, true or untrue. Had Starr even thought he could put it over that she was only a boarder? He had never seemed to care much what people thought when it came to him and women, but suddenly Innis didn't want Claire seen as some kind of tart, Starr's mistress or live-in girlfriend or whatever. Some other woman, it might not have mattered. But now they were other people's business, both of them, and "the young fella." Even so, they knew nothing about Innis, what he'd grown up with in Watertown, the gusts of merriment that at times had swept through his mother's apartment, when he was taken up and joshed, fed Saturday night snacks men and their girlfriends brought in brown bags. Or once in awhile when their noise was not like celebration but deranged almost, craziness, everyone shouting in different voices at once, the clumsy, mean jokes, roaring, bawling, the night wearing into the shocking sound of glass—tumblers clattering, busting on the floor, bottles colliding, the sharp hiss of beer caps, an ice tray splintering open like wood. And the sudden turns that sometimes happened against his bedroom wall, a jarring crash. Then the murmured sounds of cleaning up. Someone, maybe his mother, remembering he was in the next room, You want him to see the police here, is that it? And one time they did come. Their dark uniforms, which made them seem enormous to him, changed the tone of everything and Innis was afraid they had come for him. He could hear the buzz of the light over the kitchen sink, nobody talking now but the cops, sometimes polite, sometimes bullying and irritable, but regardless they were bad news, nothing good ever came in the door with them, not when he was a small boy and not later. Innis would see them again and again, the police, not because of a brawling kitchen party but to ask if Innis Corbett lived there and was he at home, they wanted to talk to him, and he might be lying in that same bed just off the kitchen, his door closed, waiting for his mother to lie or not lie, depending on her mood or how he stood with her that day, to send the cops packing or step aside. But these were things the women on the phone need never know, or Starr either.

In the stone fireplace, its mouth smeared with soot, the chimney whispered as chimneys did. He thought he heard dripping but it was the movement of a quartz clock in the shape of a square-rigger. On the wall at eye level was a brass barometer. He tapped the glass as he'd seen Starr do. The needle rose a notch, into "change." Good. No, he would not rip it off. He would steal nothing in this house.

He opened doors as he found them, looking for signs of the Captain, of his captainness and his MacQueenness. Another bachelor. Everything stowed seaman-neat, boxed, wrapped in plastic, bound with cord and expert knots. In a hall closet two navy blue uniforms hung, gold braid visible through the grey garment bags. Innis pulled out a coat and tried it on in the door mirror, the man must be shorter and stouter than himself, but who couldn't look good in this getup, all bulk and braid, anything could be an order, a demand, a dressing down with this on your back. Innis buttoned it up. Along a wall was a framed print of a Nova Scotia schooner, sails huge with wind, a river of sea over her lee rails. Underneath it two more framed ships, Great Lakes freighters, dignified in black and white iron, their blunt bows pushing into the sea, trailing grey reliable smoke. Innis had cousins who'd worked the lakeboats, they'd come through Watertown on their way to spring fit-out and after lay up in late fall, stopping for a night or two, travelling that Cape Breton road, part of the kitchen crowd. Lots of Cape Bretoners down on the Lakes, Starr said, good place for you, good pay, if you could get on with the Canadians, the American outfits couldn't hire you of course, not now. Of course.

A sink tap emitted a gasp when he turned it. Dry. His uncle's face lingered in his mind, something had sparked in his eyes Innis hadn't seen before.

Another door. It opened into dark, but he smelled it: a clay floor, pungeant with old oil. Touches of sheen, of polished metal, and he stepped almost reverently down into the garage. White winter light flared along the edges of the locked doors and his eyes adjusted to it and picked out the car slowly. He ran his hands along its cold smooth lines. Christ, it was a Cadillac, just about brand-new and beautifully kept, black, had to be black with the chrome standing out like that. The man had waxed it before he put it away. Innis bounced the bumper: yes, that ride, smooth and heavy, a dream. He put his nose to the slightly lowered window, smelled the cool leather inside, the carpeting that would absorb the hush of his own breathing. Who would have guessed a Caddy lurked in this old shed of a garage stinking of spilled gasoline, suited more to a beat-up truck or tractor? In the dusk the white sidewalls glowed, and Innis could hear the crunch of gravel, big tires just beginning to roll, backing, then the pause, the pulse of the engine as you pulled away, sweet and deep. Then you were gone.

He blew on his fingers as he frisked the fenders and panels. No. A guy like old MacQueen wouldn't keep a key here. But Innis couldn't stop touching the car: he wanted that wheel in his hands, just to sit there, light up and let it take him somewhere, the radio on low. In ten minutes that Caddy would be warm as a bed. Crazy to think about it. Fed up hanging around the house like a grounded kid, he'd find the key, he'd be back.

He returned the uniform coat to the closet, spread the rug neatly over the floor hatch, just like MacQueen would, a man who shared his taste in automobiles, then he slipped out the back door, setting the lock behind him. Piece of cake.

A miner on his day off picked him up, driving back to The Mines with his family after a spin around St. Aubin Island. The ice was pretty, one of two girls said from the back seat, bouncing up to her father's ear, lowering her voice. "Wasn't it, Daddy?" "It is," he said, turning to Innis. "It's the silver thaw we came out for, but damned if it isn't melting fast." The dad had forearms so white and bare they seemed too large for him, he steered with cramped movements as if there were fog and not a damp cold glitter everywhere, a blood-slow thaw, clear as glass. His wife spoke sharply to the two little girls sharing the seat with Innis but he said, "They don't bother me, I like kids," which was a lie, all kids were a pain in the ass, they just kept you back, curtailed you, nailed you to the floor, like he'd done to his mother. At the mailbox the girls yelled goodbye to him a dozen times.

8

Innis kept clear of the house as much as he could. Starr stayed home while Claire got back on her feet, tending to her until she grew irritable, impatient with sickness. Starr took to staring hard out windows, a cigarette burning in his hand. Innis preferred his uncle talking, he missed the easy focus it gave. Silences, then a few words Starr refused to spin into conversation, and Innis thought, fine, let it die. It wasn't for him to string small talk along. Starr was the man, it was his house. Another Friday loomed, a day Innis hated: it just dumped him into the weekend. Not even any fun in the kitchen now, Claire and his uncle strained and housebound.

Returning from the woods, he crossed the drab sod hard as stone underfoot, the day closing into cold again. He wanted to smoke, so he turned toward the barn. The culvert ditch had a membrane of ice, slivered with wan afternoon light. Earlier the sun, now a dim glare along the mountain ridge, had softened the dead grasses, glinting hillocks of old hay. Innis grabbed at brittle bush canes and snapped them as he passed. Snow, receding into the shadowy edges of woods, looked like the stranded foam of waves. He pulled down a chokecherry branch: not a bud. Saplings in the fields were no more than switches. A low shrub grey as lace, he would learn its name when summer arrived. That is, if he was still here, instead of sticking what he had in a suitcase and getting lost in a city on the mainland. Ways of getting lost. He'd be an expert, the way things were going. What about Halifax? St. John in New Brunswick? He'd have to find out about those towns.

But there was a woman in the house.

The old barn, isolated, no tracks to it, man, animal, vehicle, nothing connecting it anymore to the house or little pig barn where old lumber and junk were stored or the milk house where Starr stacked firewood or the toolshed. Innis had inspected its gloom through a stall window but had never entered, since nothing they used was kept there. It sat as he had sketched it in the fall, grey against the lower woods, waiting to be overtaken like the pasture behind it, ruined with advancing trees. One of the tall threshing doors stood ajar, sagging on its pins. Innis slipped the rope latch and heaved it just wide enough to step inside. Small low windows cast a dusty light through the stalls. The animal reek had long faded into a dry smell Innis could taste in his throat. In the lofts was dishevelled hay the color of the winter fields. Something fluttered, stirred. Mice, a rat maybe. Not a cat. Starr had drowned the last ones he found here, so he said. Shitty thing to do, dump them in a sack with stones and toss it in a brook. That was the farm way, no room for the sentimental. Yet no one, when he was in a certain mood, could be more sentimental than Starr.

Innis climbed up into the loft and settled himself in a grotto of broken bales, making a seat in one whose binding still held. A fine, musty dust hung like frost. Here and there the hay was rank with mildew. Leaks. From the CBC he'd learned about hay, its different grasses, the danger of wet bales spontaneously combusting. He was picking up things from the radio now and then, what caught his attention he remembered, just the way it had been in school. A program called *Quirks and Quarks* put him off at first, posing gee-whiz questions, What do dinosaurs taste like? or, Does the Sasquatch really exist, and if he does, should we shoot him? or, Could there be water on the moon? Innis's first reaction was, Who gives a shit? But some of it stuck in his mind, like how birds navigate over long distances, or the intelligence of a virus, or the mating calls of frogs, Brazilian tree frogs and Argentinian desert frogs and Canadian grey frogs. He fished out a thin joint, he was rolling them thinner, and lit it. The gable window was cracked and bird-soiled. The metal roof, a grey cavern pinholed with pitchfork light, shuddered in the wind and the whole barn responded, beams straining like ship timbers. A cold touch of air from some opening he couldn't see, and he hunched deeper into the hay. Would this stuff burn? Jesus, all that old dried wood. He held up a match in front of his eyes: a horny kid, am I, Starr? Dangerous in my underwear?

But after two deep hits of weed, he lay back and any wish for fiery destruction fled, revenge, anger. Friday night. He'd like to spontaneously combust. He and Ned might get stoned and cruise the glare of the Combat Zone, feel the energy of all the sexual hustling, check out a topless bar with their fake I.D.s, Ned always passed for twenty-one anyway, but Innis preferred Harvard Square, tripping with the street musicians and the girls in their funky clothes and Hari Krishnas jingling around, the guys looking more like convicts than spiritual messengers with five o'clock shadows on their shaved heads.... But Mohney was seven hundred miles away, out on the town for sure, maybe at The Groggery where live rock music could crack your skull, but lots of bodies packed in its freaky atmosphere, he liked bars more than Innis did. Was he dealing weed with a new partner? Yet Innis was only reminiscing, he did not yearn for those times exactly, they were past, used up, he didn't fit into them anymore, there was a childishness about that urge to find entertainment all the time, day and night. What would his mother be up to? For a while, she might've missed her absent son, but she was pissed at him too. I love you, Innis, that's the last thing she'd said when he left, it all got reduced to that. Was she still with that last guy she was stuck on, a jerk, an amiable bullshit artist? Funny, but now he could see his mother's situation more clearly. Alone, her husband dead, a kid on her hands. She could have gone out and enjoyed herself but there he was. What do you do with him?

She didn't drag him along at least, you had to hand it to her for that. Innis had the flavor now of confined evenings, having to stay home, and they had no taste to them. Just the phrase "staying home" was a downer. He could speak to that. And his mother had had them too, those nights when the only world worth your energy, your spirit, is out on the streets, in the lights. Of course even here he could go out, but he couldn't get anywhere, not at night. Fifteen miles to The Mines, the nearest town, and cars were not plentiful until you got out to the main highway. Could be a damn cold wait, never sure if they would take you all the way, maybe let you off at Little Bras D'Eau and you'd have to hunker at the roadside awhile longer, spirits diving. What would he find when he got there anyway? One bar, that he knew of, a serious drinking hole where he doubted he'd be welcome once he opened his mouth, regular brawls there on weekends, Starr said. He couldn't just walk around Commercial Street looking for an invitation from a sweet girl. More hitching would take him further south, North Sydney, and Sydney was where the action was, an actual city. For his mother, at least her fun was never far away.

Spoiled hay, great seat for a Friday night. It would be in his jeans before long, the dead barn smell. Wind tremored in the walls. The heavy breath of cows and horses. Innis staggered about on the lumpy hay, beating up its tired dust. The floor of the loft, exposed in places, was laid of spruce poles, unshaved, their bark dry and curling. A ladder of small boards nailed into the wall studs led up to the gable hatch. He gripped the crude flat rungs and climbed with that deliberateness grass always gave him, a microscopic attention to the physical, and to physical consequences. A crack of light outlined the hatch where they used to swing in hay bales on the hayfork, the tackle dangling as if someone had just released it. Innis flipped the rusty hatch hook loose and the small door yawned outward and suddenly his height from the field below seized him and he hugged the rung. Cape Breton from the air, that plane flight in: the thick nappy green of the forests, tiny inhabited spaces here and there as if shaved out with a razor. And the water, always water somewhere, spills of lakes, streams and bays, ponds flaring like mirrors, and the ocean or some reach of it never far, and the houses specks in the vast green, so few of them it scared him, that he would be sequestered in that. Pulp roads lay like discarded rope. Woods a bristly carpet, worn in spots, frayed. And he was living now on one of those roads maybe he'd seen from the air, pressing his face to a wooden rung, in an old barn. The weakness passed, leaving him trembling, breathless. He opened his eyes slowly to the fading light: there was the house he lived in, smoke in its chimney, set down near woods a million miles from where he wanted to be. Someone was at the back door, the glass panes, a dash of color. It was her, she moved out from behind the door and stood on the steps. She pulled a yellow scarf from her head. A regular flower, that girl.

Then she was stepping gingerly along the field. Afraid of cow turds? Snakes? A flash of resentment brought tears to his eyes: she had broken the simple arrangement of his life, he and his uncle getting on, making his way slowly and carefully and without much trouble toward September, yet it thrilled him to see her appear on this landscape. To the west the water of the strait lay slick as metal. He thought he could smell it, the salt, and the resin of the evergreens thick on the mountain among the grey leafless hardwood. Exile, you're going into exile, pal, Ned had told him when he first heard, loving the word, grinning like it was something from the movies, or a joke. Ned didn't know it was like being turned out of your own house in the middle of the night, like somebody ripping the covers off you in January and ordering you into the snow, but big-time, way up there in pain. He eased himself down the ladder, conscious of the drop at his back that even old hay might not save him from.

He hardly breathed when she came into the threshing floor below him, but he watched her poke about, brushing imaginary webs from her face. The light was poor but her hair, black as the crows Innis fed bread to in the snow, caught touches of it. He watched her tap the hard leather of a horse collar, shake a dull tinkling from harness chains hanging from nails. She was moving through a museum. Innis was sure that she, like him, had secrets. It excited him that she didn't know he was there above her. He could frighten her, but he heard her laugh softly at something on the wall.

"What's so funny?" Innis said.

She started as if a door had slammed but she didn't cry out. She raised her face to him calmly. He could see the slow light of a smile.

"A photo of the royal family, nailed to the wall here. The queen and her sister, they're just little girls."

"My grandmother's, I bet. She loved the royals, Starr says, but as far as he's concerned, they can kiss his arse, it belongs in the barn. What brought you out here?"

"I like barns."

"They're quiet."

"It's not like the house is noisy."

"Could use a little racket, couldn't it? Laugh a minute."

"I was out of sorts for a while. I'm sorry. I need to get back to work."

"No big deal. What's Starr's excuse?"

"He thought there was some little thing between you and me, I don't know what. I set him straight. He likes to talk, Starr does, but he doesn't say much about himself, what's inside of him."

"He won't like us in here then, will he, all by ourselves?"

"Oh, he's having a bath. Taking me to Sydney for dinner. I wouldn't worry about it, dear. I'm not."

"I might move out to the barn, the way things are going. Hey, you don't have a coat on. You've been sick."

"Indeed. I lost six pounds. That's enough of that."

"I wouldn't say you had to lose an ounce. Why don't you come up here? It's warmer."

"Is it?" She regarded him, her head to one side. "Help me up then."

He took her warm hand and pulled her up into the hayloft. She was wearing a purple sweater with a high collar and black bell-bottom jeans.

"Nicer up here," she said, stepping into the bales. "Like being a kid, in the hay. A long time since I've been on a farm."

"A dead farm, this one."

"There's life here yet."

"You could have fooled me, but I'm new to it, I guess."

"Yes, you didn't get that accent in St. Aubin."

"I didn't get much of anything in St. Aubin."

"You got born, didn't you? You go a long way back here, Starr says, your family."

"That isn't much good to me now, is it? I'm not going forward, that's the point."

She let herself fall back into the nest he had made. "I remember my uncle's farm when I was a girl. Fun, that warm fresh hay."

"This hay isn't fresh." Innis grabbed a handful. "Been here for years. Starr's dad took it in before he died."

"Your grandpa?"

"I never knew him. My mother didn't like him much anyway. Too religious. He wouldn't let you take his picture on the Sabbath. He got very sorrowful in his later years, she said. He would sit like a wooden man for hours on a Sunday."

"Starr doesn't have any of that, does he."

"It's under there. Scratch him deep enough."

She tested a strand of hay in her teeth. "So it's no good even for horses, but it's fine for us." Her voice was warm and easy and he let himself believe they might have planned to meet, in this very space, so close they could whisper. When she turned her head, her pendant earrings caught a dangle of gable light, a glint of silver.

"Look at this," Innis said. He huffed a breath toward her. "We've got some winter left."

"Oh, I'd kill for a summer day, just one. I want to bake in the sun somewhere. I want it to be hot and sticky and all those summer things we can't stand in July. It's a wonderful cure."

"For what?"

"Winter. We need thawing out." She stood up, unsteady in the soft footing. "The winter here gets to me. It got to the man I was living with too."

"There's bits of hay all down the back of you," Innis said.

"I can't see them."

"Should I brush them off or what?"

"If it's messy."

"Starr would wonder where you've been."

"Let him."

Innis plucked the bits as gently as he could, as high as he could reach without standing. His legs felt shaky. The weed, and the curve of her jeans. "I'm in a hurry for summer myself," he said, almost whispering.

"Are you?" She looked down at him, amused. "Well, you're young. Summer is your time, isn't it."

"Fall, more like."

Innis got to his feet slowly, braced himself against a post. He wanted to tell her, to draw her into it.

"I need to put plants in the ground," he said. "But I'll probably have to cool it till the last frost is gone, in June."

"I didn't know you were into plants, Innis. Starr never mentioned that."

"The less Starr mentions, the better, as far as I'm concerned." Innis opened his hand and peeled back a layer of tinfoil, exposing the seeds he had saved. Claire held his hand steady. She sniffed, raised her eyebrows. He saw the word come soundless on her lips: Marijuana?

"This is what you're planning to grow? Lord, Innis. Not in this country."

"Why not?" He looked into her face.

"Well..." She laughed. "The Mounties could come down on you, for one thing. We wouldn't like to see that. For another, that's not a plant that thrives here, I think."

"They grow in every corner of the States, Claire. They'll do fine here too. There's ways to encourage them, if you know what you're doing."

"Oh, I'd give them all the encouragement I could, if that's all it takes."

"It takes other things." He packed the seeds into a ball and jammed them in his jeans. "I've read up on it. This stuff grows everywhere now. Even Alaska. I'm not kidding. I'll have good buds by late August, September and I'll bag them and sell them."

"That could bring you trouble, Innis. Prison."

"It's hidden. Nobody goes where I go, way up above. I know of a trucker who'll take it all off my hands. One transaction. As soon as I get that money, I'm off, I'm splitting. I'll take up somewhere else, out west." Watching her face, her faint, skeptical smile, he wanted to kiss her mouth, hard.

"Does Starr know?" she said.

"Jesus Christ, Claire, he doesn't even smoke the stuff. He knows the world isn't flat but he's never had weed. Something, huh?"

"It's not for everybody."

"So you'll tell him?" The barn had slipped into dusk. The tiny roofholes cast no light. They stood in the uneven hay as if they had waded into a pond.

"What good would that do, any of us?" she said. "Of course I wouldn't tell him."

Innis took her hand and touched it to his lips like a sip of water. "Sealed. Look, I've got a good roach here in my shirt."

"Aren't you the eager one."

But Innis had already put a match to it and drawn a whistling toke.

"Innis, just one," she said. "I'm not real steady on my pins yet." She took it like a fly by the wings, kissed it quickly, passed it back.

"You and my uncle are pretty tight by now, I guess."

She laughed. "Listen, we'd better go. Look how the dark's come down!"

Women in his mother's kitchen, voices mingling with and cutting across his mother's. Men, the subject of men, made them talk a certain way. But none of them sounded quite like Claire, none that he remembered.

"Go on ahead, I'll come later," he said. "Here, I'll help you down." He kept hold of her hand after he'd lowered her to the threshing floor, made her look back at him. "You be careful," she said. "Bye."

He pitched himself back into the broken bales. Claire in summer. She must have been something. She was older now, true. But he liked that, that she'd been in the world longer than he had. In the flare of the match he'd seen tiny lines at her eyes and her mouth. He regretted now that he hadn't done a drawing of the ice storm, given it to her as a gift.

Lying back, he narrowed his eyes to slits. The scattered pokeholes in the roof were dim stars. Summer, summer.

When the frosts were done he'd be ready. He didn't need a barn, no kind of machinery, just himself. Smiling, he lay where she had sat, riding a buzz, until the cold crept into his feet.

9

By early May snow patches had shrunk into the shade of woods. The last snow had thudded from the eaves of the barn, leaving its metal roof gleaming, and the last tooth of ice had trickled away from the gutters. Sometimes a sunny afternoon turned rapidly cold, an east wind scooping up the chill of drift ice that still lurked in the Atlantic, beyond sight. Then the May hay appeared, a fine green in the stubbled fields where it was mown, and in Starr's, unmown for years, it found its way through the folds and humps of dead grasses winter had laid down, thickening the mat of the sod for another fallow year. The trees were still without leaves as Innis's cleared path was nearing the MacRitchies' little footbridge over their brook. In running streams blackflies bred, tiny devils that could leave you bleeding, but soon he'd be finished with this job, he could work at it fast now, slinging limbs and logs and brush, heaping them for a last burning before the woods were too dry for fire. New birds appeared, easy to pick out in the bare trees and bushes, and he'd have to look them up back in his room, he seemed to spot a new bird every day. A small brown one with a thin curved bill spiralled up the trunk of a maple, looking for bugs, no more than an arm's reach away. It seemed unconcerned about him or the noise of his axe, his saw. Innis had heard but couldn't see a woodpecker high in a bare birch drilling for insects stirring under the dead bark, a head like a hammer. Innis took a break to watch a handsome little guy, black and orange with touches of white. It was like seeing a flower bloom after months of drabness. The brook he was approaching was loud, charging through the hillside, much higher than it had been in the fall.

Sharing his secret with Claire had given his plan, as Innis saw it, some class: it was between her and himself, Starr had nothing to do with it. Or that illicit kiss, which some days he hoped she did not remember, other days he wished she did. He watched her carefully for any sign, allowed himself sometimes to think she did remember and was holding it, like he did, out of sight until the right time came to bring it up, or even that she might have, in some odd way, liked it. But Jesus, it was such a pathetic thread to cling to—he couldn't spin much of a fantasy out of it, not that it stopped him from trying. He saw little of her, he stayed in his room when he was home, came down for meals, and she sometimes worked later in Sydney, Starr arriving home ahead of her. Innis missed the high spirits of her first weeks in the house, her laughter, the way a glass of wine seemed to glow in her blue almost black eyes, her spontaneous hugs, her kidding with him, a bright headband in her blue-black hair, a silver choker against her olive skin, long earrings that twirled against the taut muscle of her neck when she laughed or turned her head quickly when she spoke. That had fallen away after her illness, after Starr doused Innis with ice. Every now and then Innis had to mock himself, ridicule his stoned scenarios, if alone in the house with her what he'd say, what he'd do, it was silly, movie stuff really and he'd end up laughing at himself. He would swing off his bed and check out his muscles in the old dresser mirror, its glass rippled like water: he'd pull back his shoulders, filled out now, broadened. He had lost the lazy fat around his waist, that little tire from lounging in Mohney's basement smoking weed and munching junk, they could mash staggering amounts of chips and dips and pretzels. He didn't even miss the TV, the boring movies, the awful afternoon shows, lame and depressing, it was just filler for living, something to jeer, then doze to. He could feel a thin sheath of muscle over his ribs now, and his belly he could pummel hard without a flinch. The ponytail had bared his long thin face, turned it more severe and serious, the hawk nose he'd been ashamed of once but had now grown into he'd got from his grandfather, his mother's dad. If you didn't feel like a teenager anymore, why look like one, hair falling over your eyes. Trim, and tightened up, that's how he liked to look at it: his arms, his hands, they were useful, not just stuck in his pockets as he slouched down a street in Watertown, Mass.

When Claire and his uncle were gone, Innis hunkered over his plants, as if just watching them were a nutrient. He kept their location from Claire, fearing something might slip, and he still liked having this secret of his own, right here under the roof. The seedlings were reaching their limits with an electric sun and a half gallon of soil. The foliage looked brave but leery. In their former lives they'd popped up under a wide, hot sun, South America maybe or California—places Claire had flown to in her stewardess days and said she'd like to visit again—but what could they expect here, ice floes lying out in the ocean in May, refrigerating the wind? No sun-struck breezes, just wan rays of fluorescence and cold darkness beyond. Innis gently massaged their stalks, turning firmer now, and he'd have to risk the early June frosts if the stems got woody. Jesus, pot was related to rope, it had to be hardy, didn't it? He rubbed the leaves between thumb and finger to stimulate their circulation. Like fingering money really, value growing day by day, if he could get it in the bank. Soon he would have to carry his plants up to their clearing in the high woods, their new home. They were over a foot high and crowding and it would be nothing short of tragic for Starr to find them now, their leaves clearly criminal even to him.

Late one night Innis woke to a soft rhythmic tapping, like rain off a roof. Just enough to pluck him out of sleep, it cut across his heartbeat, doubling it as he realized the sound was Claire's headboard patting the wall. He thought at first she was alone, moving to her own fingers, and his face flushed, he pulled himself closer to the wall. But then he heard the smothered sounds. Two voices. Goddamn them, did they think he was deaf or what? He rolled out of bed, slamming his feet to the floor, and sat there with his hands over his ears, feeling stupid, on the margin of everything.

At breakfast Starr, in a fresh white shirt that had flapped on the clothesline the day before, seemed unusually cocky for the early hour, teasing, but Claire was cool and silent at the stove scrambling eggs. Innis stood at the rear window finishing his coffee while he watched a raven with a slice of bread in its beak take two hops to get airborne, chased by three resplendent shrieking jays. He hadn't slept much but he was wide awake. A long line of thick white fog hovered above the water. He could see far along the mountain, east or west, miles. But what good did it do him, to see so far in the morning?

Starr had the radio tuned to the CBC news and was chuckling over the antics of a terrorist group called The Armed Proletarian Nuclei. "Now there's an outfit," he said, pointing to the radio like it was someone's face. "They like the big words. You notice? Nuclei? Pinheads."

"They're fighting for us, Starr," Claire said, "working people like you and me, aren't they? That's what I heard."

"That little clump of flies? They don't have a clue about work, any kind of it. Eh, Innis?" He looked from Innis's back to Claire's. "You're a frosty lot, the two of you," he said, digging into his eggs.

"You could use a little frost yourself," Claire said. Innis could feel her watching him but he ignored her.

"No, no, dear," his uncle said, "the sap is up, it's spring, not that you'd know it without a little help from me."

Innis grabbed his jacket and was out the door, heading up the driveway, Claire calling after him to wait, she wanted to talk to him but he didn't stop until he was nearly to the power line break, his breath seething. Starr had gone to her bed on purpose last night, he knew that now, in case he had any doubt, in case he'd never heard them fucking in Starr's bedroom down the hall, and he hadn't, he never listened, he didn't want that. And she'd let Starr reach for her in the middle of the night, knowing, knowing.

By midmorning he was lost in the tedium of laying tile, Finlay in the bathroom doorway giving advice, Dan Rory rocking in his chair in the parlor listening to scratchy fiddle music on an old record player. The room was steamy from someone's morning shower and Innis hated this fussy work, fitting corners and edges, but they were paying him for this and he needed it.

"That's a very good-looking woman in your house," Finlay said after a long silence. Innis could hear Dan Rory thumping out the beat with his cane. He pressed a tile into place with the concentration of a stonesetter.

"She's just a boarder," he said. He didn't want her mentioned, her name was raw in his mind.

"Yes. Well," Finlay said, drawing hard on a cigarette. "He never had a boarder before, but he knows how to pick one, God bless him."

"Only temporary, till she gets on her feet," Innis said.

"Yes. Feet." Finlay leaned over him and tossed the cigarette, *psst* in the toilet. "Likes the country, does she?"

"Likes it okay."

Did she? He knew one thing she liked. What were the

women on the telephone saying about her now, about him, about Starr?

When he broke for lunch, Dan Rory told him it was a good morning for music. "Look at that fog coming in," pointing with his cane. "But we don't get to do a damn thing, eh? No seed to get ready, nothing to plow, no cows, no horses in the barn. Just our potato patch. You like our violin music, Innis?"

"Haven't heard it much." His father had listened to it on the radio at home, and his mother still went to Down East dances Saturday nights at the Watertown Canadian-American Club, but it had never grabbed Innis. It all sounded the same, old-fashioned, distant, a hundred years away.

"Summer's the time. Not the big dances they used to have but there's music around, oh yes, good music. You'll hear it. How's the woods coming? Flies bad?"

"I got welts in places you wouldn't believe. I've pretty well cleaned up that patch, down to the brook anyway. Then the road's not far."

"I'll send Finlay down for a look. Listen, a letter come to us by mistake, addressed to you but the wrong box number. Finlay, fetch that for Innis."

"Me? I don't get letters." He didn't count his mother's, brief and mostly questions (Are you eating good? Are you still angry with me? To hell with you if you are), as if she had to imagine his life here piece by piece, and he hadn't written back.

"Well you got one now," Finlay said, lifting it off the window sill.

Innis tried to save it for later, like dessert, but he pulled the letter out of his back pocket and read it kneeling in the bathroom. *Yo!* Mohney wrote, carefully in pencil on lined tablet paper, *went down to the Combat Zone last night, great time got a massage yeah! You didn't like that stuff, paying for it but I'll tell you those ladies know some tricks. Nothing like high school. You finding any ganja there? (I hope some Canuck P.O. worker isn't reading this huh?) You get the package? The "candy" I sent? It was primo California more bounce to the ounce. I figured you could use it up there. Must be lots of space to grow "things" when it isn't snowing. Risky shit. Hope this address is okay. Deborah the girl who used to be Debbie, remember? was asking how you like the great white north and I said go up and see for yourself he's probably horny enough. Nobody can figure out how it happened to you why you can't come back. Lawyers is what they all say. You had a stinking lawyer but I told them the lawyer didn't matter fuck all. You in jail? Just goofing. Hot here today good weather for weed. The Great Order of the Leaf? Millions of members. Hope you found some up there. May's a crazy month you want to fuck around so much. You remember. Trouble is I'm getting fucked with. Remember that big prick Tony and his retard brother? Ripped me off, half a key. If you were here maybe I could do something but shit I'm on my own. Believe me I'd like to hurt them I'm broke busted. Things are getting too hot, hard for a small-timer, you get pushed out. So what the fuck are you up to? I heard its mostly trees there. I don't know what to tell you if I can't see you man. I don't have the scratch to come up there wherever the hell St. Aubin is, sounds like a church.* Mohney's voice, from a great distance. If you could not go back to a place, ever, distance in miles meant nothing, it was somewhere in space. Watertown was harder to call up now, trees and fields and water had absorbed it, diffused it, but if Ned were to show up outside that bathroom window and shout, Innis, Let's go get those bastards!, that would be a joy. They'd find a way to get even with Tony and his stupid brother, two guys tough as shit but not smart. Innis wished he could send Mohney something useful, a gun, a good knife, anything practical for vengeance. Words were worthless, but he was glad for these. He stared at the page: after Mohney had scratched the last line, he probably got in his Mustang with the dual glasspacks and drove to Izzy's to shoot pool, or maybe he didn't do that at all but something new. The day Innis left, they shook hands and said See you later. Later. Mohney pledged to visit, as if Innis were bound for jail, but Innis knew that was the last he would see of him. This called for friendship Mohney didn't have in him. Innis's circumstances nothing in Mohney's Boston could explain. A taint of strangeness in this deportation stuff, you're my best pal but, it's weird. Innis had already disappeared from their small talk, Mohney and the rest, he knew how they were, how easily they moved on if you weren't there in front of their faces, talking. Why should they care how he handled what he had become? Debbie? A fox, but snooty under the skin, not a friend you'd ever count on.

"I'm going down to the priest's," Innis said when he'd cleaned up.

Dan Rory was hunched over his record player. There was the probing scrape of a needle until he cued another 78 and said without looking around: "There's something I'd like you to do with me, Innis." He settled back into his rocker, nodding to the strains of a fiddle, a piano pounding out behind it.

"With you?"

"There's to be a Gaelic service, down at St. James Church, not many miles from here."

Church? The old guy could forget that. The priest never laid that trip on him and he liked him for it, collar and all he didn't Jesus and Mary him. "I don't go to church," Innis said.

"Your uncle doesn't take you, and he doesn't take himself anymore, so that's no business of mine. I want you to come with me to a Gaelic service. It's a rare thing now, hard to find a man of the cloth who can do it, but we'll have a minister visiting. He used to have a church down the North Shore, a lot of Gaelic speakers there in those days, still are more than a few. I want you to be there. That's all I'm asking. Your grandfather, he was one of The Men in the Knox Church. He shone, he was fluent."

"I wouldn't know what to do."

"Sit and listen."

"I don't understand a word of that."

"This might be the last Gaelic service on St. Aubin, ever. Listen to it. There's more to listening than words."

"Don't have a coat, or a tie either."

"I'll phone you up," Dan Rory said, turning back to his music, which was nothing you'd hear in a church, more a dance. "When the time comes."

The fog was coming down so fast he didn't want to hitch to Father Lesperance's, though he'd rather go there than home. He ran for a spurt, splashing through springwater crisscrossing the road. He sidarmed pebbles into roadside birches showing their first miserly buds. A car passed him and then a pickup stopped, a GMC rotting out from under the old guy at the wheel. He was heading for a tavern in The Mines, his jaw clenched upon the drinks he'd had already, too intent on steering to talk, studying the road as if it were coming head-on, his old grey fedora cocked over his squint like a salute, saucy. "Struck a deer here once," he said. "Look." He shoved his hat brim up briefly, revealing a red scar high on his forehead. "Came through the windshield like a horse."

"Wreck your truck?"

"Wrecked me. Couldn't even eat the meat. See that house? You can't, too much woods now, it's back in the rear. Last man in there he run a flower shop. Glace Bay, somewhere. Planted oh, maybe two, three hundred daffodil, up the hill behind his kitchen. Came up nice but one night, one night the deer came down, ate every goddamn one of them. Moon out and all. Trimmed them right to the dirt."

"He should've slept outside, scared them off."

"Wasn't the type to sleep outside. Who is? The deer know it. They're not dumb, they just get hungry like the rest of us."

As he pulled up at Starr's mailbox, steering the truck in slowly as a boat, the man stared at the name for a few seconds. "That one still chasing skirts?"

"No, he's almost done with that. He'll be done altogether pretty soon."

Innis was a few steps down the driveway before he noticed her car, near the toolshed. He stopped. Fog had moved up from the shore and stood white in the back field, dense, drifting over the car, the buildings. A light upstairs, and in the parlor. What he'd heard last night had shook his fantasies hard. Some of them. Awkward to be alone with her now. He'd flung himself out the door this morning, sullen and obvious. Ice. Because ice was what he'd used on his mother and she on him, not yelling, not arguments, not explaining up-front, just day after day of silence, not heat but cold. Why couldn't he have been better about this? Claire didn't have to know he cared, he'd acted like a kid. All right, she'd fucked Starr next to his wall. Did he think they didn't do it in the house, ever? But she'd been careful about that before, he'd thought it mattered to her to keep it private, keep it clear of him.

He did not want to go into the house, not without a little help from his friends. He patted his shirt pocket. The barn, no more than a dim shadow in the pale fog, was not appealing, that musty cavern. He dragged a finger along Claire's car, through a film of moisture. A drab Ford, just wheels to get her from here to there. He'd never have stolen it, anywhere, dead desperate. But he slipped inside, closing the door with a quiet thump. She had long legs but not as long as his, he pushed the seat back, settling in. A smell of solvent in his clothes. On his knees in the toxic fume of that bathroom he'd gotten jittery, panicky almost, breathing fast like he'd been running, and he'd jammed Mohney's letter in his jeans, sorry he'd received it, it yanked him back to Watertown. And now he was facing church, in Gaelic? Sorry, Dan Rory, no, can't do it, I'll never be in the mood, not even a Thai stick would get me there. Or maybe he would just disappear that Sunday morning, up in the woods. He teased a crushed cigarette from the ashtray and touched the cork tip with his tongue—yep, lipstick. Hers. The dash lighter gathered its glow, a tremble of electricity in his fingers. It popped quietly from its socket, the red coil mirrored in the windshield as he drew it to the tip of the joint. In a car. Jesus. You turn a key, you hit the road. Summer was coming, the fog would lift, sun would heat everything. Maybe his grandfather had felt this excitement in the spring, restless to work seed into the ground, his oats and potatoes and whatever other stuff he raised. But to his grandfather it was not an urge to be gone from here but to dig further in, deeper and deeper every time he turned the sod. That's what scared Innis in the old photos along the wall: people so rooted, their destinations so fixed, bound by an island within an island, Sunday stiff, in sepia tones, staring into time. Had they ever known a real city? Yet it came to him in one of those moments of stoned clarity, sighting along the hood of a stationary car, that he was afraid of the coming summer, of its openness, its energy, all the desires flooding back.

A buzz, enough toke to get him inside and to his room, past Claire. A few civil words, a joke, lighten things up.

You're not a wounded teenager. Give it up, Innis. He liked the smell of cars that women drove, they were full of their anger, their perfume, the furious smoke of their cigarettes, he could feel their hips in the seat cushion under him, share the tapes flung in the glove compartment, and the one sticking out of the tape player when she parked he would start it right there where she'd left off and let the music conjure her even if he didn't care for it, let it take him down the road as if she were still there with him. Then he would light up a joint and fly. He kept the windows up. He wanted the feeling of car: a shut-in warmth of exchanged breath, smoke and lipstick. Ashtray of stubbed butts, singed paper, gum, the sulfur of an extinguished match. The car's deep metallic quietness. No one ever knew what talk he was making with himself.

He got out of her car, tasting fog, its cool vapor. He was shivering, his jacket too light, too optimistic for the day, shirtsleeve weather in Boston now, but he knew it wasn't just the air.

"Is that you, Innis?"

He stopped in the hall at the door to the parlor. She was sitting on the sofa, wrapped in a brown flannel bathrobe that belonged to Starr. She had laid a fire in the old fireplace Starr almost never used.

"I'm surprised to see you, this time of day," Innis said, rubbing his callused hands, harder than he needed to. It was like meeting her all over again. "You're not sick, I hope?"

"I think you're a little sarcastic."

"Me? Never."

"Don't go up to the bathroom yet, it's dripping steam. I couldn't face work, I couldn't get up for it. You have a good day?"

"I made a few bucks. Keep Starr happy, I guess."

"Is that important, keeping Starr happy?"

"You'd know more about that than I do."

"Don't be mean. You're too young to be mean like that. He's treated me good, not everyone has."

"How about me?" He stood with his palms to the fire. "How did I treat you?"

Claire leaned toward the fire, her face flushed from the bath. "Like you're a little afraid of me maybe. I'm not sure what you are afraid of, so I shouldn't say that. I know you heard us through the wall. I'm sorry for that, terribly. I realized it too late. But you knew already. Hearing us had nothing to do with the truth."

A log snapped, shifted, sparks whirled up the chimney. She was wearing the wide headband he'd seen in her dresser drawer, lemon yellow against her black hair. Heat came into his face as he recalled the panties he took, pushed way back in his drawer where he'd discovered them one morning, puzzled and excited for a few moments, as if he'd slipped them off a woman and completely forgotten.

"And that night you were sick? Was I afraid that night?"

"Doesn't matter if you were. You looked after me."

"And Starr had to be an asshole about it."

"I straightened him out on that, like I said."

"I'm not sure you did, Claire. He was sending me a message last night, wasn't he? A little knee in the balls."

"He couldn't sleep and he came in my room. Some things just happen, they're not planned. Russ showed up where I work yesterday. It wasn't pleasant. I don't want Starr involved with him. I was edgy last night, I needed...I was selfish, okay. I forgot you were there."

"Thanks. This fireplace is a little smoky. You notice?"

"I felt like a fire. It's dying down anyway."

"As long as he doesn't blame it on me." Innis sat on the floor, leaning back on his elbows so he could warm his feet. "In the barn that time, I liked it with you, up there in the old hay. I want you to know that. Jesus, it's been some winter. Hasn't it? In Boston daffodils would be up by now. No deer to eat them either. My mother planted a bunch in a little backyard we had for awhile. And rosebushes. She was always on me to help her look after them but I didn't care about plants and flowers, that was for old folks. I remember spring, the smell of the ground and the grass. Everything goes to your head in May." He was tired and a little sleepy from the fire. For now, he wanted to feel nothing of his uncle in the house. Never had he sat here with Claire as if Starr were not due in any second, or already in. Her legs, sheened from bathing, were level with his eyes and gave off a scent of powder. In the weak window light her eyes seemed darker, larger. Parlor gloom, he'd felt it before. A room once set aside for guests, Starr said, visitors and Sunday-comers, the minister, deacons like his father, relatives dressed for solemn gossip on that God-driven day. "You look terrific, by the way," he said.

"In this?" She tugged at the robe's lapels. "Thanks anyway, Innis, dear. I'm glad to be away from work. Some plaid-pants politician didn't like the color of the car we rented for him yesterday. What a fuss. And Russ on top of that. Maybe I'm not cut out for dealing with the public anymore. Or my private affairs in public."

"What were you cut out for, would you say?"

"Who knows? I had the looks to be an airline stewardess, so that's what I did. It could be fun at times, exciting, and I got around, I saw a lot of places. I met a man, and then another man. I came here with one who thought cheap land and good horses would get him a lot of money. Big mistake."

"Mistakes aren't final."

"Some are. Yours aren't. You're young."

"What would you know about my mistakes?"

"Don't get testy. It's nothing to me how you got to this house. Is it?"

"He told you about me, didn't he, that son of a bitch. Who else, I wonder."

"Hey, easy, dear. Me living here, it would've come out sooner or later. Don't worry about it. What am I going to do, put it in the *Post*? Come on." She reached for his face but he pulled away. He got up and stood at the window.

"I hate this place. Ass-end of nowhere. I can't make it to September, Claire. I'll have to split, I know it. Jesus, we might as well be in the Arctic here. I can't even get the damn things in the ground. I have to start my life all over again, okay, but it won't be in North St. Aubin. I'm a Canadian after all, it turns out, not an American. I don't even know what a Canadian is."

Claire came up behind him and put her arms around him gently. "Innis, dear, you have all kinds of time. You can't know how valuable that is. Don't be hasty. I've seen a lot of that."

He didn't want to move or say anything that would release her embrace, motherly though it was. Wasn't it? In the field above the house an old cherry tree was still without blossoms. The road had disappeared, he couldn't see the mailbox, the air looked like old cotton. Beyond that slowly flowing mist there could be anything, things you wanted, things you didn't. He hardly breathed. "Smoke some weed with me," he whispered.

"Now?" She laughed, stepping back from him. "In the afternoon? Right here? It'll leave a smell."

"Only for a bit. Starr wouldn't know it from woodsmoke."

"Don't be so sure. Well...we'd best not do it in the front window, eh? There's probably enough talk as it is."

"Who'd see us now? We're a little island, lost in fog. An island in an island in an island."

They sat on the sofa, Innis patting his shirt pocket as much to soften his heartbeat as to find the roach. Smoking with a woman like Claire? Nothing better, no one could tell him different. Starr didn't have a clue. Booze made you stupid, it bruised your brain.

"A clip would help," he said.

"This do?" She handed him a hairpin from her headband and he wedged the roach into it and held it out to her.

"There's a few good hits in that," he said, delighted to see it in her fingers.

He struck a wooden match on a fireplace brick and watched her lips seek the stubby cigarette, her eyes closing tight as the flame shrunk and flared.

"Nice," she said.

He plucked it from her hand and drew deeply, lipstick in the smoke. They exchanged it solemnly until he pinched out the last hot bit. Somewhere upstairs the wind had got in and a curtain flapped.

"I left the bathroom window open," she said. "I should close it."

"Nah. Let it go."

They were suddenly quiet, inside themselves. Innis didn't care about Starr, or his shop that was so absurd it was beautiful, and Starr was in it now. Claire took his hand and turned it open. He watched her fingers as she slowly traced its lines and calluses, then closed it.

"After I was sick this time, I felt old," she said. "I saw what it might be like, needing people to look after you. That scared me a little. I have no family left."

"God, you're hardly old. And family isn't everything."

"I'm older than you." Her eyes were shiny as she gazed into the flickers of fire, low and blue. She tucked her knees up, gathering the skirt of the robe under them. Innis took her hand and turned it over as she had done his.

"Let's see," he said, "how old Old Claire is. Jesus, will you look at that." He skimmed his fingers over her skin, in circles, barely touching. "Withered up, poor girl. There's a crease, and there." He did not want to release her hand or look at her face. "Yeah, she's a right old crone, this one."

"Watch yourself, son," she said, patting his cheek. "Just like a man, serving up the compliments. I don't go for flattery."

"You know all about men, I guess. Me and Starr and the rest."

"I should know something. Shouldn't I?"

Innis slid down from the sofa and stretched out on the rug. "Did you get wild dreams while you had that fever? When I was a kid I got them. I was afraid to fall asleep when I was sick. Everything would grow huge and rush up close to my face. I'd see maybe a horse looking in my window. Awake I would've liked a horse at the window, but not sleeping."

Claire reached for his ponytail and tugged it. "Did you kiss me while I was out?"

"Out where?"

"Out of my head that night, did you kiss me or something?"

Innis stroked the worn bristles of the rug. He looked at the stuffed sofa, the ceiling light fixture shadowed with flies. He had never been stoned in the parlor. In the kitchen the sink tap dripped. Starr had told him to put a washer on it but now it was pattering out a tune in cold dishwater. Starr would not come back this afternoon. There was nothing of him in the chemistry of this room except her question: Innis could lie, easily and quickly, and that kept him from fearing it. But maybe that was not what she wanted.

"I kissed your belly. Once, quick and soft. That's all I did. It looked so tasty I just had to. Sorry." He glanced along the inside of Claire's leg where the skin looked so soft he closed his eyes. When he opened them she was staring at him, or maybe into him, he wasn't sure.

"You don't seem like the sneaky type," she said.

"It was just a kiss. Creepy, was it?"

"It didn't come back to me that way, no." She smiled. "I just wanted to ask you, now. Must be the grass. It brings... details." She stretched her legs and leaned back into the sofa. Innis saw her again in that bed, just a flash. He had given her water. He had cooled her hot skin.

He touched the instep of her bare foot, drew his hand back. "I had to do that," he said. "Sorry."

"God, your fingers are cold," she whispered.

"It's the weed. Cannabis hands."

"It's strange out here in the country sometimes," she said. "May, and the light is like ice today. Marooned in mist." She shivered, clutched the robe to her throat. She squeezed his arm, then his thigh. "That woods has hardened you up."

"A real spring day would be a gas, huh? I mean a real warm day, flat out." His voice had gone husky, barely carrying the burden of words.

"Yes, yes. Flowers, Innis. Perfume in the air." She pulled off her headband and twirled it across the room. "I want to smell lilacs on that bush out there." She tilted her head toward him and smiled, her black curls falling around her face. He tried to say something. The next step seemed to be his but his breathing took away his voice. He moved up beside her slowly, and then he put his lips against her lips, lightly, hesitating so as to save himself, his pride or whatever he had to save. But when she did not recoil or speak and he felt her hand down his back, he leaned into her arms. She felt luxurious, wholly longed for, and his hug was strong, meant. Her neck where he kissed was cool, then warm, and he wondered what this thrill he was so glad for was going to cost him. She held his face in her hands.

"You're a hungry one, you are."

"You could feed me."

"That's risky. It could be bad for us both."

"You sound like my mother."

"You wouldn't kiss your mother like that. And don't be too hard on her."

She slid out of his arms and stood with her back to the fire, warming her hands behind her. Innis looked at her slender feet, the curve of her leg. Even in Starr's old brown robe, roped at the waist, she looked beautiful.

"I saw your sketchpad," she said, not looking at him but out the window as if she was speaking to someone else. She sounded so serious he smiled.

"What sketchpad? I have lots of them, Claire, but I don't show them to anybody."

"It was lying on your bed, your door was open. I just picked it up, leafed through it. You never saw me naked like that."

"Okay, I took liberties. You can do that if you're an artist. My high school teacher told me that's what art is all about, changing what you see. There was nothing dirty there."

"I didn't mean that. There's other things though."

"What?"

She shook her head, smiled. He rested against the sofa, smiling too, his eyes sleepy. "Come upstairs with me, Claire."

"Oh, Innis," she said with a soft, helpless laugh. "Upstairs," she whispered. "Such a simple word."

He reached his hand toward her, hoping what he'd asked was ambiguous enough not to leave him looking foolish.

"I have to get a drink," he said. "Pot makes me thirsty. I can hardly talk."

"We've talked already. I should get dressed. We wouldn't want your uncle to show up about now. Would we?"

"I don't really give a damn, Claire. I don't."

"You should."

As she stepped past him she touched his hair and he was glad she didn't say anything more, his mouth was so dry.

In the kitchen he filled a tumbler from the tap and drank the cold water greedily, gasping. The spring in its dark little house, way up the hill. Yet this country was so huge, thousands of miles, thousands of lakes, and maybe he would find one whose edge he could live on. Here, he was just at the beginning of it, as far east as you could get, and out there was the rest of it, spreading westward. His pot plants were ready, but he couldn't plant them on a day like this, a chilling east wind pulling in fog from the ocean. Late frost or not, he'd have to get them up there soon, their roots were probing out the drain holes in the cans, they wanted space, a real sun. At the sink, he took in air, calming himself. If he had gone upstairs to bed with her, would she have compared him with Starr? God. He didn't want to think about it. But she liked weed, she liked that sort of magic, and Starr had none of that to give, the whole feeling was different. After one more mouthful of water, he stood in the lower hall listening to Claire's footsteps, heard her sit on the bed: he knew that sound so well, the way her weight spoke in the springs, her tossings, murmurs, rhythms of sleep. Then there was last night, and there was this afternoon.

On the hall tree, coats were hung. He punched his uncle's old pea jacket hard, one fist and then the other, then went out to the toolshed. In the big vise he clamped a straight piece of scrap iron and banged it with a ballpeen until it lay flat.

10

May slipped past, and with it the afternoon with Claire, try as he might to believe it or some version of it would happen again. She didn't touch him that way again, nothing in her voice invited him that close. She still smiled at him nevertheless, she'd hug him in the kitchen with Starr looking on, josh him, kid him. And he talked to her as if nothing had happened, too proud to let her know how well he remembered a kiss. It was just the way things had come together that afternoon, the fog closing them away from the rest of the world, her mood, the weed. He wanted her to sense that he understood. But he didn't, and trying to puzzle her out only put her in his mind more and more.

He found her swinging the mattock in a cool and windy sun. She had hacked up a small patch of pasture, torn out thick sods, exposing red-brown soil underneath. She looked happy, her hair wind-tossed, her skin darker already against the sleeves of a yellow blouse, and the sight of her got to him quick. The field greening in with new grass, and her in it alone. But Starr was always in the wings, somewhere.

"You're working up a sweat, Miss Claire."

"I am." She leaned on the pick handle laughing, getting her breath. "I'm tilling a little garden. Toiling at least. Look at the blister, will you!" She let the pick fall and held out her palm. Innis glanced toward the house where two white shirts of Starr's flapped on the clothesline. Curtains breathed in and out of an upstairs window. He took her hand and blew softly on her skin.

"Gloves, girl, is what you need. Hard labor."

She withdrew her hand and looked at him. She smiled, brushed her hair back. "I have to dig this up or I'll lose my momentum, no? Want to help?"

"I'd help you with anything, Claire." He crushed a clod of dirt in his hand. "I've got to tell you, I think about you too much."

She'd taken up the spade and was turning the soil, red-brown bladefuls, and chopping it finer.

"You remember that foggy afternoon? I bet you don't."

"Yes I do," she said. "But you know..." She nodded toward the house. "Starr will go only so far with you, and with you and me. That was full of risks, that afternoon. Sweet ones maybe, but I like it here, Innis. I want to stay awhile."

"How long?"

"Awhile. Why should I tell you how long, and you so keen to be away from here?"

"Hard for me to believe you would stay, that's all. You've been places. You've been out in the world."

"Yes. But I'm resting, you could look at it that way. A break from a bad situation."

"Then what?"

"You want to be sure about everything, Innis. I can't help you there. But we could break up this dirt and get some seeds in, couldn't we do that?"

"Might still get a frost, you know."

"But we're not afraid of frosts, are we, you and me?"

They worked without speaking. Innis chopped the soil, two-handing the spade handle, drawing it up eye level and plunging its blade deep into the dirt. Claire combed a rake through behind him. The sun was constantly attended by clouds, the air shadowed and then bright over and over, wind beating away even the persistent blackflies. Innis kept at it, his wind was good anyway, he could dig out a whole field for her if she asked him, and he could hear her breath too, behind him, a little quicker than his, and that would have to do for now.

"Claire, what're you planting?"

"Just flowers. I never had time for a garden with Russ. Horses are a lot of work, they need attention. But the horses are all gone now."

"Bulbs of some kind are coming up by the front step. Granny's, Starr says, from years back."

"Sure. Irises, I bet. Day lilies later. Then hollyhocks higher than your head. You find them around the old houses."

"That looks like an iris in the field there, where it's damp."

"It's a wild iris, a blue flag, really."

"I didn't know irises could be wild."

"Blue ones. Maybe others I don't know about."

"The lilac's out. You smell it yet?"

"Oh, gorgeous. Isn't it powerful?"

"It must get in Starr's window up there. Must drive him nuts."

"He's nervous as a cat today."

"Summer getting to him, is it?"

"So to us all. Ever see air so clear?"

"It could be warmer, if it's summer we're talking about. Be hotter in Boston long about now."

Innis shaped seed furrows with the tip of the mattock. In his face she fanned out seed packets like a hand of cards. "Take your pick. Nasturtiums, lots of those. Poppies. Petunias, marigolds. Color is what I want."

"Should've started those indoors, Claire. It's June already."

"Like you started yours?"

Innis didn't answer. He looked toward the house, took a breather. "I shouldn't tell you any more about it. I shouldn't tell you anything about myself."

"Why?" She was crouching along a furrow tapping seeds out of a packet, the knees of her jeans damp from the soil.

"A word here, a word there, and my uncle..."

"My uncle what?" Starr had come into the field, frowning, the breeze covering his footsteps. "Am I missing something?"

He looks tired, that was Innis's first thought, or something like tired. "This little garden here," Innis said, grinning, jamming his spade in the ground like a spear. "Claire wanted to surprise you."

"I'm sure she's got surprises in her."

With her shoe Claire pressed a row of soil down carefully, not looking at him. "I wanted flowers we can see from the windows."

"You'll be lucky if you do," Starr said, blowing smoke from a fresh Export. "I saw you out here slaving away. I thinks, they have to be planting, or digging a grave. I hope it isn't mine."

"Starr, don't be morbid," Claire said.

"I could think of better spots for a grave," Innis said.

"Woods are full of them," Starr said.

"What are those gulls circling for?" Innis pointed to a dozen seagulls dipping and crying above the woods to the east.

"That's the old MacLeod place. No MacLeods there anymore, but the smelt are running in their brook. Spawning time." Starr went on across the field.

"What's he going over there for?" Innis said. "Never seen him in the barn."

"He's thinking he might cut hay this year."

"What'll he harness that old mower to, the Lada?"

"He's doing it by hand he said. Scything it, I guess." Claire stood up and looked toward the barn as if to verify this. "Good thing no cows are waiting for it."

"He seems a little glum lately," Innis said. "That could be good or bad, I suppose, depending on how you look at it."

Claire balled up an empty seed packet and tossed it aside. "Russ showed up at the shop yesterday. I was helping your uncle straighten out his books."

"His books?" Innis laughed. "Some books. A mess when I saw them."

"Do you know how complicated it is?" she said, her voice low.

"What is?"

"The three of us, here. This is his house, you know."

"I didn't know that?"

"Listen for a minute. I left Russ because somehow I'd come to stand for his disappointments, and there he was right there in Starr's shop, all ruffed up and giving us both the bad mouth. He's bigger than Starr, you know, he's a big man. But Starr took him by the throat and choked him until he couldn't spit out another rotten word and then he threw him out the door, he said he'd kill him if he came back."

"Starr couldn't kill anybody," Innis said.

"Russ doesn't know that."

"Sergeant Corbett of The Royal Mounted. So now you love him, is that it?"

"Oh, I don't know if it's love, Innis, no. Do you know what that is? I don't think you do."

"I might surprise you, girl."

"You might surprise yourself, boy."

She exchanged a smile with him, tearing open another seed packet with her teeth. She chewed the bit of paper slowly, rolled it on her tongue and spat it at him. Innis smiled sadly, shook his head.

"Claire, do you think I'm a stick of wood or what?" He stomped the last furrow flat. "Am I supposed to forget that afternoon?"

"Forget it for now," she said. "Please." She touched her finger to his mouth, left the grit of clay on his lips. But, feeling his uncle behind him, he turned to see Starr making his way into the grass of the lower field, a scythe raised high by the throat like a weapon. He brought it down and then stood finishing a cigarette. Then slowly, almost thoughtfully, he swung into motion, sweeping the blade side to side, its fresh edge flashing.

"Look at Father Time over there," Innis said.

Claire punched his shoulder. "Innis, I wouldn't let him hear you. He's not in the mood."

"Oh, to hell with him, Claire. I've got a garden to get in myself."

"Not today?"

"It's a secret. I hope."

"So do I, dear."

Innis glanced up at a contrail, a slow chalky stroke in the blue afternoon sky. The plane was tiny, higher than the prop plane that had brought him here from Halifax.

"At least I'm growing something on this land. Starr's waltzing with a scythe."

11

Three days later Innis was gathering his gear from the attic, setting plants, their soil dry and light, in an old fruit basket he'd found in the toolshed loft, a few more arranged already in a backpack, when he heard the Lada in the sideyard. Starr, and Claire. Damn it. He shut the attic door behind him and edged up to the hall window. They were still in the driveway, playing around, laughing, goofy in a hot sun and a west wind. Starr chased her like a schoolboy, grabbing for her, and she ripped a handful of grass from the ground and tossed it at him, strands blowing back in her hair. Starr stripped off his shirt, his lean torso so white he seemed to Innis shockingly naked, on his shoulders blurry blue tattoos Innis had never seen: frolicking like this, he looked, for a moment, wild, a little crazy. Claire yanked the tails of her red blouse loose and tied them up under her breasts. Innis winced, that bare tummy, that sweet spot he had tasted. Starr, twirling his shirt like a flag, bounded after her, caught her at the waist and she didn't resist when he kissed her. Disgusted, Innis stepped back. Unhinged by the weather, both of them, nuts. By the end of summer he'd be gone and

they could kiss and screw till they were dizzy, any room in
the house, he didn't care, the woods, the fields, the barn. As
he released the curtain, Claire glanced up. She froze for a
long moment, Starr with his back to her now buttoning up
his shirt: like she was in a play, lost in it, and Innis, in the
balcony, had brought her up short. Performance over. She
frowned, brushing grass from her hair, but gave Innis a
furtive wave that might have scolded him for spying, he
couldn't tell.

He stayed in his room, the door shut, until Claire tapped
on it and told him they were going out for supper, she and
Starr, up to Baddeck and might not be back until tomorrow.

"Why tell me?" Innis said. "I'm not afraid of the dark."
He lay on his bed staring at water stains in the ceiling, tea-
colored phantoms, day by day he'd given them dozens of
shapes. He had a hard-on that hurt and he wanted to say
come on in, please, Miss Claire, that warm breeze, it's something, isn't it? Sorry about my big stick here. But he didn't.

And Claire didn't answer. He heard her on the stairs, and
then they were gone, Starr giving him a cheery goose on the
horn, the bastard, that miserable little beep a rabbit wouldn't
run from. Imagination, and caution, and doubt. There were
three things to keep a man occupied. Who needed sex?

He had to catch what was left of the afternoon and he
headed quickly up the old logging road, anxious to reach
the upper woods, looking back when he rested to see who
might be on the highway. Someone might drive by and spot
him and tell Starr, I saw your nephew ducking into the
woods with a big basket on his arm, and a mattock on his
shoulder. Now what would he be doing in the trees with
that? And Innis would have to come up with a nice lie. I
was up there at my pine trees, thinning them a bit, Starr,
you want a nice Christmas tree, don't you? Small stuff,
penny lies.

The woods had leafed out, were growing rich again with light and shadow, and the further in he got, the safer he felt, people just didn't go up here. He nosed the fading blossoms on a tree he didn't know, white and spicy against the thick dark spruce. Was this the Indian pear Starr had mentioned? Blossoms now, fruit later, so he'd have to watch. He moved on, Claire in his mind for a few strides until he could push her away again. How often in a day did she kiss Starr like that, drawing his face into her hands? Innis had once thought he'd lead her up here by the hand when summer came: he knew places that fairly begged you to lie down in them, thick beds of soft, dry moss. Another fantasy shot to hell. He heard nothing through the wall at night but Claire, her stirrings. Whatever she did with Starr now it was in his room, not hers. But stay cool, take the long view. That's what the window told you, all you had to do in this place was look outdoors and your sight took wing, the long mountain went as wide as your vision and the water of the strait could ebb you out anywhere east. But west it was for Innis, not seaward but into the vast green ocean of Canada, into mapspace.

He knew these upper woods better than his uncle ever had, he was sure of that now. Apart from trips to the spring, Starr hadn't walked up this far since the old fields had grown in years back. Was all cleared up there once, he said in one of his moods of recollection when the farming he had hated took on a soft, rum-colored glow, we pastured right the way up that hill. Starr didn't care to beat his way through thickets anymore, over the budwormed deadfalls, spiked with sharp branches. Leave it to the holiday hunters, Starr said, those damn fools from town. But Innis had found lots of paths, a network of narrow trails deer had cut, their hoof marks in the sod, the moss, the mud. Not that they had the same journeys in mind that he did, the same

ends, and he'd picked out his planting spot partly because
he had never seen deer near it, no tracks or scat. He pushed
on, winded but excited now, over the boggy ground beneath
the power lines, catching a whiff of the thawed mackerel in
his backpack that Starr had tossed in the garbage thinking
they were on the turn.

Through a stand of spindly maples Innis beheld his clearing. Well above the power line break, he had never seen
hunters this far up last fall. It was conspicuous in no particular way, at least on this afternoon whose sky had gone
from blue to dank white, the sun's heat strong but the light
diffused. Birch and maple ringed it, and a few spruce stark
and brittle, ashen, as if an incredible frost had blasted them,
but in fact just tiny worms, a plague that had passed. Young
spruce were straying into the clearing and that was good.
There in the new grass were the pine seedlings he'd brought
here months ago, stuck in the ground like sticks, not a
needle on any of them, rusty as old metal. Christmas pines?
More like grave markers. A forlorn time anyway when he'd
planted them, desperate to put anything down in this place,
to say *mine*. And the clearings were always attracting him
then, in the fall, he'd turn toward one and then another because he expected something living to be there, he didn't
know what.

He set to work with a pleasure no other task had matched,
spacing the pots zigzag so they would look natural, like
weeds, if someone did happen by, seduced, like him, by the
light of a clearing. He chopped through mats of sod and
stubborn roots, worked the soil clean of stones. Tougher
than Claire's little plot, but oh what flowers would be blooming here! When the reddish clay was as fine as he could
make it with a trowel, he prodded each plant free of its pot,
nesting carefully the white net of roots into its hole where
half a mackerel waited, tail, or head with its foggy eyes. He
shaped a small basin around each one to hold the water he'd

have to carry to get them started, and keep carrying if the summer was dry. A few pails from the spring. A good hike but still closer than any of the brooks. That spring only dried up once, Starr said, in the worst summer for rain we ever had, when I came home from the navy. The guy in the pot book said, Those roots got a trauma, pardner, if you know what I mean, and they need a nice deep drink of water to ease their pain. Innis whittled small branches from a willow, poked them into the ground and made plastic tents for each plant out of five-pound potato sacks. They'd keep off a late frost, and maybe deer too if they were nosing around. Would they even eat marijuana? Wouldn't hurt them to try it, might tune their ears even finer, sniff out a hunter downwind. The book writer didn't mention deer, but how could he know? He never thought about north, he didn't know these boreal woods, so removed from a pot-loving sun.

Innis stood back admiring the snug protection of his tiny greenhouses, hardly visible in the low brush. Suddenly he sensed something behind him and whirled, raising the mattock like a club: nothing. But it got his heart going, he was edgy anyway, Christ. Some animal. Maybe the cat? He made a wailing, mewing sound, friendly, not fearful, and listened again, he didn't know just what sound this cat would make. But there was only the mute trees, the misty green light of new leaf. A tall gaunt spruce, grey with lichen, creaked against a windfall it had captured in its branches. The plastic tents fluttered and breathed. Nothing but what was always here when the wind capered through woods, the subtle sounds of branch and needles and leaves. Innis drove the pickhead hard into the ragged brown bore of a stump and left it standing. No one could ruin this, not after the weeks of nursing those seedlings, whispering to them, holding his breath every time Starr walked along the upstairs hall, or was curious as to why the ceiling light in the kitchen dimmed sometimes, but he never bothered to investigate it. Well, the plants were safely hidden now, and who could prove Innis owned them anyway? Deep in trees nobody cared about, a dozen plants whose leaves and buds people liked to light up and inhale, harming no one. The whole operation here could be over by early September, maybe sooner if the weather was right, Innis gone and the pot too, not a soul this side of the island tainted by anything Innis had done. Over and out.

Innis hid the basket in a clump of young fir. He'd have to fetch a few pails of sweet water from the spring, and the seedlings, so dry from their pots, would draw it up like blood.

But first, the skinny joint he'd saved, once hoping to share it with Claire in this very clearing, to give his seedlings a lucky send-off with her lovely touch, then watch her kiss a toke, and when she passed it back to him, he would inhale a taste of her. Instead, it was just him, loading his lungs for a good buzz. The wind was cooler, the sun seemed underwater. He felt real affection for his plants, arranged there, free of Starr's house, on their own, their roots already beginning tender investigations of this new, deep ground. You live a little differently when you have room, Starr said once of the country, though he didn't say just how. Innis laughed. Love. Damn it, this was the only love he was likely to get, the hot and roving fancies of good weed, and there were lots worse things to put your lips to. He got up and wandered about the clearing, pressing his footprints down into the soft sod. He pissed against the scarred bark of a birch tree. How's this, Mr. Cat? Raise your tail here tonight if you want. The pick stuck up from the stump like a stroke of Chinese writing, black against the greening woods. He pressed his palms together: Lord, give the deer everything they love, leaves and buds and wild apples, but let them pass my *cannabis sativa* by.

From far down on the road, the faint buzz of a car with a bad muffler, soon gone. Here, out in the sticks, you'd have to be careful and clever: a stolen car could stand out like a firetruck. Be a challenge, though. He'd never stolen the cars for money—with one exception—not for anyone but himself and his own escape, a particular high. People often left the keys dangling there, asking to be turned. Richer the better, the careless ones accustomed to money, dropping things casually in their wake. All you had to do was open the door, and later a guy would come out of a bar and could not believe his luxurious set of wheels had vanished, he would rush all over the lot, up and down the street thinking he'd done something wrong, forgotten where he parked it, embarrassed. Innis was well away by then, taking the crazy back streets of Boston, laid out for horses a long time ago. Staying off the roads the cops cruised, didn't he always leave it on a side street before daylight, clean as when he'd driven it away, maybe smells in the seats and leather that weren't there before? All except that one, that Porsche he'd stolen for money because he'd been drinking then and was cocky and stupid when the hard guys asked him to steal it, Just park it a certain place and there's a grand in it for you, Innis. There wasn't, there wasn't anything in it but grief, and what was he to do about it? Go after them with a gun?

Still, he'd never seen himself as a criminal. He didn't think it sexy or macho to be hustled into a police cruiser in cuffs while neighbors looked on like he'd just knifed his mother, to be preached at by a juvenile court judge, to spend time in a detention center with toughs and fuckups. He'd just wanted the cars, couldn't stop himself from taking them, each one grooved him into a mood he needed. And the court convictions, they seemed to accumulate in a dream, and finally they'd crashed through the ceiling. As a kid, when his mother yelled him out of her hair or argued with his dad about money or about things to do with Cape

Breton—they never seemed to agree on how to think about "down home," they loved it to tears one day and the next recalled ways it had held them back—on those days Innis would wander up the street trying car doors, looking for one shiny and big and unlocked, and he would sit inside, the windows rolled up, in the deep plush comfort of its seats, eager for whatever flight. He would play the wheel that could turn him in any direction he wished, his voice for a motor. The silent hand of the dashboard clock advanced, just an instrument among others, measuring he didn't know what. And always that smell of new, all new. More than once he was found asleep in the back seat, but no one accused him of felonies, a boy sleeping in a car not his own was not illegal, not yet, and his mother was crying when they brought him home, but she slapped him too, angry because she was scared, undone. He would undo her many times more, fraying her, later, especially when a new man came home with her, he gave her a hard time. But he had never heeded what his mother told him until it was too late, the one thing he truly needed to remember: You are not a citizen, they could send you straight back to Canada some day. And after the final hammer came down on his head, he asked her why in hell she hadn't made him a U.S. citizen, for Christ's sake. Listen, Innis, she said, it wasn't my lookout, it was your dad's, he tended to things like that, not me, and he always thought we might go back home, I never thought about it later, not a citizen myself yet, I didn't think it would ever come to this, how could I?

He savored his supper that night, two salt codfish cakes fried crusty in butter, washed down with ice water. The sun was sliding into dove grey cloud above the mountain, burning like steel on the sheened surface of the strait, glimmers of sequined light, thrilling, then gone. A calm excitement in every simple action, the last bite of food, drinking cold water from a glass. He had an itch to sketch. A cat, its still-mysterious face, burning too, tufted ears alert. Paws big, the size he'd seen in snow. Dan Rory told him there'd been a mountain lion on the island once, he'd seen him, quite a beast it was, he said, but it was shot in a trap eventually. Eventually. Innis flipped a page and did a quick take of Claire, leaning into her spade, smiling, a bit tousled by her labor, her blouse undone deeper than it had been, a sexy hitch to her hip, a pose she might have assumed for a joke, if he'd asked her. He liked shaping her with his pen, now she knew he could draw her well. Okay, the impulse had been juvenile, but the nude sketches were good. This ball-point pen in his hand could turn out a vision of her, and yet she was up there someplace in the green hinterlands of Cape Breton, doing something not like this on the paper at all, her expressions would be totally different from what he had drawn, her hair would be tousled in a different way, her leg, arm, hip angled some other way from how he had her in these lines and hatchings. She and Starr now, maybe, heading for a motel on the Cabot Trail. Getting away, that's what lovers did—they excluded you. No surprise in that. Well, he'd sown his crop. Leaving wasn't just another vague, murky intention. A red spill of cloudy light, the mountain a long silhouette beneath it: it had once looked only like a wall to him, and Starr had said, if you want to go west, you got to go over that mountain, and I don't mean just by car. Through the screen door the wind turned suddenly, carrying with it distance, momentum, places it had passed through, the fragrance of trees, the sea. At night now Innis opened his window high to feel it sweep over his body.

His plants, in that cool clay, deep in a woods their genes had not prepared them for. Was there a Gaelic word for pot?

He tidied up the attic, around the loom, swept up traces of soil. Pushing a trunk aside, he found a long-dead mouse behind it: a grey puff, dessicate as bird down, its tailbone tiny beads. Not really a mouse at all but a misty grey aura that dispersed like dandelion seed when he blew on it. He was tempted to look into the trunk, but no, this was not the time to pore over the old things of this house, he was moving forward. He unfastened the lights from the loom, carried them and the warming tray out to the toolshed and stashed them in the loft, maybe Starr could use that kind of heat and light someday. One big risk, the attic risk, was over. He was sorry, in a way, it had charged the air at times. Like the evening the lights went out when they were all in the parlor. Good Christ, Starr said, why are we cooking so many fuses? I've screwed in a goddamn boxful. He dragged impatiently on his cigarette, it glowed bright, and Innis had listened to Claire's breathing, it was easy to hear it in the dark, until she said, I guess it's my turn, and went off to find a flashlight. It's the old wiring, Innis said. Something new in the old wiring, Starr said. But he never sought it out.

Just about dark, Innis hitched a ride on a propane truck that dropped him off at Dan Rory and Finlay's. He walked up the hill across the brook, through the path he'd cut, and found Finlay bent into the weeding of their potato patch below the house, Dan Rory at the end of the row talking away but not about weeds or potatoes.

"You referring to the power in those damn lines up the hill there?" Dan Rory said, waving his cane toward the upper woods. "It shoots over our heads to the mainland. What good was the Wreck Cove Project to us?"

Finlay flung aside a fistful of weeds, smacked a mosquito. "That was a feat of engineering, Daddy. That's the modern world."

"Come out of those potatoes, it's after getting dark. Listen, they blasted rock and dug out the earth and cut down thousands of trees, yiss. They messed up the old lakes there in The Barrens, linked them with concrete. What are you trying to tell me?"

"We got lakes to burn, Daddy. Important places have dams and things, for Jesus sake. The fish are fading, the mines shutting down. But the Wreck Cove Hydroelectric Project, now that's a different pig altogether." Finlay stood up, rubbing his spine. "Look, there's Innis himself. How're you now?"

"I'm good, Finlay. On my way home from Father Lesperance's, just wanted to say hello."

"We were on about the Everlasting Barrens, way up in the Highlands," Dan Rory said. "A maze of little roads there now, after the Project, I'd get lost myself."

"I shot a moose up there years ago," Finlay said. "Felt bad about it. They invite their own killing. Deer will gambol away but a moose, he'll just keep eating, he's that kind of animal."

"Or charge right at you. Have you eaten moose, Innis?"

"Never had the pleasure."

"Och, they're a big beast. Come inside for a cold drink."

Innis said no, he really couldn't, Starr would pick him up on the road any minute. He idled long enough to discuss the bats flowing out the west gable of the house, dozens of them, "We don't care, Finlay said, "they can have the attic, eat mosquitoes by the carload, you know."

A thin moon had crept above the southern hill, up toward the power line. Innis would have preferred a darker night.

"Have you seen that sight before, Innis?" Dan Rory said, pointing his cane over Innis's head. The sky above the mountain ridge pulsed with flickering, shadowy lights of unimaginable size, their source hidden by the mountain, their rays wavering in the dark blue sky. A chill rushed up his back.

"No," he said.

"Northern lights," Finlay said. "Something to do with the polar ice, I think. I've seen them brighter."

"We thought they were the breath of dead warriors," Dan Rory said. "A long time ago."

Innis glanced back at the tall upstairs windows already lit and that brought him down. They went to bed early, these old men. He bid them good night, leaving with an alibi, should he need one.

He jumped the ditch into the trees whenever he heard a car. He didn't want anyone to see him walking toward the Wharf Road, not tonight. And there was a chance that the priest might be at his cottage now that the weather was turning. But no, it was dark. Captain MacQueen's silver poplar loomed in full leaf, shadowing the little house. He was nervous, he hadn't expected that, and so he continued on past the Captain's garage, stopping for a dutiful look in the priest's window. He tried the door to see if it was busted. Nope. If he got caught in the Captain's, they wouldn't send him away, they would put him away. But at the moment he was comfortable in his innocence, he basked in it, he was almost sorry to cash it in. I'm a good boy, Father, not a Catholic but I'm okay for the moment. Have I done anything lately bad enough for confession? I wish.

He stood on the wharf, the water beneath him slapping through the blackened timbers, their bolts and pins exposed and harsh, they'd rip a hull quick. A lively place once, a ferry back and forth, cars, people, the priest's cottage was a thriving store. A rough stretch of water sometimes, squally seas when the wind tore over a strong tide. He wished he had a boat and the knowhow, he'd sail her right down that strait, under the bridge and into the ocean. Ports were great places to start over, their wharfs clustered with boats. The distances here, a glance could take in miles of mountain, long sweeping looks you wouldn't get in a city.

Telling himself it was precaution, making sure he was alone here, he plodded along the beach. A car had spun deep ruts, somebody parking for a hot session, beer bottles flung into the sand, before or after. He had not often seen cars here in the day, not in winter, except for the odd one come down for a gaze at the strait. He arced a bottle end over end into the water, a white splash in the small, steady waves. Starr could fix TVs and stereos, but there he was in a grubby old shop, a throwback, toting up bills on an adding machine you cranked, paper tape unspooling over the floor. But Starr didn't care, it didn't matter if people came to him only by word of mouth, that there was nothing in the window but the twisted, dusty blades of a dead aspidistra. And Starr didn't care, no matter what he might say in his cups, to go any further than the boundaries of Cape Breton Island, and most of the time St. Aubin Island itself, tucked safely inside it, would do him. But Claire? How long would she hang around? If she was still here in the fall, the fall...

Innis cut in behind the old garage and stood listening, his back pressed against the weathered shingles. Why couldn't a guy they called Moneybags build himself a good garage, protect that sweet machine inside? All oiled motion, that Caddy, a car that swam. Innis was shivering as he came up through the hatch and set out searching the house, moving through it confidently now, switching the flashlight off when he passed a window. What if the man didn't keep any keys here? Maybe someone else looked after them. But the old Captain, God bless him, had to be nothing if not neat, adept at hiding things from sight. Innis spent a little time in the obvious places, whipping drawers open and shut, rooting under linen. The flashlight flared in the glass doors of a tall cabinet. There, inside the third from the left of a nice row of brass-hook-hung mugs with different sailing ships on each, sat a nest of keys, among them two with a Cadillac logo. Yes.

Cracks and seams of moonlight scored the earthy darkness of the garage, caressing the car's black finish. Damn, he liked that short rear deck, the classic lines. Seville. Best looker Cadillac ever made, as far he was concerned. The key slid into the lock smoothly and he laughed as he inhaled the leathery smell and eased himself behind the wheel. But the ignition switch lit nothing on the dash. Battery. Stowed. He found it on a small wall bench plugged into a trickle charger, a half-inch box wrench lying beside it for the cable nuts. Captain MacQueen, always at the ready, gear within reach. Innis dropped the battery into the engine compartment, connected the cables. Even the engine was clean. When he turned it over, the squawk of the starter seemed disturbingly loud and he sat for a while before he tried again, his heart going hard. But who would hear it? Only this house and the priest's on the Wharf Road. The third go the engine caught, ran rough for a little and then idled quietly. He revved it but not high. Couldn't run it for long, even in a garage peppered with holes, but he knew how smoothly it would respond on the road, how it would carry him. Tank was almost on full. Before anybody discovered the empty garage, he could be miles away west, a few days' driving if he slipped out of here late at night, an hour and a half and he'd be off the island, across the Strait of Canso, go all night with the radio and just enough weed to make the road interesting, stop for doughnuts and coke when the munchies hit. He'd head out across those long, half-deserted Canadian highways where you could pull over and piss in the trees and nobody's headlights would pick you out, there would be only the silence of the endless woods and your own trickle and steam, the car idling on the shoulder, waiting to carry you as far as you wanted to go, and as you pulled away, the lights might sweep across a pulpwood road cut into the trees and it would chill you, imagining the dark woods and monotonous labor and being trapped in that kind of life. And no borders to cross but provincial ones, no cold customs officials looking him over grimly like he was a serial killer with a razor hidden in his shoe. He could ditch it maybe near Toronto, push it in a river somewhere, sell it even, cheap and quick, and start living again, city living. But he could not push his imagination into the blurry regions of this vision, he pulled back from its necessary details into the simple certainty of his plan: the plants were in the ground, growing this very minute. When the earth warmed up, they'd flourish there in the woods, flower, bring him profit. Then he could leave the way he wanted.

Smelling exhaust, he turned off the ignition. A gentle wind had risen, rustling the big poplar. He'd have to do this fast, get out quick and button her up.

The old doors, sagging on their hinges, dragged in the dirt as he pushed each one open wide. Then he backed out slowly, the space was narrow, and left the engine running without lights while he closed the garage. A quick look around and he jumped behind the wheel. Lights, reverse, ease out, into drive, and away, calmly, no rush, laying no rubber. The Seville took the road smoothly, for a stored car, accelerated without a miss. At the Ferry Road he turned west toward The Head. His breath fogged the windshield, he was breathing hard like he'd been running and he rubbed the glass with his fist. His brights picked out animal eyes at the roadside and he dimmed quickly. No unnecessary attention, please, don't look like you're running off with somebody else's car, headlights screaming down the road. Just a loan. Hey, he'd earned it, he'd paid his dues here and no one could tell him different. The brakes were a bit soft, and the steering wheel off a couple degrees, he'd have thought that would have bugged the Captain, fussy guy. But everything else was cool. Let Starr and Claire have the Lada, that old lunchbox. He was wired, had to settle down, too long since he'd driven a vehicle like this, though North

St. Aubin was hardly a network of dangerous streets. It was
not a town or even a village, but a community in the man-
ner of the Highlands, Dan Rory had told him, a run of
farms, in its original makeup, on a long single road, it never
had the focus of a village, no center, no collection of shops,
just two churches, a store, a fire hall, and in the old days, a
forge here, a grist mill there, for a town you went elsewhere,
but we were all held together just the same, he said.

The road ran close to the water, past cottages clinging to
a piece of shore land, lit with summer residents or week-
enders, but at The Head where it turned southward there
was nothing at first between him and the beach but a strip
of shingle, the hills of Cape Breton Island clear and dark
across the moonlit water, green places he did not know and
did not intend to know, just a light here and there, and the
lights of a little town, a cluster of excitement at this distance, to his eyes now it might as well be Boston, whatever
it was a long journey by car across the bridge and over the
mountain, but direct by boat or by ice the way they used to
go when the roads were poor and seasonal, terrible mud,
Starr said, and the heavy snows. The paved road ended, the
dirt smooth and graded at first, then trees closed in and it
turned rough, crisscrossed by little gullies of water, baring
rocks. He braked for ruts, groaning at every muddy splash
resounding in the wheel wells. No damage, please. Mud
spray was bad enough. The road narrowed and he swore,
he'd expected the good road would take him clear around
The Head to Southside St. Aubin, all he'd need now was a
patch of mud bad enough to mire him. He didn't dare turn
back. This was the pace of horse and wagon. He wanted to
move, bust out. God. Dense woods right to the roadside.

A skinny driveway dropped away into trees, so fast out
of sight he couldn't spot the house, just a mailbox. Summer
places probably, no door he'd want to knock on in any case.

Hi, look, sorry to bother you but I got this stolen Cadillac up there and I need to get it out of the mud quick, could I use your phone? Jesus, headlights coming his way, barely two lanes. Innis slowed even more, straddling the ditch edge as the headlights glared anonymously toward him, the stupid bastard had his brights on. Shit, talk about getting a good look. Innis averted his face as the vehicle passed by, near enough to touch, and assumed the shape of a pickup, mudspattered, the guy must live along here somewhere, no other reason to be on this goddamn road unless you were crazy enough to take a Cadillac down it. He caught glimmers of water through the lower trees, the road widened, he passed a deep field and a good house at the back of it where the land sloped away to the water, Innis knew there was water below the way the light came up behind it. He hit pavement again and picked up speed, it was like taking a deep breath, tires centrifuging mud until they cleared it and the car whispered cleanly again. He relaxed a little, tilted the electric seat back, lowered it, made room for his legs. No breakdowns please, pulled over on the shoulder with a wheel jacked up while anyone driving by could get a good gawk at him wrestling with a spare. This car had been idle for months, no telling what might balk. Moisture in the wiring, the gas. He gave it more gas, the grades and curves were gentle. A long farm unfolded on both sides of the road, up the hill and down toward the water, a prosperous spread, nothing like it on the north side. The water a good way below the road. St. Georges Channel, deep water there, Starr said, eight, nine hundred feet. A car passed him in the opposite direction, fine, it sped out of sight, but when another pulled up close behind, he slowed enough to let it pass. In Boston he had never worried who saw him in a good car as long it wasn't the alerted police, but now everyone he encountered tightened him up and he felt like he should get off the highway, not cruise on it. After all, this was not his flight out of here, he was not heading off from St. Aubin, from Cape Breton Island, from Nova Scotia, not yet. Everyone who set eyes on this car was a threat, he was exposed, might as well be driving a tractor-trailer. This was not a kick after all, not the high he had hoped for. All he wanted now was to get this car out of sight.

Innis squinted for signs of a road back to the north side, hit the brakes and backed up when his headlights caught a sign MACLEANS CROSS. Dirt road again but high, better, more clearings, some big fields, and what looked like a track for running horses. But very dark when the trees closed in again. Okay with him. He was crossing a high part of the island, surprisingly level for a long stretch, when there was a flicker of fur at the edge of his lights and immediately an ugly thump, low at the wheel well. He swerved too late, he stopped, leaped out, his heart thumping. Behind him the engine idled smoothly as he strained to make out the dark form on the road, an animal, yes, and then he heard someone calling further back in the dark, yelling a name. Innis slid back behind the wheel and screeched away, killing his lights until the road turned and descended, passing a house carved into the dense spruce and another before he reached Ferry Road and could make for the wharf again. He was sweating, the steering wheel was damp. He'd have to wipe everything, smear away every fingerprint. A dog. Jesus. Somebody's dog.

He drifted down the Wharf Road with his lights out and, after he opened the garage, steered the Seville inside faster than he'd backed it out and barred the doors. He stood in the dark listening. Then he quietly got back inside the car and touched the glow of the dashboard lighter to the tip of a joint. What a trip! If that person got the license, he was fucked. But the voice had been way down the road, they couldn't have seen much. He jabbed the radio button past classical music, a pop station, somebody talking, then hit the sweet huskiness of the French DJ. What the hell was she saying? Could be anything, just dumb DJ jabber, but a hot voice nevertheless, he could take it in his hands almost, draw it into him. Claire had French blood in her, her mother's side. Didn't she murmur Innis in her fevered sleep? But she was out of her head that night, delerium didn't count. She might have said Starr in the same voice, breathing it, puzzled or yearning, you couldn't be sure. A small scar on her ribs. Details came to him. A beauty mole, a perfect daub above her breast. If she were here in this car, in the sealed warmth of exchanged breath, of moist lipstick, that faint, inverted, intimate whistle of pot smoke, shared and held, he could forget he had just killed a dog with another man's car. Ash in the ashtray, singed paper, the sulfur of an extinguished match. The two of them, everything else shut out.

He sat in the glow of the dashlights, recycling the smoke he had made. The DJ, she had cued a record, some rock band, but Innis preferred her voice to the music. Rock? The lyrics sounded goofy in French, dubbed, unreal. Maybe they were really singing about mushrooms or wine or cheese, not about funky love, about disappointment and anger and electric guitars. Okay, he would learn French, go live up in Cheticamp on the west coast of the big island or some other Acadian place in Cape Breton like L'Ardoise or Isle Madame, meet a different kind of people. Make himself over in a new language, take another name. The priest might have some advice on that, sure. And on some things Innis didn't want advice on too. The priest. Where was Father Lesperance from? The man had a thirst. So what. Innis had a thirst too. How did a telephone get into a French rock song? Christ, the phone was ringing in the house! Radio, off! He sat rigid, each ring pounding in his ears. It was so loud he almost expected to hear someone answer it *Hello*?

He tried to count the rings, was it three longs, a couple shorts? Then it stopped. He fell back on the seat, too weak to move. Phones rang simultaneously in every house, he still forgot that sometimes: you just listen for your ring, and he didn't know MacQueen's. But other people did, and it would've rung in their houses too and somebody might be saying right now, Wasn't that Captain MacQueen's ring, now who in the world would be ringing his number now, him still in Florida? Phones were bad enough at the best of times, they screamed for attention, they brought bad news, and Innis could count on both hands the times he had used one in St. Aubin. But it was the grass that gave him the fright, the phone just plugged into it like an electrical wire. Paranoia. Easy.

He closed up the Caddy quietly, every click, and ran a rag over the door and hood where his greasy prints were visible after he took the battery out. With each disengaging step he dealt himself another alibi, in case in case, goddamn it, he couldn't take anything for granted now, if they can send you across the border for good, Look, I work for Father Lesperance over the road there, I thought I saw a couple kids sneak under the house, I heard the car doors shutting, and the engine running and I thought, Jesus, what's going on, I came in to check it out, I didn't even know the Captain had a car. The keys enclosed in his fist, Innis returned them to the mug, made his way out, feeling along the short hall where the phone's echo still hung, his flashlight was too dim now, useless. He pulled the back door behind him until the lock clicked and stood with his eyes closed under the enormous poplar, wind high in its leaves, their pale undersides rustling in the dark like water.

HE WAS GLAD to see Starr's house slowly come into view, pitch dark and empty, the high moon over it, and Starr wouldn't be there asking him where he'd been this late, walking. He was exhausted, footsore, thinking of the dead dog, he hated killing an animal like that but Christ it shot out of the dark, what could he do. Over an hour it had taken him to cover this road, scrambling for cover at the first sign of headlights, like a strafed refugee. The rest of the time it was the scuff of his feet, his breathing, a little humming and muttering to himself until the pot faded and he was merely tired, even the utility pole lights seemed unusually bright as he trotted to get beyond their reach. A buck had snorted up in dark trees, loud, driving Innis into the ditch until he heard the thump and crash of its departure. People used to walk here all the time in the old days, nothing at all to hoof it in the dark for miles, Starr said, setting out in search for a *ceilidh* or a kitchen racket or any sort of drop-in fun, through fields, woods, whatever, nobody thought twice about distance, it was a kind of walking that didn't exist anymore. Innis was only pounding along the shoulder of a paved road, straightest way home now, no shortcuts, he didn't know any. He should have been at the wheel of a car, not running away from one. Maybe Claire and his uncle had found a dance up there somewhere. She had to be a hell of a dancer, didn't she, with those long smooth legs? Do you dance, Innis? she might say. No. Yes. On the dance floor of my head. Too tired to think about it. Farming was hard work, this kind, trekking way up in the woods. Harder yet on the nerves. The Caddy was supposed to be...what? Recreation? What a joke. The woods below the house had merged in darkness with water and mountain. The mountain was a mountain of sleep, a long, reclining, quiet mountain, hushed by its forest.

Too weary to bathe, he gulped down two glasses of water and stripped, toppling onto his bed. What a downer, the whole evening, flattening someone's dog and running off, they'd want to string him up if they found him, and why not, he deserved it. Couldn't sleep, his head teeming, his feet burning as if had a fever. Should he tie salt codfish to them? That's what Granny would have done. Would she have a salve for his heel blister, for his heart? He realized that he was weeping, he could not believe the sobs that broke from him, he couldn't swallow them, keep them down. Then he gave in to it, let self-pity and anger wash over him, who would hear it after all, it was just between him and himself, the boy and the man.

Soon it passed into rueful laughter, man oh man he had fucked things up. But his plants were in, they were in the ground! From inside the pillowslip he pulled out the stolen panties, fingering the silken material. A scent of dried flowers, the sachet Claire kept in her drawer. He should put them back, this minute, this was nuts. Starr has her. You have her underwear. He went to her room and stuffed them back in the dresser, took a long, thoughtful piss, and then fell into sleep.

Loud moonlight, cold and clean, pulled him awake. In those first moments its light was fused with a cry that terrified him, fixed him to his bed. Where was it? Outdoors, not in. From the wooded gully just west of the house? In the crazy turmoil of his mind he thought it might be the dog, it had dragged itself here somehow to torment him, but no no, that road was a few miles away and this was no sound a dog could make. Like a shriek and a yowl entwining, tortured, urgent, pitched more to nightmare than waking. It rose again, raw and terrible. Was it killing, or being killed? Animal, but what? Something you couldn't shoot, couldn't kill, could you? It had come too far, he had no measure for it. He lay there stiff, his heart flayed by the sound, gripped by nothing else until it stopped. His ears ached with listening. There was no other noise, nothing of a creature. The silence seemed stunned by the moonlight spilling over his body, the deep woods sweeping away into night.

The utter wildness of what he had heard had numbed his hands and legs but under his ceiling light the room took on its familiar cast. He went from room to room switching on lights, and finally the television, whose foolish and mishapen images calmed him. Bolder now, afraid but fascinated, he went outside and swept a flashlight across the dark field, lurching along like a drunk. Nothing, nothing different: the stolid spruce and white birches of the gully, the spindly willows. The old stone pile glittered dimly with broken glass. Not a stalk of weed or grass or bush moved. There was nothing in those trees he should fear, yet the hideous cry of some animal had gutted him. "Hey!" he yelled. "I didn't mean it! It was an accident!" His voice was small, nothing. The tiniest bird would have been louder. He turned the beam toward the gully, the summer gurgle of the brook. But there was nothing there.

12

"You heard a lynx," Starr said to Innis. They were all watching the ghostly players in a Blue Jays game. The warm lazy evening had drawn Innis to the parlor where he'd slipped quietly into the old stuffed chair. The sound of the TV had caught him up, not because he gave a damn about baseball but because it was a summer sound he remembered—a background buzz broken not frequently enough by bursts of roaring, play-by-play voices on humid afternoons and evenings, monotony droning out of cars and houses and the open doors of bars, endless talk and fuss, but summer, and a sickness for home came on him like a faint.

"What's a link?" Claire, in white shorts, sat at one end of the sofa fanning herself languidly with a magazine, Starr at the other. There'd been tension in the air ever since they came back from their little trip and they clammed up whenever Innis came near. Russ was at the center of it, Innis was pretty sure, but how deep he didn't know.

"A cat, wildcat." Starr feigned interest in the ball game but it looked halfhearted. "Not big but a long-legged creature. They got tufts coming off their ear tips. Ruffy neck, stubby tail, black tail. I've only seen them dead."

"How come dead?" Innis said.

"People trap them. Nice coat, good fur."

"I hate trapping," Claire said. "It's disgusting to catch animals that way."

"There's worse traps than that," Starr said. He winked at her but she didn't notice. He had a cold Friday-night beer in his hand and a glass of rum on the end table. "They're shy as hell, lynx. Forest fire might force one out. Big feet, good in winter. They'll run down a fox, follow him slow until he gets tired out. Fox feet dig into snow but the old lynx he just floats along. Then he nails him. But that scream, God yes, strip the skin right off you. My dad used to say it was the devil."

"That would describe it all right," Innis said.

So this was the cat who'd padded around in the dark winter snow, up at the springs. It had come up that gully and shrieked into Innis's dream. Between that stupid ball game and the wild sound he'd heard lay some wide dark space where the lynx roamed. But the next morning Innis had gone looking for an animal that might match the sound, not knowing the shape of it, the day hot enough to break a sweat just walking, following the gully into the shore woods. He found almost a different climate down there, more moist and lush than the upper woods, fine damp ferns soft as hair, clearings of high grass amidst spruce and fir the budworm never got to, old grey birches with branches flexing thickly overhead. He tripped on the yellowed shoulder bone of a deer, half-buried. Out of boggy black pools mosquitoes rose like veils. Graceful moosewood were coming up in the shade, slender as bamboo, their tulip leaves fanning sunlight. He jumped down into a streambed and followed its humid, head-high banks, ducking around the arching roots of dead trees the stream had undermined and laid bare, left to fall slowly in wind after wind. By now the spring torrents had been absorbed into black mud but clear pools remained, dimpled with water skaters. Patch grass popped up in mud, mingled with dead leaves where fresh deer hooves sank deep. But no tracks of the animal he searched for, only the busy hands and feet of raccoons he'd seen crossing the back fields at night, their capering, humpbacked gait giving them away. An old bare spruce, with its thick stubs of branches, lay across his path like the spine of a dinosaur. Reduced to a trickle, the stream levelled out and wove through a boggy stretch of fine grass and thin young birches he hadn't seen up above, their bark a golden brown, thriving in the wet earth. Flowers here and there, the kind that loved muck and moisture, he'd find out their names sometime. Maybe his cannabis would have liked it better down here. Up ahead a thicket of willows, then cattails, vigorous new blades, and the stream tendrilled out into a marsh pond, clouds of algae underwater, a frog plunked before he saw it, silty clouds where he scampered across the bottom. The marsh grass was deep velvet, touched with silver and with red. Blue dragonflies zipped and hovered. He turned back, sick of mosquitoes. A big fir had come down, its underside webby, grey, its torn, dessicated roots rearing up ghoulishly, higher than his head. But that was daytime: he'd lost the terror of the dream, his confused waking. He'd skipped aside to avoid a sink in the marsh grass where the black mud looked lethal: he thrust his walking stick down to the hilt, drew it up slowly. Quicksand? Starr would've warned him. Or would he? He thought, What if I sunk out of sight right here, in that spot of suspicious mud, a clean disappearance, complete, mysterious? Who would care? And he'd luxuriated in that prospect, the tragedy of it, how sorry they'd all be, Claire upset, remorseful that she had spurned his attentions. But then he laughed, his tragic vision of himself dissolving into a jungle movie, a guy up to his armpits in quicksand screaming away, and all that shows up is a goddamn boa constrictor or a spider as big as a hamster or a woman too weak to pull him out and the last you see of him is his hand strangling a twig, and then *blurp,* he's gone. But there were no snakes to worry about in Cape Breton, and the green spider he'd watched at night outside the kitchen window, though the size of a small plum, its legs mechanically muscular, its droppings on the windowsill the size of BBs, would not likely send you to a Hollywood death. Innis's own tracks had washed out in the next rain. But was it a lynx he'd been looking for all along? They were beautiful cats. He had seen a picture of one, somewhere.

"Are they dangerous?" Claire said.

"They don't want a damn thing to do with us," Starr said. "Maybe they know we don't taste good. Well, not that good." He gave her a sardonic smile. "Clever and fierce. I heard of one that brought a small buck down, riding its back. It ripped the deer's throat out but that buck just kept leaping till he fell. Must've been starving, to get that desperate. Rabbits is what they feed on, and if the rabbits are scarce, you won't see a lynx around."

Just before the marsh bulrushes, Innis had come upon what had to be a lair, perfect in its mossy dryness, raised comfortably above the wet sod, the tall rotting stump of a fallen tree providing, with its old roots, a safe burrow. Shoulder-high spruce fenced it nicely in, and whatever animal had claimed it could—and had, judging from the slicked-down grass at the edge—nip to the narrow dark brook for a drink. Innis had stepped onto the mossy island. A patch had been recently torn up, as if the creature had raked it, maybe for insects underneath. Scat, black and dry, almost burnt, made him wary: it could be coiled right there inside, the animal that screamed, but he knew now this animal was a domestic creature, a squatter, a homemaker, all it needed was a flamingo in the front yard. The magnificent lynx would never set up house like this, it moved, it ranged out in the night, and in the day it rested, hidden somewhere different, it would never sit there and let you find it.

"I'd sure like to see one," Innis said. "But not dead. Not in a trap."

Claire was in a quiet mood, staring through the ball game toward somewhere else, her black blouse open where she was touching thoughtfully the moist hollow of her throat. It occurred to Innis like a revelation that she was bored, that she might just up and leave, tomorrow, the next day. What was there to stop her? She was free, freer than he was, and there was Russ to get away from besides. A shiver of panic ran through him: he did not want that to happen, yet what could he do to prevent it? He felt suddenly helpless and young and he hated that feeling, how little he could affect what he cared about, that other people had control of their lives and all he had was what was left over. Women had come to his mother's apartment for years, her friends hunched around the kitchen table with coffee and cigarettes, and he'd overheard their talk when he wasn't noticed, heard what they thought of men and what men did to them and he had never felt it would apply to him, those sad, bitter, sometimes humorous grievances. If Starr were to look hard at Claire right now, the distant expression on her face, her lovely legs stretched out, her bare feet wagging slightly to a beat only she was hearing, he'd be a fool to think he could keep her very long. Innis's mother told a girlfriend once, You know, a good-looking woman is never happy with one man. I don't care how sweet he is to her, she's going to try somebody else, sometime, and then more than one time.

Starr groaned as the Blue Jays pitcher grounded into a double play. The game swam across the screen: this was the channel with green faces, on the other one they were red. He looked over at Innis.

"George Morrison down at the store yesterday, he thought he saw old Moneybag's Caddy on the road. Last week."

"He thought," Innis said. "Finlay says the old guy isn't coming down this year." He didn't move his eyes from the game. He'd been afraid this might come up sooner or later. Stay cool. Your plants are in the air, leafing, rooting. You will be a man of means. You have prospects.

"So how did his car get on the road?" Starr said.

"You asking me? What do I know about him?"

"His house is across from that cottage you work at. That's all I know."

"What kind of Caddy is it?"

"Seville."

"I've seen a Seville or two on the road, one time or another."

"Sure, the roads are full of them."

"The guy, George, he say what color?"

"Pretty sure it was black."

"How could he tell at night?"

"I never said it was night, did I? You're on the road a lot, you might've seen it. I'll ask Innis, I said, he's back and forth to the priest's, you know."

Claire slipped Innis a little smile. He blushed and leaned toward the TV as if the game suddenly captivated him. On the screen the baseball moved like a tiny planet with its own gauzy moon.

"Where does he keep this goddamn black Seville anyway?" Innis said.

"In that little garage. Where else?"

"Then go check on it, if this concerns you so much, you and George. I don't care about the old man, or his car either."

"Word gets around, you know, people look after each other here, at least the old-timers do. Maybe a ghost took it for a spin."

"Yeah. Maybe. Plenty of those around here."

Starr picked up his rum and, after staring into the glass, drank it down, chasing it with beer. "You said it, b'y."

"Starr?" Claire pointed at the players and the shadows that clung to them like ectoplasm. "Can't you fix that? That's your job. That's what you do for people, isn't it?"

"It's the mountain, sweetheart. I can't fix the mountain."

"You've been looking at that screen for how long? I'm surprised you're not blind."

"Maybe I am blind. Maybe I've got to unblind myself. Eh?" He took a slow swig of beer. "People aren't getting things fixed so much as they used to, they buy new. TVs are pretty cheap now, if you think about it. When my dad brought a television home in the fifties, it set him back a few dollars, I'll tell you. Sat in the corner there big as a stove, full of tubes and promises. You could've fit a dead body in it. It was hot, you could press your hand to the wood and feel the heat. There wasn't much to watch but we sat there waiting for something good, it was what we'd all been waiting for, us country folks, some real entertainment, what the hell did we know but fiddles and Scotch music, dancing and getting drunk and shooting the breeze, stories back and forth in the kitchens? Now you don't have to say a word to each other, you just sit in a room and look stupid, and for the privilege they can try to sell you something. We used to visit. We used to talk."

"I haven't noticed you starved for talk," Claire said. "And we could always visit. I mean, it's not as if we've worn our welcome out up and down this road. I've barely met a soul. Over in Black Rock I knew people. I don't think they even know I'm over here."

"Don't kid yourself, they all know it. You want to go back there?"

Claire closed her eyes and dropped her head back against the couch. "You know I don't, Starr. Just forget it. Please? Let's talk about weather. God, it's sticky. Isn't it, Innis?"

"It is, Claire, it is. Muggiest day yet." All she had to do was pick up that phone now and again and listen. Black Rock was only ten miles away, not far for gossip. Through the gauze curtains behind Claire's head, Innis could make out the top of the lilac bush over which many butterflies were dancing, large yellow ones and brown ones, like flowers blooming and closing again and again, and he couldn't look away, they were mildly hallucinatory though he knew they were as real as the curtains or the glass or that bush they trembled on.

"We could go for a swim, Starr, down in that nice cove," she said, "that nice sandy beach."

"It'll be dark as pitch pretty soon."

"What about those bonfires on the beach you told me about? That sounded like fun."

"It was fun, but there isn't any wind. Mosquitoes would drink your blood."

"I'm not afraid of mosquitoes. Innis, what about you, do you swim?"

"Not at night he doesn't," Starr said quickly. "And the jellyfish are in."

"That water's pretty damn cold, Claire," Innis said. He

wouldn't even hint that going to the shore alone with Claire, in the dark, would blow his mind. "I put my hand in it yesterday." A lie. He'd hardly been to the shore. From the open window he heard the gully brook running louder from last night's rain.

"That's what I like about you two," Claire said, "a real yen for adventure."

"I had the idea you'd had too much adventure," Starr said.

"There's a big difference between adventure and bullshit."

"Careful, there's a minor in the room."

"Who? Me?" Innis grinned. Comic distraction. Keep the peace, relieve suspicion, he was good at it, sometimes. Maybe the Captain's Caddy wouldn't come up again, a rumor that would drift away like fog. Starr went to the kitchen for a beer. The moment Innis heard the cap hiss, there was a sensation on his bare foot: Claire had brushed him lightly with her toes, not even looking at him, then pulled her leg back just as Starr returned, his eye not on them but on the TV. He cursed the score and turned the game off.

"Hooray," Claire whispered.

"What're you doing in the woods these days, Innis?" Starr said, standing over them. "Those woods, I could go through them in my sleep."

"A pheasant almost stopped my heart this afternoon. Came blasting out of the underbrush. Protecting her chicks, I guess, trailing her wing on the ground." That was the best he could do: his mind wouldn't leave the feel of Claire's toes—sly, playful, maddening. "I just look around, pick up a little here and there. Toadstools are out." He'd seen mushrooms red as lipstick, others with caps the color of lemons he'd heard you could get high on, psychedelic stuff. You know those, Uncle Starr? And the ones that poke out of the moss like little white dicks?

"Stay away from those," Claire said. "Poison."

"Some you can eat," Starr said. "You'll see pale yellow ones later, like scrambled eggs. Chanterelles. Tasty. Don't die up there, Innis, I don't want to have to come get you."

"You'll never have to come get me, Starr. I'll make sure of that."

"I could show you a few things. You're not the only one whose killed time up there, you know. I might surprise you in those woods some day."

"If you can find me."

"I can find anything. You probably look for those magic mushrooms, eh? The kind that spin your head around?"

"Not me, Uncle Starr. I don't know a thing about it."

"Don't call me Uncle Starr. It's too hot to be anyone's uncle, yours in particular." He stared at Claire, took a slow sip of his beer. "All right, Claire, we'll go for a swim tomorrow. If it doesn't rain."

"Hardly the same thing as a midnight dip. It's really different under a moon."

"There isn't any moon either."

"Does that include me?" Innis said.

"Does what, the moon?"

"Swimming. Tomorrow."

Starr looked at him, nodded slowly. "Everything includes you," he said. "One way or another."

BY MIDDAY THE sky had cleared and Innis let Starr lead the way to the shore, trailing behind, watching Claire, her bare slender legs as she walked ahead of him, a baggy white T-shirt over her swimsuit. What was she up to, touching his foot? He'd thought about her all night, flinging the sheet off him, wishing the lynx would show up and scare her to death, frighten them all in their beds. Starr pointed out a red squirrel on a stump chomping a brown mushroom big as a saucer. "That's an eating mushroom he's got all right, but don't trust an animal. They eat stuff we can't. Like those red berries there. Birds love them but they're poison. "

Claire dropped her striped beach towel and stooped to pick it up, showing the bottom of her swimsuit. Oh, mercy. Innis nearly turned back, he didn't need this. He was supposed to fix that leaking roof for Father Lesperance, why torture himself looking at this woman he couldn't touch?

"Ah, look here!" Starr stepped off the path a few feet and returned with a thin-stalked, pale yellow flower. "Bluebead lily. Later in the summer this'll have dark blue berries on it, pretty, like beads. Pretty enough to put around your neck, Claire. But they're not for eating."

"I'll remember that, Professor Corbett."

Before it dropped down toward the cove the path rose, giving a view of the marsh that spread back to grass cliffs studded with scrub spruce and alder. A large bird was lifting into the breeze on long slow wings. "Crane," Starr said. Innis had seen that bird more than once, he'd looked it up, it was not a crane but a blue heron. But this was Starr's show. Naming, naming. The marsh grass was a lovely fine green, and dark water wove among it, but as they crossed the single plank bridge over the inlet, you could see how clear the water was, that only the black mud bottom and its twigs and leaves were dark, mottled with white oyster shells. Minnows veered in a silvery flash.

"Used to be full of oysters here, just off the shore," Starr said. "Munro and me, we'd come down with our dad and get a bucket in ten minutes. We'd have a stew of them for supper, in fresh milk."

"What happened to them?" Innis said.

"Fellas from town came in their boats and fished them out. The old story. We didn't own them, but we didn't wipe them out either."

Claire said she didn't like fresh milk, too rich, and buttermilk was plain awful, but Starr said no, no, on a hot day nothing could refresh you like a glass of buttermilk, slightly sour and just cool from a springhouse.

"Oh, Starr, please!"

On the hard sandy ground behind the beach, they passed through a few wind-bitten spruce, then a long band of daisies, laced with blue vetch. Gooseberry bushes, Starr said, plucking a translucent green berry. There were plants that looked like oats, and ropes of eelgrass, dry and stiff-white but underneath still dark, damp, laced with stones and wood bits. Small blue butterflies touched briefly upon one orange hawkweed bloom and then another.

"Starr, what about that old boat up the beach there," Innis said, "with the tarp over it?"

"Your dad's, a fella up North River built it, a Morrison. Well, we all used her at one time, after our father gave up his. She's still sound, I think, somebody borrowed her last year. I'm not for rowing anymore, not like your dad was. Now your Granny, Innis, she knew the wild medicines. See that? Cow parsnip." He fluffed the big white flower heads of a sturdy plant, waist-high. "She made a tea from the roots. Good for sore throats, headaches. But that over there." He led them to a tall solitary plant whose white umbels, just emerging, were more delicate, loose, its thin stalk streaked with magenta. "People have confused this with other ones you can eat the roots of. But any part of this will kill you."

"What is it?" Claire said, stepping back.

"Water hemlock. I heard of a kid—see, the stalk is hollow—he made himself a whistle out of it. It killed him just blowing on it, the juice got on his lips, his tongue."

"Good Lord, yank it out," Claire said. She was backing off toward the shore.

"Why? We know what it is," Starr called after her. "Doesn't attack, never bites. So we'll just leave it alone. Right, Innis?"

Maybe he would and maybe he wouldn't. He lingered there, barely touching, as if they were electrified, the leaves, the stiff squarish stalk. He wiped his hand hard on his jeans. He'd seen this plant somewhere. The shorebank maybe, near the marsh pond. But knowing he'd seen it was not enough. Suppose he had chewed on it, made a peashooter for the hell of it like he had as a kid out of hollow canes from a backyard bush. He could feel his lips on the hollow stem, the poised breath—*pooh*, a pebble stinging someone's head, but that little meanness, if he'd done it here, could have cost him a sudden and surprising death simply because he did not know what water hemlock was. He pulled a small pad from his back pocket and sketched the still-forming flower heads, the stalks, the fern-like leaves. No strange markings, just another weed, like an alder or willow shoot. He heard Claire calling him and he backed away slowly, thinking.

Down in the soft sand Claire was pulling off her shirt. A one-piece swimsuit, a dark wine. He had tried very hard to keep her out of his mind, but there she was. Now he seemed to forget everything except her, sorting out every little thing he had observed, heard, felt, for her, from her, about her. And the pages of drawings she had not seen, hidden under his mattress, a few of them harsh when he was angry with her, others erotic, flattering, true to his fantasies.

"You going in, young man?" She was lying out on the long beach towel, her hands folded across her tummy. Her eyes were shut to the sun and she was smiling. Innis watched Starr, pale and wiry in a pair of khaki shorts, stomp into the water, roaring until he dove and disappeared. The surface of the wide cove was barely skittered with a breeze. In the shallows, redbrown seaweed swayed, clinging to small rocks, its shadows moving on the light sand that faded away into dark water, and a mile across was the long green mountain, feeling higher, nearer, extending west toward Red Head, east toward the bridge, the wooded slopes losing their wooly texture and becoming tight and fine. In the high sun it took on the easy green sweep of a sea swell, streaks of lighter and darker green, like light on a rising wave.

"No swim trunks," Innis said. That wasn't true, Starr had lent him an old pair that showed his balls if he wasn't careful, but he felt paler than his uncle, awkward, his body lanky and white, wintered. He used to slouch into his height, too skinny to bear it, too visible. Claire looked darker than before, as if she belonged on sand with the sun above her. Sitting on a stump of driftwood, Innis pulled his shoes and socks off and wormed his feet into the cooler sand.

"Go in without them," Claire said. She lay like a sleeper, none of her moving but her lips. Without lipstick they looked soft and innocent.

"Without what?"

"Trunks."

"You kidding?"

"Chicken."

"Starr would love that."

"Don't do just things he would love."

"That's not what you told me before."

"No, it isn't. It's something else I'm telling you."

"Jesus, Claire."

"Come sit next to me." She patted the sand, let a scoop of it run through her fingers. "Take your shirt off. It's summer." Starr was swimming out into the channel, pounding the calm surface, all arms and legs and spouts of water. Starr had to be out of shape and yet there he was churning away, not far from those long, snaking currents where the light reflected differently.

"Look at Mark Spitz out there. He better make it back. I can't save him."

"Would you?"

"Not while you're around." Innis looked frankly at her, from her red toenails, painted for sandals, up her legs, up the wine suit, to her chest, her composed face, her closed eyelids. "Are you bored, Claire?"

"Summer is a different time. This is good as Bermuda. Are you?"

Innis lay belly-down in the sand, looking out. Starr was returning, swimming slowly on his back.

"Sometimes. But I've got plans." It had now occured to him that he might chop that hemlock plant into bits, wrap it tightly in plastic and send it to Ned, with instructions. A dangerous weapon, bad magic from the north woods. See how the likes of Tony T. and his stupid brother could handle that. "A little pot helps too."

"I suppose it might."

Innis brushed his finger over her leg, barely feathering the faint golden down of her skin. He could hear Starr staggering through the water, yelping at the stones, his tender feet. Innis groaned. He gave her leg a light smack.

"Deerfly," he said. "Bite like a bitch."

Claire smiled, opened one eye at him. She patted his backside. "You have a nice hard butt," she said, folding her hands serenely over her stomach. Along the edge of her swimsuit, on the inside of her thigh he could see a few short curly hairs. He wanted to touch her so badly he ground his teeth. Starr tiptoed up the sand, shaking himself like a dog.

"She's brisk, b'y, but good for the blood. What are you two doing, lounging at poolside? Let's see you in the water."

"He forgot his trunks," Claire said. "And I'm too hot right now for water like that. Maybe later."

Starr dried off, his head lost in a white towel, muttering. "You said you wanted a swim, not a sunbathe."

"The sun's good for you too, Starr," Claire said. "There's a long winter to burn away."

"Burn's the word. There wasn't a lot of sun way back in the Hebrides. Our people aren't noted for browning up. Look at Innis there, half an hour he'll look like a lobster."

"I'm okay." Innis laid his head on his arm. His face, turned away from Starr, was inches from Claire's leg and he could smell the coconut oil, so redolent of girls in bathing suits, arranged on towels just as Claire was, bare, all midriff and shoulders and legs, it might have been an aphrodisiac. The sun soon made him dozy and Starr was dancing on one leg, struggling into his trousers, beating sand from his shoes.

"I'm not much for lying around like this," he said. When he was dressed, he stood looking out to where he had swum. "We used to use that water, all of us. We'd go back and forth shore to shore, up and down here. Was like a road. Damned few around now jump in a skiff at two in the morning and row home. People drive across the bridge, they don't know it anymore, that water. Just fishermen. We lost something there, lost another hold on things. We came into houses the back way, up from the shore. A little thing, that way of coming, but it gave us...a different look at each other, another way of greeting. Eh? Yes, you come by boat, you come different." Innis felt the long pause of his uncle's shadow. "I don't want to keep telling you stuff like this, I know it doesn't matter to you. I don't want to tell you this cove was full of oysters and we could rake up a bucket in minutes. Why should you care? I could tell you we swam here in October, me and my brother and our cousins, in our clothes, the water would turn your balls to stone. But we'd build a big fire on the beach and steam ourselves in it. It was just something we did, maybe no one else in the world swam like that in October, I don't know. And why tell you about Peter MacAulay, depressed so bad he wanted to drown himself, he couldn't get it up anymore. But he only waded out to his waist and then he turned back and went home. Too cold, he told his wife, I think I'll hang myself instead, but by summer he died in his chair."

"You're awful cheerful today, Starr."

"We need to get away for a few days, Claire. Let's try some other part of the Island, a place you haven't been. I need to get away."

"Starr, I'm working, I have a job."

"Quit. Dump it."

"I can't. I don't want to. Can I just soak up a little sun?"

He was quiet, folding and refolding his towel. Innis knew Starr did not want to leave them like this, even though Innis was lying next to Claire head to feet, even though he only had his shirt off and was sleepy and probably a bit singed. But fuck him, let him say so.

"I'm going back up," Starr said. "You coming?"

"I'll be up in a little, I just got here," Claire said, frowning.

"Even you can get a sunburn, miss," Starr said. Innis heard his uncle's shoes chopping through the sand and he was gone.

Innis did not want to say a word. Proximity, just lying there with her, he'd settle for it, it couldn't last long. He waited for Claire to speak but she didn't. Something hit the water, too quick and sharp to be a fish.

"He tossed a stone from the woods," Claire said. "Ignore it."

"I'm not moving. He's probably spying on us. Not that he'd get an eyeful of anything."

"We won't give him an eyeful of anything either. Right?" Claire, her face toward the sun, did not move, just her eyes, barely slitted. She smiled.

Innis took his time buttoning his shirt. Starr was right, his shoulders were tender.

"I guess I don't understand you, Claire," he said. He squeezed a small warm stone in his fist.

She wiggled her toes, raised her head slightly to observe him. "Why would you want to, Innis? There's no fun in that."

13

The rain had passed, but every minute or so the ceiling above the priest's bed produced a single drop that fell emphatically on the plastic tarp below. That sharp splat made the room seem derelict somehow, and though he didn't like asphalt roofs, Innis intended to silence it. He pulled a crude wooden ladder out from under the house and crawled over the roof where a patch of black shingles broke into coal-like bits when he pried them and the wind whipped them about. Last autumn the colors had flamed along the miles of that mountain, making him ache for October afternoons back home, the sidewalk leaves he'd kicked through, the smell of their dust, their smoke. He was rubbing grit from his eyes when he heard a car below, a honk. Father Lesperance, in a summer outfit, his portly belly expanding a big blue T-shirt. Bermuda shorts, a bit too long, but neat black stockings in black shoes. He was clutching a bag of groceries. Innis climbed down to talk to him and as they shook hands there was a whiff of liquor in his words, then it was gone.

"St. Swithun's Day, Innis. A healer and a bringer of rain. Forty more days of it if it rains on St. Swithun's, but I think we're safe by the looks of that sky."

"You been enjoying the cottage, Father?"

"I'm happy you're after that leak. I had to sleep on the blasted couch last time." He whipped off his battered khaki hat and stepped back a few paces, squinting at the roof. The purplish tinge in his cheeks seemed deeper today. "Yes, yes. Good, Innis, good. Not much rain, but a damp bed is misery. Did you find those bundles of shingles? Two will do it you think?"

"Plenty, Father. It's just the one spot."

"Come in for a rest then, come in."

The priest hustled about in the kitchen, pulling open curtains and drawers. Innis noticed the painting had been hung and he moved closer. THE JESUIT MARTYR-SAINTS OF NORTH AMERICA the caption said and listed their names. A watercolor? A group of priests, eight, in cassocks, standing or kneeling, one holding up a crucifix, all suspended in the sky and gazing toward a heavenly radiance of pale blue where angels and cherubs hovered. But below them, in the nasty world of frontier Canada, a smaller scene of their martyred deaths, a mayhem of Indian treachery. A peaceful campfire in the center of a loghouse settlement, three seated Indians, one in full headdress, poking sticks in the embers under a big kettle, getting ready to torture a priest who was bound to a stake. Around them there was plenty of tomahawk action, priests knocked to the ground or crouching in fear or unwittingly shaking an Indian hand while another Indian reared up behind, two-handing a tomahawk toward the father's skull. No blood yet, it was all stilled in the act, hatchets raised but yet to fall, the consequences clear. In the background a lake, spiky spruce trees, Canada wilderness but little different from what Innis wandered in every day. He didn't know the story behind these murders or who was to blame for what, but that's where the action was for sure, hatchets and blood. The upper part of the picture didn't have much going for it—serene, the angels cute and sweet.

Weren't angels ever mean, little streaks of meanness in them? Innis would have drawn them that way, and he wouldn't have the priests floating in clouds of pale yellow and blue. Too hokey. These had to be tough men.

"Interesting, isn't it?" Father Lesperance said behind him, holding a can of orange juice in each hand. "Not great art of course, but it's direct and innocent. And the little narrative below."

"They had a hard life, I guess."

"They did that."

He listened to the priest in the bedroom. A drawer opened, the clink of glass, a pause, the drawer closed.

"Nobody's broken into the cottage, Father, not that I could see."

"No, no," he said, returning. "We're still intact. I brought a few kids out last week, we tramped the shore and up the woods. They liked it until it rained and then they were disappointed I had no television." He leaned in from the kitchen. "You know one of them has cousins up on Mac-Lean's Cross? Their cousins' dog was killed a while back, at night, struck by a car. The bastard just drove away. A terrible thing to do, and them heartbroken. A car chaser, that dog, true, but they loved him."

Innis looked closely at the painting, tracing its surface with his finger. "They see the car that did it?"

"A dark car, that's all the kids could recall. Shiny, new, they said."

"What was its name?"

"Name?"

"The dog, that they hit."

"I don't know it myself, Innis. It wasn't much more than a pup."

The priest spread the front window curtains wider and stood looking out. "Innis, the old Captain, he keeps a very nice automobile over there, stores it until summer."

"Yeah, that's what I hear."

"Funny but somebody saw it on the road. Captain Mac-Queen's not there yet, so of course that's a curious thing. But I went over and there it is, the Cadillac sitting in his garage. I looked in the crack."

"Somebody was mistaken then."

"It would appear somebody was. People see things in the country, of course, that aren't always there for the rest of us. Take Dan Rory. He's got the second sight, they say. Forerunners and that sort of thing."

"He can tell when a person's going to die," Innis said. "I don't believe that myself."

"I'm skeptical too, Innis, yes, I am, about those kinds of powers in a man. But if you're here at night, you know, it's not like the city at all. I saw a single firefly in a warm night breeze, against the trees it moved more like a bird, in dips and sweeps, a bleep bleep of light, uncommonly glowing. Almost supernatural. Wouldn't take much to see it that way, I suppose. But then again, I didn't want to believe it was anything but a firefly. Other eyes could see it easily as something else, a premonitory light perhaps, a spirit. In the Celtic world, there are sites they call 'thin places.' I love that term. Places where we're likely to experience the spiritual. These were ancient sites, already spiritual, and so churches were often built on them. There might even be a thin place or two around here. My mother was Irish, a Roche. Norman name, like yours, Corbett. Oh, they got all around, Ireland, Scotland. But we're not superstitious, not you and me. Eh?"

"I don't think so, Father. Well, sometimes."

"Of course, I knock on wood, I fling a little salt over my shoulder. I grew up with that." The priest turned away from the window. "You have a boarder where you live, I guess?"

"Since a while, Father."

"Claire Wiston, yes? I knew the man she used to live

with, over there in Black Rock. Sometimes he showed up at the church where I assisted. Stress and strain brings a man back to the church sometimes, they want the comfort. They fall away from it when life is smooth, but give them a rocky spell and there they are at the door."

"I don't know him at all, Father."

"No, I guess you wouldn't. You getting on with Claire? She's a nice woman, from what I could tell."

"Sure. We're just boarders, the two of us."

"Of course, of course. What do you think of this?" From behind the sofa the priest pulled out a large kite of wood and red paper emblazoned with the golden head of a roaring lion. He held it up high. "The lion is my idea. I like lions."

"It's a good day for them. Isn't it?"

"Lions or kites? Oh, both. A man I don't like very much, Innis, I had to give him some hard advice. He told me, Father, why don't you go fly a kite? Yes, I said. I'm perfectly capable of that, and it's a pity you are not. Shall we?"

They strolled down toward the old wharf, the strait lively and blue under a brisk sun. Two young children were in swimming, shrieking at the small waves that washed over them, their parents, dressed, sitting on a blanket watching, smoking cigarettes, dad's trousers rolled up his white calves, mom with a cup in her hand. Innis looked for girls in bathing suits but it was not that kind of beach, not enough action, there weren't any boys making fools of themselves with a Frisbee. Innis sidearmed a flat stone at the water but the first skip was swallowed by a wave. Downbound toward the sea, a sloop, driving hard under the westerly wind, galloped along in midchannel, cutting the chop, spray cracking white off its bow.

Father Lesperance inhaled deeply, beaming comically at the sun, the kite close to his chest like a shield. "This island was all French once, did you know?"

"I wondered about the name."

"Eighteenth century, a Frenchman owned the whole works, every square meter of it. His own farm was up on the eastern end. Good farm, sophisticated in its day. But the fortunes of war overtook him. After the Battle of Louisburg, it all fell to the British, and he was a French officer, decorated one in fact. And later on of course, you Highlanders came in, Innis, my man. But we had a foot here first, oh, yes. I know a very old woman down the road who remembers French gravestones in her woods when she was a little girl. All swallowed up in trees now. Sooner or later, the woods have the last word here. Give me a hand, Innis, if you would."

Innis held the kite while the priest backed away, spooling out line.

"Do you like boats, Innis?"

"I wouldn't mind riding along on that one out there. Where they heading, do you think?"

"Oh they're out of Baddeck, I'd say. Maybe they've been cruising the lake. Might be making for somewhere up or down the coast, anywhere. They'll be in the Atlantic soon, at any rate."

"Could they go all the way to Boston in a boat like that?"

"Why not? That's got to be about a forty-footer. Why, you want to go to Boston?"

"I wouldn't mind a trip back."

"No money?"

"Not yet. I'll be okay."

"What are your plans, Innis? Long-range, I mean?"

Innis laughed. He almost felt he could tell the priest the truth, he seemed like a guy who might understand it: Father, I've got a little crop of dope up in the woods and it's going to get me out of here and into a new life. "Nothing specific, Father. Not since Boston."

"What happened?"

"Oh, some bad habits. And my mother and me didn't get along too well. So...I came up here."

"What kind of schooling?"

"High school." Schoolbooks, he never had the patience for them. He could not concentrate on them at home, though he could draw for hours, shaping things to his own eye. The television had always been there, a murky voice in the living room. He filled small tablets, then larger ones until he started buying sketch pads and decent paper, good pencils. A teacher or two had captured him for a while— Innis, look, you're far smarter than the work you're doing, you can do better than this. An art teacher in high school said he had talent, he should think about art school or college, but Innis said I just do sketches, that's all I want. "I almost graduated. I didn't like it enough."

"Schooling comes from all directions, Innis, it never stops. Okay," the priest yelled, "let her go!"

Innis lifted the kite and the wind took it up and slashed it back and forth, paper crackling, tail whipping. Father Lesperance laughed, his battered hat blew off, his bald head glistening as he unreeled the kite higher and higher over the water until it was a bit of red dancing against the long green mountain. Innis raised his fist high, feeling only sun and wind and water.

14

The black roof shingles had soaked up the day's heat and Innis tossed in his bed, tormented by a mosquito's needling, looping drone. A moth flittered across his cheek, startling him. In the lamplight, blots like brown ink on its creamy wings. He dozed again in the dark but a bat woke him,

veering near and away, a flutter of warm air, and he made
no move to drive it off. Was she scared of bats? He lay with
his arms flung back, waiting for window light, thinking of
Claire, angry he couldn't keep her out of his mind. Amaz-
ing. One kiss, weeks and weeks ago, but the taste of that
ran all through him when he had nothing to do but lie here
and remember. The house was too quiet. No snoring down
the hall, no stirrings on the other side of the plaster. If he
held his breath he could just make out that distant rustling
of the tide, the sound of broad water moving on a still
night. Starr had finally persuaded Claire to quit her job in
Sydney, she wasn't that keen on it anyway, I'm too old to
smile when I don't feel like it, she said, and Starr said
Amen, and forget about money, we're fine. Innis didn't see
how that could be true, but off they'd gone for Isle
Madame, Starr hadn't much business anyway, people were
outdoors, it was an uncommonly warm summer so far,
more sun than Starr had seen in years, fine as long as the
spring didn't go dry. He told Claire if she liked beaches so
much she'd love the sand of Ingonish up north, softer
than sugar, and on the west coast the water was warm
from the Northumberland Strait. She was dark as a Greek
now. A summer person, she bloomed. What would she
want with a winter man like Innis? He'd been a small diversion once, on a foggy afternoon.

A muggy morning shower arrived, over by the time he
got out the door. He tramped into the upper woods, there
was his little plantation to attend to, thank God. Starr had
told him again to check the level of the spring, the water
seemed cloudy. But Innis knew what silted it: the bucket he
drew through it a dozen times one afternoon. Steam rose
faintly from the rocks and rough clay ditches and he was
sweating under the backpack that held a small shovel, a
bottle of fish fertilizer, a baloney sandwich and two apples.

The grade was steep until he reached the power line. He rested on his walking stick by a shallow puddle where tadpoles, saved by the rain, squirmed and skittered. Innis flicked a pebble into the water, scattering them, but they soon clustered black again, nibbling for air. That little round ditch was their very life and a few sweeps of his boot could fill it with dirt. But that wouldn't give him a kick anymore. Anything alive here now he'd rather watch than kill or scare, except blackflies, deerflies and mosquitoes. He looked back down the overgrown road he'd come up through: trees framed a short section of the highway at the bottom of the hill, and the old hay fields and the house deep at the rear of them, small and distant, and the flat, calm strait burnished after the rain, and the mountain, the sky, the watery strokes of cloud—everything lulled and hushed, as fixed as a photo. Not far from the barn he could make out a meandering path of mown hay Starr had cut with the scythe, charged up that day with some crazy urge, and maybe Claire had cured it.

Cut brush and slash flung every which way told Innis that the power company workers were afoot. Their half-track vehicle had dug deeply across a patch of soft rushes but at least they weren't spraying chemicals. Bullet holes splattered the *Do Not Spray* sign his uncle had nailed to a line post. There's springs all along that hill up there, Starr had said, and we don't want weed killer in our water. A chainsaw rattled into life: in the east, where the corridor crossed the next property, three men were wading into alders that had sprung up in the break. Innis moved on before they could spot him. If things ever got hot up here, they would allow him an alibi: why wouldn't they, just fellas like himself, be tempted to bootleg a patch of marijuana where nobody but hunters showed up, and easy ways to disguise it? Those hunters from town in their camouflage outfits probably wouldn't know a pot plant from a raspberry bush, and

Innis would be long gone by deer season anyway. He had seen them last fall when he was new to the woods, prowling and crouching through the trees like movie commandos. Stay out of those woods for a while, Starr told him, unless you've got a neon sign on your back, sneeze and they'll plug you. Higher up the slope, west of the deer trail his comings and goings had now widened, Innis caught sight of his clearing through scrawny maples and moosewood, a small oasis of light among the shadows. He pushed through the last of the ferns, ferns helped, they hid the path.

He tended each plant, rubbing its leaves gently in his fingers. Spend time with your green things, pardner, the man in the book said. Talk to 'em. They like to know you care, and they like company too sometimes. Give 'em a little chuck under the chin, sing 'em a little song. Good vibrations are everything, happy plants make happy weed. Sure, okay, that guy had been smoking too much of his own stuff, and it had to be a lot stronger than what Innis was looking at. Though green and growing, free of their little tents and high as his knees, they were coming along more slowly than Innis had imagined. The weather had been dry, sure, but he'd hauled water like a donkey, brought up hay from the barn and packed it around the bare circles of dirt to hold moisture. Water was the magic now, and surely that and a few more weeks of decent sun would shoot them up. They could grow very fast. They were weeds, right? Fragrant collas by September, flower tops, that's where the money was. But the summer was dragging. He was trying to be patient. That was part of it, wasn't it, of leaving Boston behind? He knew what he had to wait for and what he could get right now. Not Claire. He didn't even know how he wanted her or how he could have her. Much older than him. Yes. But at ease with herself, not like girls his age, edgy, too aware of how they looked and what you were making of it, not sure, some of them, what kind of woman they wanted to be one day to the next, and they all had marriage in their eyes if not on their lips.

Work. Keep moving. He fetched the plastic pail from under the low, winglike branches of a hemlock fir. Starr had worked the farm when he was young, and now, except for a fit of pointless scything, he had Innis mow the grass out front the house and made sarcastic comments about Claire's little garden. Yet he must have learned a lot of things from his own dad, Innis's grandfather. Fathers pass that on. But in that cramped apartment in Boston, what had Innis learned from his while he was alive? His dad worked night shift, his face puffy and numb at the supper table, not much to say. Never a talker, your dad, Starr said, I made up for it I guess, your dad was a good fella, but he was a bit soft in the heart, and your mother, she worked it in her hands, she could stroke it or wring it, and she did both. Then he was gone for good, took that flight above a city street where, in Innis's memory, he remained suspended. Torn up, his mother drank at home quietly for a while, later with a woman friend who said, Listen, girl, you're young, you can't bring him back, the two of them started going out, and going out some more. His mother brought home a man Innis had never seen before, hungover and clumsy in the kitchen, nothing for Innis but pats on the head and bar tricks that didn't amuse him. His mother sometimes let him roam outside in the evening if a man came by, and he fell in with other boys who liked streets and had time on their hands. But he knew very early that he would want to do it alone, that he would find the cars he wanted and do his own thing inside them.

Coming on the weathered wood covering the spring, hidden in alders and grass, always gave Innis a flush of pleasure. Something about that little house sheltering the water of his own life, and it had come out of that rock ledge year after year in a steady, unfailing trickle, for him, for his uncle, for all of his family who had lived here. The warped grey boards were warm to the touch as he unlatched the low door and ran a stick around the dark opening. He couldn't blame the spiders, it was such a lovely cool cave out of the wind, but he hated the cloying webs. He dipped the pail through the small pool. Silt rose like ink. Innis, why is this water murky? Starr would say. The spring is low, I guess, Innis would tell him. Starr would threaten to go see for himself but he never did because in a day or so after Innis had watered his plants the clay particles had once again settled on the bottom of the shallow reservoir. His uncle would take a tumblerful from the sink tap and hold it to the window while the spring water swirled with tiny bubbles. A bit better, he would mumble, and then he'd drink, declaring, without fail, this was the best water in the world, a goddamned tonic.

Purple fringed orchids had poked up here and there in the grass. They were not luxuriant like their name, their blossoms tiny, but they were pretty and he plucked a few as he walked. They didn't grow down below, they'd be new to Claire. Rasping chainsaws were not far away. That power line crew, they made him nervous. He took up the pail and the flowers and got himself out of sight.

By noon he had soaked a dark ring around each plant, a pail as full as he could make it and a dollop of fertilizer dissolved in each. Tired and sweating, he ate sitting on a stone where the clearing caught a breeze. The baloney sandwich tasted wonderful, washed down with spring water in an empty soda bottle. He chewed slowly, satisfied that his labor would show results. Wasn't that what kept a farmer going, day by day?

Partway through his first apple a wild thumping approached the woods and seemed to percuss the whole area.

For a few seconds he could believe it was a diesel gypsum freighter chugging up the strait, but the sound grew louder too fast and he was running through a hail of vibration, the helicopter beating the air above his head. A tempest smeared through the grass and weeds and saplings and he caught a glimpse of the pilot, his dark visor, before he fell to his belly in the ferns. He thought he might pass out, he was hyperventilating, but he didn't move and the *chunk-chunk-chunk* faded off toward north over the strait. Christ. They weren't police, he knew that, knew it was probably the forestry patrol or a spray plane but God. From the air what could they see but trees and brush? He didn't even have a plot here, just a few staggered plants, it was pathetic, nothing, not worth a bust even. Why did the bastard come in so low? Power lines maybe. Somebody lost. His hands trembled for a thin joint deep in his shirt pocket. Come on, Innis, you're not a hick in the boonies, you know what choppers sound like, and sirens, the noises of alarm and pursuit. But it had been awhile, been awhile since he'd heard them.

He let the smoke sit in his lungs until he could hold it no longer, then the breeze pulled it slowly from his mouth. Spring water might be a great tonic but some things it couldn't cure. Later that day after the three of them had returned from the beach, Starr had cornered him alone in the toolshed: I'll put it to you plump and plain, he said, you have the hots for Claire, don't you? Well I'm telling you to forget it, there's no room in this house for that. This time Innis did not protest or deny, he just smiled and said, Sure, Uncle Starr, whatever you say, and Starr said, Stop calling me Uncle Starr or I'm going to pop you one.

Wind came through the clearing in soft, calming sweeps through grass and ferns. The leaves of his cannabis shivered, turned like feathers and flashed the paler green beneath. The hardy young spruce, the fir, the dead pines barely moved. A woosh as faint as a whisper ran through the maples behind him. Where was the lynx? Cowering? Never. It was a master of its territory, of concealment, of stealth.

15

It had been an afternoon of blue calm, a bluish cast to the air, trees, the mountain, and by early evening the sky was pearled with blues and creams. Everything clear, quiet, the water a brilliant matte, a flatter shade of the sky, so calm Innis could pick out voices from the other side, their tones almost intimate though a mile away. A dog's bark echoed across the water, solitary, sharp. Saturday night, people getting cranked up for the weekend over there on the other shore. Innis sat in the skiff he had uncovered and turned on its keel. He was sure he could row it when the surface of the strait was like this, the tide slack, no wind stirring it up. The oars needed varnish by the looks of them but they were functional. He might try his hand at them here in the cove, but he hadn't quite the nerve yet. He had seen those swirling eddies, this wasn't a pond and it could shift in a hurry into yelping whitecaps, a dark surface of mad white hounds. No, he'd sit on the thwart for now, work the oars in the oarlocks, get the feel of it. He watched a power-boat cut through the silence until it was beyond the next point, its wake opening in a graceful V, a smooth wave that touched the shore. A motor could take you someplace on a night like this. Innis slung the tarp over the skiff and left.

Before he reached the house he could hear Claire's raised voice, and he stopped shy of the screen door. Starr had a letter in his hand and she tried to grab it but he held her off.

"You have no business opening my mail, Starr, any of it. You knew it was from Russ. Now give it to me."

"And what's he need to talk to you for? Eh? Wants you to meet him in Sydney."

"Starr, for Christ's sake, we had a long relationship. You wouldn't know anything about that, would you, but I can tell you it has a few loose ends. None of them have to do with love. We shared property and money."

"And what's this he's saying about me?" Starr turned the letter toward the light. " 'If you want to hitch up with that two-bit TV repairman, suit yourself.' " Is that all I am? Maybe so, maybe so. It's not a sexy business, it's just a living, and barely that."

"The letter has his name on it, Starr, not mine. I didn't ask him to write it, those are his words. And I didn't ask you to read it either."

"I don't want to see anything of that son of a bitch in here, I don't even want to see his handwriting in the mailbox."

"You're being ridiculous, Starr. I won't even talk to you about this, it's none of your affair."

Innis clomped noisily up the back steps and they both went quiet as he opened the door, slapping the salt cod, now little more than a tailfin. "Good evening to you too," he said, passing between them on his way upstairs. From his room he could hear only the heated murmur of their voices, then Starr going outside, his feet on the gravel. Innis saw him out the hall window smoking at the toolshed door, staring into the field. The house was quiet for a while, then Claire went out to him and they talked there at the door. She came back to the house and called up the stairs to Innis.

"There's a dance over at the community hall. Let's dance." She looked up at him, her foot on the bottom step. She had the letter in her hand. Innis, who'd grown up in apartments, had come to believe two storeys were clearly superior: upstairs gave you another perspective on those you lived with.

"What's that got to do with me?" That was not how he wanted to reply, he wanted to say, Hey, Miss Claire, let's go, let's do it, but Starr was around. There seemed to be nothing in this house he could seize for himself. Whatever he had was on hold.

"Oh come on, Innis," Claire said. The hall light caught the skin of her throat, the silver hoops in her ears, the lustre of her dark hair he'd heard her washing in the tub before supper, pitcherfuls of water cascading through it. "Come with us."

"That's the trouble, Claire."

"What is?"

"With us." He leaned on the railing and spoke lower. "I'd go with you in a second. Anyway, I can't dance." He had danced in high school, but mostly stoned flailing to the blare of rock music, or slowstepping in that sweaty hug you hoped would lead to sex. "Not the way they do it here."

"Time to learn something new. Innis, I know you're a dancer, dear. You can't fool me."

"What about Starr?"

"What about him? We need to get out of the house and I want you to come too."

"He doesn't want me tagging along. You know that, so why are you asking me?"

Claire swung around the balustrade and came up a few steps, beckoning him in a loud whisper, "So I can get you off in the bushes! Now come on, step on it."

"Jesus, Claire, give me a minute or two." He splashed cold water over his face, sniffed the armpits of a denim shirt that was not too wrinkled. From his stash box he plucked out half a joint, just in case. Starr hit the horn. A quick look in the mirror: he ran his hands along his temples, his ponytailed hair felt sleek and tight, aerodynamic, wind would flow over him tonight, a slipstream.

Innis squeezed in the back and stretched his long legs across the seat. Claire smiled at him, then gave Starr a buss on the cheek as if everything was just fine, though Starr did not seem festive, not his usual Friday night self. He drove slowly toward The Head, letting a car pass him, ripping by at high speed. "Jackass, he's half-cut already. Be dead before he gets there." In the rearview mirror he noticed Innis scratching his neck. "You got bites there, b'y?"

"Down at the shore. The mosquitoes are brutal."

"Jewelweed for bites. Used to be some growing by the brook. My mother made a salve out of it."

"Did it work?"

"She didn't use anything that didn't work. I wish I'd listened better, or written them down. She had remedies for everything, body or head."

"Bad dreams?" Claire said.

"You having bad dreams?"

Claire just smiled and looked away toward the mountain, a dark cloud lay along the ridge, a long fish trailing raggedy fins. High above it a contrail picked up the lost rays of the sun, moving like a cut in flesh across the blue-grey sky.

"I've had a few bad dreams," Innis said, just to keep things going, "but I wouldn't talk about them."

"Sex dreams, no doubt." Starr fixed him in the mirror until the car wandered, then he looked back to the road. "She had a treatment for that too, your Granny. I heard her telling old Cousin Willena about it once, she didn't know I could understand the Gaelic good enough, but you pick it up all right when they don't want you to know. Some fella came up in their conversation, he'd been bedevilled by randy dreaming, and my mother said, There's something for that, you know. Garden lettuce, the leaves, pound them up soft and mix them with camphor, then rub it on the man's testicles. She didn't say testicles but I knew what she meant. That'll kill those kind of dreams all right, and maybe a few other things."

"Did she say you had to get the man's permission?" Claire said.

Starr glanced her way. "You wouldn't, would you, girl? You'd slap it right on. You got any lettuce in your garden there?"

"I have nasturtiums coming along nicely. But I can't say much for the rest."

"Och," Starr said with mock pity, "no flowers for Claire."

"Not true. Innis brought me lavender orchids from the fields. They're on my dresser, if you want to see them."

Innis hid his smile against the window.

HE HAD EXPECTED a big hall like he'd seen on TV in Boston, couples swirling over a dance floor, print dresses umbrellaed above chaste legs, the men hearty and grinning and good at the steps, square as their plaid shirts and string ties, some guy calling out indecipherable instructions over a loudspeaker. Instead he was crowded just inside the entrance of a small community hall, a former schoolhouse. A few men out front were gathered at the open trunk of a car, drinking. Innis had already resisted Claire's attempt to tug him onto the floor, into an energetic circle of couples, but more spectators so far than dancers. Claire looked great out there, her skin a shade darker against her mustard green blouse, he loved her black hair, she just brushed it or the wind blew it and the thick curls still fell beautifully around her face, her blue eyes glowing black, a shine of excitement in them, maybe a little wine too, that easy laughter when she'd had a couple glasses, he could see all that in her dancing and it didn't seem to matter who her partner was, maybe it was all for herself. Were those steps she could teach Innis? Not publicly. Let her whirl around with that local fellow, short and earnest, a grin that said I can't believe my luck, and those who were watching could stoke up their gossip about the woman who lived with Starr Corbett and his nephew, Innis knew that, had overheard it when they first arrived, as he had on the phone, and he didn't want to put himself in the middle of it right here, all the wondering and the details they didn't know but filled in for themselves.

Pressed to the wall, he stiffened against flashes of panic: it was just the weed, he'd had a few tokes in the trees hoping it would loosen him up, he'd seen a single firefly flash like an eye, just once. He didn't know any of the people packed around the cleared space where half a dozen couples, their ages and abilities mixed, stepped off to the music, it wasn't square dancing after all, there was no caller just whoops and exclamations, onlookers turning to each other to gab or nodding along to the strong beat of a fiddle, appraising the dancers, some eager, waiting their turn. The fiddler, lean and brown and old like the instrument on his shoulder, was tucked into a dim corner, Starr standing behind him, bending suddenly to say a few words in the fiddler's ear, then moving off into the crowd. The fiddler smiled as he played, maybe at Starr's remark or from the tune or just his mood this evening in a hot and excited room. Innis lost sight of Claire, she was somewhere in the back now, resting, after dancing, pretty clear she came here to dance, with Starr or without. And to take Innis into the bushes. Innis laughed, his voice mingling with the random yells to dancers and fiddler, close to the floor, b'y! Me, I'm just a wallflower, poor b'y that I am, Innis whispered to himself in the local accent, in that broad rhythm he could mimic now, making Claire laugh if Starr wasn't in earshot. He was good with voices, you needed to be when you spent a lot of time alone, and these Cape Breton voices he had heard often in his mother's kitchen, and the "down home" visitors even made fun of each other, the people from town mocking the slow country cadences, and someone from New Skye taking off on someone else from Tarbot, a place not fifteen miles away. Starr had imitated Innis too, his Boston talk, the r's that disappeared in the back of his throat. Right now Innis wanted to be that kind of stranger, just dropped in from Boston to have a look around, not from here in any way, just passing through, on the road. Had anyone in this room been a name in his mother's kitchen, in gossip there about St. Aubin? In his memory, their voices were an atmosphere, a feeling he got in that noisy room, cigarettes going constantly, bottles and glasses and ice and laughter, and once in awhile a fiddler there too if they were lucky, if not, his dad or later his mother would play records and the guests would argue that so-and-so had a better bow or was better for listening than dancing, they seemed to know them all, the fiddlers from St. Aubin, from Inverness, Mabou, Cape North, each with a distinctive style, they could pick one out without any clue but the playing, what the fiddler put into the notes.

Behind Innis, outdoors, men were lounging on and in a big Oldsmobile as in a bar, illuminated by the dome light, the driver seated, his legs swung out the open door. Why couldn't Starr get himself a real vehicle like that instead of that balky Russian crate he was fixing half the time. Innis turned back to the crowd. There was almost no one here his age, save for a lanky girl in a long brown braid dancing with her dad, it looked like, or maybe an uncle, which might account for the bleary-bright desire in his eyes, for her or somebody, a patch of white belly behind a broken shirt button, a dark tooth in his smile. All right, sure, he would love to get laid, take a woman to bed, if he could find one willing to skip the weary preliminaries, go with him into those woods out back, he knew what the moss would feel like, the scents that would be in the air. But not while Claire was here: he wouldn't want her to know he was even thinking about anyone else, as if that, absurd as it was, would reduce whatever wild chance he had with her. Through the moving faces he caught his uncle squinting at him until whatever he wanted to see came into focus, then he looked away. Was he wondering what his nephew was doing here, alone against the wall, two steps from the doorway? Innis was never sure anymore just what the man was thinking. Sometimes he could hardly remember what it had been like when there was only the two of them in that house. B.C. Before Claire. But he did know that high-flying feel-good smile of Starr's, knew it well, the look that said Fuck it, I'm in a long slow dive into a night of drinking and you can watch me or not, I don't care. A joy Innis could not move with, fed as it was by a pint of rum and a case of Moosehead Ale in the trunk of the car. Tomorrow Starr would be glum with hangover, tonight would be ashes in his mouth. Innis hated the blearing, dulling euphoria of alcohol, your mind muddled, foolish. Give him weed any day, his head was clear, and travelling. A little paranoia sometimes, but it gave him no excuse at all for not understanding what he did.

Jesus, there was old Dan Rory planted in a chair, his cane making do for dancing, thumping to the fiddler's foot, a brown, paint-flecked shoe with a bit of shine on it. Where was Finlay? Innis flushed, remembering suddenly the felled pine tree like it happened this afternoon, the anger and embarrassment of being surprised in the woods. Too late, Dan Rory had seen him and motioned him near, what could he do but push his way over there. Innis bent down to hear him and the old man shouted into his ear, "We'll take in the Gaelic pretty soon, you and me, Innis, it's coming up. Having a good time, are you?" Innis smiled and nodded and eased away as the fiddler ended with a sharp cut of his bow and waved it to clapping and shouts. Innis was afraid this was a break and he would once again be pulled into intro-

ductions and versions of his autobiography, whose family
he was attached to, they always insisted on that, *Co leis thu?*
as an old woman he'd shovelled snow for asked him once,
not who are you but *whose* are you?

But the fiddler hardly drew a breath before he swung into
another tune. Most of the dancers moved to the sidelines,
fanning their faces, plucking at their clothing, but others
stepped out. Claire had been drawn out by the hand and
Innis paused to study her partner, a guy maybe her age, late
thirties, jeans faded to a warm blue, black hair thick about
his neck, his white teeth taking Claire into his smile. Innis
didn't know who he was but he could see how tightly he
swung her into him, Claire stepping deftly around his clumsi-
ness, the muscles glistening in her neck under the ceiling
bulb as harshly bright as a kitchen's. Kitchen rackets, his
mother had called them, house dances and *ceilidhs,* Cape
Bretoners loved them even in Boston, and it was this very
closeness that they seemed to enjoy so much, a small, intense space to spin in. Claire had that look his mother had
on Saturday nights when dancing was in the air and her
restless all day, jumpy, irritable. Who needs a kid to look
after when you want to be out, happy in the clamor of a bar,
iced bourbon, a man near your face? His mother would go
out no matter what the weather. She craved that kind of attention available nowhere else, even as a boy he had figured
that out. On those nights Innis kept out of her way. But she
called him to her affection in the morning. Innis, honey?
You awake? Come in here and see me, hugging him, covering his face with kisses.

Claire could dance, yes, she knew the steps, and she made
up some of her own. Slow dancing was Innis's style, turning slow and easy with a woman all up and down you, feeling her waist in your hands, her smile, the muscles of her
back, her legs. Innis tapped the toe of his shoe on the floor,

just barely, as he watched: she was breathing hard but she didn't miss a step, not that he could notice. That lingering ache arose in him: there was not any lovely part of her his mind hadn't made warm in his hands, his mouth. Why in hell had he come here? To watch that guy fling himself around in front of her, chest hair peeping out of his shirt?

Suddenly Starr was beside him, clamping his arm in those wiry fingers, hard, like a bite. "Be honest," he said into his ear, "where'd you find a racket like this in Boston, eh?" Innis could have said, More places than you'd think, the town is lousy with Cape Bretoners, but he just smiled. His uncle's white shirt was stained with sweat, his eyes that darker grey they sometimes turned, their color deepened by how he felt, high or low.

"You don't drink and you don't dance, Cock Roddy," Starr said. "What're you good for?"

"Where's all the young folks?"

"Like you? There's a dance across the water, in that big trailer park. Rock' n' roll is what they like."

"I can live without it. Who's the guy with Claire?"

Starr narrowed his eyes. "Buddy Marr? I'll be in bad shape before I worry about him. Beating your time, is he?"

"Not mine. Yours maybe."

"No maybe about it. But I'll dance when I'm ready. I feel good enough to die."

For a few moments Innis felt the camaraderie they'd sometimes had months ago, as if Claire were a strange and desirable woman they were both appraising on equal ground, uncle and nephew, two men with needs, two bachelors: didn't they both love to be high, in their own ways? Everything seemed to be revolving pleasantly—the brogues, the pounding feet, the fiddle, even the big ceiling lightbulb seemed to have a spin, a glow. Starr pulled him outside where he'd stashed a bottle behind a tree, but Innis said no, he didn't want any, and Starr said yes you do, you'll find that out someday. The air was a relief, a soft breeze cooling their sweat. Innis looked over where cars were parked, caught sight of a man in a red sport shirt as an arriving car swept its headlights over him. Father Lesperance? Jesus, it was, gabbing with some guys beside a car, a paper cup in his hand. Innis wanted to say hello, talk to him, but only if the priest were alone. Starr raised the bottle and drank while Innis took in the rich river of the Milky Way. Stars seemed to trickle like bright dust. A shooting one crossed his vision like a scratch on a dark window.

"You can gawk at the moon anytime," Starr said. Another splash of liquor, the bottle catching light from the doorway. He seemed drunk in some way Innis had not seen before, plunging downward, blind. "Listen." He pulled Innis close, spoke low, a fume of rum in his words: "Oh, I don't think, dear, you'll get it near hard enough," this in a mocking voice whose source Innis did not recognize. And then, as if Innis were suddenly a confidant, "She likes it very very hard, you know, none of this halfhearted stuff. No one-eyed worms for that girl or she'll send you away. Tight as a buttercup."

"You're drunk, Starr, come on."

His uncle stepped back and laughed, as if Innis were somebody he'd bumped into in the dark. Two men who'd just left their car stopped as they passed by.

"Jesus, it's Starr Corbett, he got no legs under him," one said, the other laughing behind him.

Starr whirled around at them. "I got legs enough for you, you shit-arse."

Innis could feel all three of them stiffen. The man let a few seconds pass before he replied, his voice tighter. "Try that on me a little later, Starr, b'y, I'm not in the mood yet."

"I'll break your jaw if you're in the mood or not, Neilie Campbell. Wouldn't be the first time either."

"Maybe. That your nephew back there in the dark?

Good place for him, from what I heard. The States shipping us their bad apples now, eh?"

"You better fuck off, Neilie. You won't get a dance with blood on your puss."

"Isn't he the tough character now? You'll get yours, Starr, you'll get what's coming."

"It won't be from you, or that piece of shit next to you either."

The men moved off toward the entrance, glancing back, muttering but not loud enough to be heard. Innis knew there were fights in his uncle's past, even without proof or demonstration. It was there in his eyes sometimes, a flash of icy grey. He never bragged or told stories about it, but they were there in the small scars around his eyes, the nicked cheekbone, the swollen bridge of his nose.

"Looks like it's all over the place now," Innis said, "my life story."

"I wouldn't flatter yourself that it's all around. Fuck them. They didn't find out from me. Anyway, you'll be leaving in a few weeks. Right?"

It surprised Innis to hear it put that way, in weeks, to hear Starr say it. "You bet."

"Enjoy it while you can, b'y. You're in the land of opportunity."

Starr, sobered a bit from his clash with Campbell, lurched away toward the music, firing the empty bottle into the trees. He bumped into Dan Rory and Finlay coming out the door and stopped to talk with them before they came on toward the cars parked at odd angles, some nosed up on the grass, little parties going on inside them. After Finlay had helped his father inside their old Chevrolet, he hailed Innis and met him by the rear bumper.

"Innis, listen, I just wanted to tell you Daddy and me walked way up in the woods a couple days ago. He wanted to go up there, that's a long haul for a man his years. Stubborn, and he's got a heart like a horse. You happy, Innis, you taking care of yourself?"

"I'm okay, I'm getting by."

"I only have a minute. Listen, Daddy saw you at the old spring."

"Up your way? I haven't been there since the winter, since that day."

"Sure, but he saw you, you see, bending to the water. Clear as day, to him, to him. He didn't want to tell you but I'm telling you. Good night. Go back in there and get some dancing done."

Not a chance. He watched Finlay back the car out slowly and carefully, the same way he drove. What did he mean? Nothing fearful in it that Innis could detect, Dan Rory saw things other people didn't, but he was eighty-some years old. You'd see all kinds of stuff at that age, wouldn't you, so much crammed in your brain, memories and sights? But a cold feeling trailed through him, a little chill. Just the weed, providing highlights, as it could do.

The strait, over the woods behind the hall, lay out dark and still. The mountain above it was blank but for a solitary light at its shore, tiny in the long blackness. A range light? A house? Not many people lived over there. Were there lynx in that dense steep wood, wood that had never been cut? On the water, if he watched it carefully, were traces of current. He'd like to tell Starr, Listen, I'm a light year ahead of you, I've been places with that woman, right here inside my head, where you'll never get to, not with your head or your hands or your prick. A commotion arose inside the hall, a confusion of shouting. The fiddle went louder for a few bars, then quit. People drifted outside and stood smoking and exclaiming about the heat. A few went to their cars where matches flared in the windshields. Innis thought he heard Starr's name tossed about, and not kindly. Claire appeared in the doorway, noticed him, came over to him at the edge of the trees.

"We should be dancing out here," she said. "The heat inside is tough on tempers. You have a cigarette by any chance? I'm dying for one. No, you don't smoke, just those damned roll-your-owns that flip your head around." She swiped her hair back from her face, jammed her hands in the pockets of her jeans.

"What're you mad at me for?" Innis said. "I'm just an innocent bystander."

"Your uncle broke up the dancing. Carrying on. He cut in on me and some Neilie guy. Oh, he's spoiling for a brawl, that one, and he'll get it too. More than one man here who'd punch his lights out. Have you said anything to him?"

"About what?"

"Anything."

"Jesus, Claire, what's to say?"

He watched her bum a cigarette from the men gathered at the Olds. One lit it for her with a flourish of his lighter and she lingered, blowing smoke over her shoulder, taking in their langorous banter, their laughter. To a man, their eyes followed her back and it wouldn't be hard to imagine what they were murmuring.

"I think they like you," Innis said.

"That's a polite way to look at it. And you, do you like me?"

"Get serious, Claire."

She glanced at the little white building where the fiddle once again had been taken up, and then she grabbed his hand. "Let's get out of here."

Innis tried to read her face. "Where to? He's got the keys anyway."

"I don't mean the car." She pointed behind him, the sharpness gone from her voice. "I mean the shore, down there."

His eyes were used to the dark now and the night had an odd clarity, the way he thought a cat might see it, darkness being just shapes defined by what little light was out there, the flicker of a car on the mountain highway, back in the woods, the pulse of fireflies, the bow light of a small boat steady in its barely troubled reflection. The shadows on the woods had a sheen, like velvet. If he could have called up such a sound as the lynx made, he would have, because he knew now what had been in it: joy fused with terror, a cry to chill the world around him, to make him, the lynx, the center of everything.

"Sure, let's go down," he said.

Claire pulled him away through a dark field. "Lord, it's black," she said, letting go his hand. "I can't see where my feet are falling." She was still in the dance, he knew that, but maybe he could take her somewhere else. Quiet water showed in the trees as they pushed through unmown hay and grass until they found a path cutting into the lower woods, the ground soft at first, a smell of pitch and dank fern, like sweet tobacco, and the black sooty mud of the boggy places, and the brooks, all smells conjuring his own familiar woods. She stumbled on a tree root and he grabbed her to stop her fall, then he kissed her without hesitation. She seemed surprised for a moment, then she laughed and kissed him hard before pulling away down the path. The rolling stroke of the fiddler softened, grew faint, the yells of the dancers intermittent, far off. She ran ahead of him as the path twisted and dropped to the beach, eager for the fine sand he'd guessed would be there, and he heard the chuff of her knees and her hands as she threw herself into it, kneeling. Out on the water something small splashed, a silvery burst in the dark. The sky was shot with stars but their light touched nothing but the eye, and Innis's magnified everything, a swathe of oxeye daisies floating brilliantly in the dark, a driftlog shaggy as a pale horse, the spine of a big stone splitting a tidal stream whose ebb at the water's edge was absorbed in soft quick laps. A luminescence eased through the water like curtains in a breeze.

"Innis, let's swim."

"You're out of your mind, Claire."

"Sissy."

"It's not midnight."

"Near enough, come on."

There was no moon to relieve the blackness, but Claire's blouse unfurled from her, fell to the sand. She was humming some tune. What songs did she like? Why didn't he know? Her back was the color of light wood where her swimsuit had covered her and he wanted to enclose her in his bare arms. He was removing his shoes, clumsily, one foot already cool in the sand.

"Jesus, Claire, that water's got to be cold." But he was wrestling his shirt off, his jeans were slipping down. "Starr—" but then he didn't know what to say about him. Maybe he just had to put his uncle's name out there, toss it in the sand like their clothing. Claire, dimly naked, flung her jeans away. Her shape moving toward the water's edge made him wait, turn into a watcher again: what more could he want than this that seemed to be happening?

Bold as Claire was, she shrieked when the water touched her, her arms high over her head, then she dove under, surfacing quickly, mewing, laughing. By the time Innis winced over the gravel and stones of the shallows, she yelled it was lovely now, once you were in it was great, but Innis, busy imagining crabs and eels his toes were probing toward, took one good grunt of breath and held it. He flinched at strands of eelgrass caressing his ankles. When the water lapped his crotch he yelled out. God, he'd never get hard again in his life, his cock so shrivelled it was numb, just a bit of fish bait between his legs. Claire swam with smooth strokes that seemed the only sound on the whole water. Innis was afraid his mood was turning into gooseflesh and clamped teeth, but when he finally shut his eyes and plunged, Claire was right: half a minute of agony and his body soothed out, his nakedness grew warm and sinuous. He'd never swum at night except once in a public pool roiling with chlorine and lights and hysterical kids. Now his pale limbs seemed liquid themselves and he stroked his way in a slow dog paddle toward Claire with hardly a splash, pleased with his stealthy passage. He could hear her breathing as she floated quietly on her back, her face a light mask in the darkness until he was near and then he could see her skin beneath the clear water, her hands weaving circles to keep her afloat. He reached out, brushed her leg.

"Oh God, I thought you were a fish!" She was breathing hard now but Innis felt barely winded. Claire turned toward shore. "We'd better get back to the shallows, Innis. There's no one here to save us."

"Good."

But Innis let her go, he drifted where he was, treading, wheeling slowly on his back. Stars and water. No one could touch him, a man immersed in this that most of the world was made of, his eyes leaping to the sky. The stars flowed in streams, yet he was solid as a diamond, glints of light on his wet skin. He arched his back and lay out his whole length, poising for sips of breath. The merest motion of his hands buoyed him. The water seemed to clutch his face lightly, acquainting itself, nervous touches on his temples, salt in his mouth. At the corner of his eyes a long ripple from the darkness of the strait surged quickly over his face and he coughed it out, righting himself, scrabbling for air. He swam defensively, fighting for his breath, his limbs suddenly heavy, to where he could stand. But as he extended his legs toward the bottom, his feet touched not stones and sand but a zone of water so cold it scared him, and he pushed further on where Claire was standing in water to her waist. It streamed from her hair and shone on her skin. Innis pulled up, his feet dancing on bottom, crabs or not.

"Did you catch that layer of cold water out there?" His voice shook in the warm air. "Ice to the bone."

"It's a spring, I think," she said, her voice low, as if they'd be overheard. "They come up offshore sometimes." She rubbed his chest briskly, then hugged him. "It's a kick, isn't it? Don't you feel good?"

"Jesus," he said. He nuzzled her salty wet hair, the salty drops on her skin. He had taken care of her, a long night, put his lips to her belly, her body burning, too hot with life.

"I think there's creatures around our feet," she said.

"They must be friendly, they're not biting anything."

"You're not afraid of them?"

"Right now I don't care. I wouldn't even feel it." He drew her tight against him, kissed her neck, her ear, her mouth, and she returned it, working her mouth in his, a murmurous language formed only by their lips. They pulled tightly against each other, barely rocking. A wind was coming up the strait. The water lost its polished blackness, rising and falling along their bodies. Claire shivered.

"Let's go in," she whispered.

On the beach they dried each other slowly, using each other's shirts. She teased him about his tender feet.

"Starr will be suspicious of everything now," he said.

"It's too late then," she said, rubbing his back, hugging him from behind. She moved her hands over his chest, down the tightened muscles of his belly. "Oh my," she said.

They lay out on the sand, cool, then warm as they pressed into it with the slow rolling of their bodies. A small shell cut into Innis's knee but the pain was distant, lost in all the sensations of her, and further still a sound like Starr's voice, calling their names from somewhere up the hill, hers, then Innis's, again and again in different voices, querulous, angry, softer and louder by turns, smothered in the wind, but Innis didn't hear him at all for the roar of his own breath. Above them the shorebank trees were stirring in the wind like horses walking, and the world was nothing but her and him.

16

Innis pressed the receiver against his chest. "It's Dan Rory. The Gaelic church service in Big Bras D'Eau, it's this morning."

"So?" Starr was sipping black coffee, black as his look. Innis had stumbled downstairs, surprised to find him at the table, ignoring the phone.

"I was supposed to go with him. I have to do it, I said I would."

Starr took another thoughtful sip, watched him. There was a small black cut on his cheekbone and a swelling over his eye. Innis shifted the receiver in case Dan Rory could hear his heart.

"You asking my permission or something? That's a first," Starr said. In the window behind him white mist had lowered the mountain ridge to a flat line.

"Look, I don't know what I'm in for here, Starr. I don't want to embarrass anybody. I been to church maybe six times in my life."

"You ought to go more often. They talk about right and wrong there. But this is the service for you, b'y. You won't understand a goddamn word of it."

"You're the one who should be going, not me."

"My Gaelic's not good enough. It's for the old folks."

"Like me?"

"Like you. Can you handle it? I thought you'd be shagged out till noon."

"I didn't drink a bottle of rum."

"I don't see how that matters." Starr drew slowly on a cigarette, squinting through the smoke. "The princess still sleeping?"

"How would I know? It's not my bed she sleeps in."

"Well now, I'm glad to hear that. I was worried. Tell Dan Rory you'll be up at the mailbox, wearing my necktie with the hangman's knot, and the worst sport coat I can find you."

IF INNIS HAD any prayer in him, it was please God, no rain, he didn't want the church with rain, he should have insisted Starr come instead of him, Look, you phony, dropping Gaelic when you don't want me to know what you're saying, this is your kind of church, not mine, but there it was, rain steady and oppressive, streaming from the steep roof of the white-shingled church, people ducking for the front door, huddling in the vestibule, nodding and exchanging a few quick words as they shook out an umbrella or a hat. They'd been deprived of the social gathering out front where, Dan Rory said, the older folks liked to meet before the service, some had come miles away for this, and Innis felt maybe the rain was better after all—he'd been spared the introductions, And who's this young man with you, Dan Rory, no, is it Munro Corbett's boy, well, well, and you're liking it here, are you, sure, not like Boston, but less rush and fuss, eh?

With Starr, there might be plenty fuss and rush this day. Innis was worried, leaving Claire, not sure yet just how she felt or what his uncle knew or what he'd throw at her when she came down to the kitchen. Would they have it out, him not even there? But what could his uncle know? Innis and Claire had separated on the path to the dance hall, returned from different directions, she back into the music, Innis out at the cars, feeling tired in a lovely and powerful way Starr might even have smelled on him when he came out of the trees, Jesus, where the hell were you two? Two? Innis had said, I went off for a piss. Starr, fresh from a fistfight that had been broken up, put his face close to Innis's and said, there's a lot more than pissing going on here tonight.

Innis inched along behind Dan Rory, the old man halting nearly every step to greet someone in a husky whisper or clasp a hand while he talked. They fell in and out of Gaelic, hitting points of reference that English didn't seem to touch, and Innis was sure some of it bore on him, this lanky youth in bad clothes. Did they think him a grandson or what? Finlay, up ahead, or Dan Rory would explain. He shouldn't have come, his head was back with Claire, he was unsure where and how he would take up with her after last night, what daylight would do to them, but he had to get alone with her to find out, away from Starr. Innis looked at his wrists thrust out the sleeves of a coat Starr must have hidden away to humiliate him in, some kind of polyester fleck like seat covers in a cocktail lounge, and a tie with tiny red horseshoes on it. Dan Rory leaned into yet another pew, huddling in a little circle of Gaelic while Innis waited, his cheeks flushed, there for all to see and whisper about, oh Jesus, he'd have to go through it all when this was over, Who, who, *Co leis thu?*, whose are you? Why couldn't they just sit down? But he couldn't tug the old man's coattail, these exchanges meant too much, the old folks craning their necks, checking out who was still in the aisles, the knock of a cane, the squeak of shoes, the labored sigh as someone found his seat, coughs and murmurs and the slick sound of raincoats coming off. Further down sat a girl, a young woman, her blonde hair fanning almost white down her back, bent into a hymnal, she was a wonderful distraction, the grey glass window light on her hair, he wanted to slip in next to her, hey, what's with you here, all these old folks, are we in the same boat, you and me? Maybe she knew Gaelic, there were young people who did, determined to carry it forward, Finlay said, more up west than here. That would seem sexy to Innis, hearing her talk that tongue, asking her words, interesting words, since he'd heard it only from older people, Dan Rory and Finlay exchanging a private line or two, sometimes Starr on the telephone. Maybe she would sing when the time came, if they sang hymns in Gaelic. Listening to the radio in a car with her she might be ordinary, but here in church, as Dan Rory directed Innis into the pew behind her, she seemed beautiful, mysterious. An old man in a brown suit scooched over to let him sit, taking in a good glance through his fogged lenses. Then Dan Rory settled his long body against the pew back. Only laughter will save us, Starr had said once. He wasn't laughing this morning. Was Claire up now? She'd had a lot of wine. Innis had wanted to see her first, blowzy with sleep, that incredible hair that nothing could muss enough to make her look plain. But Starr would see her first. Starr, you bastard. What do I do now?

The old guy beside him leaned forward quickly as the minister ascended to the pulpit, a little rumpled in his black robe. He plopped a Bible down and spread his elbows as if he were at a windowsill. Dan Rory said he was a retired minister, originally from lonely St. Kilda fifty miles out in the Atlantic beyond the Hebrides, he'd been evacuated to other parts of Scotland off that isolated island with the last of St. Kildans in the 1920s, so an island man too, what was it with these island men. A part-time chaplain in a British Columbia prison now, he'd once had a church up the North Shore when they all had the Gaelic at home, Dan Rory said, no English until school, and He was *Dia* before He was God. The man looked rough and ready, that nose had been busted. Thick grey hair, boyish, unkempt over his forehead. He didn't seem to be preaching when he began to speak, it was more like conversation, just talking to these people, a few of them from his old church. A nod, a faint smile. The language washed over Innis, it hadn't the schoolteacher edge Starr gave to it, Famous Gaelic Sayings to Inflict on Your Nephew or snatches of nasty comment he didn't want you to hear, though Innis could tell when it was raunchy. The minister's voice was gentle, almost bemused. If he had fire in him, he must have burned it out earlier, having preached in English at another church this morning. No, he was here for them, the old people, and they for him. Innis fixed his eyes on the long blond hair in front of him, sometimes he believed he could put his thoughts into someone else's head if he concentrated exceptionally hard and wanted to tap into their mind bad enough, so he let an intimate wish drift toward the blond, nothing dirty, just frank and cool desire, he still had momentum from last night when everything with Claire seemed to occur in some smooth and natural sequence toward a sweet combustion. But the girl was not picking up his silent signals, she was listening intently to the minister, chin lifted, though maybe, like Innis, not to the words themselves.

Then Innis too perked up: the minister had switched to his burred English to welcome visitors who hadn't the Gaelic, and then he referred to "the men downstairs" who would lead the sacred singing of the Psalms. Below the pulpit sat a row of eleven men, in dark suits that might have had a shine in the seat some of them, facing the congregation. They had the bearing of Sundays, long Sundays, so it looked. It wasn't that they were all so old, not as old as Dan Rory, and a couple not much older than Starr, but to Innis there was something ancient about them, strange in their privileged solemnity, plain, without vestments, hands folded around black books in their laps. These men were all from down north, Finlay said on the drive over, where good Gaelic speakers were still found, though almost gone on St. Aubin, and this no doubt the last generation of "good and tone" Precentors, no young Gaelic voices coming along trained or inclined to take their places, and why anyway since a Gaelic service like this was only a rare event now, a piece of our churchgoing past.

The Precentors stood up, a line of uneven heights and postures, and the lead Precentor put out the first lines, *Arduicheam thu, mo Dhia, 's mo Rìgh, d'aim beannaicheam gu bràth,* the other men picking it up on the last word, repeating the line, carrying through, and then the leader soloed out another line, continuing the pattern. This was the traditional way, the old way of The Fathers, Dan Rory said, the way your grandfather did it. The men drew out their wavering intonations, unsweetened by any youthful or feminine sounds, to Innis a dirge, slow, unmelodious, not even an organ swell in the background, no adornments or flourishes, unlike the robed, roundmouthed choirs he had heard in those Easter churches back home singing hymns with the enthusiasm of a glee club. Dan Rory's lips were moving silently, Och, those fellas, they learned the precenting tunes with their ear and their heart, he'd told him, and you'd never hear this in a cathedral. Innis thought that was likely as the lead Precentor held the final dour note until his tenor faded away, the minister gazing down at the men gratefully while they took their seats, coughing and clearing their voices.

The minister put on blackrimmed spectacles, surveyed the congregation once over the tops of them, and began to read from his *Biobull,* putting more feeling into it than Innis had sensed in the Psalms. Innis was watching the girl's long, slender fingers comb slowly through her hair when Dan Rory nudged him and placed an open Bible on Innis's lap, tapping the passage in English the minister was reading in Gaelic. Innis nodded, dropped his eyes dutifully to the page. Job, it said in the upper corner, and okay he would pretend to follow, and then he did read in case Dan Rory asked him about it later, the minister's voice moving behind these words, rising and falling: For there is hope of a tree, if it be cut down, that it will sprout again, and that the tender branch thereof will not cease. Though the root thereof wax old in the earth, and the stock thereof die in the ground, yet through the scent of water it will bud, and bring forth boughs like a plant. But man dieth, and wasteth away, yea, man giveth up the ghost, and where is he? As the waters fail from the sea, and the flood decayeth and drieth up, so man lieth down, and riseth not: till the heavens be no more, they shall not awake, nor be raised out of their sleep. Oh that thou wouldst hide me.... The minister had stopped and Innis looked up to see him pull his glasses off and tuck them away as he moved into the sermon, his Gaelic soft and easy, almost casual. If that passage he'd read was a grim note, it didn't sound like it now. Innis handed back the Bible to Dan Rory, smiling thanks, but the old man was absorbed in the words from the pulpit, savoring them, his eyes shut. Rain streamed faintly down the grey translucent windows, gothic but without stained glass color in the light. The church had warmed, the air had a humid scent of damp clothing. Innis's eyelids drooped but he jerked them open, fingering the small cut on his kneecap to stay awake. Afterward Claire had joked, we don't even have a cigarette, either of us. Innis couldn't stop touching her, tracing her face, her body, he wanted to call it all up in his fingertips later, like now, brushing sand from her skin, from the curve of her back. Did you hear Starr? he'd said, I thought he might find us down here, and she'd said she wasn't worried, he was just some noise up in the woods, but he must never know about this. Innis said, what will he suspect? Anything he wants, she said, suspicion has its own joys, doesn't it. They dressed slowly, dreamily, it seemed to Innis now. They didn't talk much, the stars were gauzing over with high clouds. The mood was broken by the thrum of a gypsum freighter moving up the strait and they lingered until they saw its running lights and its wake hissed along the shore, and Innis kissed her again, and perhaps, recalling it now, his lips were more eager than hers, more hungry....

The Precentors were standing, clearing their pipes for another Psalm, but this time the congregation, still seated, joined them as another Precentor led, a man with sandy grey hair who ignored the Psalm book in his hand, putting out the long slow line and the worshippers picked it up and sang it back, and the volume rose now with all the added voices, old voices gathering strength. But there was something else: they had begun to rock slowly, almost imperceptibly, as they sang, Dan Rory too, and the others around him, even the girl slightly, she could not resist, Innis himself could barely hold back when he detected a slow tapping that soon turned into a measured thump of hidden Sunday shoes, at first only here and there as if some were shy or it had been so long they had to be roused to it, no hand clapping or wailing or crying out, only this diffident thumping of feet out of sight, marking the beat, to Innis it was the rhythm of his axe, of his tree felling, this cadence of their singing. It echoed something deep in them that went a long way back, this foot beat, he could feel it even though he didn't know what it was and his foot was going, if lightly, discreetly, after all this was beyond him, before his time. These people did not rock in trances or weep on their knees, this was the only passion you'd see from them in this holy house, this was their opening up, rocking in the cradle of the old tongue. There were two more Psalms before the eleven men, eyes high and hymnals closed, brought the singing to an end, and the minister delivered a benediction in Gaelic, *Deanamaid urnaigh,* surely the last one some of them would ever hear from a pulpit.

Amid the shufflings and stirrings that followed, people rising into talk, Innis slipped out a side door, he didn't want to repeat that agonizing processional, him the mute relative lost in others' reminiscences. The rain had lightened to a blustery mist and he clutched his collar shut, wandering into the churchyard. Jesus, be a shame if he ruined this coat and tie, in Boston they'd arrest you in a getup like this. He hunched under a birch tree, looking out over the gravestones, granite, a few newer with polished red faces, older ones white or grey, their lettering abraded, obscured by lichen. Beyond, the strait, its grey water snarled with white, widened toward the ocean. Last night they were in the dark, after all, he and Claire, it was all touch and breath and tongues in the darkness. He wished he knew what was in her head. She was older, she had other things in her life, other men. The girls Innis had known, they had all been new to it just as he was, just as clumsy, uncertain, blindly excited, no other intimacies in their past, or so he'd thought. Starr, on the ride home, had said not a word, his steering a bit unsteady but good enough to stay on the road, Claire staring out the passenger window humming quietly, inside herself, Innis in the back seat again like the kid after a family outing, strapped for any line of conversation that would draw in the three of them. He hadn't wanted to talk anyway, only to reach out and touch Claire, lay his hand on her shoulder to remind her, listen, we have been somewhere tonight, for a little while we left everybody in the world behind. It drove him crazy that he could not be alone with her now, that Starr was there, worse in his silence than in his gab.

Innis wandered among the headstones, reading names and inscriptions. So many died young, years and years ago, young and sometimes close together. Sickness probably.

Two MacLeods, brothers, drowned at sea 1886, one Innis's age. Well, if you had to die young, that wasn't a bad way, was it, sink in a storm? Would have been a sailboat of some kind, that. So man lieth down, and riseth not. The truth of that was all around him. But it only sharpened his sense of luck, that he was wet and breathing and could smell fresh roses on the next grave. Maybe he could get work on a fishing boat. That was suddenly appealing, rain streaming down his face, there was something about this weather that thrilled him. But he remembered that on the way here they'd passed through Big Bras D'Eau where most of the fishermen moored, selling their lobster at the government wharf, but the season was over, the boats were hauled out.

17

It did not surprise him that Claire went cool on him. Not that she wasn't friendly or wouldn't talk with him, she just wouldn't talk about them, her and Innis. She would hug him hello and goodbye in the kitchen, Starr looking on, she'd even kiss him, a loud cousin kiss, self-conscious, almost comical, though Innis didn't laugh. Only once, when they met at the top of the stairs, she gave him a quick, fierce kiss as if it were a hit and he'd have to take whatever high it gave him. He went along, maybe he was colluding with her to douse whatever Starr remembered or thought he remembered about the night of the dance. The man had nothing but suspicion to go on, and instincts, which were, in this case, too sharp to take lightly. All right, Claire blurted out at supper one day, tired of his barbs, flinging her knife on her plate, we went for a swim, it was hot, so what, for Christ's sake, leave it alone. A swim? Starr said, turning to Innis, and what is it you're good at, breaststroke? Backstroke? Of course you had your suits on under your clothes, eh? His uncle's sarcasms went on until Claire blew up, told him she would leave if he didn't quit. So he let the subject fade when she was around, but prodded Innis with it like a sharp finger in his back. You sneaked off, you little bastard, he said to him when they were alone, the two of you, don't ever do that to me.

By himself at the shore, leaning against the old skiff, Innis called up Claire with a fine-tipped ballpoint, in detail meticulous as an engraving. Can you do this, Starr? There were the faintest of lines at her eyes, the almost invisible beginnings of middle age, but her eyes, gorgeously large, were what the drawing noticed. He gave her body little quirks and flaws, but they only enhanced what he loved about it. He was watching her differently now. He was sure that it would happen again, that mood and day and circumstance would come together, but it was nothing he could demand. When he finished, he flipped back through the pad, pausing at certain pages. A tiny flower with twin, nodding blooms. A truck abandoned in the woods whose rusty blue patina had caught his eye, an intricate orb web in its windshield. An osprey's hefty nest on a powerline pylon, all twigs and branches in the crossbeam. A dead bat lying in grass like a discarded glove. Claire at the dance, her face hidden in swirls of hair. A bouquet of marijuana collas, the way he hoped to see them up above. A crow on the clothesline plucking a button off one of Starr's shirts. The hemlock plant—he'd forgotten it, his plan to harvest it for Ned. He went off down the beach to see if it was still there. Yes, taller now, its tiny flowers fully formed in radiating clusters. Was it getting stronger, did it mature like pot? He would get back to it soon, it wasn't going anywhere.

He worked hard on the wooden boat, sanding flaky spots and painting the hull. It was sound enough, Starr said, but the seams would leak for a spell, and so they had while

Innis rowed back and forth in the cove on calm days, teaching himself to work the oars, to take the boat on a straight course. Turning was too damned easy, the oars yanked him this way and that the first week, so he was often one-oaring it, re-sighting the bow at a shore mark again and again until he could put the boat directly there with both oars pulling. Water sloshed at his feet until he got nervous and dragged the boat up on the sand, bailing it out with a cut-down bleach bottle. The wood soon swelled and closed the leaks and it was just the hollow clack and swivel of the oarlocks as he ventured further out on a slack tide, but even then there were subtle eddies, and when he had to row against them, when he could feel the boat respond almost eagerly to a current he couldn't even see, he pulled hard for the cove, his heart pounding, tasting sweat. It never looked like a mile across to the mountain shore until he was out in the water a ways and that's when he lost his nerve, afraid the tide would turn on him. And that was all it was really, nerve, he'd get it, he had to.

He hiked into the upper woods, glad to see the power line crew was gone, though their slash was tossed wherever. They'd cleared out not just alders but every mature tree in a gulley that traversed the break, birches, maples, not one of them a threat to the power lines above. You could see a long way now in both directions, the crests of the break as they climbed into the distance. He approached his little clearing as he always had, on a slim, curving path through trees and ferns, you would have to look for it, and even then it could be a deer path, the woods were laced with them. But as he came into the open he stopped dead: his plants were waist high and sturdy in the breeze, their fan leaves fluttering, but he felt that someone had been there, and not an animal. So palpable was it that he walked the perimeter of the clearing, spreading bushes aside, peering into the trees behind. He knelt in places where maybe the grass had been disarranged by a foot, a patch of moss pressed flat. But maybe not. He was not an Indian, not a backwoodsman yet, he couldn't read broken stalks of soft rushes as anything more than that, he couldn't say what bent them. Like Starr, he only had suspicions. But the feeling was strong, and sometimes you had to listen to that. Once assured that he was really alone, he went from plant to plant, rubbing their stalks in his thumb and finger, then sniffing his skin: yes! resin! not turpentiney like conifers, but with a sweet component, a tingle in the nostrils, designed for inhaling, it would never thin paint, not this. Three were showing male flowers but he couldn't bring himself to pull them out, to hell with it. So the females would not be *sinsemilla* after all, he would still get good money, even males were okay smoke and more than good enough, who'd know the difference here, weed was weed. Nobody could have been here, could they? Too far up, no action up here but the trampings of animals, their night forays, sheltered in darkness. After all nothing was really disturbed, not a leaf was missing or nibbled. He could hardly stand guard up here anyway. The plants were getting serious, another few weeks. There'd been decent rain, so he wouldn't have to haul from the spring. More damn sun would help. A day of lowering sky, threatening rain, but the clouds were wan and thin, marbled grey and unmoving. He circled the edge of the clearing several times, he would lay down his scent, like the lynx, this territory is mine, enemies take notice. He stood at the head of the path, watching his plants as if they were his flock, straining to detect any sign that a wolf had been through.

But hell, what more could he do here this afternoon? He had a job painting an old barn up the road, Mrs. MacKenzie's, she wanted it red the way it had been years ago, and its dry shingles were sucking up gallons of stain. Today, on the highest rungs of a long ladder, he would reach the first high gable. And then, in what was left of the afternoon, he would go down to the boat.

His garden was still on his mind as he rowed from one side of the cove to the other, rocking in the gentle waves, thinking. Of all the spots in those woods he might have chosen, had he picked a dangerous one? To lose those plants seemed more terrible than any prospect of arrest. But there was no real evidence of anyone's having been there, or was he just failing to decipher it? Lulled by the splashcut of the bow, he shipped the oars for a rest, letting the boat slowly revolve. And there she was on the beach. White blouse, a gay striped towel over her shoulder. Innis took a deep breath, waiting for Starr to appear out of the trees, but he didn't. Claire saw Innis and waved, but he pretended he hadn't seen her and with one oar pulled the boat around until the bow was shoreward and he was looking out at the strait. If Starr was on his way, if he was due to show up, then Innis would take the boat further off, up the shoreline, out of hailing. He did not want to be on that sand with her and his uncle, he wouldn't listen to his talk, not today, no one could make him. But he heard her voice, she was calling to him. He rowed as slowly as he could, his back to her, not looking over his shoulder until the keel scratched gravel and she waded a few steps in and grabbed the bow.

"Dreaming out there, were you?" she said, helping him haul the skiff clear.

"Not really. Starr coming?"

"He went to a funeral, in Sydney. An old cousin." She cocked her head at him. "He was looking for you to go with him."

"He'll have a long look, if it's the cousin I'm thinking of. You should've gone. Can't beat a good funeral."

"I'm not in the mood for a funeral, thanks. Innis, you're getting tanned. That winter pallor is gone."

"Is it?" He set about scooping water from under the stern thwart. "I wouldn't think you'd notice, Claire. You notice anything about my uncle?"

"Some things you do, I suppose, and some things you don't." She reached for his collar and tugged it straight. "Youth is fine, even beautiful, in someone like you, but it isn't everything, kiddo."

"Tell me, Claire, do you think I don't know much?"

"You just need a few more years under that beltbuckle there."

"You like it? It's World War I. I'd like the army cap that went with it, with the cocky green feather."

"You're cocky anyway."

"My mother used to say that. I don't think it's true anymore."

"Was she pretty, your mother?"

"Still is, I guess. Was yours?"

"She still got looks at fifty, my mother. But that mattered to her too much, getting whistles, winks from the butcher. I thought, God, I don't want to be that way, wanting looks. I know it has to end. But if you want to give me a look, Innis, I won't complain."

"You got your suit on under those jeans? I think Starr requires that now. It's a regulation."

"Oh yes, I'm observing the law." She smiled. "I didn't know you were a boatman, Innis."

"Better day for it than swimming." The light wind had vanished. There were no waves in the cove and the water sat against the shore as if it had been poured. In the clear green shallows a purple jellyfish bloomed and closed, bloomed and closed, others just helpless blobs in the sand. "I'll take you out, if you like."

She wrapped the towel around her like a shawl, looked at the sky, its dark, still clouds. "All right, Innis. Be my boatman."

His shoes were wet anyway, so he pushed the boat off and stepped in, Claire in the stern seat. She sat comfortably, her hands clasped between her knees as he poled out of the shallows. He set the oars in the locks and fell into the rhythm that was becoming familiar to him, Claire looking past him out into the strait where he pointed the bow. If he rowed hard he could make the other shore on this slack tide and what happened after that he didn't care. He was in good shape, he could pull this boat all day if he had to, his wake was good, straight as a road. The cove slowly receded into shorebank backed with woods. Ah, the ever-present woods. Innis felt liberated from them, there was no sound but clatter of oarlocks, the synchronized splash of the blades.

"Everything looks different out here," Claire said. "You can see so far down the strait."

"Only a few miles to the sea. Beyond the big bridge you can just make out the narrows there. After that, hey, it's the ocean, Claire."

"Some other day, all right?"

"I never get other days with you, Claire. That's the trouble."

"Let's enjoy this one, captain. Look up there!" She pointed above the cove where Starr's house appeared on the hill, black-roofed and white-sided, and soon, further east, the grey barn, the wild fields.

"I like it better from here," Innis said, picking up his pace, leaning deep into his strokes.

The rain was at first so light it turned the smooth grey surface to sandstone. They both laughed at its touch, raising their faces, opening their mouths. A cormorant, up from a long dive, took fright, its wings skipping water until it was barely airborne, propelling its long black neck seaward. Even the currents seemed just tones, the texture of fossil. Save for the whisper of rain, the stillness extended deep and wide and they were suspended in it: that was what brought Innis up short—the sensation of not moving anywhere in spite of his muscular rowing. He glanced behind him over the bow: this was farther than he had ever rowed and, Jesus, they weren't but a quarter way across, the mountain hardly nearer. His wake was meandering.

"Look out," Claire said. "Here it comes."

He heard the drops before he felt them, loud plinks like on glass, then their sting, so hard he shut his eyes. They both hunched down as the rain beat on them and in seconds it fell in long curtains, straight as beads, then slowly moving in long waves as the wind followed, and then the water came alive. He raised one oar, the boat seemed to be sliding sideways, and he turned it back toward the cove with the other. Claire had hold of the gunnels, bracing herself as waves began to hit broadside, easy for his first few strokes, but the troughs grew deeper, he could hardly believe how the surface of the strait was rolling and leaping. In the wind the shore was a dark green blur.

"The current's taking us, Innis!"

There was no wake to see now but she was right, the waves were coming out of the west, shoving them eastward, away from the shore. He could make out her dark hair, her blouse.

"Bail with that bottle! Under your seat there!"

There were moments when he lost all sense of where they were headed, he was just thrashing against thick rain and choppy waves heeling them over. He managed to get the boat around so the bow met the waves, but that headed them the wrong direction. The pitch was violent, the bow lifting, plunging. Water washed over his shoes.

"Innis! Where are we going?"

He didn't answer, he was glad she was afraid. He was tiring, but if he could work the oars enough to keep them into the waves, they might make shore, the sea was pushing them sternward. But their drift was too slow, Claire had stopped bailing, the plastic scoop rolled fore and aft at their feet. He would have to come around and ride with the waves, not into them. He lifted the oars to ready himself. He had never been so soaked, so without shelter.

"Hold on, Claire!"

She said something he couldn't hear and then he pulled hard with one oar, he had to do it fast, 180 degrees, but the troughs were short, the boat lurched down, then up, taking spray, and again until he had the bow angled toward land. As the stern lifted under Claire she cried out, water slashing across her back. The rain had slackened but the wind was blowing it about as Innis pulled against the current, it could hit five or six knots when the tide was ebbing, Starr said, but there was always an eddy just offshore running opposite the tide. Innis forced his leaden arms to move, keep moving, he didn't look behind him until he knew he'd have to rest, and by then the boat did not seem to be slip-sliding anymore, he was free of the current, the shore not thirty yards away.

"Innis, you can beach it now!" Claire said.

"I can make the cove."

In the eddy he got his second wind and pulled for the cove. The swells were abeam and rocked them good, Claire had to grip the gunnels hard, but there were no whitecaps to raise the water washing at their ankles. When the shore was close he gave the oars three loud heaves, driving the bow onto the sand. He slumped on the thwart, grinning at her. Her blouse was translucent against her skin. She wasn't wearing a swimsuit. The boat rocked under them, keel grinding in gravel. The rain was merely steady now, nothing dangerous.

"Claire, you look drowned."

She ran her hands slowly over her face and through her hair. "Good God, Innis. Don't be funny."

Together they beached the skiff. Innis tied the bow rope to a tree and flopped on his back, his arms outstretched. Claire knelt beside him. She wiped rain from his face. "We should go up. You'll get chilled."

"I don't want to see Starr. I just don't."

"He won't be back, he's having supper there."

Innis opened his eyes. "He's always jabbing at me. What does he know?"

"He doesn't know what happened that night. But it's in the air between us, you and me, and he walks through it every day."

"Just air?"

"I'm trying to hold my balance, Innis. Maybe our balance."

"I don't know what you mean. It was just messing around, was it, on the beach that night?"

Claire touched his face but he turned away. "That? That was wonderful, it was. Listen, Innis, I have a whole history you can't imagine and it doesn't disappear in one night. That isn't possession. I'm not yours or you mine because we made love. You're so young yet, you're too serious about it. You don't see these things, you don't know that sometimes you take what comes your way, and then it goes. It might come back and you'll be happy if it does, but you can't expect it to, it's not yours or mine, it's just the way things happened at a certain time. God, there didn't seem anything else for us to do that evening but what we did. I won't forget it, I won't. I used to think I could get something from one man, something different from another. But it's so difficult, the two of you tied up with me that way, here."

"Nobody can keep a secret like me."

"Come on, you're shivering." Holding his hand, she got up and pulled him to his feet.

They walked slowly without speaking up through the woods, the dripping trees, Claire ahead. "Wait," Innis said. He plucked two stalks of bluebead lily, dangled the indigo berries at her earlobes. "Beautiful." She smiled and kissed his face and they went on. At the house she stopped in the kitchen for a small glass of rum. "Take a swig," she said, "it'll warm you."

He winced, it burned his throat. "Not used to it anymore," he said.

Upstairs they parted to their bedrooms. Innis peeled off his shirt, his jeans, wrung out his shorts in the crockery basin. He stood at the window and dried himself slowly, under his arms, between his legs. He buried his head in the towel and rubbed it vigorously, flung the towel away. Bending to the mirror, he combed his hair back with careful strokes and tied it with a piece of leather bootlace. He closed his eyes: it felt so good to be naked. He wanted a joint, but there wasn't time for that. Sometimes he wondered what there was time for. When he was as old as Claire, what would he have? Hearing her singing, too soft to make out, he went to her open door and stood there, his arms at his sides.

In her robe, her back to him, she was brushing her hair. She saw him in the mirror and turned, setting the brush carefully on the bureau. "What're you singing?" he said. She looked him up and down, smiling almost sadly. "It's French. My mother." He didn't move. "Innis, what am I going to do with you?" "Something good, I hope, Miss Claire." She came over to him, caressed the muscles of his shoulders, his chest, his neck. She reached behind him and tugged loose the bit of leather that bound his ponytail. "There," she said. He spread her robe open until it slipped from her arms. "Claire in the daylight. Something else," he whispered. "Yes," she said. "I haven't been whispered to in the daylight for a long time, like this, close." She kissed him quietly on the lips and he cupped her face in his hands, her flesh against his flesh was incredible to him, everything was spinning down to this. His voice was gone but he took her hand and led her into his room. "No," she said. "You lie down. Go on." He lay there and watched her, she pulled the window curtain closed, then leaned over him and ran her fingers lightly down his torso, kissed the hard muscle of his belly before she slid over him on her knees. "Lie back," she said. "I'll row us out to sea."

18

Claire flung open all the upstairs windows after she got out of bed. "Let that rainy air blow through," she said, "it'll take us out of here before Starr gets back." Innis had lain there listening to her, the sweet feel of her cooling over his body. "I'll get myself out of here," he said, "I'll hitch down to the priest's. I don't feel like talking to Starr, or listening to him, not today, Claire. You know what I mean?" "Yes," she said, "I know what you mean. I'll drive you, this time." When she dropped him off at the Wharf Road, he said, "I should have thought of this sooner, you driving me places." "Believe me," Claire said, "this is soon enough. And what places?"

The priest was not at the cottage. At the wharf Innis watched the mountain sundown through a drizzle, a mixture of white vapor, smoke, small apertures of brilliant light, altering moment by moment. Into the darkening water he sidearmed a stone, cutting the surface in neat accelerating skips. Seven, maybe eight. The taste of her was still on his tongue.

A stone looped high over his head and plunked in the water. Innis turned to see Father Lesperance on a drift log, rocking on his heels, his hands clasped innocently. Behind him stood another priest, dressed clerically, even Father Lesperance wore black, except for the small yellow feather in his stingy-brim hat.

"Innis, my man," he said. "What's new?"

"Not a lot, Father. I've finished."

The two priests looked back at the cottage, with its fresh white shingles, the blue-trimmed windows. "Brighter inside and out. It needed that light, yes. Innis, this is an old friend of mine, Father Swaydo. We're off to Antigonish, Father Swaydo and I, to visit a few brothers. We all went to school together."

"Hello, Father."

Father Swaydo stepped forward and shook Innis's hand. "How do you do, Innis." He was a thin, erect man, his blackrimmed glasses magnifying his eyes. From his black fedora to his black shoes he was all priest, but there was something about the cut of his coat, his trousers, that seemed out of date, from another time.

"Let's get out of the weather," Father Lesperance said. "I want to settle my account with you, Innis."

"There's no hurry, really."

"Odd, but I have a feeling that there is."

Innis led the way to the cottage, as if he were showing it for sale. Inside there was still a smell of paint.

"We'll all be comfortable here now," Father Lesperance said, clasping his hands together. "Gloomy, wasn't it? Before?"

"I didn't think so, Father. Maybe sometimes."

"I heard the Captain is coming down after all, later in the month maybe. Did you know? It'll clear up the mystery when he does."

"What mystery?"

Father Lesperance peered out the front window. "John J. MacKeigan has a key, he looks in every few weeks or so. The wheels have mud on them, John J. said. Well, I said, Captain MacQueen might very well have parked her in that condition. And John J. said, He very well might not, he's a fastidious man." He took Innis aside and spoke low to him. "It's a small place, St. Aubin, Innis. Lots of space, lots of separation, but still small. Keep that in mind, eh?"

"I have, Father. I know what you mean."

Father Swaydo had spotted the prie-dieu. "Ah," he said, and knelt carefully on the bench, pressing his palms together. "Do you put in a lot of time on this, Henri?"

Father Lesperance winked at Innis. "Don't pray yet, Richard. We have a Protestant in the room. We wouldn't want to give away any secrets, would we?"

"You can trust me, Father," Innis said.

"I have not the least doubt of that, Innis." He pulled out a white envelope from his coat and handed it to him. "I hope that will cover your work, for good work it was. Count it."

"No need to, Father. It's fine, whatever it is."

"Suit yourself. I might find other work for you, you know, later."

"Thanks, but I...I'm kind of winding down."

"Not leaving soon, I hope? Back to the States?"

Innis smiled and shrugged. "No, not back there."

"Well," Father Swaydo said, rising from the prie-dieu, "at least you don't have Pierre Elliott Trudeau back there."

"Oh come now, Richard, you old Tory," Father Lesperance said. "The man has charm, admit it. It's his wife, poor girl."

"Ah, yes. Her and the rock stars." Father Swaydo adjusted his glasses delicately to examine the painting of the Jesuit Martyr-Saints. "Henri, where on earth did you get this kitsch?"

"We like it, Innis and I. Kitsch isn't even relevant to what we like about it. Not so, Innis?"

"That's right, Father. There's a lot going on there, from the top to the bottom."

"Exactly. See, Richard? That's art. Now we're on our way. I won't say goodbye, Innis. I will see you again, I'm sure."

"Don't forget the key." Innis held it out to him.

"Listen, you hold onto it for now. Use this little house when you need to or want to. All right?"

Innis shook hands with them and walked them out to the road. Before getting inside the car, Father Swaydo picked up a stick and whirled it high toward the shore. "I'm better with a football," he said, straightening his hat brim. He waved as they drove off, Father Lesperance's muffler noisier than before. Innis envied them, off to see old friends. There was something about them he knew he could never have, never understand. He squeezed the key. There might be a night when he'd like to crash here, alone. But the Captain was coming back. What could you prove from muddy tires? Nothing. Still, Innis had been on this little road more than anyone else these last months, people knew that. The car was over there, it was waiting. The urge to be free of Starr felt almost maddening, but how could he leave the house, his plants in the ground, unharvested, unsold? And Claire.

He stood in the shelter of the front door and inhaled a roach, rocking on his heels until a gentle buzz put him on the wavelength of the rain, light and steady, the staccato drip from the eaves. Don't rush, Claire had told him that afternoon, it's a slow meal. She asked him to caress her lightly, to kiss slowly, to linger afterward until the air between their mouths grew hot. She showed him there were other places you could kiss, that lips were sweet wherever they touched, here and there too sweet to talk about. Wait, she said, sometimes waiting is even better than getting there.

What if Starr were gone, not here at all? Just Innis and Claire?

The question moved untethered in his mind, arriving from nowhere, going nowhere. "I'm just stoned," he whispered, "my heart is beating on my brain." He made a bowl with his hands, gathering rain and wiping it over his face. With a wince of guilt, he remembered what Dan Rory had given him after the Gaelic service, the framed quotation from Isaiah, handing it to him as he got out of the car. For your wall, he said. Just that, nothing more. Innis had hidden it away in his dresser. How could he hang that among his drawings? He was not religious. It would seem as phony as if he'd hung a crucifix there. Nevertheless he liked the words and sometimes he took it out and read them. *And the Lord shall guide thee continually, and satisfy thy soul in drought, and make fat thy bones: and thou shalt be like a watered garden, and like a spring of water, whose waters fail not.*

A FEW DAYS later Innis hitched out to the TransCanada where thumbing a ride would be easy in the tourist traffic, and the August weather had turned fair. A couple on their honeymoon, from upstate New York, gave him a lift in their station wagon, thinking him a local, and he did nothing to disabuse them, muting his accent as much as he could, and what would a college professor and his much younger wife know about how locals talked anyway? They'd never been here before and had just pulled out of the motel at the intersection, so for a mile or so there was a high view of the strait, calm as stone this time of the morning, and of the mountain west almost to Red Head and east clear to the Cape. The new wife, whose dark-rimmed glasses could not hide her pretty green eyes, had been to Norway and said it reminded her a bit of a fjord along here, but her husband disagreed amiably.

"Not high enough," he said, "or deep enough, I suspect."

"It's deep on the other side of this island," Innis said, "Nine hundred feet."

"Really?" the man said. "Well."

Then they hit a dull stretch of island highway, ragged woods as far as you could see on either side, they didn't make you want to wander through them. Innis handed them information freely whether it was accurate or not, enjoying their confidence in him and his status as a local.

"Yes, I was born down that road near your motel. My great grandfather was a pioneer." A term he had never used before. He knew it was true, but the word had always conjured up Western movies, it didn't seem to fit here somehow. The woman asked him if he had any favorite spots up north in The Highlands and he nearly blurted out that he'd never been up in The Highlands but he caught himself. "Ingonish is terrific, great beach." Then he told her he was going into town to get a birthday gift for an older cousin. "What do you think would be good, what would she like?"

"What do you mean by older," the woman said, smiling, "fifty?"

"Maybe thirty-eight, I never asked her."

"Perfume?"

"She's not much for perfume."

"A piece of jewellry could be nice," the woman said, glancing back at him from her seat. "What is she like?"

"Yeah," Innis said. "I thought maybe earrings. She looks great in earrings."

HE WALKED THE main street in The Mines, realizing quickly he should have gone on to North Sydney, to the mall, the store fronts here were depressing. The jeweller's window featured watches and rings and the dim interior didn't seem to offer much. Innis had never shopped for something like this. He wanted to spend money on it, it had been a long time since he had a packet of bills in his pocket, but it had to be unusual, this gift. Not just any earrings would do. Maybe there'd be something at the North Sydney mall, but he hated it, the people milling around there like it was the only thing in their lives, the bingo games going on in the big hallway, all those old folks hunched over cards, cigarettes burning down in their ashtrays. He passed an old guy he'd seen before, when he'd been here with Starr, "How're ya t'day, buddy?" the man said, they always spoke on the street, the older fellas, more than a few of them had a limp or a stoop, they walked like some part of them had broken way back, a hiss of pain through their teeth, but they were friendly. Only one coal mine was operating anymore, it ran miles out underneath the sea. When he came abreast of Starr's shop across the street, he saw that his uncle was not there today, the sign on the door hung lopsided. That foolish plant in the window. Jesus, was it dead, nearly a fossil. Come on, Starr, just a tumbler of water once in awhile. Why did he even bother with a Closed sign? Everything about it said closed, said I might be back tomorrow or never. A car went by honking at two girls outside the drugstore, drivers honked a lot here, hailed people on the street with their horns. The girls were looking him over from across the street. Younger than him, but maybe on an earlier day he would have crossed over to them and said, What's happening? Know where there's some fun in this town? He might have, if they seemed hip at all, asked where he could score some weed. But not today, not anymore.

The stores ended and he walked on toward the shore road that led to North Sydney, passing old miners' cottages, the only ones left on this street, a section of small rowhouses. At the curve where he planned to hitchhike there was a sign at the roadside pointing in the other direction down a north road: JUNE BUG ANTIQUES: ONE QUARTER MILE BUT WORTH THE WHILE. The day was hot, hotter here than in St. Aubin, but the sea behind the houses was blue and fresh. Innis turned down toward the shop, curious, he'd never been in one, just heard Claire refer to things she'd bought in them when she had her own house. His mother had always scorned antiques, Oh Lord, stuff my dad would've burned they want five hundred dollars for.

The shop, whose wooden sign featured a royal-blue beetle, was in a made-over front porch, enclosed with windows, and when his entry tinkled a bell above the door, a blond woman stood up from behind her counter. "Hi how are you?" she said, "I dropped my lighter. I'm trying to quit." She waggled a long thin cigarette. "Four a day, that's all I'm allowing myself. But this is my third, and what is it, noon?"

"About that."

"You go ahead and look around. Shout if you need me."

There was no theme to the objects arranged on every surface in the room and Innis liked that, lamps impossibly ornate, glassware that caught the window light, blues and greens, china on an oak table with big claw feet, a ship's lantern hanging from the ceiling. Smaller items Innis picked up carefully, turning them over in his hands, wondering what they were. A butter mold. Sheep shears. A moustache cup. A pair of opera glasses. A salt cellar, crystal, Ireland, the sticker said, and a crystal pitcher. A coal scuttle from England, brass and embossed with a ploughing scene, a pair of fireplace bellows, horse brasses, a spinning wheel made of fine wood, like his grandmother's in the attic, a crockery churn, a Victrola with a horn, framed photographs of Cape Breton, black-and-whites the photographers had hand-colored, Margaree Valley, Cape North, Loch Lomond, places he had not been.

"What's this?" He held up a pronged instrument.

"They used to spear eels with that, maybe still do. You ever eat eels? I like them myself, if they're fresh."

There was a commode set, pitcher and basin and toothbrush vase, in yellow roses, but not quite as good as what he had in his room, even with its hairline cracks. Whisky jugs in wicker. A big wooden bread bowl that looked home-made too, like the weaving shuttle of hard, worn wood. A huge copper boiling pot had seen hard use over a fire. A Scottish dirk with a jewelled pommel. "That came out of an old house," she said, "not far from here. Full of things from the old country."

"My uncle has a few antiques," Innis said, "but we sit on them and eat off them, so I guess he wouldn't sell. His kitchen table might be worth a buck or two. My grand-father made it. Rock maple."

"I wouldn't doubt it. Nova Scotia furniture. Carloads trucked off to the States after the War. They'd come up from Boston or someplace and just go door to door in the coun-try. What do you want for that old bureau there? Lamps, commodes, spinning wheels, buy it up for a song. Five or ten dollars cash was a lot of money then, out in the country." She pointed to his belt. "You're interested in militaria?"

"This was given to me. I like that gun though."

He held up a long rifle whose tag said circa 1850, it had a ramrod and touches of brass and an oiled stock. But what he fell in love with was a navy telescope covered in worn brown leather. He extended its four brass parts and aimed it out into the afternoon: the Atlantic was perking up in the wind, the foreshortened waves carrying sun on their backs. A seagull out of focus blurred past. Whitecaps huddled and leapt. The woman watched him as he put it to his eye sev-eral times in different directions. "That's English," she said, "I got that from a retired captain, saltwater, he picked up a lot of things in England." The tag said a hundred and fifty dollars, so he set it down. "Do you have earrings?"

"Over here." Her jewellry was arrayed in a glass case be-neath her counter. She began to lay pairs of them on the top, telling him what they were and what she liked, some of them had been hers, "I bought them for myself," she said, "I've got dozens of them, I can never get enough jewellry, if it's something I like. These are malachite and silver. Elegant, eh? Victorian." She dangled them at her earlobes and smiled, she had light blue eyes shaded with mischief, and she was older than Claire.

"I don't think they'd suit her, she's sort of dark, like, well, a Greek or Italian. Except her eyes, you wouldn't see them on anybody else, blue as ink."

"She tall?"

"She is. A long neck. It's beautiful. Can I say that about a neck?"

"Absolutely. How about these, with her black hair?" She tinkled them like bells. "Navajo." Discs bigger than silver dollars, with moons of turquoise, silver beads. "I bought them in New Mexico maybe twelve years ago. My boyfriend thought I was nuts. That's one reason he isn't my boyfriend anymore."

"How much?"

"Oh, gee. I'd have to ask a hundred. Less than I paid. But I can see you like them."

"Not just any woman would look good in them."

"Me, for instance. Listen, I can tell you like that telescope, you handle it like its your own. You can have that and the earrings for two hundred, if that's in your line of sight."

"Hey, I'm fat." He smiled and patted his breastpocket. "Great. Thanks. I need something for an old guy too. I'll look around just a bit more."

He wanted to blow every bill in his pocket right here, go out the door broke with a sack full of these old things, he loved them. He turned over a set of black rosary beads, fine for Father Lesperance, but it was Dan Rory he was buying for, something. A pipe. He fingered its carved bowl, deep ruby wood, the head of a stag whose antlers flowed back like hair, joined to the stem. Innis took it to the counter.

"Strange, isn't it?" she said. "Somebody brought that over from the Highlands, so they tell me."

"I know a man who might like it."

"Ten dollars?"

"Thanks, fine. And this, for my uncle. He'd get a kick out of it. I think." He handed her a Lucite cigarette holder, a nude woman in a classical pose.

"1930s. You can have it, it's yours. I hope your uncle's not religious."

"Not that I can tell."

ON SUNDAY MORNING, Innis squatted in the sand and studied the plant, amazed by its seeming harmlessness, swaying softly, a good five feet now, its flower heads resembling the Queen Anne's lace in the upper fields. He supposed any part of it was death, so he pulled on work gloves before he gripped the stalk and yanked it out by the roots. As he plucked the leaves and dropped them into a paper bag, he could feel his heart rising. He found he was holding his breath, as if he might inhale the vapor of its juices, and by the time he'd sliced the stalks into short pieces, leaving only the flowers scattered in the sand, his hands were trembling so hard he had to laugh. Jesus, this wasn't nitroglycerin, it wasn't going to scorch his face. He shucked the gloves and closed them inside the bag, then washed his knife in the shallows. The waves were small, falling lazily ashore, the wind east and a little chilly, smelling of salt. Salt water would clean the blade. The skiff lay hull up in the sand. He'd had a scare thrown into him, he had to admit, but he would row again, when he was ready. Now he had other things on his mind. Near the shorebank he stopped to inspect a dead bird, but it was only curved, burnt wood, its charcoal glistening like the feathers of a crow, sometimes they woke him early, their morning noises, crawking, jittering, mewing on the roof.

In the toolshed, with the heel of a hammer handle he carefully crushed roots and pieces of stalk in a crockery bowl, working them, along with leaves, into a pulp. Twisting that in cheesecloth, he squeezed out small amounts of juice into a jelly jar. Claire was in Sydney to see a friend about a job—this time Starr did not object—and Starr was at the shop, but Innis kept an ear out for their cars. He wouldn't want to explain this little project to either of them, pleased though he was with the success of his extractions, a touch of the scientist about it. How many people up and down this road knew what water hemlock could do? He held the bottle up to the window over the tool bench, tilting the liquid in the glass: not a lot, but if the taste on a peashooter could kill you, this portion could do it in spades. Greyish-green, it looked harmless as spit. He screwed the cap down tight. Indians in South America tipped their arrows with poison, something from a plant. Not the sort of work for a Sunday morning maybe, but a man had to move when the spirit was upon him. He'd wanted to see if he could do it—capture that lethal sap. It was sort of like hunting, wasn't it, but better since he'd never want to bring an animal down. He took the leavings in the paper bag he'd soaked with kerosene, to the edge of the woods and watched them burn to ash. Then he returned to the toolshed and hid the jar in the loft where no one would come upon it.

Last night Starr had been in a good mood after supper because Claire fried him marrachain and potatoes. And while he was drinking his tea Innis reached across the table and set the cigarette holder by his plate.

"What's this?"

"Stick your Exports in it. Smoke through a holder, Starr, it's better for your health."

But he'd known immediately he should have given it to him without Claire at the table. Without her, they might've joked it away.

Starr held it up to the light, turned it round. "I couldn't smoke a cig in this. They'd think I was a fairy."

"Not a chance, Starr," Claire said.

"It's just a naked woman," Innis said.

"No such thing as just a naked woman." Starr handed it back to him. "You know that as well as me."

NOT LONG AFTER noon he heard Claire's car but he waited where he was. She leaned in the door of the toolshed, a bright sun behind her.

"You're not in the house much lately," she said. "Have you eaten?"

"Not hungry." His axe was in the vise and he gave the blade a few listless rasps with a file. "Starr will be, though."

"We have to get on with each other, all of us, Innis."

"I get on with you. Isn't that good enough?" He smiled.

"Don't be saucy. Listen, I'd like to go over to the Gaelic Mod. I've never been, and Starr hasn't been for years he said. It's a lovely afternoon. We can all go together."

"No, you guys go."

She stepped inside and pulled his face close to hers. "It's Sunday. Together. That means you too."

"I have a present for you."

"What's the occasion? It's not my birthday, it's not anything."

When she saw him take the earrings from under a newspaper, she frowned, but she stood still as he hooked them into her pierced lobes, delicately, as if he were threading a needle. He stepped back.

"Innis, they're lovely but I can't take them. Jewelry like this is expensive. Please."

"Turn your head a little, slowly. Far out. They had your name on them, Claire."

"You need your money, Innis. Please don't spend it on me."

"You have to take them, Claire. They're a gift."

"I have no choice. Is that it?"

"That's it."

"I'll wear them until Starr shows up. Better that he doesn't see them."

"I don't care if he does."

She kissed him. "It wouldn't be worth the aggravation, now would it? Let's keep things calm until..."

"Until what?"

"I don't know yet, Innis. Do you?"

He didn't want to answer and so they walked out into the lower field, in the strong sun the silver earrings flashed against her hair, her skin, the turquoise like flowers, and he thought she had never looked more beautiful, the golden-rod higher than the hay, it was like pausing in a river with her, in currents of windswept grass, the trees thrashed with sound, flowing and subsiding. The strait was deep blue between woods and the dark mountain, waves on the water like quick strokes of chalk. He was about to ask her to walk to the shore with him when he heard the Lada grinding down the driveway. Claire said nothing, but before she turned she slipped the earrings off and pushed them into the pocket of her jeans.

"I'll ask him about the Mod," she said.

Innis squinted past her at his uncle climbing out of the car, looking over at them, cupping a cigarette to his mouth.

"That grove of old hemlocks, in the lower woods. I was hoping we'd go back there."

"You want to draw me in those trees again? This wouldn't be the day for it."

"Is there going to be a day?"

He watched her make her way back through the field, combing the heads of goldenrod as she went. They were both watching her, he and Starr, but each other too as she moved between them, and Innis would have to give her up to him for another afternoon, another day, another night. He remembered that first afternoon when she meant nothing to him but a woman in a wide-brimmed hat, kissing his uncle, but she did not kiss him now, she did not linger in his embrace, and after talking briefly they went into the house, Claire waving to Innis, motioning him home.

Innis moved deeper into the field, skirting that grassy depression in the ground marking the only time the spring had gone dry, the well Starr dug drunk, angry, coming home from the navy, they had to lug pails up from the brook, and he told his father, Dig a decent well, for Christ's sake, why are we still without water in the house? And he'd grabbed a mattock and a shovel and started digging, right here in the field, he still had his uniform on, and it didn't take longer than this shallow bowl in the soil for the rum to burn up the energy he had left in him after a long ride on a train, civilian freedom driving him again and again to put that bottle to his mouth, to pass it around, to sing, to lean over the seat of a pretty woman coming home to Cape Breton too and tell her all the bullshit things he was going to do, and then finally he'd stood up there at the mailbox, here he was, home, and everything looked the same down to every detail just as it had the day he left. I would've dug that well to China that afternoon, he'd told Innis, just desperate to get away and I don't even know why. It had me again, home, I wouldn't leave, couldn't leave, I knew that. But how? Innis had said, troubled that there might be something in this place that could shortcircuit your own will. How? Starr said. I can't explain it, it's just there. But Innis didn't believe that anymore, he could feel his departure gathering inside him, not clear and exact, not day, means, destination, not written down and paid for, but there.

On his way back to the house he stumbled and pitched forward into the grass. Jesus, the scythe Starr had used weeks ago, just cast it down here and left it, the blade rusting away, an ugly cut waiting for someone. To hell with it, let it stay here, let Starr search it out when he's in his haying time again.

19

"You think they'd let me in this college, Starr?" Innis said.

"Not if I was running it." They stood in a hot sun on the grounds of the Gaelic College waiting for Claire to come out of the gift shop. The mown green was flanked by neat log structures local men had built before the War. Bagpipes wailed in and out of song, down a hill, out of sight, but a girl in Highland dress seemed to be tuning up in the center of the green. "It's not a real college anyway. Some minister's notion, back in the thirties. He figured we weren't keeping our heritage alive so he got this going. Oh he was Scotch all right, from the old country, but he couldn't even say pass the bread in Gaelic. This is all it came to after a while. Summertime classes, piping and dancing, kids mostly, some Gaelic tossed in. Good Scotch fiddling here now and then, our music, I'll show up for that."

"That fiddler at the dance we went to, he ever play over here?"

"He's dead."

"You're kidding."

"I went to his wake. If it wasn't him, it was somebody who damn well looked like him."

"Why didn't you tell me?"

"You? Now what would I tell you for?"

"I was there, I saw him at the dance."

"That night's cut into your memory, has it? But it wasn't the fiddler, was it. It's not his tunes you're calling up."

Innis tightened his jaw and concentrated on the girl piper who was fixing her lips primly on the chanter. She pumped the bag full and wailed and Innis had to smile at the martial shrill of her pipes, her frilled blouse, her earnest slender fingers, the way the pleats fell neatly along the curve of her butt. Tourists who'd emerged from a bus milled around her briefly and moved on. Innis watched her foot, tapping time, too soft to hear, not like those shoes at the Gaelic church service, beating time under the pews to something he could feel and remember but not explain. She sounded a little rough around the edges and he guessed you couldn't get away with a lot of that on the pipes, not without somebody killing you. Maybe the tourist geeks made her nervous. Pretty knees, what he could see of them between the stockings and the hem of her kilt, her fingers doing a slow dance on the chanter, hugging air under her arm. A long braid down her back, and those fine pleats. He'd draw her if he had his pad. He'd done a sketch of the fiddler too, from memory, but he wouldn't tell Starr that, not now, not anymore.

"Maybe I should move out," he said suddenly.

"Sooner the better."

Innis didn't want to answer, his heart was in his tongue, it had just popped out of him, he wanted to tell Starr, Listen, I'll be out of this place sooner than you think, I got buds coming in up on the hill, they'll be big as your fingers in a while, sweet as roses. He could see his uncle drawing hard on his cigarette, the cords in his neck flexing. There seemed no way for them to talk anymore without it whirling down to that night, that beach, and they always seemed to pull back just before crashing. Dangerous swimming in the Great Bras D'Eau at night, currents there can sweep you out to sea, Starr would say out of nowhere, a walking hard-on is one thing, but a swimming hard-on, now that's a danger to navigation. The weeks had only inflamed his suspicions, far from fading them out: what he hadn't seen was more powerful than what he had. In those early months with his uncle, Innis had joked with him, shared humor with him, it had made things bearable, they'd listened to *Dr. Bandolo's Pandemonium Medicine Show* on the CBC, though Innis found the skits funnier than Starr did. If you knew what a man laughed at, you knew something about him. It troubled Innis more that things had gone sour between them than if they'd had a solemn relationship from the beginning: the bitterness felt deeper, even dangerous. To become so serious and unpredictable, to fear something you can't kid about anymore, that hurt, that put you on edge. Just talking made them feint like boxers.

"Maybe I was kidding," Innis said.

"Maybe you weren't."

He did not want Starr to kick him out. He did not want to be ordered away from the house. Stronger than the memory of the fiddler who'd died so fast, he remembered the immigration officer who had escorted him into the plane at Logan Airport: they had to board first, with cripples in wheelchairs, the man took him straight to his seat and watched him as he fumbled with the seat belt, stood there until he was settled into that seat and staring out a misty porthole at the ground crew manhandling luggage, and then the agent waited beside the stewardess at the forward door while she greeted passengers, his eyes never leaving Innis, as if Innis might, before takeoff, burst out the emergency door and flee into the back streets of Boston, miles away. The guy had told him while they were waiting in the airport lounge, Innis's face stuck in a magazine, that Innis would have had an Immigration officer on either side of him if he were dangerous, a dangerous criminal. There'd be two of us, one for each arm, he'd said. And we'd take you all the way into Halifax, the airline wouldn't accept you otherwise, we'd all fly together. Innis had said, turning a page, Sorry I spoiled it for you guys, a free trip to Halifax, gee. The man looked at him sideways. The Mounties already know about you over there. They know about you at Immigration Canada. There'll be a lookout posted when you land, he'll watch for you. When you get to where you're going, the Mounties will have a little talk with you probably. You're on a list at the border crossings, every one. Cross at the Yukon, won't matter. You're a known man, Mr. Corbett, but I wouldn't be proud of it. The officer did not leave his post until they were ready to close the door, he stepped out of the plane at the last minute, a final, sealing glance at Innis. The stewardess was polite, gave Innis her smile, but she and the others had him in their eyes, he knew that, and he'd wished just then he was dangerous as hell, manacled, all suppressed fury, wedged between two burly INS. Barrier for life, the man had reminded him while they were killing time. I hope you like it up there, he said, don't expect it to be Boston, they don't even have a baseball team. At Halifax an official had plucked him out of the line and he had to prove himself a citizen of Canada, the birth certificate his mother had dug out, registered Sydney, Nova Scotia. Then they let him go. He could've gone west just as well as east, all of Canada was out there, rolling away, endless, and nowhere in that direction would he be a known man.

"There's Claire," Innis said. His peripheral vision had caught her immediately, those white shorts and long brown legs, her red sandals. Her hair wonderfully black, a lush flower. "We should let her enjoy herself."

Starr flicked his cigarette into the grass. "Who's stopping her, me?"

"Not yet. We only just got here."

Starr said nothing but reached into his pants pocket and pulled out a wad of paper. He opened his hand long enough to show Innis, then slowly stuffed it away as Claire came up to them smiling. She pulled out of a bag a doll in Highland dress, bonnet to brogues. "For my little neice in Toronto. Cute, eh?"

"Is it male or female?" Starr said. "Hard to tell from here."

"A little man, I think," she said. "It won't matter to her and it doesn't to me."

"It would matter to our Innis here. He likes those things correct, in the drawing of them, I mean. Not so, Innis? Well, good fiddling this afternoon, they tell me, and there's a man who would appreciate it." Starr moved off through the tour bus crowd fanning out over the grounds.

"He's strung pretty tight today," Claire said, watching him shake hands with a man who seemed to be breezily observing the fresh visitors.

"Rum," Innis said. "Under the car seat." He thought about the wad of white paper in his uncle's hand. "He say anything to you?"

"About what?"

"I don't know. Me and you."

"Nothing we haven't heard before. He has an imagination, your uncle does, and it's on overtime. Most of it he keeps to himself."

"Good. I guess."

"I have other things to do, so I'm seeing him less." She shaded her eyes: Starr and his friend were heading toward the trees. "Less and less."

Innis felt the sun and Claire beside him and he wanted to put his arm around her waist, naturally, easily, pull her close to him and walk off with her, nuzzle her face if he felt like it, kiss her discreetly so as not to rile anyone with public display, his lips sliding lightly across her ear, her neck. There was an ache in him to have her in his arms.

"That sounds rather grand," Claire said, pointing to The Great Hall of the Clans. "Let's have a look. Starr seems to have disappeared."

Inside the new log building, in the dusky lighting of the corridor, Claire strolled from one exhibit to the next, peering through the glass, scanning the commentary beneath them. Innis hung back, caught up in the charts and the histories, his eyes roaming over the maps and along the arrows of a long wall display that flowed from Ireland up into the west of Scotland, the Hebrides and the coast. Dalriadic Scots. "I didn't know they came from Ireland," he said out loud, but Claire was too far down the hallway. He moved along the major clans and their histories, stopping to study the Campbells, liking, for the moment, the idea of being linked to their powerful lineage, to a name famous in the Highlands, if not always nobly. There was a chief, kilt blown against his thighs, his face to the wind. Innis wanted a couple tokes to get into it, the spirit of it, but no chance here. A museum, people shuffling along the hall, talking low. He came upon a Highland male in a glass case. The dummy was done up in kilt and sporran and buccaneer shirt, bonnet, wool hose, a knife in one cuff, a *sgian dubh*, the plaque said. The pane was smeared with fingerprints but Innis kept his distance and gave it a hard study. Maybe a secondhand mannequin did not make the best Highlander, its arms arrested in a half-wit pose neither menace nor alarm, a senseless gesture where nothing terrible had occurred, no howling enemies had rushed him with murderous eyes. On one awkward arm had been affixed a targe, a round leather shield, but towels or neckties could have hung there just as easily, the other arm holding a sword aloft like a tennis racquet, the warrior gazing blandly from beneath his feathered bonnet: if there had ever been a fierceness in this dress, it was lost in the stunned, khaki eyes of the dummy. Might be better if they just hung the clothes in there, forget about the mannequin.

"Lift that kilt, you wouldn't see much," someone behind him said. "All smooth there, like a doll."

Innis laughed. It was an old guy, a local by his accent, still in his church necktie, his dark coat slung over his arm, his silver hair carefully parted and slicked down.

"The kilt doesn't quite hang right on him, does it?" Innis said, stepping back, tilting his head.

"He's got no arse, that's why. And too much knee there, for a laddie. You ever wear one of those?"

"Me? No. You?

"I don't play in a pipe band and I wasn't in the army. My dad got Gaelic from his mother's milk, but you wouldn't get him in a rig like that."

"I saw older people in kilts out on the grounds there. Not students, are they?" Innis said.

"Och, no. They're for this Gathering of the Clans thing, they're mostly from away, you know. They travel around and get dressed up from one do to another, you can see the stickers on their cars. It's them that got those booths set up out there with the names of clans on them. You find your clan and they have brochures and bits of paraphernalia. I'm a MacLachlan myself. 'These Are Your People,' the sign says on the MacLachlan booth. No, they're not, I says to myself. Never set eyes on them. My people were in church with me this morning. They don't care about castles."

They drifted along together toward a portrait of Bonnie Prince Charlie and Innis read that this was the Stuart Pretender who had rallied his supporters toward the disasterous battle on Culloden Moor, the deathknell of the clan system.

"Some think him a hero but he's no hero of mine," the man said. "A lot of romantic foolishness fixed to that name. At Culloden he was worthless. He was half-Polish besides."

"Says here he inspired a lot of songs and stuff."

"Songs are fine, but they're not history. People don't want the facts. He came from France and he went back to France. That's where he grew up." He nodded at the effigy of the Highland Woman. "I think I've seen enough. I'm getting cranky in my old age anyway, so my wife tells me. Good day to you, sir."

"See you around."

The Highland Woman was arrayed in a long tartan skirt and white blouse with a sash of matching tartan—the correct garb, the text pointed out, not the short kilt, the *philibeag*, the kind the men wore. Claire should be down at the beach, this kind of afternoon, lying in the warm sand, and he with her. Then it came slowly into his mind, his face flared, his heart swelled as he stared at the painted flesh behind the glass: that ball of paper, he knew what it was, he had not a moment's doubt but it was the drawing he had done of Claire, in the grove of fine old hemlocks, their trunks like columns, under their warm open shade he'd said, Could I draw you, would you let me draw you nude here? Now? He'd liked the sound of "nude," it had a ring to it. You already did, Innis. Weeks ago. But from memory, Innis said, I made you up, it's not the same. Nevertheless, Claire said, it looked convincing. Innis already had his sketchpad on his knee. One sketch. For my eyes only, he said. She was darker by that part of summer, her skin was like creamy coffee where her swimsuit had covered her on the beach. Posing her, Innis touched her shoulder lightly as if he had never touched her before. His head had felt light and threatened to start him trembling, but the soft scratch of his pencil calmed him: he would, though he'd never been to art school where women modelled naked every day, draw this woman coolly, capture that something about her more desirable than any woman he wanted to imagine. That slight smile, her graceful limbs against the hemlock bark, it was more than sexual, he knew that and felt that, he couldn't say what it was, but it had kept him drawing until the breeze died and he watched Claire pull her clothes on quickly, shooing mosquitoes from her face. And now that study of her, of her in that afternoon—and him, every line and shading of it was himself too—was crushed into a ball in Starr's pocket.

He located Claire circling a tall wooden figure of Angus MacAskill, the Cape Breton Giant. "Look at the pictures of him," she said. "He's handsome, but this is a cartoon."

Innis smiled and shrugged. He couldn't think, he felt hollowed out. He stared at The Giant's belongings, the enormous boots, the waistcoat that could envelope two men, the walking stick as tall as a staff. Starr must have gone through his things, he'd hidden his bigger sketchpad underneath the mattress. Starr had no right to do that, none.

"Innis?"

"You almost done with this place? It's stuffy."

"You go ahead, I'll meet you."

"Where?"

"Oh...in that tea shop at the entrance. Will that do?"

"For what?"

She touched his face. "For now."

Outside, the sun struck him, dazed him, but he sat on the warm dry grass of the green. His plants would thrive on this heat, there had to be buds by now. He had to go up in the higher woods and see, he'd hung around down below lately whenever he could, nearer Claire when she was around, the water. Jesus, he had to get up there. Soon.

He felt a shadow over him and squinted up at his uncle. They regarded each other as if there were no one else around. Innis got up slowly so he, half a head taller, could look Starr in the face.

"That's my room upstairs," he said.

"Is it?"

"I don't want you digging through my stuff."

"You got nothing to dig through. You should be more careful when you strip your sheets. Things pop out." There was rum on his breath and the man he'd been talking to earlier, a florid man with thin sandy hair, came up behind him laughing.

"Jesus, Starr, the clans are massing, b'y. You going to march or fight?"

"What? Ah, Joe! With that crew? I couldn't keep a straight face. Let's you and me march to those trees and have a snapper, eh?"

"Let's have a gander at these characters first, all that kilted folk from hither and yon. This your nephew is it? Pleased to meet you, b'y!"

"Hi, Joe. Innis."

"How's business, Starr?"

"All but boards over the windows, Joe. I don't give a damn if every TV in the world goes up in smoke tomorrow."

"That's a terrible thing to say, Starr. What would we do with ourselves?"

Pipes had struck up, an annoucement came over loudspeakers that a march of the clans was assembling. Clansmen kilted and otherwise were lining up on the hill leading toward the ampitheatre.

"This is the International Gathering of the Clans?" Starr said, amused.

"I guess the word didn't get around," Joe said. He pulled a flask hidden behind his belt and gave it a buss. "Internationally, like."

"You should be up there, Starr," Innis said, "a Gaelic speaker like you."

"Find me one kiltie up there that speaks Gaelic and I'll kiss him."

"Bit thin in the ranks, the whole bunch," Joe said. "Must've been a bad year for cattle raiding. Keep an eye peeled for MacIvors. Seen any milling about?"

"They don't have a booth, Joe."

"Ah, well, Jesus, what a shame. I'd've dragged in a few of my own, if I'd known they were scarce. My cousin Murdena, she can't get enough of the old country falderol. Loves the aristocrats, oh Jesus, truck in some chief or duke or somebody in his knobby knees to cut ribbons and, God, she's off. Clippings on the wall."

"The same crowd that sent us over here in the first place, for Christ's sake, and here we are kissing their arse."

Two pipers led the procession, a motley parade of men and women, some in various interpretations and portions of Highland dress, some in streetclothes, but all solemnly out of step. Clan banners rose here and there in the ranks. One young man wore running shoes with his kilt, another a T-shirt that said UNIVERSITY OF NORTH CAROLINA. The tourists lining the route looked unsure. Where was the big band of pipers and drummers all dressed in uniforms? An old man in full regalia came sweeping along, huge in a bloused shirt and shoulder plaid, kilt swinging, he could have stepped out of a painting in the Great Hall, one of the chiefs on a mountain pass, flowing white hair under his bonnet, long beard, planting a big staff in the ground with each exaggerated stride and a serious squint ahead of him.

"A Scotchman, by God," Starr said.

"A right old actor, he is," Joe said. "Straight from the movies."

"Jesus, he could be your chief, Joe. Where's your chief?"

"We left him way back in the fog, b'y, the mists of the ages. He got nothing to do with me anyhow. Say, is it too early for a drink, Starr?"

"No, and it isn't too late either. Car or trees?"

"Too hot in the car, and the trees are so handy like. You coming, Innis?"

"He's a pure young man," Starr said. "Forget him."

Innis watched them go off to the woods behind the buildings, Joe's arm around his uncle. Thanks, Joe, keep him there awhile, will you?

The Tea Room featured Scottish fare—tea and scones and shortbread—but hadn't forgotten the motor homes and cars parked in the lot. Innis bought a Coke and two bags of chips and sat at an empty table. Tartan clan plaques shaped identically like coats of arms were displayed along the wall, too neat and uniform somehow, but Innis studied them as he downed his Coke. Two children, brother and sister, hot and bored, fidgeted at the table next to him, their parents preoccupied in a whispered, tight-lipped disagreement. But the corner table caught his eye, a middle-aged man and woman lounged imperiously in their Highland gear. Innis had seen them climb out of a big van with New York plates, decals in the rear window from Highland occasions they'd hit all over North America—Stone Mountain, Grandfather Mountain, Santa Rosa—and they were chalking up another one here, though they seemed aloof, above the mere civilians around them, people who possibly were not even of Highland descent. The man, his balmoral cocked on his ear, had a lean, wizened face, and the bearing of his sharp chin seemed to express some notion of breeding which his dress was meant to declare, but a pair of mirrored aviator sunglasses, slightly askew on his nose, marred the effect. His wife, skirted in tartan, sipped her iced tea and nibbled a scone and jam. They didn't talk. The man's attention seemed to be elsewhere, maybe in some glen, misty with the romance of his race. "What clan are you folks from?" Innis said as they got up to leave, gesturing with his Coke bottle at the shields on the wall. The man gazed down through his mirrored lenses. "Clan Snodgrass," he said curtly, his voice surprisingly deep for his wiry build, his wife adding as they turned away in a swirl of pleats, "Snodgrass of the Isles."

"Ah!" Starr, wearing his sunglasses, had suddenly appeared behind Innis's chair. "God bless you! Fine people, those Snodgrasses!" The couple didn't look back but kept on through the door while Starr addressed them, a little louder. "Distinguished themselves in the battle of Killie-Something-Or-Other, if I remember rightly. Not often you run into a Snodgrass, I mean of the Highland sort. We better get you into the Great Hall over there, seems you've been overlooked."

"Where's Joe?" Innis said. He was already missing his genial diversion.

Starr, after squaring up a chair with some difficulty, sat down. "They need a booth, those people. What's a clan without a booth? Where's Claire?"

"Said she'd meet us here."

"From where?"

"Last I saw of her she was checking out Giant Mac-Askill."

"Wouldn't she, though? Just like her. A major distraction, The Giant. Gets women thinking."

"Gets you thinking."

"Ah. Miss Claire. Miss Claire doesn't think along those lines, eh?"

"Not the way you do."

"You're a lily-white pair, the two of you. My, my." Starr lit a cigarette and blew out the first drag in a long sigh. "You an expert now on what Claire's thinking?"

"She's lived with us for how many months. I ought to know something about her."

"Something?" Starr leaned back in his chair, smoking, staring at Innis. The other tables were empty now. "The question in my mind is, should you know this!" His hand disappeared under the table and he brought it up and fired the ball of paper at Innis's face, hitting his closed eye but it stung, flared red when Innis opened it, and he was on his feet fast, he shoved his uncle in the face, staggered him, they both yelled something Innis would not remember, but he would remember the speed, how fast they came together, Innis's heart shaking, he hardly knew what he was doing, he was taller than Starr, he'd never felt so strong in his life, he'd sawed those goddamn dead trees up with a bucksaw but Starr had an instinct Innis couldn't find in himself, a punch stunned him, not its force as much as its surprise, it was quick and on the mark, and Innis, hurt but jacked-up, swung wide and caught Starr off the side of his chin, then danced back, shocked, hot, ready for damage, words, for the pushing and shoving of the fights he was used to. Starr hit him three times—yes, it was three, later he could count each one—fast, in the face. Innis shouted, blood in his nose, flailing, overwhelming Starr but not hurting him, and they bounced off tables, the wall, crazy with anger, they clawed their shirts, ripped them, scratching, digging, but Innis knew he'd already lost whatever it was, the fight, the chance to push Starr back and get some room with Claire, to save something he needed to save. They hit the floor in a desperate and raging hug, and then Starr released him suddenly and rolled away, Innis flopped on his back, tasting blood, gagging it up. Somebody tossed him a wet kitchen towel and he sat up and pressed it to his face, his lips stung, his nose was throbbing. He'd got it in the ribs too, a chair, something wooden, maybe Starr's fist, Christ, his fist was all bone. He could hear the manager or someone above him shouting about the Mounties as he set the table back on its legs. Innis grabbed the wad of paper, got to his feet and pushed through a family jammed in the doorway like on-lookers at an auto wreck. Starr was over at the Lada, staring at the road and smoking. The parking lot was filling with cars, sun broke from a windshield with an aching flash. Innis arched his head back, pinched his nostrils. He felt people staring, he hated that more than the hurt. He was patting his mouth for blood when he saw Claire coming to-ward him, but she stopped far enough away so that her con-nection to him would not be apparent, and when he tried to smile, wiping his nose on his sleeve, she turned back into the crowd.

20

The morning was cool, rain trailing from the eaves of the toolshed. At the bench under dusty window light, Innis spread his hand across the wrinkled sheet of paper over and over, but the figure remained grotesque, he couldn't smooth his uncle's fist from it, his own sweat smudged the pencilled lines. Finally he folded it carefully twice and pushed it into his back pocket. He wiped his eyes quickly, angrily. Two days ago, that Sunday, Claire had gone off in her car, she didn't say much except that she'd be in Sydney for a bit. Starr did nothing to dissuade her, just smoked at the kitchen table, but after she was on the road, Innis saw him out in the back field, waist-deep in fading goldenrod, his head thrown back like a runner getting breath.

In his rain jumper, an apple in his pocket, Innis went out into the grey, drizzly morning, kicking moisture from a patch of browntop. He paused by the little garden, lusty weeds now, underneath them the reds and yellows of her sturdy nasturtiums. He plucked one for luck, stuck it in a buttonhole.

He had hoped he'd get sun for this trek to the upper woods, that he'd be able to see the resin glinting in buds, in collas even. He didn't need any gear, there'd been enough rain and the fertilizing was long over. Later, when he harvested...but how much later was there? Only weeks ago he would have done anything crazy just to break up his life, but now with Claire not in the house, everything seemed fragile, suspended. He did not know what to do, she'd left no address, no phone number. Not seeing her every day, hearing her pass his door, knowing that there would be chances, if he was vigilant, when he could embrace her for a few seconds in the hall. But she would be back. Most of her belongings were still in her bedroom, she had not left: she did care about him, or she would not have talked with him the way she did. No, she had never said she loved him, but if they had a stretch of time alone, without the threat of Starr, a string of days together, travelling....

A day of stillness, hushed in soft rain. Even the poplar leaves were soaked and still. The rain soothed his sore mouth, hood back he opened his face to it. Moisture brightened the foliage, all shadings of green reflected light, inclined ferns in one direction like long feathers. Under trees leaves twitched, jumped, a riff of drops tapping. Water rose quietly in hollows, ruts, hoof tracks, the depressions of stone, spongy sod sucked at his boots. Woods and water, weirdly powerful.

With a noise like fleeing birds, wind gusted through wet alders and was gone. He ran the fight back through his mind, touched its sharp edges. Somewhere in himself he had known it would happen, he might have been eager for it, but yet it was all surprise, humbling. After he'd stopped his nose bleeding, Innis got into the Lada, telling Starr, You better find Claire, she isn't happy about this. By the time Starr returned to the car without her, Innis had the blood off him and passersby weren't eyeing him anymore. Starr said, I can't find her, I'll come back and not one word more about her, you want me to take you to a doctor? Fuck, no, you sucker punched me anyway, Innis said, and that got a grim smile out of his uncle but he looked tired, spent, the rum had burned away in a flash point. Jesus, he'd said as the Lada was grinding up the mountain in the slow lane, this'll light up the switchboard in St. Aubin, probably has already, phones ringing off the hook. Do you give a shit? Innis said, I don't. His uncle did not reply until they had passed over the summit and could see the green girders of the St. Aubin bridge below, the strait an afternoon blue east to the sea. I'll survive talk, he said, I always have. But it's over for us, Innis. Innis didn't ask exactly who he meant by us, he didn't care. In the kitchen Starr had cracked open a tray of ice and Innis wrapped cubes in a dish towel and went upstairs to rest it on his swollen mouth. The room was hot and close and he rolled the ice back and forth on his skin. He dozed until he heard Claire's voice rising downstairs, Starr's muted and curt. When she passed Innis's closed door, he tensed: whatever she had to say, she could chew him out, fine, but not now, him here like this on his back. He jammed the ice pack under his pillow and listened to her opening drawers in her room. Suddenly she'd tapped on his door and pushed it ajar.

"Don't get up." She took his hand and held it gently. "Looks like you could use a few boxing lessons."

"We flared up. That's all." He wanted her to sit on the bed where he could touch her. "It's over."

"Over? I wish I could believe it."

"Where did you get to?"

"I ran into Russ at The Mod. I knew he'd drop me off if I asked."

"I thought he'd more likely drop you off the bridge."

"Russ, he moves on, he gets over it. He has another woman anyway." Her eyes skimmed over his drawings on the wall. "I'm going to Sydney for a few days, Innis."

"Days? Why?" He raised himself up on his elbows.

"I need to get away for a little. I'll stay with a girlfriend there. Be back midweek or so."

"Or so?" He noticed an overnight bag in the hallway. That wouldn't hold much, she'd had two suitcases when she arrived. "Listen, Claire. I'll patch things up with Starr. You and me, we don't have to stay here much longer anyway, neither of us. Do we...?"

"It's looking that way." She touched his face, his tender nose, his chin, the brass belt buckle.

"You checking my parts?" Innis said. "Don't stop now."

"You seem to be all here, all in one piece." She kissed his bruised lips so softly it frightened him. "See you."

"Claire?" She picked up her bag in the hall. "You wouldn't leave without me, without telling me, would you? I mean *leave*?"

She smiled and pushed her hair back from her face, that beautiful hair, it broke his heart to see her hand run through it. He hadn't noticed the dark green hat in her hand, a velvety felt. She placed it firmly on her head, tugging down the wide floppy brim.

"Without you?" she said. "No, Innis."

He wheeled off the bed but had to catch himself, his ribs hurt, and he'd sat there doubled over, breathing fast, listening to her car go up the driveway, hesitate at the top, recede down the road. He flopped in his chair, his head back. Then Starr was in the doorway, frowning at him.

"You going to live?" he said.

"I don't think I can handle that right now, Uncle Starr."

"Hit first, and hit hard. Remember that."

"Yeah, I will. Especially when you're around."

"You hungry? I'll scramble some eggs."

"I'm cool. That was a shitty thing to do, rifle my stuff."

"It was lying under your bed. Was I supposed to pretend I didn't see it?"

"It was just a drawing, Starr."

"Don't say such a stupid thing. I don't want to hear any more of that."

His uncle lit a cigarette, squatted in the doorway. He took a deep drag, and another. Through smoke he stared at the floor. "We're better off without her."

"Speak for yourself, Starr."

Starr squinted up at him, nodding slowly. "It was you I was thinking of."

INNIS CROSSED THE power line corridor, thickly grown by now, boggy water in the grassy ruts the lineworker's half-track had made, soft rushes spiking up, tough shrubs of sheep's laurel blooming, poison, lambkill, and the alders seeding out, and further up the last lavender bits of fire-weed's splendor, he'd picked her a bunch when it first appeared within the old stones of a foundation, some old burned structure, and she was pleased even though they hardly lasted the afternoon, some flowers don't take to picking, she said. The ferns, their green freshened with beads of rain, had lost the vanilla smell that rose from underneath them on the hot days of July. But there were still surprises, the swab of mustard yellow on a dead birch trunk, as soft and brilliant as fresh paint, maybe a strange fungus, and tiny brown mushrooms had sprinkled up under spruce bows, maybe they were magic, he'd heard they grew here, but he didn't need hallucinations.

His jeans were soaked to the knees as he turned up

higher, leaving the ridge of springs, *fuaranach* Dan Rory called them, the water all along this hill, several miles of it. He left the path, disoriented briefly by the shimmering light the rain made, without shadows everything stood out brightly, but he pushed on into the thin maples, his clearing just beyond them, finding that he was oddly nervous, an excitement in his chest that was not pleasurable and he stopped where he was, wiping his face, trying to slow his breath. He unzipped his jumper, fumes of sweaty rubber. The red nasturtium had dropped from his shirt somewhere. He listened to foliage shedding rain, staccato plinks and splats beneath the trees. A few more steps took him to the edge of the clearing and he stopped. A shot of fear hit him first: not one of his plants was visible. He thought police, Mounties, they've raided, born them away for evidence, but that yielded quickly to a sickening hollowness as he stumbled into the open. They were all there, he counted out loud, his voice shaking. One by one they'd been cut off at the base and flung about, viciously it seemed, leaves torn, stripped. Not the work of an animal, not four-legged, nothing eaten or chewed, it was sheer human destruction. He held a limp stalk: the flower top between his thumb and finger was just beginning to form, there'd been promise in these tops, but they were mashed, this deed had been done a while ago, long enough to wither the leaves. The resin was ruined. Trashed.

He sat on the ground, his face to the sky. The rain resumed, gentle, steady, and he caught it on his tongue, swallowing. But this was a thirst he could not slake.

Aware that the seat of his pants was wet, he got to his feet and crisscrossed the clearing, parting the taller grasses, the clumps of spruce. Could be foot marks pressed into the sod, but hard to be certain if shoe or hoof had flattened the grass, or just the weight of rain. He sheltered against the trunk of an old birch, hunched and shivering, cupped enough fire to light a tiny roach. It wasn't even cold really but the trembling ran through his body as he sucked the sharp smoke, bit it off in his tight lips until the ember burned them. Fuck, this was just about the last of it anyway, and there lay his plants. Slaughtered, that was the only word for it. He thought wildly of gathering them up, maybe cooking them, he'd read about that in the book, something about butter, but shit, how would he do it, in his uncle's kitchen? And who'd pay money for butter with pot in it, he didn't even want to eat it himself, he wanted smoke in his pocket, the feel of rolling it in paper between his fingers, fire, the quick high that could, sometimes, make things interesting again. He took the apple from his pocket and bit into it, ate it slowly down, and as his eyes followed the tossed core, they caught the sheen of cellophane, wadded green paper on moss. Cigarette packet. He opened it out, sniffed the tobacco shreds. Exports. Unfiltered. Navy Cut.

He made his way down through the trees, staggering, dazed, as if the woods were strange again, his feet clumsy on the terrain, city feet, sidewalk feet. At the break he turned west, he hadn't been west since March, since he'd brought the pine tree down. The power lines swooped overhead, trailing droplets in the still air. He walked on, through vigorous alders, across a narrow brook where he thought a fish skittered out of sight. He only wanted to keep moving through the high scrub, motion was what he needed now, the illusion that he was under way. A drizzle resumed, fogging the air, and he hardly realized he was near where the winter spring had been, leafed-out trees obscuring it, maples and ash. It was there off to the left in the hill. Moss marked the mouth of the small dark cavern, you could miss it easily, and he knew that close to it he would hear that tiny echo, water ticking faintly out of rock. But he didn't stop, he walked a full circle around it, hoping he might find some track of the lynx as he had in the winter, then he turned down toward the pines, their long needles lush with moisture. The one he'd felled lay out dark and thinning amid their green, its greying branches still holding needles, the stump top black. He tried to pry loose a piece of sap but it had hardened. He almost expected Finlay to appear, but this time he would hear him, and after all, the deed was long since done, they were friends, Innis had nothing to lie about now, nothing to hide. Jesus.

When Innis came out of the woods into the MacRitchie field, someone in a black sou'wester stood at the far end of the path like he'd been waiting for him. Innis paused when the man waved a stick in the air, then he went on: it was Dan Rory. He had never thought of him as part of the sea but of course they'd all had boats in the old days, men on this island, they'd all known them.

"On your long walk again, are you?" Dan Rory said. His sou'wester was shiny with rain. Sweet smoke rose from his stag head pipe.

"You going in a boat?"

"Old barn leaks. I move things around in there, when there's a new one. Were you up at our old spring?"

"I didn't drink. I went round it."

"But you didn't go round it sunwise. Och, you're free to take that water, it's wonderful water there."

"I took it once, in the winter."

"I know. But you'll be thirstier now."

"Is there fish in the brooks up above?"

"Used to be trout there but I don't think so anymore. Did you catch one?"

"Saw one, I think."

"Almost as good. Come inside out of the rain, man, you're looking weary."

"I have some things to do, Dan Rory. Do you know if Captain MacQueen is back yet? I'd heard he was coming."

"Wanted to meet the Captain, did you?"

"I thought he might have some work, is all. Around the house."

"I suppose he might. He's mostly recovered, from the surgery. Heart. They put a thing in his chest so it fires on all cylinders. He likes it here, he likes coming back home. Any day now, I suppose, we'll see him. You're right drenched, stop for a little."

"I can't today. I'm sorry."

Dan Rory looked into his face. "You're too young to be hurrying like this. Is it a woman that's got you pale and your lips thin?"

"I'll be okay, when I get going."

"You afraid? I'll tell you what an old man is afraid of. It's that first time a stranger comes in to look after you, when they look around at your life and are already thinking how they'll bring it into line with theirs, what of you is to be kept or tossed away, what they'll let you do and not do. I wish I could shut it all out, close a door."

"Finlay's still here."

"He could go before me. He's not young. His teeth are whistling. Well, you go do what you have to do, Innis. I'll leave you with this much, kinship will withstand the rocks. *Ge fad an duan ruigear a cheann.*"

MIDWEEK PASSED AND she wasn't back, and by Saturday Innis was missing her badly, already worked up over his plants. Not the same without her in the house: just Starr and himself, dangling like two bare wires waiting to touch. She'd lightened so many weekends, even when all Innis could do was listen to her getting dressed and watch her leave with Starr, an excitement trailed behind her, and he'd known he would see her again, hear her voice. Now it was Sunday and he had yet to tell her what had happened up in the woods. That was all that was holding him together now, that soon he could tell her, as he had told her about his plants that winter afternoon in the barn. This was a setback he was afraid to absorb alone, he was only talking to himself about Starr and what he said was disturbing. They hadn't exchanged a dozen sentences, he and Starr, since Innis came down from the woods. Without Claire, there seemed to be no next step, only a sliding backward.

Sunday afternoon he walked aimlessly through the lower field, buffeted by a sun-driven wind parting the russet grass flaxen, like the coat of a dog. Goldfinches were fading to green, goldenrod to brown, but blue asters were out and at the edge of the brook nightshade was in flower, its blooms intricate as jewellry, yellow stamens in indigo. He should call his mother, how long had it been? Months? She had gotten through on that old phone system one Sunday but sounded as if she were under water, an urgency to her voice that Innis didn't want to hear, he'd have rather she scolded him than ask him question after question, all with a fearful edge, Don't yell into the phone, Ma, he'd said, I can hear you, I'm not an immigrant. You calling underneath Boston Harbor or where? Don't be wise, she said, there's ten people listening at least. Starr said you had plans for leaving, when? Where you going from there? I've got cousins in Truro, on the mainland, they might help you find work, it's a fair-sized town, and Halifax isn't that far. Are you broke, do you have money? I have enough, Ma, I don't need much money to get out of here. She said, Are you angry with me still? It's not fair if you are, Innis, it isn't. No, Ma, I'm not, not with you. Okay? This isn't a telephone we're on, you know, it's a radio station, I'll call you in a while. Put Starr on, I love you, you know. I want to say hello to him.

Hello, Starr. Uncle. What in hell drew you up there to that very spot, that little clearing of mine? What harm was it to you or anybody else? You could have walked on by, cost you nothing. Innis lay back in the grass, spreading his arms and legs like a snow angel. He fixed his gaze on the peak of a spruce tree: clusters of small cones, resin clear as raindrops. Every time he breathed he took in Claire, every shift in the wind. The sun lay over him, the high white clouds complicated and cool and rushing. Hay and sweat, and all its fine gradations. A tinge of red in that maple, in a leaf that had been distinctly green, when? Last week? Yesterday? Starr, passing through the kitchen, had said that he had seen geese the evening before, not the soaring arrowed formations of fall but early flocks, ragtag and scattered, nervous about the season. Then he got in the Lada and left, returning after dark.

Innis circled his way back through the grass, through a tangle of wild roses, all hips and thorns now, and stood staring up the driveway, its gravel rutted with summer mud. Wind whipped the weeds along its edges, crackled in the unpruned branches of the cherry tree. Across the road white birches swayed against the dark spruce. White woods. Black woods. The futility of his waiting, of his vigil, was suddenly everywhere he looked. Why hadn't he seen it? He rushed for the house, past Starr in the kitchen and on upstairs to the open door of her room. He didn't have to go inside, didn't need to look any deeper into the half-closed drawers. Hangers and someone's old coat hung in the open closet. God, when had she been here, when had she packed her things and carried her things to the car? Or had Starr carried them for her? It was not surprise that hit him, that dipped his heart like a sudden fall: he had almost expected to see what he was seeing. The hurt was entirely new, bitter, an exhilarating mix of love and affront and despair, beyond his controlling. The telephone shrilled from the kitchen and he counted the rings. Another house.

Starr sat facing the west window, the kitchen table

cleared and clean, its scarred maple surface warm with afternoon sun. Placed neatly near his hand were a small glass
of rum and a tumbler of water, casting streaks of light on
the wood. He didn't acknowledge Innis but kept his eyes
narrowed as if he was looking a long distance, at the strait,
the mountain. His chin had the shine of a fresh razor and
his shirt was so white Innis blinked.

"I knew it was you right away," Innis said from the hall
doorway. "How did I know, even before I found that empty
packet of fags?"

"What did you think?" Starr said evenly, almost wearily.
"That I don't have eyes, ears? That I never walked in my
own woods anymore? Maybe you wanted it to be me. Eh?
All right, goddamnit, I obliged you. Worse could have
happened."

"Not much worse. Claire is gone, isn't she?"

"I was supposed to keep her around here for you? Christ,
get some sense into you before it's too late. I don't need a
woman here anymore. Find your own, one with fewer years
on her, and you'll be better off."

"What the hell did you say to her?"

"I'll tell you one thing, I told her if she wants to strip for
randy young men half her age, there's plenty of them in
Sydney, she doesn't have to do it here."

"In Sydney where? Where is she?"

"She's left the Island, she's gone."

"I don't believe you, Starr."

"Who else you going to believe?"

"I'll find her. You won't be around to fuck it up when
I do."

"Be my guest, b'y. She's got a wicked head start on you,
more ways than one. You've got the time, and the money,
eh? You flying, by the way, or taking the train? You could
go by car, see the sights. And there's always the bus."

"You bastard, I would've had money. I'd've been okay. More than okay."

Starr looked at him calmly, then resumed his gaze at the back field. "If you mean what I think, I'd see you sent to Dorchester first. You brought that shit here. Take it away with you."

"Nothing to take. It's worthless. You don't know anything about it, any side of it."

"Tell me what I'm missing."

"It wouldn't save you anyhow. You're past whatever it could do for you."

"Did great things for you, didn't it." Starr lifted the rum to his lips, set the glass down. He raised the tumbler of water into the slant of sun and peered through it, rays on his face. "You better get a move on," he said. "Maybe she's waiting somewhere."

"When I'm ready to go, I'll go."

Innis waited for his uncle to say you'd better go now, I want you out of here, but he said nothing more and Innis went up to his room and closed the door. A whimper of rage swelled up in him, his eyes teared. He wouldn't do a damn thing tonight, he wouldn't take one step toward getting out of here, nothing, he didn't even know where she was, where she was travelling to. But then he was tugging tacks from the corners of his drawings, letting them flutter underfoot. He pulled out the suitcase from under the bed and flopped it open, his dad's, black pebbly old-fashioned leather from another time, it had embarrassed him at the airport, lugging it like hand-me-down clothes. Smuggled whisky, shattered on a baggage cart, had stained the paisley lining, Cost me a customs fine, his dad had said. Just looking at it made Innis feel helpless and he left it empty and picked up the limestone rock from his dresser. He ran his fingers slowly over its sculpted curves and hollows, he had seen just the tip of this rock in the lower brook and he'd pulled it out of the mud, its buried curves revealed themselves, shadings of grey, light, dark. The skull of the eight-point buck, a spiderweb spun on the antlers, he'd have to leave it, like the stone, behind. Starr was wrong about that, the skull had not frightened her at all. What I want you to do, she said here on his bed, after the boat and the squall and the bluebead lily, after the taste of rum, I want you to dance your tongue, slowly, from my lips to my toes, around and around, everywhere, anywhere, even behind my knee, yes, that's a lovely spot, whatever excites me chances are will excite you. I want you to cover me with you.

Why didn't she wait for him before she left, talk to him? Leave him a note, a number? Starr might have told her anything. Anything.

He dug out his stash box and scraped from it every bit of dust and leaf that remained, from which he rolled, with conscious ceremony, one last joint, to be set aside, now was not the time for its sweet distractions.

The framed Isaiah? He liked the old man, so he would take it, there might be a room, in some city, some town, where he would want to hang it.

He gathered his drawings from the floor and laid them in the suitcase, the sketchpads on top, there was a little history in those pages he wanted to save, there would be a better time than this and he would go through them leaf by leaf, woods, fields, shore, ice, snow, people. Claire. Even his uncle. What had he failed to see in Starr, what clues were there that he would come into the woods the way he did, deep, off the beaten paths? Or that he was saving one rotten deed for the end of summer? Innis pulled out the pencil drawing he'd done of him and studied it: if that bit of meanness was there in his face, he had missed it. He balled the paper up and flung it at the wall.

21

His uncle had not returned by dark. Innis hoped Starr would be gone for the night, wherever he took himself now that he never answered the phone.

Innis did not dare hitch a ride down Ferry Road, he walked the whole long way as he had the time he took the Caddy out for a dry run, leaping off the roadside at the first glow of headlights. But this was a Sunday night, more than usual traffic from the cottages at The Head. He'd get a stretch where he could cover some ground before cars showed up, some at such rates of speed the ditch was safer than the shoulder. Only two kinds of Cape Breton drivers, his dad said years ago, go like a scalded cat or a cow with a calf in her. The houses he passed were far apart, set back a long way in fields or trees, but if one was nearer the road with lights in the windows, Innis crossed to the other side. One here and there he'd worked in, like Mrs. Melchuk's, an elderly widow, her father came from the Ukraine, Innis had cleared her snow, repaired her sagging steps, her eave spouts ripped by frost, she fed him meat pastries in her steamy kitchen, he'd love one right now, she liked to talk about her husband, a steelworker in Sydney for years and years, and this little yellow house in the country they were to enjoy when he retired but he died of silicosis. The MacLeod house with its wide white verandah, bought by Americans as a summer place where last fall Starr got Innis hired on a re-modelling crew because the contractor was a friend, but Innis quit after a few days, the men asked too many questions, What're you up here for, b'y, no work in Boston? and Starr, disgusted, said, What the hell did you expect with an accent like yours? Sure they're going to ask questions. There was Reverend MacLennan's place, a huge old house he couldn't get the bats out of, a retired minister, he hated them with a passion that made his big blue eyes widen when he talked about them, and Innis had waited one night in his yard, the minister standing behind him, watching bats stream out of the attic gable, startling gusts of them in the moonlight, and to pass the time he told Rev. MacLennan about the anthropologist he'd heard on the radio who'd eaten bat soup in Maylasia, tiny bones in it that crunched in your teeth, and the Reverend made an awful sound in the back of his throat, Look at them, look at the little devils, he said, shuddering, they scratch in the walls at night, horrible, and Innis went into the attic and plugged every gable opening he could find while the minister waved a flashlight under him, Hurry, hurry up before they get back. But there was no moon tonight.

He trotted down Wharf Road breathing hard until he saw that both houses were dark, the priest's, the Captain's, but he circled MacQueen's quietly, what if the old guy was inside and sleeping? He banged on the front door. No light, nothing, so he slipped under the house, last time for this funky hole, in through the hatch. He could tell someone had been here cleaning up, maybe MacKeigan getting things ready for the Captain, a smell of Lysol, and the curtains had been spread wide, but Innis didn't need a flashlight anymore, he slid through the house like a cat burglar. The ship's clock chimed and brought him up short, he'd not heard that before, and he froze until it stopped. Seven bells, whatever that was. The keys however were not in the mug and he went through the whole cupboard, Christ, who moved them? that was the Captain's hiding place. There was not time to search elsewhere, he had to get out of here, could he hot-wire it? But in the garage when he opened the Caddy's door, the dome light lit: battery already installed, keys in the ignition, dangling, ready. Sorry, Captain. It's only a loan, no one will take better care of it.

Driving back, only three cars passed him from the other direction, he drove at a sensible speed, if the car was seen they'd say, Well now, I didn't know the Captain was down, but there he was on the road last night, couldn't wait to get into that nice Cadillac, no. Innis's plan was to pull down behind the toolshed long enough to fetch his suitcase and get away, hit the mainland before sunrise, but shit, the Lada was parked at an odd angle in the lower driveway. Damn you, Starr. He idled on the shoulder, his eyes at the rear-view mirror, where in hell could he hide this now? He buzzed the window down. Car coming around the curve behind him, he could hear it, and as he started off again he remembered the old logging road on the MacLeod property, long unused, could a Caddy get up there? He was afraid he couldn't spot it fast enough in the dark but he saw a culvert and he turned and crossed it, headlights meeting the thick weeds, he gunned the engine, the car fishtailing, skidding in and out of the old ruts, the lights of another car zipped past in the door mirror, Innis hoped the guy hadn't seen him. He worked the Cadillac just beyond a turn, alders and young spruce and willow bushes raking the undercarriage, he couldn't take it further than this, he'd get hung up. Lights off, engine. He leaned his head on the seat back. What time was it? The dashboard clock was screwy, must be getting on for midnight. Crickets, no longer shrill, resumed their muted, fading notes. The nights were colder. Later, he could back down without the engine, ease her onto the road when it was clear.

INNIS WALKED AS casually as he could down the long driveway. Seaward in the east, clouds were rising rapidly into a starless sky. There was one lighted window upstairs but the rest were dark, the fields as black as the woods. Starr was silhouetted in the door of the toolshed, a bottle of rum sitting on the bench under the dirty lightbulb. Innis turned past him toward the house.

"Where the hell you been on foot?" his uncle said.

"I don't drive. Remember? And I don't have to answer any questions."

"A man has to answer somebody's, sooner or later." Starr flicked his cigarette into the darkness. "I thought you were in your room. You left the light on."

"It isn't my room."

"Funny, I could've sworn I saw you there, oh, the last few months or so. Well, *fàgaidh sìoda is sròl is sgàrlaid gun teine an fhàrdach.*"

"Save it, Starr, whatever it means."

"Silk and satin and scarlet, b'y, they leave a fireless, cheerless hearth. Claire called."

"She did?" Innis came nearer his uncle.

"She didn't." Starr showed his teeth in a slow smile. "I just wanted to see the look on your face, Innis. Move into the light a little better, yes, you look like a puppy. Hoping for a pet, a little bone."

Innis's fist flew out before he even thought and sent his uncle sprawling into the toolshed, clawing the air. Innis took a fighting stance, breathing hard, fists cocked, he didn't care, but Starr sat on the floor looking out at him. He touched his chin, pushed it side to side, then laughed quietly, shaking his head. "Go on," he said. "Get away out of here."

His uncle did not come in from the toolshed and Innis paced in his room praying the man would crash. His hands were shaking as he spread them out before him. Funny what hands could do, what they could take hold of, let loose. Claire. Here. Once. He flopped back on the bed, but soon sat up. No, no sleeping here anymore. He raised the hall window a few inches, he could hear Starr growling to himself but couldn't see him, he'd finish that damn bottle before he quit. Innis would never get past him to the Caddy now, not with a suitcase. He pulled out dresser drawers in case he'd missed anything that belonged to him. There was the jar in the toolshed loft but that would have to wait. He poured water from the pitcher into the bowl and soaked his hand. His knuckles hurt, but it was hurt he could live with. Puppy? Jesus. I'll give him a bone. He dozed in the chair. Claire was in his mind when he woke, he thought he was in Claire's bedroom, where was she? Not here. Sick or well. The phone rang out, repeated, he lost the count. They were after someone else, too late to call this house anyway. He took his telescope from the dresser top and aimed it out the hall window: toolshed light still burning. Had Starr passed out? Trees were hissing with wind. Mountain was indiscernible from sky until slowly tumbling clouds turned livid with lightning. Thunder rumbled in the soles of his feet. He directed his telescope at the strait: above the thrashing tree-tops dim whitecaps raced by in darkness. Soft explosions of light. Christ, a nightmare, out there in a boat. The storm broke over the house as he was thinking could he slip past his uncle, past everything, but water was pelting the windows like gravel, and then in his head the tension of lightning, a sizzling blue beyond the barn, this was how he would remember it, a brightness bearable only for the second it took to strike, any longer and it was the light of madness. The lapse between flash and thunder grew shorter until they ripped the sky almost at once. Suddenly a pitchfork flash caught Starr, like a photo negative, leaping a puddle, making for the back door. The lights went out quietly, a pylon had been hit somewhere. Innis drew back from the window, slammed it shut and stood behind the closed door of his room. Soon his uncle came clumsily up the stairs, stumbling, pausing, his footsteps lost in a long erratic break of thunder. "She'd be here!" he shouted outside Innis's door, "if it wasn't for you!" then slammed it with his fist. Innis's heart surged, what bullshit, what lies, he tried to shout back but only a croak came from his throat, he wanted to yank the door open but they would only tear into each other, things that had to be said could never be said. Lightning snapped close by, throwing the deer skull into absurd shadow. Trembling, he raised his walking stick like a club, he felt he could kill or be killed now, at this moment, this very spot.

Innis didn't move. He heard nothing further from his uncle, only rain shifting across the roof as the storm spilled away into eruptions of distant thunder and fading light. He opened the door slowly, but Starr was not there, nor in the hallway. Still grasping the stick, he found him flung across his unmade bed, a snore mashed beneath his face.

The house was still dark when Innis stopped in the toolshed long enough for a good toke, and then climbed the wooden ladder to the loft, descending with the small jar in his fist. In some mean city he might need it.

He took up his suitcase and started up the driveway in the rain, disguised under the hood of his jumper. Streetlamp out, nobody driving, but they'd have to wonder about him this late at night, hunkered in their headlights, hauling an old gladstone bag. He wheeled around and walked backward for a few steps to take in the darkened house, the barn. Where was the excitement of leaving, the rush? Too much excitement, the wrong kind. Maybe on the highway, an accelerator under his foot, it would hit him.

When he reached the Cadillac the rain had quit, there were rifts in the clouds, whitened by a moon somewhere. He dropped his suitcase in the trunk, struck by how odd it looked under the lid light. With the trunk closed, there was just the darkness again and himself. He was thirsty. How far to the spring from here? Couldn't be a long hike. He found a dim flashlight under the seat and pushed off up the hill, slipping in rut mud, he was tired, there were deadfalls to climb over, the rough hair of lichen in his hands, dead bark, he'd never been this route and the line break was further off than he'd thought. He rested, saving the flashlight, but the dark seemed to fall in on him so quickly, dizzying him, he forced himself ahead into an alder thicket, a smothering maze of thin branches. Crashing through on the edge of panic, he was breathing too hard, but he was in the open, in the break. The power line rose up overhead. Between this pylon and the next, just above the break, was the spring. Somewhere along here in the wet grassy sod he had found purple-fringed orchids and picked them for Claire, he could smell their faint scent now if he tried, she'd put them in a slim vase of clear glass.

That grey little hut, not easy to pick out with weak batteries, he missed a landmark and backtracked. But there it was, the wooden peg in its doorlatch. He knelt to the door, the peg was jammed tight and he had to work at it, his fingers cold, clumsy. Flashlight flared off the water when he opened the door, spiders trembled in their webs, sorry, fellas, tearing up your hard work, I know how you feel. He angled the beam into the still water, down to the quiet silt of the bottom. Then he put his mouth to the cold surface and drank, it hurt his teeth and he quit, his lips numb. With his head hunched just inside the shelter, out of the dripping trees, he put a match to the roach, toked deeply and nipped it out. He pulled back into the darkness. Maybe another squall moving in, above him long sighs of wind showered moisture from needles and leaves. I don't know the Gaelic for car thief, Starr said many months ago, don't make me learn it. The Cadillac, so long hidden, a treasure in a box. Maybe they could have left together, he and Claire. Maybe she would still be here, if. If something. Innis rocked gently on his haunches. A lynx swims like a dog, he had read, and if a foe awaits him at the shore, a lynx will not turn away, but land and fight to the death. Rivers are women, oceans are men. Somewhere he'd heard that and wanted to believe it, it sounded wise and balanced and true, but he still didn't know what it meant. Claire liked blouses in plain but striking colors, with dramatic collars. How clear that was to him now. She would never come back, not here. Suddenly, his heart beating wildly, he tilted the jar over the water, held it at the verge of spilling, heard the liquid hit with scarcely a sound. He snatched up the flashlight and clicked it again and again, he wanted to see the water but it wouldn't light and he smashed it on a stone. He threw the jar into the trees, then pegged the door fiercely tight, pressing his forehead hard against the wood.

His legs were shaking as he started down the hill. Jesus, only a little, in all that water, what could it do? Maybe trembling was how poison kicked in, then what? A hot shaking flash, your whole body coming undone, muscles, bones, vessels, cells, every thin little thread you breathed and moved with, all shorting out, every bit of wire burning, a smell on your tongue, black bile searing your voice so you couldn't cry for help, and who would come anyway, who would hear you melting away while this stuff coursed in your blood like fire, killing every microscopic thing it met there, putting out every light? Would your mind go first, or last? Details rose at him vividly, indulgently, moaning, gagging, convulsions, a chalkwhite face, a hideous swollen tongue, guts churning. But these visions had their own life, they were not attached to anyone, not yet, not even his uncle, and the rain began again, washing them from his mind, it was not easy going, he stumbled hard into a water-filled rut, soaked to his knees. In the back seat he struggled out of his wet boots and socks and jeans. If he left now, by daylight he could be well off the Island, by noon maybe out of the Maritimes altogether. Just a few minutes rest on this soft leather. He hadn't been this whacked since that first week in Dan Rory's woods, yet what had he done but hike to the spring and back. Claire's skin, how unbelievably smooth it was, how soothing to think of it.

When he woke, uncomprehending, his head thrown back on the seat, his mouth gaping and dry, everything around him was so strange that for a few seconds he only moved his eyes. Too much grey light in the steamy windows. The first sound was not rain but the claws of a crow on the roof, and as Innis sat up, it flapped away, cawing to its raucous mates in the trees. Jesus, daylight! The wet glare of woods, the sun was already burning behind that lowering sky. He could see up ahead his ragged path of last night, the stomped weeds disappearing now in white mist. He hopped in his bare feet to the trunk and dug out dry jeans and socks, his feet were freezing. Damn it, he'd lost the night, let it get away. Shivering in his undershorts he pissed into the cold grass. The Caddy looked abandoned, they did that to old cars here, drove them up in the woods and walked away, but the Caddy was new, out of place. A chainsaw was snarling up above somewhere, much too near.

He dressed quickly, letting the engine warm up as he backed slowly down, playing the brakes, gritting his teeth at the sounds underneath the floorboards as the car combed back over crushed saplings and brush, skidding, scraping, but gravity got him to the shoulder where he stopped, and after a quick look each way, he backed out onto the Ferry Road and turned, for what he was sure would be the last time, toward the main highway.

The Seville took the road smoothly and he let out his breath, he had to settle down. Raining again, that was in his favor, in rain a car passes and people, huddled inward, might glance up, someone might even say, Wasn't that Captain MacQueen's car? But they wouldn't be sure, the pavement slicked with light, the hiss of tire mist swirling off a black car already gone by, well Jesus, John, was it his, you think?

No, no, it couldn't be, not Moneybags's, the man's in Florida still. Let them talk, let them get on the phone and speculate, that could take up a good part of the day, there were other Cadillacs on the TransCanada, he'd be off Cape Breton Island in a couple hours, and by the time they determined the Captain had not arrived, Innis could be in New Brunswick, the car on a side street in St. John or someplace, another few days before anyone would know it was ditched. At the TransCanada intersection, he waited for three cars and a truck to pass, revving the engine, checking the rear-view mirror. They were barrelling all right, the traffic was sparse. He turned west, descending the long curve toward the strait, he was in the flow, ahead of him the elegant arches of the bridge. He didn't need the radio yet, only motion, flight. The rain had let up but still flew from the metal of the car, like the stormy light off the strait as he levelled out onto the bridge, smoothly, rocked suddenly by wind, girders slashing past the window and through them the waters of the strait turning west like a wide river, the surface all silky metal, disappearing beyond the point that hid Starr's cove, and lined by the wooded hills of St. Aubin on the side he was leaving behind, and by the high woods of the mountain ahead, and east out the passenger window the weather was rolling off the sea, dark, fast-moving clouds, the sun roiled in them like light in a school of fish. The causeway dipped into a level stretch of highway, past a trailer camp at the base, the bare brown cliff rising behind it where they'd blasted all the stone and fill for the bridge. He sized up two hitchikers as soon as he saw them though he didn't slacken speed, two young guys hunched and miserable under backpacks. Sorry, fellas, my nerves are tight. Not cool to give you a lift in the Captain's Cadillac, I'll lose my momentum, I want to wind up that mountain highway fast. And then he was pushing it upward, keeping speed, the tires screeching slightly as he cut into the first banked switchback where semis sometimes lost it downhill and careened off into roadside trees, he slipped into the outer lane and passed three cars up that long grade, he could feel the strait behind him, there was a motorhome parked in the lookoff, its passengers staring east toward the Atlantic, a wide dramatic view he couldn't glimpse from his direction, a postcard, he'd seen it in a drugstore. Another squall burst upon the road and he eased back, the curves were nicely banked but too easy to speed on. He tinkered with the electric seat, backing it a little, tilting it, until it held him just right, he was airborne, cresting the mountain, heading down, the silvered light of St. Ann's Bay north of him, tapping the brakes now and then, letting a car pass him, easy does it. Through the wiperwash he saw the Englishtown turnoff coming up, the ferry route across the mouth of St. Anne's Bay, but he wouldn't take that, not this day, he wasn't going north. If he did, he'd stand out on that small ferry, handing a quarter out the window to a crewman who'd have a great chance to remember him, just the sort of witness a Mountie would pump for information. Could you give me a few details of description, Mr. MacTavish? Oh, a ponytail of red hair he had, not real red, brownish, a sort of hawk nose in high bones, his face, the glass was a bit steamy.... Ahead on the roadside a girl, young woman, long skirt, a shoulder pack, and she turned her head calmly as he went by, smiled, not thumbing, as if walking in rain were just fine with her. Innis didn't hit the brakes hard, all taillights and skidding, but came to a controlled stop, gliding onto the shoulder until she was a blur in the rear window. In a Caddy, you just sat waiting, engine ticking over, you didn't back up. He was watching a car approaching in the side mirror, feeling suddenly conspicuous, when he heard a fingernail tapping glass. He buzzed down the passenger window and the opening framed her face, long light hair corkscrewed by rain, freckles across her nose, a pleasant face, tilting her head, smiling.

"You going down north by any chance?" she said. He was going west toward the Canso Causeway. But the Captain's garage doors were still closed and his Cadillac behind them so far as anybody would know, and here was a girl he didn't want to say no to.

"How far North?" Innis said.

"Ingonish, or thereabouts?" What would Ingonish cost him, an hour? It wasn't as if there was a radio alert out for him.

"I can take you a ways."

"Great. You could turn around and take the ferry, it's shorter."

"No, I'll go around the bay. Sometimes the ferry's a wait."

She brought into the humid interior of the car a refreshing current, like a cool spray of water, her cheekbones red, she'd been in the sun. A long madras skirt and a short buckskin jacket stained with rain. She set her pack on her lap.

"You soaked?" Innis said, waiting for a car to pass before he took off. "I'll turn on the heat."

"No, no. I just got dropped off a little way back."

The turn toward St. Anne's came up quickly, then they were off the TransCanada, passing a lobster restaurant.

"You hungry?" he said.

"Not for that place. I've got fruit. You want an apple?"

"Maybe later. I'm more thirsty than anything." He had no time to pull in there anyway, stare over coffee at the water of South Gut, a shivering smoothness after the squall, and just chat with her, talk of no consequence. She poked around in her pack and brought out a pop bottle, held it out to him uncapped.

"Water," she said. "Here."

His face went hot, he didn't look at her. "I'm okay," he said. She was talking to him but he only heard her voice. His breath was coming fast. They passed the Gaelic College, the road wound along the bay, down and up. The spring, their spring, his.

"Some bus you have here." She ran her fingers along the dash.

"It's not my car."

She laughed. "What's a cah? Are you Boston? Maine?"

"Boston. Visiting."

"You don't look like a tourist. Nova Scotia plates."

"You're not with the Mounties, are you?"

"Am I bugging you? Sorry."

"It's ... my Uncle Angus's. He can barely drive anymore, his eyes are bad."

"Angus who? Where from?"

"Oh Jesus, no family trees, okay? Please? A MacNab, that's all."

"Sure, fine." She muttered at her window, "Never heard of any Angus MacNab around here. Look at that pony in the rain! Poor little devil." On a hillside field a small shaggy Shetland, head bowed, its rump to the wind. An herbal smell seemed to rise from her clothing, and of damp leather. Was Starr up? Hungover, he'd be thirsty too, gulping water at the sink. Jesus. But it wouldn't have arrived yet, couldn't, not down that long hill.

"Going to see someone?" she said.

"Just driving."

"My mother, she's home with my aunt, and no men anymore, either of them. It's nice when you haven't been home for a while. It's all easy for a day or two, smiles and love and treats of meals I like. But then she takes a long look at me, with her eye cocked just so, stitching a tear in my skirt, say, a skirt she doesn't like on me anyway. She can't help it. She has it in her mind I'm a hippie and won't let go. I love it there, above the sea. I just can't stay home anymore, not for long."

"I want to get away too." Acts of moral turpitude, the immigration judge had said, a hardnosed Irishman, as an alien you get only one, Mr. Corbett, two at most, and then we send you home.

"From Boston? Live up here you mean?"

"Somewhere west, a long way from here. A real city."

"Boston not city enough? I loved it for a while, around Cambridge there, around the university. Down there most of a summer. Great music. Awful hot some days."

He braked for a sharp turn where the road went round a cove, his mind was drifting. He wanted to put mile after mile behind him as if nothing had happened, away so far he would never hear what turned out, not even in a newspaper. But his tongue lay bitter in his mouth. A car resembling a Mountie's flashed past in the other direction, he hadn't noticed it coming. He picked it up in the mirror and watched it disappear in the blowing rain.

"There was a bar there we liked," he said suddenly, "my buddy and me, it had a submarine torpedo game, you aimed torpedos at passing ships, slow ones to fast ones. All hand/ eye coordination, and we racked up scores, Ned and me, we were damn good at it. But a college kid came in one day and showed us how to beat the machine. He just held the trigger down and swung the sight from one side to the other real fast, he didn't even aim it. Free game after free game, he ruined it. It's easy, he said, don't let them rip you off. But he didn't get it. We played for the skill." He was just yammering, filling the air that sometimes felt too thin to breathe.

"College guys," she said. "There's plenty they don't know, but they don't know that either."

When they came out of a long valley and reached the east coast highway, Innis hesitated at the intersection. The Atlantic lay behind trees across the road. He wanted to inhale that rainy ocean light.

"When you're past Wreck Cove," she said, "there's a little cemetery. Could we stop? I wouldn't be long."

"That's a good bit north."

"Not as far as Ingonish."

"I'm in kind of a hurry. What's your name?"

"Jessie." She studied his face. "You're awful pale. You okay?"

Feeling a car behind him, he turned north with a squeal of rubber. "Me, I can do without cemeteries. What's there, relatives?"

"My dad's there but they had to wedge him in. Sure, it's relatives. Yourself must have a few around here, under stone."

The old spring was ringed with stones, he'd knelt against them. "Jessie, I have to be somewhere else, I don't have time for this place."

"Cape Breton you mean?"

"I mean here, now."

"What about your uncle?"

"What?"

"Angus, his car."

"What's the time, Jessie? How far do you live?"

"Not far."

A white church, he couldn't catch the name, see what saint was on the sign against the white shingles, sometimes it wasn't a saint but he preferred them, St. Margaret's, St. Joachim's, St. David's. The sea was distant through trees, then moved near the highway, a sudden broad grey, bringing gulls, throwing itself white over the rocks, reaching, falling back. It wasn't as if Starr was lying on the kitchen floor with a knife in his heart. One glass of water wouldn't harm him, he'd have to drink more than one. Wouldn't he? Gallons and gallons of water in that long waterline to the house, a dollop of hemlock couldn't be lethal, not diluted like that. Could it? And the toilet flush, and wash water, all that would go down the drain, he might never put it to his lips.

"Piece of orange?" Jessie held a section out to him on the

point of a jackknife. She had quartered the orange in her lap, flicking seeds into the ashtray.

He took it in his mouth, the tart sweetness, his mouth was dry. He thought for a moment he would weep, that it might well out of him and be over, but that passed, he wasn't even stoned. When they finished the orange, Jessie shared an apple with him, slicing it carefully and placing each piece in his mouth as he drove. He let her find music on the radio, she liked CBC classical in the morning, but today it was organ music so doleful even she agreed it was a downer, like a rainy day in church. They passed an enormous concrete structure set into a steep hillside, gated and fenced, and beside it a road ran up into the high trees. "Wreck Cove Hydro Project, that's the power plant there," she said. "Looks like science fiction, doesn't it?" "Yeah, sort of." She mentioned a general store, they could get a bite there, a drink, but when he saw it was right on the highway, he told her he'd wait. He listened to her talk about Boston, about swimming in Walden Pond Reservation with a boyfriend, and Innis remembered swimming there too, he and Ned Mohney, but there'd been too many people that day, even in the woods. Jessie said she liked The Garage on Boyleston Street, the shops with folk art, far-out clothes, but when she came home she didn't wear outrageous things. Innis asked her did she know the New England Aquarium, he and Mohney would get stoned and watch scuba divers feeding ocean fish in a huge tank, a real trip, more than weird to see them swim behind that glass. Jessie was quiet for a stretch and he could feel her brown eyes on him. No need for panic. Still lots of water between Starr Corbett and the spring. Small amounts moving down that line. One glass here, one glass there. A kettle. A basin. What if he took a bath?

"Jessie, could I make a call from your house? Your phone's in the kitchen, isn't it. Never mind. Everybody listens in."

"Not everybody. Innis, you're sweating."

The little cemetery was just above the sea, on a strip bare of trees, but the narrow dirt road to it sloped downward and, parked, the car was mostly out of sight. Innis showed her the roach he'd been saving for later, and she said sure, and after they exchanged a couple hits, she took his hand and led him down to the older stones, some with Gaelic inscriptions, the dead had been born on the Isle of Harris, of Lewis, early 1800s. Her father had a new headstone of white granite, he was the last one, the place was full, some of the original stones no more than grassy hillocks.

"In the early days," she said, "they'd just pick a stone from the beach, one they liked, and put it over the grave."

"I bet the sea could climb right up here sometimes."

"High tide and wind and you'd get waves up here sure, a lot of the bank washed away over the years."

"But nobody here is feeling the water, they don't care," Innis said.

"We don't entirely know, do we, Innis."

He pulled the telescope from his back pocket and offered it to her. She laughed.

"I'll look for a white whale, will I?" She found a freighter, hull down in metallic glare.

"That's where I'd like to be," he said. "Out there, farther than any spyglass could find me."

Huddling in the misty rain, they put an arm around each other and watched the ocean breaking loud and white beneath them. In a sandy stretch a plover on its clockwork legs buzzed back and forth, always at the heels of the shore wash. Innis turned them back toward the Caddy where he warmed her hands in his.

"Jessie, I have to split now, head back south."

"You want to come meet my mother first? It's only her and my auntie. They cook one hell of a meal."

"Jesus, I would, you know. I just can't. Can't. Not this time."

"What makes you think there'll be another time?"

Innis rested his forehead on the steering wheel. "Nothing. Nothing makes me think that."

She squeezed his hand. "Come anyway, when you're ready. See you when I see you, then. Okay? Safe home."

He thought of getting directions to her house, but there was no point. She assured him she'd get a ride easily, she wasn't that far from home, but when he left her at the roadside and waved to her out the window as he turned south, he felt desolate and alone. He would have loved to go with her, he could imagine the warm kitchen, the strong tea with milk and sugar, there'd be bannock, maybe with raisins, his favorite, butter and jam, he'd just be a guest, laid back, he wouldn't have to come up with a lot of lies, a few harmless ones would do, Jessie wouldn't care, she wasn't suspicious, her mother and her aunt might even like him. He overtook two cars before he calmed down, cursing softly, tears in his eyes, come on, this is stupid. So here he was driving fast for St. Aubin back toward the spring. The sun hurt, flaring off wet pavement, he'd had sunglasses somewhere. Then two things caught his eye almost simultaneously: a Mountie car with its dome light flashing, pulled onto the shoulder up ahead, and, coming up fast on his right, the looming structure of the Hydro Plant. Innis braked just enough to swerve onto the road running into the highlands, it seemed perfectly logical that he avoid that police car no matter what.

As he climbed the steep road he was aware that it followed a deep brook hidden in big maples and birches, the asphalt looked fresh, and it was easy to believe he was being hotly pursued or soon would be, that he was climbing into the Everlasting Barrens with a Mountie on his tail and he'd have to put the Caddy to the test, do some real driving, there were other roads in and out of the Barrens, he could slip that patrol car and find his way back, but that urgency faded the higher he went: he could see wind in the foliage but an odd stillness descended over everything and he slowed down. The area felt recently abandoned, like a military site. Unearthed rock still lay about, huge pieces blown out of the landscape, but the road crossed over dams built of neatly piled rocks, in places bare earth looked newly healed. There was no person anywhere, but a little building off behind a cyclone fence, and further along on the other side of a small lake, a solitary trailer, accessible only by a causeway with a locked cyclone gate. A day's workclothes beat like drab flags on a line strung from the trailer to a pole. Shirt, trousers, socks. Something forlorn in all that, fluttering out flat in a cold wind, the guy shut away inside the trailer by himself, his lonely stuff hanging outside, his underwear.

Innis drove on, more slowly, the asphalt gave over to graded dirt. Had Claire taken a plane off the Island, or was she driving too, on a road somewhere west? He would never find her now. He shut off the radio, no more than a murmuring hiss. Rocks had been no obstacle here, or woods. Dynamite, dust, an immense plowing. But all that was over. A strange calm, still settling. Like after a one-sided battle, everything had been buried, piled up, reconstructed. The engineers call it a flowage, Dan Rory had told him, from the old waters that were up here they had to, they said, correct the mistakes of nature. Imagine that. The way they looked at it, the engineers, there was all this water up there going to waste, running down little rivers and streams into the sea, such a waste of water, eh? So they made these new lakes and poured concrete canals and made spillways and sluices, stepped the water down faster and harder, into Wreck Cove Tunnel, into the great turbines there. And so the power went out over the land. Not to us. Over us. That's where it always goes. Amen.

In the distance a single windmill, the wind was blowing hard but the blades were not turning. He was thirsty, he should've stopped at that general store like she'd wanted, got gas.

Had Starr already opened that cupboard over the sink, taken his time selecting a tumbler, raising it first to the ceiling to see if his nephew had wiped the glass clean? He would open the tap, he would not fill the glass right away but run his fingers under the water, feeling almost immediately that surprising cold. No reason for Starr to hesitate. Free of silt. Nothing swirling there, nothing to the eye.

On the upper side of the dam Innis was approaching lay a cold nervous lake, its surface darkly blue, charged with small, rapid waves. He turned down a short road to the windward shore hoping for a drink. The wind was immediately cold and steady when he got out of the car. The sun seemed to have no heat, though the air was bright. Deep behind the beach driftwood had banked up high, white and dry as bones against a concrete wall. Hundreds of pieces must have been driven there by storms, jammed into a long windrow of bleached wood. Newer wood not yet dry was scattered along the shoreline. Innis ran his hand over a piece like huge misshapen antlers, its grain a satiny silver, polished and damp. Tree stumps, most of that driftwood, and the lake was still giving them up, working them loose like teeth from the flooded, cut-over woods. He couldn't see any wood floating, maybe they were still submerged in that dark water, like seabeasts, each one different, malformed, rising from the depths. Sunlight sank only a short way into the clear water, at first faintly yellow, then a rusty tinge deepening into a red darkness. Iron oxide. The lake's surface seemed jittery in the wind, excited somehow, hurried, its choppy waves striking the shore in quick succession. You'll still find trout up there, he'd heard. Hard to believe down in that bloodred darkness there'd be fish.

Surely it was fresh enough to drink, only the rock colored it, and Innis cupped out a few cold mouthfuls tasting faintly of metal. Maybe Starr had deserved a touch of poison. But just who deserved what, and why, was still a mystery.

The squalls seemed to have passed, shreds of cloud cooling across the sun. Could this be a thin place like the priest had mentioned? He picked up a piece of wood whose whorl of knots caught light like wet stone. There were interesting rocks lying about, fractured in attractive ways. He patted his pocket for a sketchpad but he'd forgotten where he put it, in his bag maybe back in the car. But how would he draw this anyway, this strange lake where all the blood had run? An army had been through here and what remained was the blown rock, the ruined trees, the concrete channels, the dams, the stilled windmill. There was no room in this wind for drawing, the wind was growing colder, it cut into him and he was glad to shut himself away in the car, every time that engine shot into life, he was comforted.

But signs for a road out, where were they? He drove carefully across a damn of earth and stone, a deep lake on one side, on the other a mean plunge to a thin afterthought of a brook, its water tracing off into a valley, a mere leak beneath the dam. From this maze of roads, any exit at all, he didn't care right now where it would land him as long as he could continue south.

Scrub spruce and alders stretched away and away, and there was the bright wet grass of bogs, a stunted terrain to which had been brought dams, and deserted roads to get lost in fast, they would suddenly merge with the ground as if they had turned into the earth. There'd been a big fire across the Barrens back in the sixties, Finlay said, roared right over it, and the trees were stunted anyway, always small up here where the rocky soil is thin. A scrabble of dense little trees no bigger than they would ever get in this windy space, branches curled and huddled, roots twisted into the soil. When he deadended in a muddy clearing, he turned the car around, spinning clay, and retraced, he was certain, the same road, but once again other roads opened into it enticingly, they looked the same, and he bounced down one side road, then another, ending like the one before in a pile of bulldozed stones and he had to turn the mudsplashed Caddy again. He'd bottomed it already too many times, the muffler had a low rumble when he gunned the engine, a sound that in high school he would have thought cool but now it was a flaw, a worry, in this fine automobile. A highway car. That thought amused him at first, so sure of this car, no way you could keep it off the highway for long, but its shocks were intended for good pavement, not ruts and gravel and rainholes. Main road, mean road, little difference here.

He fingered out the roach stub from his breast pocket and lit it, sucked its smoke in deep. There was poisoned water everywhere, wasn't there, diluted versions of it, people drank it every day, Starr was not putting hemlock in his mouth right now, the plant was a long long way from him, its stalk, its stems, even its deadly juice. Maybe. Wind jostled the car. Jesus, there was not a road sign anywhere, who was all this designed for, God? He took a turn where a road looked wider, better graded. Was that a human being, had he spotted a man, dark, solemn, maybe an Indian, fishing below the road half-hidden in the thick bushes, casting high into a brook? Innis was not sure. Of course the man would see the car and ask him questions, like what in the hell did you bring a Cadillac up to the Barrens for? He didn't want to leave the car anymore, he felt safer moving, any temptation to stop quickly vanished. Conversation? For what? Who are

you, where you from? *Co leis thu?* He was in the high Barrens now, had to be, best for berries, they said, maybe he
could find some. He could see a long way, the windbeaten
trees as low as bushes, some road just a tan scar in the distance. He stopped to pan his telescope across the land, but
there was nothing it could pull close enough to matter. He
went on until the road he was following quit in a small
cleared turnaround and he sat there idling. With the window cracked, the wind whistled over the car, it was still August, for Christ sake, wasn't there a touch of summer left
to lift him up a little? In his mouth an aftertaste of the
lake, a tinge of iron. He scooped out the contents of the
glove compartment and found half a roll of stale mints. He
popped them all in his mouth, cut the engine. Wintergreen.
The Captain's breath. How much gas would it take to get
him back to the highway, if he could find it? Encirclement
was creeping into him and he would have to beat it back,
worse than being lost in the woods last fall: these were
roads and roads took you places, they didn't lock you in,
they didn't dazzle you, make you stupid. He folded his
jacket into a pillow across the steering wheel. Just a few
winks, he was hungry but resting his head, his eyes, seemed
to matter more, clearing his mind. He could manage only a
dozing, fitful parade of his unease, sleep would not let him
arrive, anywhere. He slid down sideways to the seat, his
mouth agape with weariness, eyelids trembling. Starr's white
shirts flew on a clothesline, three of them, sleeves snapping,
pins could not keep them, they writhed away in the wind
one by one.

His face felt mashed when he woke, his eyes gritty,
squinting at the long late sun as he stood outside the car to
piss, wind shoving at his back. Maybe Starr had taken no
tainted water yet, not run a tap at all during the day, if he'd
gone to The Mines. There were good reasons why he

wouldn't have put any in his mouth yet, that tiny cloud of poison was still diffusing, slowly, invisibly into that long hill to the house, under the road, then diagonal through the front field, a long run of line, so much water coursing through it, backed up behind the taps. Kitchen. Bathroom. A spigot near the back door. And the toilet. How many flushes would...? Maybe it was all there, collected in one small space, and something as innocent as a piss would disperse it, that few pints or quarts or gallons of danger. Suppose Starr simply was not thirsty for water? There were three beers in the fridge. Distinctly. Three brown bottles of Moosehead Ten Penny Ale, Innis could describe if asked the design of the label, the logo, the color of gold, the styles of lettering, the name, the origin of the brewery, the percentage of alcohol, higher than beer in the States. Starr liked a beer sometimes first thing in the door. But the weather was not warm, he wouldn't reach for a Moosehead today grumbling about the sticky, windless air, wind was everywhere and it carried autumn, chilling summer away. Autumn light. Warm, yet cold on your face.

He tried to concentrate, he couldn't be fooled anymore by roads that went nowhere. He'd been trying to get off that Cape Breton Road, hadn't he, the one that ran from here to Boston and beyond and back again, a great circle of sentiment and memory, of love and anger and disappointment and hope, leading back to this Island, even to here?

The prospect of darkness had focussed his mind, he found he was moving beyond the Barrens, the trees were coming taller, the road straighter but monotonous. Stacked pulpwood appeared at the roadside, this had to lead to a highway. He was daring to pick up speed, the muffler grumbling louder, when the headlights caught the dark brown hide of an enormous animal, like suddenly encountering a zoo creature, a runaway from a circus, its size seemed so out of place in front of his car, claiming the center of the road. Innis skidded to a halt, headlights freezing the moose as it wheeled its great head around, like a comical horse with its bristly dewlap, exaggerated snout. Innis expected it to flee like a deer but the horn, that smooth Cadillac horn, seemed only to arouse it, it lowered its immense rack of antlers, then, with a deep grunt, reared up impossibly high, all belly and legs, a mighty bull. Innis reversed hard but not before its hooves thumped heavily on the hood, he kept backing up until he felt the impact of the ditch, his head flew back, the Caddy suddenly askew, stopped, stalled. He could hear the moose crashing away through the trees. Holding his whiplashed neck, he turned the engine over and over until it started and then listened to what he was afraid of, wheels whining in the wet ditch, spitting out mud and stones until the car barely rocked. The moose had smashed one headlight, the other was angled upward, illuminating uselessly the high branches of a tree.

Innis sat in the listing car, the thought of leaving it he could not handle, not yet. Bugs danced in the cockeyed light. Was that a wisp of fog or his own dust settling? He punched every button on the dash, the radio leapt from white noise to white noise, the aerial withdrew into the hood, the fan breathed cold air, he lowered all the windows, then raised them shut. Shit. A goddamn moose, and no Bullwinkle either, it must've been ten feet high, pissed off. Innis was sure he'd been on a road out, all he'd need have done is keep going. To a gas station, a house, a phone, anyone's phone. Starr, don't drink the water from the tap, just don't, don't ask me any questions, never mind where I am, goodbye. Goodbye.

The darkness was unbelievable, even as his eyes adjusted to it he was straining to keep to the road. But oh God, the stars, they blinded him, they made him stumble, they were brighter than the night with Claire when he spun slowly in that midnight water, weightless, certain he would soon feel her against him. He looked behind him just once, the Caddy's headlight like a carnival beam, barely visible in trees. Jesus, he was thirsty, he'd never been so thirsty, there had to be a brook along here, why not take the woods, didn't he know them, weren't these the same trees that grew on St. Aubin, everywhere here? A terror seemed to flame through him, furiously cold, like his hands in the spring water. He was going downhill, the woods were thicker than any back home, but a hill would lead him somewhere he needed to go if he could stay on his feet, where was his walking stick, lying in the upstairs hallway, he was afraid of tumbling headfirst, of sinking in a bog, he had no gas left, his legs could not match the obstacles, the deadwood, the tangles of tough young trees, but he knew too that this momentum would drive him the rest of his days, to better or worse, he saw flowers, yellow, were they primroses, his mother wanted him to dig holes for roses, outside there by the back window, Innis, please, I can't get a spade into that soil, it's hard as cement, but his pal was waiting at the curb and Innis didn't want to be seen putting rosebushes in the ground, they were blooming even, cream and red and yellow, petals dropping to the pavement, but he regretted it now, that he hadn't done that little thing for her, that if nothing else, roses in the garden she could look at, and she had tried anyway to plant them herself but they turned to brittle sticks and thorns. He tripped on a tree root, his knees dug into dirt, his palms, the breath knocked out of him, but he was up again, wiping his eyes clear, that had to be a light he saw, it was, yes, and he pushed on toward it, crashing drunkenly, never taking his eyes from it, it had to be a house, a dog was barking sharply, or was it a fox, there would be a telephone there, and he could crank out those rings, crank them like a fire call, loud and long, and Starr would count them out without even thinking, four-ring-three, and he would get up from wherever he was, the big chair in the parlor, the kitchen table, maybe even his bed, what time was it anyway, and he would say hello, and Innis would say, It's me. It's me, Innis.